THE WHITE MIRROR

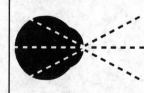

This Large Print Book carries the
Seal of Approval of N.A.V.H.

THE WHITE MIRROR

ELSA HART

THORNDIKE PRESS
A part of Gale, Cengage Learning

GALE
CENGAGE Learning·

Farmington Hills, Mich • San Francisco • New York • Waterville, Maine
Meriden, Conn • Mason, Ohio • Chicago

LIBRARY OF CONGRESS CATALOGING-IN-PUBLICATION DATA

Names: Hart, Elsa, author.
Title: The white mirror / by Elsa Hart.
Description: Large print edition. | Waterville, Maine : Thorndike Press, 2016. | Series: A Li Du novel | Series: Thorndike Press large print historical fiction
Identifiers: LCCN 2016037158| ISBN 9781410495372 (hardcover) | ISBN 141049537X (hardcover)
Subjects: LCSH: Librarians—Fiction. | China—History—Qing dynasty, 1644-1912—Fiction. | Large type books. | GSAFD: Mystery fiction.
Classification: LCC PS3608.A78455 W48 2016b | DDC 813/.6—dc23
LC record available at https://lccn.loc.gov/2016037158

Published in 2017 by arrangement with St. Martin's Press, LLC

Printed in the United States of America
1 2 3 4 5 6 7 21 20 19 18 17 16

To Robbie

PROLOGUE

It was more than ten years after my brief acquaintance with the scholar Li Du that I heard his name again, and it came from the unlikeliest of sources.

The year was 1718, and I was in Saint Petersburg. There were hundreds of foreigners in the city that summer. We were in Russia at the behest of the Czar, who wished his new capital to be a place of surpassing beauty and refinement. The canals were to be Dutch, the gardens French, the palaces Italian. My task was to contribute something of the English botanical perspective to its apothecary gardens. This occupation delighted me, not least because I had ample time to conduct my own survey of the plants, imported and domestic, growing in the city.

One day, late in the summer, I had reason to consult Dioscorides, and inquired as to where I might locate an edition. I was directed to an estate at the city's edge, a grand, two-storied hall set on a flat lawn with a forest behind it. Inside, I was received by an apologetic official, who explained that the estate was being converted from a private residence into a new royal library and cabinet of curiosities. The collection was incomplete and in disarray, but I was welcome to examine it.

I soon despaired of locating the volume I sought. Many of the books and objects were still packed away in crates, and those that had been unpacked had not yet enjoyed the ministrations of a librarian. I would have stayed to peruse, but found myself uneasy under the stares of half-assembled automata and preserved fishes. I learned later that the estate's former owner had plotted to murder the Czar and had, in punishment for this treachery, relinquished not only his property, but also his life. Perhaps the rooms retained a certain malevolence.

After abandoning my search, I set out to explore the forested grounds. Soon I was surrounded by the red trunks and dark needles of Siberian pines, my boots sinking into soft moss, the drone of insects loud in my ears. I stopped to rest beside a small lake, and was enjoying the blurred reflections of silver poplars and white birches in the water when I was hailed by a man walking toward me on the path. His clothes were richer than a peasant's, but worn and muddy at the knees. The hair beneath the brim of his hat was white. He carried a trowel in one hand, and a basket of iris roots in the other.

He told me his name was Étienne Laporte. He and his wife had come to Russia from France, he as a gardener, she as a lady's maid, and had served the estate for fifteen years. I questioned him eagerly, and found him particularly knowledgeable on the subjects of rhubarbs, lilies, and mosses. When he invited me to sup with his family, I accepted, and followed him to a modest residence separate from the main house, where I was received with gracious hospitality.

After a pleasant repast, Laporte led me to a parlor and poured two glasses of the Russian liquor. As I examined the room, my attention was arrested by a flower in a vase beside a small window — a red, waxy blossom that drooped from a thick stem curved like the neck of a swan.

The sight of it transported me. Before my eyes, I saw gray, sloping rooftops and courtyard gardens. When I drew in my breath, it seemed to me that the air held juniper smoke and the scent of angelica. I knew the flower — a species of peony — but I marveled at its presence, for I had never seen it growing outside of China. I remarked on it to Laporte.

To my disappointment, he did not immediately address the subject of the plant. Instead, he spoke of his employment before he came to Russia. He had been an under-gardener in the palace of the Sun King, in that monarch's Labyrinth of Fables. Years of tending its hedges, he explained, had engraved the shape of the labyrinth into his memory. He would never forget its corridors or its thirty-eight statues and thirty-eight tales, stories of imprudent ravens and malcontented frogs intended for the moral education of the young dauphin.

Then he pointed to the red flower and told me that it had grown from a seed given to him by a traveler in gratitude for his recitation of those thirty-eight fables. Laporte laughed and said that this man, a talkative fellow, had insisted that one year the plant would produce a green flower, and from it would crawl a turtle with a jeweled shell that would grant any wish, so long as the creature was acknowledged the king of turtles.

I gave little credence to the improbable

amalgam of plant and animal, and yet the traveler's manner, as conveyed to me by Laporte, was somehow familiar. I asked for his name. Laporte replied that no name had been given, but recalled that the man had a princely bearing. I asked whence the traveler had come. Laporte did not know, but told me that his eyes were dark as the seeds of the peony, and that he wore a short beard, oiled and pointed. Finally, I asked what stories the man had told of his travels. At this, Laporte rose to light candles and refill our glasses. The traveler, he said, as he returned to his chair, had told only one story, about a caravan on a path between empires, and a librarian who had once been an exile.

And that is how I came to learn, ten years after I returned home from China, what befell the friends I made there. I have endeavored to set down the account as Laporte related it to me, supplemented with my own memories of that part of the world, and with my researches into the Edifying and Curious Letters sent by men of the church.

Of the location where these events took place, I can say little. I do not know the path my friends took after I parted from their company. I know only that it lies

11

somewhere on that branching trade route that connects the forests where the Chinese grow their tea leaves to the arid plateaus of Tibet, where it cannot be grown and is thus greatly valued. These paths, which wind through vast and treacherous mountains, have been claimed over the centuries by at least three powers: the emperors of China, the kings and monks of Tibet, and the Mongol princes of Tartary. Who rules there now, I do not know.

My survey of the plants of Saint Petersburg remains incomplete, my notebooks from that time being devoted, so unexpectedly, to the further exploits of Li Du.

— FROM THE MISCELLANEOUS PAPERS OF HUGH ASHTON

CHAPTER 1

In high places, a single storm takes many forms. A wise traveler knows to be wary of what the clouds and the mountains are saying to one another. So when Li Du observed a raindrop strike his mule's bridle and bounce into the air instead of slipping quietly down the leather, he stopped and looked up with some trepidation. Through dripping branches, the sky was like rough silk stretched tight across a frame.

A gust of wind pulled at the tops of the trees. Li Du's mule shook her head, upset. The wind had loosed the flap of a saddlebag. It fluttered and snapped at her flank. Li Du freed one of his hands from his coat sleeve and stepped carefully around the animal, aware of the precipitous drop to his right where the edge of the path fell away through gnarled oaks into a deep ravine. At its base, cascading water frothed and pooled around boulders and forest debris.

Once he had secured the saddlebag, Li Du patted his mule's shoulder and tucked his hand back into his damp sleeve. It had been precipitating since dawn, an irresolute rain that was now assuming the colder, sharper guise of sleet. Ahead, the trail rose steeply, slick stones and black mud churned by booted feet and shod hooves. He resumed his progress, stepping automatically into the footprints that were already there.

Li Du was a small man of middle age with a smooth, oval face, unassuming square eyebrows, and eyes that smiled when he did. It was his tendency to walk with his head thrust forward and his chin slightly tucked, as if he was scanning the ground for a lost item. His rumpled wool hat was worn and faded. His long coat, cinched at the waist by a belt, had been mended many times.

For Li Du, there was a rhythm to each day of mountain travel. In the mornings, he opened his eyes to the blue half-light of dawn with a feeling that he had become part of the cold dirt beneath him. Later, after a hot breakfast and the effort of packing up camp, his fatigue left him and he was eager to set out. There followed a pleasant interlude of walking and noting with interest the varieties of vegetation, the vistas, and the birdsong.

By midday, the morning's energy was spent. Small pains broadened into aches, breath became an exhausting necessity, and fears of injury insinuated themselves into his thoughts. Fortunately, on all but the most difficult days, this discomfort passed and Li Du settled into his own steady afternoon pace, content in the knowledge that nothing was expected of him except that he match his slow stride to that of his mule until the caravan stopped for the night.

This afternoon was different. Li Du was anxious. Over the last ten days, they had not seen anyone outside the caravan except for a single farmer in a distant barley field who, upon observing them, had hurried out of sight. The air had been growing steadily colder. That morning, Li Du had witnessed a worried exchange between Kalden Dorjee and his men as they discussed signs of an approaching storm.

Li Du was nearing the top of the ascent when a sound reached him. He gave a little sigh of relief as he recognized the bells of the caravan's lead mule. He crested the rise and, blinking away stinging ice, peered down. In front of him, a steep declivity led to a wide clearing on the bank of the stream, where the caravan had halted.

The sleet imparted a wraithlike uniformity

to the shapes of the men, but he knew them. Bundled in their coats and hats, the six muleteers stood among their laden mules. Li Du had often remarked that, in dismal weather, the bright red plumes affixed to the lead mule's bridle seemed lit by remembered sunshine. They were clearly visible now, despite the precipitation.

He took hold of his own mule's bridle and began to make his way down. The bells jangled again. He looked at the clearing. The animals had shifted, and he could now see a narrow, flat bridge over the stream. On the far side, a spur path disappeared into the forest.

Distracted, Li Du stepped onto a loose rock and slid forward. He flung out an arm to stop his fall. His hand found an overhanging branch and he clung to it. When he had recovered his balance, he released the branch. As it sprang back into place he felt a pull and heard a rip as part of his sleeve tore away. He made a quiet sound of exasperation as he looked up at the threadbare strip of wool, now a forlorn pennant.

Down in the clearing the lead mule shook its head impatiently, and the bells rang for a third time. It was then that Li Du discerned another figure beyond the clustered men and horses. The stranger — a monk, judg-

16

ing by his crimson robes — was sitting cross-legged on the bridge, his back to Li Du. *A disciplined ascetic,* Li Du thought, *who would meditate here, far from a hearth, with a storm coming.*

As Li Du lowered himself from a rotted tree trunk down into the clearing, he felt the air become colder. He could no longer hear the skittering sleet. Not one of the muleteers raised a hand to him in greeting. Li Du's eyes were drawn to the man on the bridge. He approached to where he could see the figure clearly.

The seated monk was still, his head drooping forward. His robes, crimson and saffron, hung in sodden folds around a thin body. As Li Du tried to make sense of what he was seeing, snowflakes began to collect on the shaved head and crimson cloth. Still the figure did not move. This was not a man meditating on the bridge. It was a corpse.

CHAPTER 2

It was the forty-seventh reigning year of the Kangxi Emperor of China, the year 1708 by Western reckoning, and the earth rat year of the twelfth cycle in Tibet. In the in-between lands where Li Du currently found himself, he was unsure which, if any, of those measurements applied.

That it was autumn, at least, was beyond question. In the scattered enclaves of human activity, villagers cut crops of buckwheat and millet in fields and spread maize and sliced apples on flat roofs to dry. Outside those enclaves, the passes were filling with snow and ice, sealing off the paths that formed the great network of the Tea Horse Road. In coming months, many of the passes would become too dangerous for any but the most foolhardy travelers, and villages would draw themselves in close to wait for winter to end. For some, this would mean telling tales and whittling wood by the hearth while enjoying rich stores of salted meat, dark tea, butter, and roasted barley flour. For the less fortunate, it would mean a grim season of hunger.

Along the branching system of roads that ran through these lands, mules and yaks carried tight-strapped saddlebags and boxes heavy with furs, herbs, salt, gold dust, copper, and, most important, tea. The caravans too were preparing for winter, choosing their paths with care. When the passes closed, the blood pumping through the veins connecting the Chinese empire to its neighbor Tibet would slow. Only the roads near market towns were paved with stones. The rest were rough, and required travelers to navigate ledges carved into cliff walls and rope bridges strung high above icy torrents.

Li Du had joined this small company of Khampa muleteers eight months ago in the market town of Dayan, after unforeseen events had altered his status from political exile to independent traveler with silver to spend and freedom to go where he wanted. The caravan was headed north on its return journey, first to Lhasa, where the tea it carried from China would sell at the highest price, then home to Kham.

In the weeks since they had left the trade

19

outpost of Gyalthang, the larches had turned brittle yellow. The mornings were colder, the afternoons darker. Kalden, gruff and impatient, had pushed his caravan to travel greater distances each day. The muleteers, who built shrines at every campsite, had begun to burn extra juniper as they looked at the leaden skies.

The dead man sat upright, propped against the crude railing built on one side of the bridge. The fingers of his right hand were curled around the protruding hilt of a knife buried low in his abdomen. As Li Du took in the wound, he felt an involuntary jerk through his own body, an imagined echo of another's pain. Blood soaked the crimson robes below the waist and overflowed the cracks and crevices of the bridge's planks.

Above the wound, his clothes were rent and parted, exposing a pronounced collarbone and faintly outlined ribs. Across the center of his chest, these human contours were obscured by a thick layer of paint. Vivid pigments, beaded with frozen rain, were smeared into the shape of a white circle framed in gold and blue.

The dead man's chin rested just above the mark. He appeared to be staring down at the destruction wrought upon his own body.

Li Du knelt, facing him. The white circle was tinged pink where blood had mixed into the paint. Li Du identified the impression left by a fingertip that had slid through the blue pigment, spreading it into a sinuous trail at the base of the circle. His gaze dropped to the hand that clutched the knife. Its fingers were crusted with paint as well as with blood.

The man's left arm was flung out, palm upward, the hand suspended over the rushing water. Dangling from the fingers was a string of wooden prayer beads. The lowest section of the loop danced and jumped as the current tried to pull it away.

"We should not cross the bridge." The speaker was Norbu, the caravan cook. He stood beside a mule whose saddlebags bristled with pot handles and tea churns. The fragrance of herbs and aging butter that usually emanated from this mule was reduced to a trace as snow accumulated on it.

Kalden kept his eyes averted from the bridge. "The manor lies on the other side of the stream," he said.

"Then we should change our plans and keep clear of the place," said Norbu. He gestured at the body. "It isn't safe to cross into a valley with a gatekeeper like that."

Kalden frowned. "We are expected at the

manor."

As the oldest and most experienced member of the company, Norbu was the only one permitted to argue with Kalden. He pointed at the path that led out of the clearing, away from the bridge. "We can reach the pass before the snow is too deep and camp on the other side."

Kalden's reply was short. "It is too dangerous."

"Dangerous? And what of him?" Norbu looked again at the bridge.

Kalden moved closer to Norbu, which emphasized his height and strength relative to the older man's. "If the snow is falling here, then it will already be deep up at the pass. We will not attempt it."

Li Du, who by now had a good command of the language common to the trade routes, awaited Norbu's capitulation. But Norbu resisted. "I'd rather face weather than demons," he said. "I still say we leave this place." He stopped. It was as if, like the trees around them, he was pressed into silence by the muffling snow.

Kalden raised his voice over the rushing water. "We will cross and go to the manor."

The debate was over. Kalden instructed two of the muleteers to lead the animals ahead and find a place shallow enough to ford. The other muleteers crossed the bridge one at a time, each placing as much distance between himself and the body as he could. Li Du stood with Kalden waiting for his turn to cross. "Should we carry him with us?" he asked.

Kalden shook his head. "It is better to leave him as he is."

"What do you think happened?"

A shadow of uncertainty crossed Kalden's face, but was gone by the time he spoke. "It has nothing to do with us."

Kalden's turn came to cross. The snow was falling heavily, and Kalden had not yet reached the far bank before Li Du lost sight of him. Li Du took a careful step onto the bridge. It was slippery under the snow. Li Du took another step. Then, perceiving movement out of the corner of his eye, he turned.

The string of beads looped around the dead man's outstretched hand had crept to the tips of his fingers. Li Du watched as a final tug from the water pulled the beads away and sucked them into the rapids. The current carried them spinning and bobbing down the mountain in the direction from which Li Du and the caravan had come.

Li Du looked down at the body again, and noticed two small, square items beside it, almost covered in snow. He bent to pick one up. It was a strip of rawhide that had been folded over itself to make a square packet. Li Du unfolded it. The inside was coated in a thick, sticky residue of white paint. Quickly, he examined the other one. It had held blue paint.

He set them down and straightened up. He was about to tuck his hand back into his sleeve when he noticed a glint of color from several particles that had adhered to his fingers. He raised his hand to look at them. They were deep red, and sharp, more like sand or shards of stone than dirt. He squatted down and ran his fingers over the planks of the bridge. More granules were scattered there.

A familiar voice called to him from the other side. He wiped his hand on his coat and continued across. As he rejoined the caravan, he turned and looked once more at the bridge and the figure they had left there, framed and confined by inexorably spreading ice.

The path up through the forest was steep but short. After a few minutes, they emerged from the dense trees and continued uphill until the ground became level. Li Du had the impression of open space, but the actual size and dimensions of the valley were impossible to ascertain through the falling snow. Luckily, there was not enough snow yet to cover the path worn down by feet and hooves into an uneven trough.

A dark shape like a boulder loomed ahead of them. As they neared it, Li Du smelled smoke and identified the obstacle to be a tiny hut. He hurried forward and reached the front of the caravan just as Kalden received a shouted answer from within the hut. The wind pulled the sound apart into indecipherable syllables, but Kalden seemed to have understood. He opened the door and ducked through it. Li Du followed.

Inside, a man sat cross-legged near a hearth. He was lean, with eyes set in fanning wrinkles above sharp cheeks. Three metal basins hemmed him in. Each was filled with opaque liquid: one white as the snow, the second white as a lotus petal, the third yellow as parchment. The man looked, to Li Du, like a frog surrounded by lily pads. In one hand he held a ladle, which he set down beside him in a shallow bowl.

Kalden introduced himself. "We are seven men and twenty mules."

The man nodded. "The family is expecting you. Your friend arrived yesterday." He reached behind him and pulled two knobby canes from the cluttered corner of the hut. He levered himself up and, leaning heavily on them, skirted the basins and went to the door. He peered outside at the caravan.

"I am called Yeshe," he said, returning to his seat. "This is where I live, but there's another place like this one. The manor lord invites you to stay there." He pointed. "It's not far. If you put your mules in a line, the front nose of the leader would touch the wall."

"And the manor?"

Yeshe swung his arm in the opposite direction. "It's farther away than the hut but you won't miss it — even in the storm. It is a grand place with walls all around."

Kalden nodded his thanks.

"There is cut firewood in the hut," said Yeshe, with a hint of impatience, "and Doso Targum will want to meet you." Yeshe looked at Li Du. "You must be the Chinese scholar. There is a room ready for you at the manor."

When Kalden still did not turn to go, Yeshe raised his voice. "You don't understand my words?"

"I understand," said Kalden. "We are grateful for the welcome. Excuse my hesitation, but we bring disturbing news. There is a man on the bridge in the forest. A monk.

26

We thought he had come to greet us. But when we approached him we — we saw that he was dead."

Yeshe's lean body tensed. He picked up his ladle, gripping it so tightly that his skin strained around the knuckles and tendons of his fingers and hand. "An older man or a young one?"

"Older than I am, younger than you."

Yeshe's fingers relaxed slightly. But if he knew who the dead man was, he did not volunteer it. He lowered his gaze to the bowl in front of him. "Some wild beast?"

"No." Kalden described what they had seen. While he spoke, Yeshe's eyes glittered, unreadable in the firelight. When Kalden had finished, Yeshe gave him a hard look, then shrugged. "Take this news to the manor," he said. "I can't tell you anything about it."

Once they were outside, the door to the hut pulled shut behind them, Kalden issued instructions. He shouted to be heard over the wind. As the muleteers led the animals away in the direction of the promised shelter, Li Du guided his own little mule out from the group and, following close behind Kalden, set out through the agitated, whirling snow.

27

CHAPTER 3

The manor's façade loomed above them. Li Du craned his neck to take in the shuttered windows and brightly painted eaves. At first he could not understand why the building seemed to float in the air. Then he realized that he was looking at a second story, which was supported by an expanse of windowless white wall.

Li Du and Kalden located a set of heavy doors that stood open. Passing through, they entered into a dim corridor. At its far end was a second set of doors, also open. As his eyes adjusted, Li Du saw that the walls of the passage were decorated with painted animals. A whiskered blue dragon, a grinning tiger, and a griffin with a snake in its talons floated across an ocher background, chipped and smoke-blackened. Above their heads, wooden beams shook with the faint vibrations of footsteps on the upper floor.

They emerged into a courtyard, and were once again engulfed in snow. Li Du discerned vague shapes of buildings, and glimpsed their ornamented exteriors. Vivid medallions in rows of alternating colors winked at him through the snow like hundreds of eyes.

"Welcome, brothers!" The salutation came from their right.

They followed the sound into a long barn open to the courtyard. Its back wall was formed by the same solid fortification that they had seen from outside. As Li Du caught his breath and stamped snow from his boots, he felt his chest and shoulders relax involuntarily at the warmth surrounding him. It was the heat of living animals, of their breathing flanks and fur and dung. The space smelled of sweet hay and milk and manure, and was populated by the hulking shapes of yaks and the comforting silhouettes of horses and shaggy ponies.

A low, masculine voice repeated the welcome, and a man strode out from among the animals. He was of such unusually large stature that he made the yaks seem suddenly smaller. The expansive shoulders of his black goatskin coat were flecked with snow. He held his hands outstretched, palms upward, in greeting. As he came closer, Li

Du saw gray hair at his temples and a loose-ness in his cheeks and jaw that suggested he was older than his strong, upright gait implied. Even Kalden, who was tall, had to look up to meet their host's eyes.

"You are to be congratulated," announced the man. "The way to my family's land is not easy even in good weather. I, too, have only just come in from the storm." He gestured behind him at two yaks whose backs were beaded with melting snow. "I am Doso Targum. It is the tradition of my fathers to offer largesse to tenants when a child is born. Fortunately, I set out before the storm became serious — we will be cut off from the village for several days at least."

Doso ushered them deeper inside the barn. Something in his enthusiastic welcome struck Li Du as forced. His behavior re-minded Li Du of an inexperienced actor who is too aware of his audience. Doso continued. "Please settle your mule here in the stable. I am sorry that there is not room for all your beasts. But do not be concerned. I will give you good hay for them. This storm will pass quickly. It is not winter yet."

It was Kalden's turn to speak. Li Du had seen him navigate tense interactions with other caravan leaders on narrow bridges, of-ficials inspecting permits and tax receipts, and soldiers on patrol. Kalden was a taciturn man by nature, but he had an innate ability to balance deference and confidence when speaking to powerful strangers. He gave his name, his place of birth, and a description of his caravan. He offered formal thanks for Doso's hospitality.

Doso waved a hand. "Only my duty, only my duty," he said, sounding pleased. "But come upstairs. My wife, Kamala, will make you butter tea, and I will introduce you to my children."

Kalden had a hand on the bridle of Li Du's mule, and she began to dip her head restlessly. Li Du guessed that she perceived Kalden's apprehension. "We came across the bridge," said Kalden.

Doso nodded. "That is the easiest crossing. The others are only notched logs that would be treacherous in the snow. That water is deeper than it appears and the current is violent. Your company are all safe?"

Kalden cleared his throat. "We found a body there."

"A body." Doso stooped and cocked his head a little to the side as if he had not heard correctly.

"A man is dead there on the bridge," said Kalden. "A monk."

Doso's demeanor changed instantly. His

affable mien vanished, and a hand shot forward to grip Kalden's sleeve. "What monk? A young man?"

"No — he is not young." For the second time, Kalden gave an account of what they had seen. He acquitted himself well, and Li Du observed with some relief Doso's apparent willingness to believe what Kalden was telling him.

When Kalden finished, Doso looked out at the gusting snow. It was difficult to see across any distance, but there was still light. "You left him there?"

"We did not want to interfere."

Doso nodded his approval. "It is the province of a monk to help a dead man."

A silence fell between them. Doso appeared to be gathering his thoughts. When he addressed Kalden again, his voice was stern. "You and I will go together to the bridge," he said. "And I will give you fair warning. We know the tricks of thieves on our roads. If this is treachery, the men of the village will not spare you. We know the paths through this valley even when the snow covers them. You do not."

Kalden held Doso's stare. "We are not thieves," he said. "You have met our ambassador." He looked at Li Du. "And here is a librarian from the court of the Chinese

Emperor himself. Show him the letter."

Grateful for the warmth of the barn that had thawed his numb fingers, Li Du deftly lifted an oiled leather flap on one of his mule's saddlebags and drew from the pocket beneath it a document wrapped in silk. He handed it to Doso, who unrolled it. Li Du could see the fiery red ink and the great seal of the Emperor through the back of the paper.

Doso returned the document and bowed to Li Du. "I am honored to host a guest of such high nobility and reputation," he said. His voice was distracted, but he seemed determined to be solicitous despite the circumstances. He switched from Kalden's language to slow, formal Chinese. "Tell me what you require, and I will provide it."

Li Du returned the bow. "The warmth of your home has already brought me comfort. And my mule will be grateful for the shelter tonight."

Doso looked faintly surprised by this humble response. "My home is your home," he said. "There is a room prepared for you. When you have unburdened your animal, my wife will attend you in the kitchen." He gestured toward an open staircase that led from the barn up through a cutout in the ceiling to the second story. Li Du heard

33

light, pattering footsteps — children's footsteps — above.

Doso glanced up at the ceiling. "I will speak with her."

He climbed the staircase. Li Du and Kalden heard something drop with a clang on the floor, followed by a muffled conversation. They exchanged glances. "This is not so bad," whispered Kalden, with obvious relief. "It could have gone much worse for us."

Li Du agreed. "Be careful on your return to the bridge," he added. "We do not know what happened there."

Kalden looked at him. "The monk held the knife's hilt as if he had thrust it into himself — I have heard of it being done that way before." Kalden lifted his eyes to trace the faint outlines of buildings through the snow as if he was searching for something. He shifted his shoulders uncomfortably. "We must hope that the storm is brief," he said.

They heard footsteps on the stairs, and looked up to see Doso descending. He went to the back wall of the barn, against which an assortment of gleaming weapons was arranged. He selected a sheathed sword and fixed it to the wide belt at his waist. Then he slipped a bridle over the head of a sturdy mule and turned to Kalden. "Let us go now," he said, "before we lose the light."

Li Du's mule was a gentle, steady animal not in her first youth. He had a rule that whenever he enjoyed a comfortable room he did his best to secure her a place in a dry barn. He led her to an open corner. Once he had unburdened her of bags and saddle and examined her hooves, he used the blunt edge of a blade to scrape the melting snow and water from her back. He looked for signs of injury or inflammation where the saddle had rubbed.

Who was the man on the bridge, and how had he come to such an end? In these mountains, from what Li Du had seen, village monks and lamas were present at every birth, at every death, and on all the ritual days between. They were there to celebrate the beginning of the harvest and the end of it. To lose by violence someone so integral to family life would, Li Du thought, be devastating. Yet neither Yeshe nor the manor lord had displayed the emotional reaction that Li Du might have expected.

Over the years, Li Du had learned to enter each unfamiliar village, inn, and estate with a flexible attitude and an acceptance of his own ignorance. No books he had read had prepared him for the variety of traditions scattered through the hillsides, valleys, mountains, and forests of the borderlands. Each high pass or wide river was a barrier behind which languages changed and religions evolved. And then there were marriages and wars and traveling teachers to change everything like a child shaking a jar of colored pebbles.

He removed a pot of mayvine salve from his bag and smoothed a layer of it over a raw spot on his mule's flank. He glanced around for a cloth to wipe the thick oil from his hand. Behind a small bamboo screen where he expected to see barrels or bales or stacked saddles, he found himself instead in someone's room. A low bench covered with furs was balanced on large stones. A butter tea churn and a bowl rested against a wall beside a blackened, dented pot. There was a basket full of rawhide strips on the floor. On the bed, among the furs, were several lengths of twine braided and tied into knots. Aware that he was intruding, Li Du stepped away and returned to his mule. He knelt and wiped the salve from his hand on a bit of clean hay.

For an isolated manor that did not often see caravans passing through, the barn was well stocked, filled up with sacks of barley, maize, and peas, and tea bricks wrapped in bamboo sheaths. A bright row of pots sat against one wall ready to be filled with fresh milk each morning. There were racks of saddles on the wall beside the numerous bows, arrows, and blades of various sizes.

Li Du was just about to climb the stairs to the upper floor when a young man, stooped under the weight of bundled firewood, hurried into the courtyard. He dropped his hands to his knees as he tried to catch his breath. His hat fell into the snow, but he did not pick it up. He made his way to the barn where Li Du stood, hidden from the young man's view by the animals and the thick painted columns.

As soon as the young man was under the shelter of the roof, he let his burden fall to the ground. It was only then that he caught sight of Li Du and stopped. Confusion competed with distress in his expression.

"I am a guest here," Li Du said quickly, silently amending his first impression. This was not so much a man as a boy. He was thin, the last roundness of childhood just recently gone from his cheeks, the left of which was twisted by a long scar. His eyes, when he was close enough for Li Du to see them, were very dark, the expression in them elusive. His hair was roughly cut and stood up from his head in matted clumps.

"You came with the caravan?" he asked nervously.

"Yes."

The young man's hands toyed with the fraying cuffs of his sleeves. "Then you saw —" He stopped, uncertain. "— on the bridge?"

Li Du nodded. Interpreting the youth's apparent distress as grief, Li Du spoke gently. "I am sorry," he said. "Was he from this house?"

The young man seemed to close in upon himself. He shook his head, then looked behind him. His hat was a black spot in the center of the white courtyard. He said, "I must go up to the temple. I have to bring the Chhöshe to the bridge."

A woman's voice called from upstairs. "Is that Pema who has come back?"

They looked to see the lady of the house descending the staircase into the courtyard. She did not come all the way down, but paused and bent slightly to address them. Li Du observed a round, smooth face and fastidious attire. Her dress was so neatly arranged that she resembled the painted latticework that decorated the manor. Her forearms were wrapped in cloth to protect her sleeves from becoming soiled in the kitchen.

"Pema," she said, addressing the young man, who winced slightly in response. "The children are frightened," she said. Then her voice became hushed. "Is it Dhamo who died?"

Pema nodded.

"What happened to him? Why was he at the bridge?"

"I don't know."

The woman made a sound of impatience. "Where are you going?"

Pema pointed upward toward the mountain. "To bring the Chhöshe."

The woman nodded and waved her hand, ushering Pema away. "Hurry then."

Pema looked as if he might say more, then dipped his head and ran out into the courtyard. He scooped up his discarded hat and left the manor.

The woman's glance took in Li Du standing with the saddlebags on his back. "I will show you your room."

The building housed the family's animals in the barns on its lower level, and the family itself, as well as their guests, in the rooms above. It comprised two wings of equal length joined at a right angle to enclose the courtyard on two sides. The guest rooms were connected by a hallway that ran the length of the building adjacent to the courtyard.

Li Du's room was a large, spare chamber located at the far northern end of the wing. Dim light entered through gaps in the shuttered windows. The bed was heaped with wool and yak fur blankets. A candle stood on the table beside it. A copper brazier hung from a ceiling made from slats separated enough to allow smoke to be drawn up and out from under the raised roof.

Shelves attached to the wall were stacked with wooden bowls and ornaments. As he explored the space, out of the corner of his eye Li Du glimpsed his own reflection, warped and spectral, moving through the polished lid of a copper pot. He set his saddlebags down in a corner beside a small shrine, a silver statue and an unlit butter lamp arranged in front of a painting mounted on black silk. He put his mule's bridle on the table by the bed. Its bells clicked into silence one at a time as they hit the wooden surface.

A voice startled him. "I had charmed the whole household, and then you bring them a dead man."

Li Du turned to see a familiar figure in the doorway, a man with a black pointed

40

beard and a graceful set to his shoulders. He wore a blue hat brightly embroidered with birds and leaves.

"Hamza," Li Du said. "I am very relieved to see you."

"And I you, librarian," said Hamza.

Hamza was a fellow traveler on Kalden Dorjee's caravan. He was a storyteller by profession, a master of languages, and a self-proclaimed collector of local tales and names of gods. A man of apparent youth, he might have been twenty or forty, and affected one age or another as it suited him.

Since Li Du had met him, seven months earlier, Hamza had never told the same story of his past twice. Once he claimed to be the sixth son of a family of gardeners from Akbarabad. On a different occasion he insisted that he was born in Istanbul and left home on a ship bound for Athens. On a night when he had drunk a bottle of wine around a fire in the Gyalthang inn, he spoke with vehemence of the death of his noble family at the hands of the East India Company in the narrow alleys of Hooghly, only to claim on the next night that he had been raised by spies and cutthroats.

Hamza's features offered little clue to his place of birth, but when he sat with the muleteers around a campfire, wearing his plain hat and rough coat, he could easily pass for a trader from Kham. His polished manners and skill with languages had earned him the role of ambassador for the trade caravan.

Now he stood in the doorway wearing a critical expression. "There are many acceptable gifts that a traveler can offer his host. You might have brought news of foreign kingdoms, trinkets for the lady of the house, or half a torn map, perhaps, or a cart full of wondrous objects. Instead, you present a corpse."

Li Du gave a small smile, which faded quickly as he remembered the inert, icy figure on the bridge. "How did you hear?" he asked.

"From the old man in the cottage who is making cheese in a snowstorm," said Hamza. "Perhaps it is a delicacy — curds separated amid snowflakes and clouds. Like tea leaves dried in moonlight." Several months earlier, in the market inn at Dali, Hamza had spent a day composing a tale about moonlight tea that he swore would double the tea's value in the Lhasa markets. It was something to do with the ghost of a poet searching for his fox wife.

Li Du recalled the crippled man making cheese in his hut. "We met Yeshe. I think he knew who the monk on the bridge was, or guessed, but he was not eager to speak with us."

"He is not warm with strangers," said Hamza. "But the lord of the manor displays enough geniality to balance twenty gruff gatekeepers."

"Is Yeshe a member of the family?"

Hamza shrugged. "The children call him Uncle."

Li Du nodded abstractedly. He was turning his hat over in his hands, twisting the worn wool.

Observing him, Hamza frowned. "Was it so bad a death?" he asked.

"A nightmarish end," Li Du replied. "Violent and inexplicable." As Li Du described the scene at the bridge, he watched Hamza's expression flicker between surprise and curiosity. When he came to the paint applied to the corpse, Hamza's brow furrowed, as if he had not understood the words.

"Painted?" Hamza raised his hand to stop Li Du's account. "But are you sure this was not some trick on tired minds? This apparition on the bridge strikes me more as a spirit than a man. Perhaps this white and gold and blue was an illusion?"

"It was real," Li Du said. "The paint was

thickly applied. I saw the image clearly." Li Du traced a finger across the surface of the wall, sketching an invisible copy of the shape he had seen.

"A white circle framed in gold and blue," said Hamza, thoughtfully. He was leaning against the wall beside the table. He picked up the silver bells and began to polish them idly on his sleeve. "I have seen courtesans painted blue and green to intrigue princes," he said. "I have seen a sorcerer's arms etched with black serpents that writhed, living, across his skin. I have seen eyes painted on the closed eyelids of the dead." Hamza's gaze was focused on memories Li Du could not see, as if he was turning the pages of a book quickly, searching for a half-remembered illustration. "I have never before seen a dead man painted this way," he concluded.

"And you did not even see it," Li Du reminded him.

"No," Hamza said. "No. When I arrived here yesterday, there was nothing on the bridge. Nothing living, nothing dead."

Hamza set the string of bells down again on the table, now polished so bright that the walls of the room were reflected in each one. Li Du looked at the string of identical stretched reflections. His glance shifted to the round copper lid on the shelf, then to the painting in the corner. "I think," he said, "that it was a mirror."

Hamza, who had followed the direction of Li Du's look, lifted his eyebrows. "In this part of the world, mirrors are carried by gods."

Li Du nodded in the direction of the shrine in the corner. "In paintings like that one." He stood up and crossed the room to examine the little devotional painting. It was a delicate piece of work that depicted a woman seated in an open flower against a background of green and blue. She held a curling plant with red and white blossoms. Open eyes stared from her palms, the soles of her feet, and her forehead. Her red garments floated around her.

"There is no mirror in this thangka," Li Du said, "but I have seen them, held, as you say, in the hands of gods and goddesses." Li Du recalled the visible outline of the fingertip that had pulled the serpentine length of blue paint from one side of the dead man's chest to the other. "It was roughly done: the white circle, gold frame, and handle wrapped in blue ribbon."

"And you say that he did it himself?"

"That is how it appeared."

They were both silent for a moment, Li

Du remembering the paint-smeared fingers and the terrible wound. "Did you meet a monk here?"

Hamza shook his head. "There is at least one monk, but I saw him just before I heard what happened, so he cannot be the dead man. There is a mountain temple not far from here — he is inside it lost in prayer."

"You visited a temple?" Li Du raised his eyebrows slightly. Hamza was adamant in his wariness of monasteries, which he insisted were dangerous places.

Hamza shrugged. "In the name of exploration, not of worship. In the morning I went to the village, but I came back and had nothing else to occupy my time."

"You did not return by way of the bridge?"

"No — the village is on this side of the water. There was no one about at the manor, and the pines were emitting a green light before the storm. I found stairs in the mountain like dragon's teeth. How could I resist? So I climbed them, and of course I came to a temple. It's always a temple or a shrine in these mountains. The snow became so heavy I feared I would become lost in it. I returned, and now I am here. My room is that way, closer to the kitchen and not so cold as this one."

"And the family — what are they like?"

"The usual kind of family. A lord, his lady, children to inherit the land and coin coffers and animals. The wife is young, and seems to know all that occurs in the manor. I heard her recite the amount of payment received for every animal they sold last year at the market as if she had only just struck the bargains." Hamza glanced behind him and lowered his voice slightly. "Doso is from an old family, and he will tell you how his ancestor did some service for a king. And then he will tell you about all of his ancestors. And then he will talk about crops and the value of different yak breeds." Hamza sighed. "And there is a mother, Doso's, who turns her prayer wheel by the fire and does not speak. And the other visitors, of course."

"More travelers? In this remote place?"

Hamza nodded. "For a valley so difficult to find, an unusual number of people have found it. There is a dignitary from Lhasa. He is a man of high status who asks uninteresting questions about taxes and crops and the state of the roads and the health of other families of rank. But it will please you to know that one of your favorites is here — a foreign monk."

"A Jesuit?" Li Du had studied with Jesuit priests in the Forbidden City. They were the only Westerners currently permitted to enter China.

"I did not ask. He can communicate in Chinese, but has a translator here with him for the local language. If the translator's expression is anything to go by, I would guess that his employer is not an easy companion."

"Strange company to find in this place." Li Du rubbed his forehead, aware of his fatigue.

"There is a woman, too," Hamza said. "A traveler. There is something odd about her — a religious fanatic, perhaps, or an abandoned mistress chasing a man who made false promises."

"Have you met a young man, not much older than a boy, with short hair and a brown coat threadbare at the elbows?" Li Du told Hamza about his encounter outside the barn.

"No — a village boy, perhaps, performing required service for the manor." Hamza seemed to lose interest. "Temples," he said, "are dangerous places."

"You have never explained to me why you think so."

"Have I not?" Hamza looked surprised. "I have never told you that I once offended a demon spirit? I did not know, at the time, that the demon in my tale was a real demon.

48

So I spoke of him to my audience — the harem of the sultan across the sea — in a private room that no man was allowed to enter. I was an exception. The sultan's favorite consort demanded a tale from me (I will tell you how I first met her another time), and the sultan was so enamored of her that he could not refuse her request. So I told the tale of a demon who posed as a saint. As it happened, my words were so well chosen and so accurate in their depiction of this demon (who I did not know existed) that they summoned that very spirit to the room. He challenged me to battle. I put him off — it is always wise to have prepared at least three ways to convince a demon to wait awhile before killing you — but I expect him to force the issue one day. I avoid monasteries because this particular fiend tends to frequent their paintings."

"Of course," said Li Du. "I knew there must be some explanation."

CHAPTER 4

To reach the kitchen from his room, Li Du had to traverse the full length of the building. He passed four closed doors, then turned left into the wing above the main entrance. The kitchen was at the far end.

It was the largest room in the manor, and the warmest. The floor retained heat rising from the animals in the barns below, and the fire on the hearth was big enough to light the whole space. The hearth itself was a flat, raised platform surrounded on three sides by low, wide benches. An opening in the eaves drew smoke out into the twilight.

Dinner preparations were in progress. Kamala worked beside her children — two boys and a little girl who cradled a swaddled infant. Savory fragrances rose from a large pot set on the hearthstones, to which Kamala was adding pieces of meat. Her hands were shiny and slick with melting fat.

There were four people sitting around the

fire. The first was a man in yellow silk robes trimmed with fur. His face, defined at the chin by a wispy white beard and at the forehead by a red hat, seemed too small for his voluminous attire. He held, cupped in his hands, a bowl with a golden rim that caught the firelight. The second was a younger man with a starved look to his cheeks and a suggestion of a reptile in his wide, thin mouth. He was looking at the fire as if he wanted to rearrange it.

The third person was a woman. Her hair was haphazardly tied and braided away from her face in a matted, knotted tangle, a document of moments when a braid was added in one place, a strip of leather tied to another, and piece of yarn twined in on some different occasion. When Li Du and Hamza entered the room, she glanced up briefly. Her eyes were bright, the skin around them faintly creased, like a page of a book that had been crumpled and smoothed flat. After a quick assessment of the newcomers, she turned her attention to the fire and retreated into her own thoughts. Beside her was a very old woman whose dark clothes blended into the corner so well that she was almost indistinguishable from her surroundings.

Kamala noticed Li Du and Hamza, and

nodded toward the hearth. "Please sit," she said, and returned to her work, issuing soft commands to the children.

Li Du bowed to the assembled strangers and sat down. Hamza remained standing, and after a moment began to walk slowly around the room, examining the vivid painted panels on the wall, the carved wooden bowls displayed on shelves, and the family shrine in one corner framed by translucent white scarves.

The man in yellow introduced himself first. He was Rinzen Ngawang, the dignitary from Lhasa. "I understand from your friend," said Rinzen, with a nod to Hamza, "that you serve the Chinese Emperor. Do I take his meaning correctly — you are one of the Emperor's librarians?" His speech was formal, but not pompous. His affect suggested that he considered Li Du an equal.

Li Du accepted the cup that was handed to him by one of the children. "That was my formal title," he said, "a long time ago. I am just a traveler now."

The man who had been staring intently at the fire raised his eyes to Li Du's for an instant before looking down again. "I am called Andruk," he said. "I am translator and guide to the foreign monk. He wishes to know what has occurred — it was your caravan, I am told, that found the body?"

Li Du nodded and was about to speak when a sound on the stairs announced Doso's return. The manor lord brought the cold in with him. It emanated from his coat, which he removed and hung on a hook in the wall. Even empty, the coat retained a formidable presence. Doso's footsteps vibrated the floor as he crossed toward them.

He looked shaken. The strong lines of his face were drawn, and he clenched and unclenched his hands as he held them to the fire. His eyes moved restlessly around the room as if he needed to ascertain that nothing had been taken during his absence. This scrutiny encompassed equally his wife, his children, stacked cups on the shelves, and glinting knives fixed to the wall.

Doso picked up a bottle and refilled his guests' cups before pouring the clear spirit into his own, filling it to the brim. He raised his glass and they drank. A soft rumble of pleasure sounded in Doso's chest. Then he turned to Andruk. "Where is the foreigner?"

Again, the translator directed his response toward the flames. "He is praying for the soul of the dead man, according to his own rule. He wants to know what happened."

Doso rubbed his large hands on his knees. He cast a quick, fond glance at his children. Then he frowned, raised his cup in invitation for them all to drink again, and drank it down.

"The man who died is known to us," he said. "He was called Dhamo. He lived in seclusion in the temple up the mountain."

Andruk was the first to speak. "What happened to him?" His glance flickered to where Doso's eldest son, a boy of six or seven, listened wide-eyed.

Doso drank again. "He took his own life."

"I heard that something was painted on his body," said Andruk. He looked at Li Du for confirmation. Li Du nodded.

Rinzen's aged face creased in distress. "Paint on the body," he said, with a shudder. "What horror has visited this place?"

Doso nodded. "There was paint. But he applied it himself — his hand was covered in it. We found leather pouches in the snow — he brought the paint with him."

The people around the hearth were silent while the flames whispered and crackled. Doso drew a breath and offered the bottle around the circle, poising it over each cup in turn. He filled his own cup to the brim again. "I would not speak of the dead," he said. "It is known that the subject attracts

54

bad spirits. But I will explain, because most of you are strangers here, that this event is not so impossible to comprehend. Dhamo was a man of peculiar fixations." Doso paused. He looked at Rinzen, as if seeking affirmation.

Rinzen nodded. "Dhamo saw what most people do not see. He lived in a world a little removed from this one. He was a man of visions, and he possessed the gift of being able to express these visions in his art."

"His art?" The question came from Hamza.

Doso took another drink. "Dhamo was a painter. He came to our mountain temple thirteen years ago, and we have honored his request for solitude ever since."

"The white mirror." Andruk said the words slowly. "Why did he paint the white mirror on his flesh?"

Doso shook his head. "That is not for us to understand. We did not communicate with him, nor he with us. He lived in his studio and painted there alone."

Rinzen set his cup down on the floor. "It is good that the Chhöshe is here. You are sure that a monk cannot be summoned from the village to assist him?"

Doso was running his thumb along the edge of his cup, his face tense with concentration. "Not until the snow melts. The Chhöshe is at the temple. He will do all he can to protect Dhamo and our family."

The Chhöshe must be a lama, Li Du thought. He remembered Hamza's description of the young monk he had seen that morning.

Kamala approached silently and added a root to the stew that Li Du did not recognize. She withdrew to the table and began to carve out pieces of preserved ham with a glinting blade. Andruk's eyes followed her, then returned to the fire.

Li Du became aware of a soft buzzing sound in the corner. The old woman was spinning a prayer wheel, its beaded string creating the high droning sound as it revolved around and around. Her listless expression suggested that she did not understand what was being said. Her rheumy eyes were fixed on the hearth, watching a charcoal cave fill with blue flame.

Kamala ladled stew into bowls. In the firelight her soft face glowed. Her braided hair, thickened with yarn, was pinned up and ornamented with an engraved silver disk. When she brought food to the old woman, she took the prayer wheel away gently, and replaced it with the bowl.

"I heard," said Kamala in a clipped, tense

voice, "that his body was not facing our home. That is good."

The boy standing in the corner widened his eyes. "Mother," he said, "is Dhamo going to walk through the village tonight? Is he going to —"

Kamala's voice softened instantly as she replied, "Of course he will not. He will travel far away. And you will stay close to me."

The boy looked unconvinced, but Doso was speaking again. "It is unwise to confuse the night by talking about spirits, and it is not a subject for children. My children," he said, "Sangyal, Tara, Tenzin, and the little one has my own name." Doso looked with pride at his family. "My line is a very old one," he said. "I will tell you how responsibility for this land first came to my ancestor, who was only a poor traveling laborer from south of Tsang with no hope of advancement, and of how he built this house, and of his descendants."

Doso proceeded to give an account of his family's history while the guests silently ate their dinner. The litany seemed to calm him. He spoke of his ancestor who had impressed a king with a feat of strength, of his great-grandfather who had fought the Mongols in the north, and of his grandfather who had traveled to China and to Lhasa and into the Mughal kingdoms, and had restored the manor to new strength. He spoke modestly of his own travels as a younger man. "My firstborn, Tashi," he said, "was called to a religious life."

In the corner, Kamala plunged the dishes into the water so that they clattered against each other. She began to scrub noisily, the water sloshing over the side of the bucket. Doso went on, "A beautiful boy, Tashi, who learned to shoot an arrow and ride a horse not long after he could walk, and impressed everyone who saw him because his skill was so great."

Doso was interrupted by the sound of dogs barking somewhere within the manor walls. A hollow pounding resounded below them on the manor's outer door. It grew louder. There was someone outside, someone who had traveled through the storm and the darkness and now demanded entry.

The solitary traveler who entered the kitchen beside a scowling Doso stamped the snow from his boots and shook it from his coat and hat. He was a man of about Li Du's age, dressed in dark traveling clothes brightened by a red sash tied diagonally across his chest. His long hair, ornamented with silver and turquoise beads, was loose around his shoulders, mingling with the white fur at his coat collar. His nose, very thin and straight at the bridge, widened into a crooked tip.

"This is Sonam Dhargey," said Doso.

With a smile, Sonam strode forward to the hearth and took a seat. His quick eyes took in the faces of the guests, then shifted to the corner, where they lingered on Kamala. He pulled a bowl from a pocket of his coat and gestured at one of the children to fill it for him.

"You have a full house, old friend," he said to Doso. "I hope that you have room for another and will not turn me out into the storm." There was something unpleasant in his speech, a subtle disrespect in the half smile on his full lips.

Doso filled Sonam's cup. "You know that I would never refuse hospitality to a traveler," he said. "But how have you come so late? You cannot have crossed the pass in this weather."

Sonam lifted his cup to Doso and drank deeply. "It is a bad storm. If I had been caught on the pass any later I would have been buried with my horse. The wind beat the cliff so hard that I thought I would be pounded into the stone — become a mountain spirit. It is fortunate that by the time darkness fell, I was almost at the bridge and could find my way to this house with no moon or stars."

Appearing not to notice the tension in the room at the mention of the bridge, Sonam leaned forward and inhaled savory steam from the pot over the fire. "I dream of your wife's cooking," he said. "It is better than all the food that the government officials buy to impress each other in Dajianlu."

"Dhamo died today," said Doso.

Sonam looked around the room, as if seeking confirmation of Doso's words. No one spoke. His features slackened in surprise, making him appear less intelligent, and less handsome. The veneer reasserted itself quickly. "Well," he said, "Dhamo was not a young man. It will be a pity to lose the income from his paintings."

Ignoring Sonam's remark, Doso gave a terse summary of what had happened. As he listened, Sonam's eyes shifted around the circle, assessing the company one at a time. "I have seen corpses on mountains before," he said when Doso had finished. "And on these roads, even monks are not safe from cutthroats. I have seen the remains of the diseased, the starved, the frozen. But suicide in the forest — that is not so common."

Sonam's spectral corpses seemed to insinuate themselves into the kitchen. Shadows spread across the wall with new menace. Sonam tore a piece of bread from the plate Kamala had set down and began to eat. "Tell me then," he said to Doso, "what drove Dhamo to such an end? When I last saw him, he was painting in his studio as if he had no desire in the world but to continue. I would have expected him to refuse death out of fear that in his next life he wouldn't know how to paint."

The last statement earned Sonam an appreciative nod from Hamza.

"Dhamo's path was his own," said Doso, with stern finality.

Sonam shrugged. His eyes moved to the woman sitting across the fire from him, and remained there. She did not return his stare.

"I have not seen you here before," Sonam said.

She looked up. "The lord and his wife are so kind to let me stay," she said, but did not offer anything more.

Sonam shrugged, then looked around him. "I saw Pema downstairs with the animals," he said. "So he is as slow with his work as he ever was."

61

Listening to him, Li Du felt that he had heard Sonam's voice before. Something in the rough, low syllables resonated in his memory, but he could not connect them to a specific time or place.

As the conversation turned to speculations on the duration of the storm, Li Du felt the unease beneath the clipped, polite voices. *We are all thinking of the dead man,* he thought. *We are all wondering what form he will take in our dreams tonight.*

Beneath Li Du's feet, the wooden floor of the hallway felt old and sturdy, as if the manor had adopted some of the hard permanence of the mountain into which it had settled.

He had almost reached his room when a rattling sound made him stop and look to his right. The light from his taper, a sliver of pinewood saturated with pitch, illuminated a door, and he saw that the bolt holding it shut was not secure. He reached out to adjust it, but in doing so accidentally released the bolt entirely. The wind caught the door and slammed it outward. Li Du's taper was instantly snuffed, and he was pulled, stumbling, out onto a platform engulfed in snow.

The freezing air knocked the breath from

him. He could see that he was at the top of an exterior staircase leading down to the courtyard. Nothing else was visible through the snow except for a faint glow coming from a building he could not identify. He grappled for the edge of the door and hauled it closed as he retreated backward into the hallway. Then he slid the bolt into place and hurried to his room.

With shaking fingers, he used a flint to light the candle by the bed. He held three pine tapers to the flame and slid them into the hanging brazier. Light glowed through perforated shapes — triangles and diamonds — in the copper. As soon as he had pulled off his boots he sat on the bed, his back against the wall, and drew the blankets up around him.

In the sudden burst of cold, a memory had escaped a chamber in his mind. It was a memory of a winter afternoon in Beijing. He had been leaving the library, and the wind had caught the door, blowing it wide open and almost pulling his hat from his head.

In the cold manor bedroom, Li Du tried to clear his mind and return to the present. He did not like to think of Beijing. But as fatigue began to creep over him, he could not contain the memory.

Was it ten years ago? Twelve? The wind whirled dry leaves around him as he climbed the hill from the library to his favorite teahouse. He looked down at what remained of the rice crop in the Emperor's pleasure garden. The neat square pools were covered in a transparent glaze of ice, from which the browning leaves of rice plants protruded sadly, drooping toward each other as if they were discussing their bad situation. No one had expected the Emperor's agricultural experiment to succeed, and it hadn't. But the Emperor was away on a campaign, and when he returned he would almost certainly be consumed by some new interest.

The teahouse was warm and fragrant, crowded with conversations and hazy with steam. It was a favorite haunt of scholars. Two Jesuits argued over a sketched diagram unrolled across a table. Across from them, two court scholars looked forlornly down at their cups and watched the pot grow cold just out of their reach. The foreigners had used it to hold down a corner of the paper. Li Du found Shu, and they fell into a discussion of the Emperor's campaign against Galdan, leader of the Dzungar Mongols.

Li Du followed the paths of dream and memory out of the teahouse and into the courtyard outside his home. It was evening now, and the moon was full. Its light slipped down the curving roof tiles like water and cast shadows of plants on the door. Li Du heard steps within, and the voice of his wife. She was talking to her sister, who was going to have a child, and their aunt, who was giving them advice. He heard the clatter of game tiles on the table. He looked up at the moon. It was uncommunicative, a flat, featureless disk. *A circle,* Li Du thought, *a circle painted white.*

CHAPTER 5

Li Du woke the next morning to a gray dawn seeping through the shuttered windows. For several minutes he did not move, except to trace with his eyes the unfamiliar map of cracks across the ceiling beams that had been invisible to him in the dark the night before. Half awake, he attempted to impose on it the route the caravan had taken. If that cobwebby rift there was the gorge southeast of Gyalthang, then that knot could be the trading post. But the trails disappeared as he looked at them and his wandering gaze lost its way. He pushed away the blankets and got up.

When he had readied himself to quit the room, he rummaged through his saddlebag for his bowl. It was a silver-plated wooden dish that he had purchased on the outskirts of Kunming almost a year before. "You are in our territory now," the merchant had said, proud to be explaining things to

66

someone ignorant of local custom. He held up a silver bowl, the outside of which was engraved with a simple depiction of leaping deer. "If you are going to be traveling with caravans, carry a silver bowl. Silver jewelry for luck, silver chopsticks for food, and a silver bowl for avoiding bad water. If you dip the bowl in a stream and find it turns black, that's poison, and you had better not drink it."

Li Du had thanked the man, bought the bowl, and managed to avoid being talked into the bracelets and chopsticks as well.

He was halfway to the manor kitchen before he realized that, in such a fine house, it was unnecessary to bring his own bowl to the fire. He turned around to take it back to his room, but stopped at the door that had blown open the night before. It was open again now, and someone had swept the stairs leading down to the courtyard. He stepped outside.

Below, the snow was crisscrossed with footprints, ridged and shaded blue in the half-light. Now that the view was clear, Li Du saw that two sides of the manor were defined by a high wall that connected to both ends of the long residential building, forming a square that enclosed the court-yard.

In the middle of the courtyard was a square tower. Li Du counted four stories, the top three of which boasted ornate exteriors. In the far corner was a smaller building, a temple with orange and gold pillars. Outside its open doors, a cauldron filled with lit incense sticks sent thin undulations of smoke into the air.

Still holding his bowl, Li Du descended the stairs carefully. It was no longer snowing, but a quick glance at the sky suggested that there was more to come. Hearing his name, Li Du turned to his left and saw, at the edge of the open barn, a fire cradled in an iron brazier with several stools arranged around it. One of these was occupied by Rinzen, the visiting dignitary, who raised a hand in a gesture of welcome and an invitation to sit with him.

"Please let me serve you butter tea," said Rinzen as Li Du approached. "The others have gone, but I am making a fresh pot now." Li Du thanked him and sat down. It was a large fire, built high with kindling to last through the morning. The flames rose around a pot filled with water, its rough, blackened sides clothed in flame. It rested on three stones, beneath which the hollow heart of the fire devoured itself in hungry gasps of white and blue. Flakes of ash fell away and were lifted into the air by imperceptible currents.

"Like many forces," Rinzen said, his eyes also tracing the path of the ashes through the air, "the power that moves the ashes is invisible and must be inferred from the effect it has on those objects light enough to be moved by it." He held out one hand and gestured for Li Du to hand over his bowl.

Li Du passed it to him. "Thank you."

Rinzen took the bowl and set it down beside his own on the swept, cobbled floor. He drew out a small knife from a sheath on his belt and used it to chip a portion of dry tea leaves from the brick that rested, half wrapped in its paper, on a flat rock beside the brazier. The sign of the tea's maker was still visible in the middle of the brick, a raised seal that came from the mold into which the tea had been pressed. Rinzen dropped the clump of leaves into the pot. The water had reached a boil, and the leaves disappeared instantly, pulled down into the roiling bubbles.

Rinzen sat back. "I am happy that we are meeting at a time when our empires are in such good accord. It has not always been so."

Li Du had heard little of the relationship between Lhasa and Beijing in the six years

69

since he had left the Forbidden City. He had paid scant attention to news exchanged by travelers around hearths and wine bottles. He knew that in remote areas, reports were often just distorted echoes of events long past: rivalries, exchanges of power, concealed deaths, marriages, and murders. To distinguish true from false, current from outdated, was almost impossible. To do so successfully was the task of spies in search of information important enough to merit a king's notice.

"For six years," said Li Du, "I have been almost entirely separated from discussions of empires and delegations and oaths of allegiance." He gave a self-deprecating smile. "I have floated down a different stream, with quiet trees and stones for company."

Rinzen smiled, an expression that almost made his eyes kindly. They were eyes more intelligent than warm. "But you have heard that Tibet now has a king in Lhasa."

Li Du tried to summon memories that were like neglected tapestries left too long to fade on a sunlit wall. "I recall that the regent to the Fifth Dalai Lama had the governance of that city after the death of his master."

"He does not have it anymore," said Rinzen. "The regent is dead."

70

"And there is a new one?"

"Not a regent — a king. Lhazang Khan has ruled for five years."

Li Du absorbed this information. "And he is allied with the Kangxi?"

Rinzen nodded. "Your Emperor has supported Lhazang Khan's claim against many challenges. Old grievances are forgotten. The ancient oaths between the empires have been renewed: *They shall not plot against us, and we will make no preparations against them.*" Rinzen raised his eyes to meet Li Du's. "The frontiers will no longer be garrisoned. Our empires are like brothers to each other now."

It was possible to forget many things in six years away from the imperial court. Li Du had endeavored to forget as much as possible. But he knew with absolute certainty that the Emperor of China would never leave a frontier ungarrisoned. Deciding that a noncommittal response was more prudent than silence, he said, "That is good news for travelers. These roads are treacherous enough without armies marching across them."

Rinzen peered into the bubbling pot and nodded briefly, as if satisfied. Using a thick cloth to protect his hands, he poured the tea into a cylindrical wooden churn, and

71

slid the lid down the churning stick to seal it. "It does not surprise me that you have lost the thread of current events," he said, as he began to mix the butter and tea. "In these hidden places, a village could go on believing itself sworn to a king even after the king, his son, and his grandson have been buried. Places like this connect empires, but they are too far from the centers to feel their power. These are the safest places, and at the same time, the most dangerous."

Observing the old dignitary who had witnessed, Li Du was sure, a bloody change of power in his city of Lhasa, Li Du was reminded of the officials and magistrates he had known. He saw the travel fatigue in Rinzen's sun-burnished skin and beringed fingers stained with frost poisoning that hadn't yet healed. The bright yellow silk and fur was, on closer inspection, beginning to fray, though the colors remained a brilliant reminder of Rinzen's high status.

As if sensing Li Du's sympathetic gaze, Rinzen stopped churning for a moment and stretched his back. "I did not sleep last night," he said. "Yesterday's events were heavy on my mind."

"You spoke as if you knew the man who died."

Rinzen nodded. "I did. I had not seen him in many years, but the delicacy of Dhamo's nature was obvious even then. Perhaps he should not have been allowed to stay here, alone, so far from the supervision and guidance that a monastery would offer."

"It was my understanding that he wished for solitude."

"He did, but if solitude meant that he kept company only with his visions, perhaps it would have been better for him to be with other monks. He wanted nothing to distract him from his work. He saw the world around him in pigments."

There was a short silence between them while Rinzen removed the lid from the churn, placed a rough straw strainer over Li Du's bowl, and poured the butter tea into it. The dark leaves caught in the straw, lifeless and glistening. Rinzen filled his own bowl and set the strainer on the rock beside the tea brick. He handed Li Du's bowl to him with both hands, and Li Du took it. The opaque circle of liquid was velvety; its steam carried the fragrance of fat and musk and black tea. Li Du sipped and felt strength spread through his chest and limbs.

Rinzen picked up his own bowl. "You are wondering, perhaps, what brings an official from Lhasa so far from that city."

73

Li Du's general dislike of questions about his reasons for going from one place to another made him less likely to ask those same questions of others. But he was curious.

Rinzen continued, "I am accompanying the Fourth Chhöshe Lama on a visit to the place where he was reborn."

The Chhöshe. Doso had uttered the name the night before, as had the boy in the courtyard. Li Du knew about tulkus. They were guides: reincarnated, discovered as children, and taught to embody the sacred lineage of a master, enlightened beings who chose to walk the earth in human form and lead others away from harm. The most powerful of all was the Dalai Lama, the one man whose existence had proved capable of uniting even the most belligerent northern clans. But there were hundreds of other incarnated lamas, some of older lineages, some newly discovered, some possessed of wealth inherited by rebirth rather than bloodline, others living in self-imposed poverty and solitude in mountain caves.

"I have not heard of that lineage," said Li Du.

"It is a minor name, a wandering monk bound to no monastery," said Rinzen. "But in this incarnation he shows promise of elevating the lineage to greater fame. Already his fellow students at the university follow his teachings. Even his instructors listen to him when he reasons through the most confounding doctrinal contradictions."

Li Du tried to piece together what he had been told. "In the vast expanses of the mountain range, it is a strange coincidence that your journey with the Chhöshe should lead you to a temple occupied by a monk you knew long ago."

"It is no coincidence. The Chhöshe was born in this house, and it was for him that Dhamo first came here."

"I do not understand."

Rinzen leaned forward to adjust a log. One end of it fell apart in a cloud of powder ash and blackened, charred flakes. "The Chhöshe was born Doso's son — his son by his first wife. Thirteen years ago, when word reached Lhasa of the death of the Third Chhöshe, the search began for the Fourth. It was Dhamo, then a painter in a Lhasa monastery, whose vision guided the emissaries to this valley. He saw a mountain pass and a boy climbing stairs cut into stone. When we arrived, Dhamo's visions were affirmed. The signs were very clear, and the boy was identified."

Rinzen's gaze moved to the courtyard,

where a thin eddy of snow had been picked up by the wind and scudded smoothly across the surface. His brow crinkled. "The Chhöshe has almost completed his education. He wanted to visit the place of his rebirth. I was sent to accompany him." Rinzen finished his tea and set down his bowl with a clink on the stone. "Now," he said, "I have told you why I am here. It is your turn to tell me about yourself. Why are you leaving China?" He asked the question lightly, but his tone did not match the piercing attentiveness of his gaze as he waited for Li Du's response.

Li Du felt his mind shrink from the question, as it always did. "I am drawn to travel," he said. "I wish to — I find at this time in my life I wish to travel." He paused, embarrassed by his own ineloquence.

"And your work as librarian?"

"There are many libraries to see in the world."

"Of course," Rinzen said, "but visiting a library is not the same as knowing one."

Li Du was honest. "I will not deny that I miss the library at the Forbidden City." He paused. "But I am fortunate to have a rough duplicate of it in my mind."

An idea seemed to strike Rinzen. "There is a small collection of books in the mountain temple," he said. "If you wish to study them, I see no reason why you should not. The Chhöshe has assumed the duties of the temple's care while the storm keeps us here."

Li Du glanced up at implacable gray sky.

Rinzen reached out a hand. "Please," he said, "allow me to refill your cup, and I will tell you the way to the temple."

Li Du floundered through the snow to the caravan camp, around which the mules, now unburdened, stood unconcernedly in the drifts. Scraps of hay and grass littered the snow, suggesting that Doso had kept his promise and shared feed from his own stores.

Outside the hut, Li Du paused in the clearing that had been dug in front of the door. From within he heard the clatter of bowls and pots, and Norbu's voice. "So cold," Norbu was saying, "that it makes this storm look like a bit of dust blowing through our village in the summertime."

Li Du ducked inside. The muleteers had settled into their temporary shelter so naturally that the saddles and packs had become part of the building's structure, fortifying the weak walls inside and out, and insulating the inhabitants from the wind.

Planks, branches, and rocks had been set up to accommodate the group seated around the fire. The place smelled of leather, wet wool, smoke, and dank boots.

Hamza was already there. He gestured toward an open space, and Li Du squeezed into it. Norbu was accepting bowls, filling them with butter tea, and passing them back to their owners. Hands reached across the fire. They were scarred, callused hands, the skin burned and frozen and healed so many times that they were impervious to levels of discomfort that would hinder others. *You must experience injury before you can develop resistance to it,* Li Du thought, as he listened to Norbu recount a storm from his youth.

"We were at the Sho La," Norbu said. "You see this bowl of tea?" He held the bowl up. "It would be frozen in the time it took me to fill it. The snow was blowing, but it was too late to turn back. We had to continue forward, or stay where we were and die. Then the animals stopped walking. It was ice between the iron and the hoof."

The others nodded and murmured acknowledgment of this disaster.

"The mules would not take another step," Norbu went on. "And by that time the snow was up to our chests." He raised a hand and held it horizontally across his heart. "So

78

what did we do? We took the saddlebags from their backs. Each bag was as heavy as a man. I carried two of them on my own shoulders. Without the weight, the mules agreed to walk."

Norbu handed a full bowl to Kalden. "Your brother was leading us," he said. "We didn't lose an animal, a man, or a pack. That was a good year."

Kalden was looking up at the ceiling of the cabin as if he were seeing through it to the sky. He took the bowl. "We are all eager to move on. But it is not winter yet. In a few days the temperature will rise, and the snow will melt."

Norbu poured butter tea into his own bowl and set the blackened pot near the embers to keep warm. "We should have taken our chances on the pass yesterday. I don't like being trapped near the spirit of a man who would paint a mirror on his body and slit his own belly. It isn't safe."

The smoke from the fire, illuminated by thin daylight filtering through the roof beams, swirled restlessly. Kalden glared at Norbu. "We would be safer if you kept your attention on our food supplies."

Norbu ignored him. "Something was chasing him through the forest," he said.

"Why do you think so?" The question

came from Hamza.

Norbu leaned forward and extended his arm slowly. His bony wrist and gnarled hand protruded from the greasy cuff of his sleeve. He opened his hand flat, his palm inches from Hamza's face. "I know because of the mirror," he said. "Hold a mirror to a demon, and it is frightened by its own reflection."

Hamza looked slightly startled, and Norbu lowered his arm. "I will tell you what happened," said Norbu. "The man on the bridge was the victim of a demon who followed him into this world. He was a painter, so he turned to his paints for protection. He painted a mirror on his body to frighten the demon away. But it did not work. The demon gripped his hand between its own and thrust the knife into him." Norbu paused. "And now the demon searches for another —"

"Peace, Norbu." Concern vied with exasperation in Kalden's expression. He put a hand on Norbu's shoulder. "This is why we should travel with a monk in our company," he said. "To prevent baseless speculation."

Kalden's words did nothing to dispel the sense of unease that had filled the hut. Norbu's dog, a long-legged hound with a golden coat who was curled in the corner, growled softly. The fire was burning low and starting to smoke. The three hearthstones at its center hunched like plotters amid the embers.

Hamza broke the silence. "I will not argue that there are no monsters in the forest," he said. "But I know a tale of a mirror that is not so ominous." He straightened his back and flexed his fingers. "It is the story of a man who went fishing for the moon in a pond one night."

Hamza drew in his breath to continue, but was interrupted by a creak at the the door. A woman stepped over the threshold onto the dirt floor. It was the traveler from the manor. Hamza, his hands still lifted like those of a conjurer, stopped talking.

"Are you telling the story of the fish who kept the moon's secret, even though it separated him forever from his love? That is a sad tale."

"That is not the ending I tell," replied Hamza, affronted.

"Oh? I did not know that it had any other ending. Please continue."

Hamza opened his mouth to speak, but the others were now paying attention to the woman. "I will tell it another time," he said.

She turned to Kalden. "Pardon me for intruding on you," she said. "But I hope you will sell me some tea leaves. I hear that you have the spring flush from the Pu'er groves. I know that it is expensive, but my sister whom I am going to visit has a particular fondness for it. Would you sell me a small portion? I am Seratsering," she added, "a guest at the manor."

"We did not intend to trade here," Kalden replied. "That leaf sells for a high price in Lhasa."

"I would not offer for it before I have seen it," she said.

Kalden hesitated. Then he rose, removed a round slab of tea from a bamboo sheaf, and handed it to her. She lifted it to her nose, then squinted at the compacted leaves. "It is not the finest quality," she said.

Li Du saw Kalden's eyes brighten. "If you think so," he said, "then I assume you do not want to buy it." He held out a hand, but she did not return the tea.

"I am considering it," she said. "But I won't pay Lhasa prices."

They haggled good-naturedly for several minutes. As she spoke, Li Du noticed that Sera's eyes traveled lightly over every sack and box and bag in the hut. The appraisal was conducted so subtly that he doubted anyone else noticed it, except, perhaps, for Hamza, who was watching her through narrowed eyes.

An agreement reached, Sera dropped the silver taels into Kalden's hand. "Thank you," she said. "My sister will be pleased."

"One less brick to be taxed," muttered Norbu.

Kalden silenced Norbu with a look, then bowed to Sera. "May you find your sister in good health," he said.

After she had gone, Li Du stood up and moved toward the door. "I wonder," he said, hesitantly because he had never questioned Kalden before, "how you knew that the manor would be here when you sent Hamza ahead to find it."

Kalden shrugged. "It was described to me by some villagers. They said we could rely on the manor lord to be hospitable."

Li Du considered this. "You said when we were staying at the Gyalthang inn that you intended to explore a new route, one less accessible than the road through Dajianlu, in order to establish new trade relationships. But we have passed at least ten villages since Gyalthang, and you have not traded at any of them."

"My brother taught me that the man who explores new paths is the man who becomes rich," said Kalden.

There was a loud clatter, followed by a

hiss. Norbu had lost his grip on the pot of tea and dropped it into the fire. "Go on," he said, gesturing toward the door. "You are blocking the way, and if we don't add kindling to the fire it will smoke us all out into the snow."

Li Du stepped outside. Norbu called after him from within. "Never question the leader of your caravan. It's in Lhasa that the tea is worth the most, and it's in Lhasa that we'll sell it."

CHAPTER 6

A fine, quiet snow dusted the air as Li Du made his way to the place Rinzen had described. Behind the manor, not far from a towering woodpile, he found a trickling stream and followed it until he came to stairs set into the mountain, their shapes barely discernible under the snow. Li Du raised his eyes and traced the steep ascent up through firs studded with blue-black cones. With a sigh he bent down, knotted his long coat above his boots, and began to climb.

He stopped to catch his breath beside a bulbous hollow tree. When he reached out a hand to lean on it, a layer of old, rotting wood crumbled away under his fingers. The snow had stopped, but the hush it had imposed on the forest remained. Li Du thought of Dhamo descending these same stairs the day before in his crimson robes.

Resuming his climb, Li Du found that his

memory from the night before had invited others, which now competed for his attention. The higher he climbed into the thinning mountain air, the less able he was to ignore them.

His mind began to paint the black and white forest with greens: the dark green of bamboo in the shade, the shining yellow green of leaves with sun passing through them, green moss on the stones by the pond, green water reflecting the moss and leaves, and a green glazed bottle full of wine.

With a sigh, he gave up and stepped once again into the past. It was fifteen years ago, and it was springtime in Beijing.

"The Emperor is right," said Shu, pouring the clear wine into their cups and leaning back in his chair. A dragonfly skipped across the surface of the pond, disturbing the reflection of the trees.

"He is right," Shu went on, "because he is the Emperor and what he says cannot, by definition, be wrong." He lifted a finger, as he tended to do when he made a point. "But also, he is right."

They were discussing the exhibition that had occurred the day before in the Garden of Perfect Brightness at the palace. The Emperor had granted a foreign painter, a

Jesuit residing at court, the opportunity to demonstrate a technique that he claimed would advance the art of painting beyond what had yet been accomplished in China. This technique, he said, involved manipulation of lines informed by new understandings of the human eye.

The result — a sketch of an open courtyard crowded with columns — earned polite murmurs of appreciation from the small audience of invited courtiers and officials. The Emperor examined it closely, and at a distance. "It is of some technical interest," he said finally, "but it is not artistic in any way."

The dismissive comment was softened in translation for the foreigner, but it was agreed afterward that the Emperor's indifferent reaction was yet another in a series of indications that the foreigners were falling out of favor. There was a rumor that he intended to banish them from China entirely.

Li Du picked up his cup, watching the wake of a dragonfly spread across the surface of the water. Golden light caught on the ripples. The sky was filled with changing color around the falling, ponderous curve of the setting sun. "I may speak plainly?" he said. It was only half a question. He always spoke plainly to Shu, who had been his teacher ever since Li Du began his formal education.

"You may," Shu replied, "and it is correct of you to ask. But no matter what someone says to you, you should never speak plainly unless you are very sure of your audience."

Li Du nodded, acknowledging the warning in a general way, then setting it aside. "In my opinion, it would be wrong of the Emperor to send the Jesuits away. I think that we should pay close attention to what they can teach us."

"About the Christian god?" Shu's white eyebrow quirked.

"No," said Li Du. "That is not what I mean. I am speaking of all they can teach us about science, about the movement of planets and the properties of time, and yes, even how they achieve illusions of depth in painted canvases. The Emperor treats their knowledge like a collection of curiosities. He sees a clock and tells his craftsmen to replicate it, but he does not ask *why* it was made. The foreigners do not simply know things that we do not know. They think differently. Why would we banish them when they have so much to teach?"

Shu raised a hand to shade his eyes against the setting sun. "Yes," he said. "They are intelligent. They express themselves well. They offer intriguing explanations for the world's secrets. That is all true."

"But you agree that they should be banished?"

Shu raised a finger and tapped his own ear. "I think you should listen more carefully. You were so eager to say what you wanted to say that you replied thoughtlessly to my question."

Li Du was abashed. "What question?"

"I asked about the Christian god."

Li Du's brows drew together. "Their faith does not seem relevant. They do not force it on their students. When I converse with Jesuits in the library, we rarely address religion."

"And so you forget that they were sent here on a mission of conversion. You are distracted by their science. But the Emperor has not forgotten."

Li Du considered this, then shook his head, unconvinced. "But the Emperor cannot see their religion as a threat. They have almost no converts. No one is interested."

"Not yet. The Jesuits have not discovered a way to make a convincing case. When they wax philosophical, they embarrass themselves because they are ignorant of our literature and prone to basic mistakes. It is difficult to imagine anyone being persuaded by their paintings of men with wings." Shu paused to sip his wine. "But they traveled a very long way and endured great hardship to come here. I think that there is power behind them that we have not seen. And now that power — the ruler they call the pope — sends them letters chastising them for their failure to convert the Emperor of China."

"That is arrogant," Li Du admitted.

"Yes. And to produce such arrogant people, this faith must be very powerful in the West. And so the Emperor is cautious. He is wise to be cautious."

"But to banish them? Or even to kill them, as he has threatened to do before?"

"I do not think he will banish them. In my opinion, he will keep them here and learn from them, as you want him to do. But he will make sure they know that he is not some credulous scholar who is easily manipulated by these 'tricks of the eye.' Their faith may not seem likely to win converts, but the Kangxi knows never to discount religion. After all, think of Tibet. Even the Mongols, who are never at peace with anyone, will follow the command of the Fifth Dalai Lama."

Li Du sighed, unable to dispute this.

Shu smiled. "But perhaps you think I am just an old scholar set in my ways who does not want foreigners coming in and offending my ear with their incorrect pronunciations."

Li Du raised his glass and bowed his head in a gesture of deep respect. "If you were like the other old scholars, I'd be imprisoned, dead, or exiled by now."

"It is true," Shu said. "I am very patient with your irreverence." Shu's expression became sad. "I do not like to think that we would never again sit and watch the sun fall into the bamboo grove."

They were silent for a moment. The wind carried the soft voices of their wives exchanging opinions on other matters as the loose threads of their embroidery floated like spiderwebs through the air.

Li Du looked across the pond at the sunset. "It is so pleasant at this house outside the city. When I am here, I never want to leave. And then I return to the library and I say, 'Now I am here, and I never want to leave.'"

Never want to leave. Li Du was pulled from the memory back into the snowy forest by the shadow and flutter of an unseen bird, a raven, perhaps, or an owl. He thought of Rinzen's question that morning. *Why are you leaving China?*

With a determined frown Li Du adjusted his worn hat, as if by doing so he could control the thoughts in his head. He resumed his climb, and was relieved when the next turn in the stone stairs brought him to an open mountain meadow.

CHAPTER 7

There were no more trees above Li Du, only the suggestion, through the clouds, of bare mountain summits. Ahead of him in the snow, strands of fluttering prayer flags stretched from the top of a pole to the ground, to which they were pinned by rocks. Many of the flags were faded and threadbare. Others glowed like liquid glass against the gray sky. Like the red plumes on the bridle of the lead mule, the flags asserted human presence in an inhospitable landscape.

Beyond them stood a modest temple with a sloping roof. Two sets of stairs led up to two separate doors, one at the far left of the building, the other at the far right. A narrow porch, from which the snow had been swept, extended between the doors. Set into the outer wall was a row of weather-beaten prayer wheels.

Seeing that the leftmost door was ajar, Li

Du climbed the corresponding stairs. At the top, he touched the handle of a prayer wheel. He spun it a quarter turn clockwise, and by doing so exposed a section that had been turned toward the wall. It was blackened and traced by an irregular grid of cracks. His gaze moved to the building's columns. Beneath their peeling paint, they too were charred. He went to the door and, without stepping over the lintel, peered inside.

The temple's interior was initially so dark that Li Du could see nothing but flames floating in the blackness. As his vision adjusted, he saw the rims of copper chalices cradling each flame — butter lamps in a row on an altar. The eight identical butter lamps looked duplicated, like a trick of mirrors, differentiated only by the flames that moved independently, intent on their unique conversations with the air.

Prostrated in front of the central altar was a monk. Li Du could make out nothing about his appearance except for his shaved head, broad shoulders, and robes of crimson and saffron. *The Chhöshe,* he thought. Between the huddled monk and the altar was a recumbent figure — a human body — covered by a sheet of rough cloth.

Bending over the monk was another man, who appeared to Li Du as a pale face bobbing atop a black robe. This man was speaking, but just as his eyes struggled to adjust to the darkness, Li Du's ears fought to understand the sounds. Slowly the syllables formed sense in his mind. The man was speaking Latin.

"It is a holy and salutary thought to pray for the deceased so that they may be released from their sins." The man gesticulated like a performing dancer, as if by the extension and movement of his arms he could amplify his speech. He pronounced his syllables slowly and with emphasis. "But the words you speak are whispered by the devil. Cease your false prayers. *Cease* them."

Li Du stood transfixed as the man raised his hand to his mouth and gestured as if he were pulling an object from between his lips. "Words," he said to the monk, who showed no sign of response. "Do you understand? I am speaking to you of words, of speech." He gestured at the shrouded form in front of the altar. "You think that you guide his soul to heaven, but you are leading him instead to the inferno. You condemn him."

Still there was no answer. The man raised

his arms to encompass the wall behind the altar. "Do you venerate these demons?" he asked. Li Du raised his own eyes to the wall. Behind the flickering butter lamps, color coalesced in the darkness. The wall was covered in paintings. Hundreds of faces stared out from within frames of gleaming silk. There were entities seated and standing, their smoke-darkened features outlined in red and blue and green. Tongues emerged from fanged jaws. Heads were crowned in rows of skulls. White eyes stood out like snowflakes against dark earth. Figures in crimson sat on floating clouds.

Li Du stepped carefully over the high wooden threshold into the room. The standing man had begun to repeat his entreaty, as if time had completed a circle. "It is a holy and salutary thought to pray . . ." He reached out a hand as if to place it on the monk's back, and Li Du saw the crimson-robed shoulders tense.

Li Du coughed. The man looked up, startled. As he took in Li Du's small stature, patched clothes, and tentative demeanor, he relaxed. Li Du walked toward him and introduced himself in quiet, perfunctory Latin.

The other's eyes widened in astonishment. He raised his hands as if in supplication to some presence in the shadowy rafters above them.

"The language of the Church," he said, "in this, of all places, and from a native." He took a step toward Li Du. "I am Paolo Campo."

"Perhaps," Li Du said, in a whisper, "we might speak together outside?"

The man shook his head. He did not lower his voice to match Li Du's. "I cannot in my conscience allow him to continue. He condemns his own soul, and the soul of the deceased."

Li Du spoke firmly. "He will not stop his prayers."

Seeing the foreigner hesitate, Li Du pressed his case. "I see that your translator is not here. I speak the language of these roads. If he pauses in his prayer, then I will translate your words to him."

Campo relented, and after a final glance at the monk, turned toward the door. As Li Du prepared to follow him, a flash of reflected candlelight caught his eye. It drew his attention to a small collection of objects arranged near the shrouded corpse. Moving closer, Li Du recognized the ornate handle, now clean, that he had seen clutched between bloody fingers the day before. But it was the silver blade, exposed for the first time to Li Du's gaze, that had gleamed.

Outside the building, Li Du had the opportunity to observe Paolo Campo in the light. He gave the impression of a man who had once been round, and was now deflated. There was a mottled, slightly bruised look to his face, as if he had not slept. His hair, interspersed with gray, was pulled back and tied at the nape of his neck. His robe-like coat, Li Du now saw, was not black, as it had appeared in the temple, but brown.

Campo spoke first. "You address me in Latin," he said. "How is it possible? Can it be that we are in proximity to one of the lost Christian kingdoms?"

Li Du pulled the door of the temple closed and descended the stairs. "The lost kingdoms?"

Like a deer stretching its nose toward food, Campo followed him down. "You are, perhaps, descended from the realm of Prester John?"

Li Du shook his head. "I was not born in these mountains, nor am I of the Christian faith. I learned your language from the Jesuit scholars in the court of the Chinese Emperor."

"Ah," said Campo. He looked so crestfallen that Li Du, to his own surprise, was tempted to change his answer, and to assure the man that he *was* a Christian in order to comfort him.

Campo went on. "So you were taught by the Jesuits," he said. "That explains how you can speak the language of the Church and yet not follow its teachings. For more than a hundred years there have been Jesuits in the Chinese court, but they spend their time building clocks and astronomical observatories instead of saving souls. The ignorant cry out for salvation while the Jesuits enjoy the luxuries of palace life."

Li Du knew something about the strife between Christian orders competing for influence in China. "Are you, then, a Dominican?"

The question seemed to please Campo. "So you know something of our orders," he said. "But to answer you, I am not a Dominican. I am a Capuchin, an adherent to the teachings of Saint Francis. I have come to these mountains to promote true belief in the —"

A gust of wind bore down from the encircling cliffs and carried away the rest of Campo's sentence. Li Du felt the chill through the seams and patches of his old coat. He shielded his eyes against the particles of snow that whirled up, filling the air and stinging his cheeks.

Campo's face contorted in a grimace of pain. He tucked his chin and hunched his shoulders as if bracing himself against an attack. "The people who live in these places do not feel the cold as I do," he said, his voice muffled by the wool and fur of his collar. "I will never become accustomed to it."

"Then let us go in out of the wind." Li Du indicated the closed door on the right side of the temple.

Campo lifted his face slowly out from his voluminous scarves. He directed an uncertain look at the door. "That is where the dead man lived," he said. "It is where he performed his demonic conjurations."

Li Du hesitated for a moment, then started up the snowy steps. He spoke over his shoulder. "Whatever the history of this place, it is first and last a shelter from the mountain's inhospitality. We offend no one by using it for that purpose."

He heard Campo's step behind him. The wind blew again. The beams of the temple creaked. Li Du stamped the snow from his boots, took hold of the iron ring of the door, raised it, and allowed it to fall with a sharp clang. He listened, but no sound came from within. He pushed the door open and went inside.

100

There was an odor in the air at once pleasant and disturbing, oily and leathery. Li Du inhaled deeply, identifying other scents: metal, wood, smoke, juniper. Perceiving movement in the upper periphery of his vision, he tilted his head back to look. Hanging from the ceiling were what appeared to be ribbons. They were flat and pale like skins discarded by snakes, and they swayed gently, caught by currents in the air.

He examined the rest of the room. There were two doors in addition to the one through which he had come. One was to his left, and must, he thought, connect to the chapel. The other was directly across from him. Both were closed.

With the exception of space allotted for doors, the walls of the room were lined from top to bottom with shelves cluttered with bowls and pots and jars and boxes. As his gaze rested on a tall jar of black ink sticks, Li Du recalled the similar jar that used to stand on the desk in his own tranquil copying room in the library.

Campo had gone directly to the hearth in the corner. His boots left wet prints through the fine layer of ash that had been scattered by wind through the ventilation opening in the roof. Campo crouched and lifted a blackened pot from where it rested on an iron frame. He set the pot down on the floor beside several others and held his hands above the little pile of ash and scaly blackened wood. With a disappointed shake of his head, he stood up. He rubbed his hands together, then cupped his fingers and blew on them.

"The hearth is cold," he said.

Li Du continued to examine the contents of the shelves, marveling at the incongruous brightness of powdered pigments. "Did you meet him?"

Campo sniffed. "I spoke to him."

"What was he like?"

"The devil held his tongue. He would say nothing to me."

Li Du glanced at Campo, who was now also examining the shelves. "I understand that he was preoccupied with his work and with his devotions," Li Du said. "He abjured company and conversation."

Campo reached out to touch an open wooden box. "He behaved as if he could not see or hear me. He stood where I stand now, arranging and rearranging these vessels. I might have been invisible to him." Campo sighed. "Perhaps I was. The devil deceives."

Campo drew something from the box and held it up. It was a thin, circular wafer as red as a poppy petal. "What is this?"

Li Du took the wafer and turned it over in his hands. "It is cotton," he said, "saturated with dye." He returned it to Campo. "This is how it is transported and sold at markets. The red color is extracted with heat and water."

Campo replaced the wafer. "My translator insists that his works were masterful. You have met Andruk? He intended to commission a painting. Of course, there will be no painting now."

There was a short silence between them as Campo shifted his attention to a bowl filled with gold spheres the size of acorns. He picked one up and rolled it between his fingers. "Precious gilding," he said, as he watched the light gleam and curve across the surface of the sphere, "wasted on the Deceiver." He dropped the sphere back in the bowl. "Brother Achille finds beauty even in the most grotesque pagan paintings. He says that they give us hope for the souls of the Tibetan infidels. For, he says, if they are capable of honoring false idols with gilded splendor, then they are capable of honoring the one true deity."

Li Du raised his eyebrows in question. "Brother Achille?"

"Achille di Spiritu is my companion in

travel," explained Campo. "But we are temporarily on separate errands."

"You are a great distance from the centers of empires," Li Du said. "What errands bring you so far?"

Campo cast an assessing look at Li Du. "Our purpose," he said slowly, "is to find remnants of the Christian kingdoms that ruled here. Achille is in Zogong, where he enjoys the hospitality of the lord of that city, a man eager to be reborn in Jesus Christ through holy baptism."

"And you have come here."

Campo nodded. "I make an initial foray in search of ruined Christian churches rumored to exist on one of these remote passes."

Li Du searched his mind for a memory that would support Campo's words, but found none. "I did not think your faith had ever reached these lands."

Campo bobbed his chin. "It was long ago. But it is in the devil's interest to isolate the faithful from each other, and so he caused these terrible mountains to divide the devout from the holy Church. They were left here unprotected, and they degenerated into sin. The people of these lands have forgotten their faith, and must be led out of ignorance." Campo raised fervent eyes to meet Li Du's.

Li Du was curious. "And have you found evidence? I have seen only the temples and monuments of the Buddha in these valleys."

Campo's shoulders slumped slightly. "As yet I have found no churches, nor have I spoken to any who remember them. The task is easier when Achille is with me. He speaks the language of these roads — it is a hardship to travel without him and to rely on Andruk, who is not even a Christian."

"Do you and Andruk converse in Latin?"

"No — in the Chinese language, which I speak when I must. But if you will continue speaking with me in the language of the Church, I would be grateful. It is a comfort. Andruk talks so rapidly that I sometimes cannot understand him. He is a tiresome man. And now this man's death has thrown him — thrown us both — into distraction."

"It was a terrible death," said Li Du, quietly.

Campo repeated the word. "Terrible? Yes. But this is a barbaric land, full of horrors." Something, perhaps uncertainty, flickered across Campo's face. "You saw him in the snow?"

Li Du nodded. "It is a sight I will not forget."

"And he — he inflicted the wound upon

105

himself?"

"It appears that he did."

Campo murmured a brief string of words that sounded to Li Du like a prayer. He began to pace the room. "We must not listen to enchantments," he said. "The painter listened, and now he is dead." Campo's gaze moved to the door that separated them from the chapel. The low intonations of the monk were faintly audible through it. Campo began to pick at the skin of his knuckles. Li Du saw that they were raw and scabbed.

"Do you know something of Dhamo's death?"

"I? Of course I do not. I cannot know what evil he brought upon himself."

Li Du waited for him to continue, but Campo seemed to have drifted into his own thoughts. When he spoke again, it was on a different subject. "The snow fell so quickly," he said. "I did not expect to be trapped here. I am afraid."

"What frightens you?"

Campo did not answer.

Li Du tried again. "Do you perceive some threat?"

"No." Campo shook his head as if to clear it. "It is nothing. I am only tired and upset. And I am very cold. I cannot remain still here where there is no warmth. You will return with me to the manor?"

Li Du shook his head. "I will stay here awhile. I came to find a library."

Campo rubbed his hands and blew again on his fingers. "Be careful of the books you find here. Their words are corrupted. They will poison you."

When Campo had gone, Li Du stood listening to the prayers through the wall. He had not observed any shelves containing scrolls or bound books in the chapel. To return and search for them seemed inappropriate. A draft spun down from the eaves and spread another trail of ash across the floor. He looked at the hearth and imagined the room warm and lit.

A tea churn, a kettle, and two pots rested on the floor. One pot was coated in layers of old grease, to which blackened morsels of pepper and millet adhered. The other was filled with a smooth, almost translucent substance. Li Du bent to touch its surface. It was cold and hard as glass. He looked up at the dangling ribbons above, realizing that they were thin sheets of glue. Melted in the pot, the glue strips would be used to bind pigments. *Would have been,* Li Du corrected himself.

He pictured the solitary monk alternating pots on the fire: judging from what he had been told, Li Du guessed that Dhamo had considered one as essential to his subsistence as the other. Who had Dhamo been? How had he lived? The closed door at the back of the room beckoned. Li Du crossed the room and pushed it open.

While the workroom was a tumble of supplies and tools, this room was free of clutter. One corner held a small cot covered in blankets of brown fur and unembroidered brown wool. The walls were bare. In the center of the room was an easel, in front of which was a cushion that retained the indentation of knees that had recently pressed into it. On the floor beside the cushion was a single wooden bowl that held the crusted remnants of azure blue paint. Three brushes dangled from an unadorned brush stand.

Suspended in the easel was a rectangle of heavy cloth pulled taut by string sewn through its folded edges and tied to the surrounding frame. Its surface had been smoothed by a wash of white paint, on top of which faint charcoal outlines had been applied. Li Du had to bend down to discern the image. The closer he looked, the more intricate it became.

A figure dominated the center. It had seven faces, each of which wore a different expression. Its body was draped with chains of human heads and beaded garlands. Numerous arms fanned out from its torso; the topmost set of hands wielded scarves decorated with eyes. Details had been drawn with equal precision at the borders, which were crowded with animals and clouds, each one unique.

While the subject of the thangka had been meticulously sketched out, its creator had added only two pigments before abandoning the work. A background of sky and mountains was depicted in rich hues of blue and green.

Li Du stepped back. He could almost see the painter kneeling before the easel, right hand lifted, muscles subservient to the mind that commanded them.

"This was Dhamo's room," came a voice behind Li Du.

He turned, startled. In the doorway stood the young man from the manor house, whose name, Li Du remembered, was Pema. He was stooping from the weight of a basket on his back, from which protruded three rolls of thick white cloth. He lowered the basket to the floor.

"I am sorry," Li Du said. "I should not

have intruded." He backed away from the easel and joined Pema in the other room. Pema closed the door to Dhamo's studio, his expression blank.

"Were you his assistant?"

The question appeared to disconcert Pema. "I helped him sometimes," he said.

An awkward silence followed. "Does your family live in the village?" Li Du asked.

Pema's mouth quirked in a humorless smile. "I am the eldest son of the manor house."

Li Du tried to conceal his surprise. "I apologize. I misunderstood."

Pema moved to one of the shelves and began to fiddle with a bowl that contained rough rocks. He picked one up. It was veined with bright green and pale quartz and sprinkled with a glitter of gold dust. "I was adopted when I was an infant." Pema replaced the rock.

Li Du considered this for a moment. "I learned this morning that the Chhöshe also was born into this family. Then you and he are brothers?"

Pema's hand went still. "We were," he said. "When we were very small."

Seeing Pema's shoulders slump, Li Du searched for a more welcome subject. "I am surprised to see these rare pigments and minerals in such a remote place," he said. "How were they acquired?"

Pema brightened. "I bought them for him," he said, "at the markets of Dajianlu."

"A long journey from here?"

"A week, or a little more."

"Dhamo never accompanied you?"

Pema shook his head. "He gave me lists of what he needed. Dhamo never traveled." Pema moved to a rack of brushes and selected one. He pressed his thumb to one end, absently testing the give of its bristles. "I liked the journey," he said. "It is the farthest from this valley I have ever been, or will ever go."

"There are scholars," said Li Du, "who claim it is possible to experience all the epiphanies of travel within the mind, to move through distant landscapes without leaving home."

Pema's mouth quirked. "I would not want to be transported into one of Dhamo's paintings."

"Why not?"

"Because," said Pema, "they were like the wildflowers in the fields where I take the goats in the summer. They are beautiful, but every year they are the same flowers, only in different places. I would rather see what I have never seen before. You are a traveler — is that not the reason you travel?"

Li Du hesitated. "Not at first," he said, "but perhaps it is now."

Pema sighed, and returned the brush to the brush stand. Then he crossed the room, removed the rolls of white cloth from his basket, and, with a nervous look at the closed door of the chapel, set the cloth down on the floor. "I must return to the manor," he said. "There is more to carry."

He was about to leave, then paused. "There is something I cannot stop thinking," he said. "Perhaps it is not important."

Li Du looked at Pema's wan, scarred face. "If you are thinking it, then it is important to you."

"It is about Dhamo," Pema said. "It is only that all my life I watched him paint. They are not uncommon. I have seen them in thangkas in Dajianlu. But —"

Li Du's voice was gentle. "What is it that is bothering you?"

Pema kept his gaze on the floor. "In all the years I knew him, I never once saw him paint a mirror."

Alone again, Li Du gave the shelves a final perusal. He would not have noticed the empty bowl except that it was set a little apart from the others, poised precariously at the edge of a shelf as if it had been set down in a hurry. He pushed it to a more secure location.

As he drew his hand away from it, however, he saw that several dark grains had transferred themselves from the bowl to his fingers. He was about to brush them away when he stopped. He lifted his hand and looked. Tiny red shards gleamed against his skin.

He frowned, and cast his mind back to the bridge the day before. He saw again the snow beginning to cover the dead man, recalled the wooden beads bobbing and pulling away from the stiff, hooked fingers that could no longer clutch them. He remembered the red shards that he had found in the snow by the body. The ones that now clung to his hand were identical.

There had been a time in Li Du's life when he had been able to find the answers to all of his questions on the shelves of the library in Beijing. Now he closed his eyes and searched the duplicate library housed in his memory. He saw a room in the southeast wing. A lacquered screen in one corner depicted the story, in gold and green, of the sisters who abandoned a god only to be summoned back and turned into mountains.

Deep in the memory, Li Du paused to look at the painting. He thought about how time was spread across it, the future mapped across the same surface as their past. Someone who did not know the tale might see a painting of nine women and three mountains, when in fact it was a painting of three women at four moments in time. At the top of left of the screen, the three mountains that had been women rose into the clouds, each the same color as the silk robes of the woman it had been, the clouds around them like sashes blowing in the wind.

Li Du scanned the shelves to the right of the screen until he found the text that he sought. *The Making of Pigments.* The neat columns came into focus in front of his eyes. *Vermilion,* the text read, *comes from cinnabar, an ore of mercury, and can be recognized by its color and heavy weight. The mineral is ground in mortar and pestle and cleansed of impurities with water. Care must be taken in grinding it. A circular motion will turn it unpleasing white. A pounding motion will turn it useless black. Proper grinding alternates these motions and uses only the minimum of water . . .* Li Du skimmed to the section below: *On Locating Sources of Cinnabar . . .*

CHAPTER 8

Li Du had almost reached the base of the stairs when he saw three people below him through the trees. He recognized Rinzen immediately; the yellow silk of his coat was an incongruous blossom amid the dark wood and faded green lichen. Beside Rinzen was a tall man with a basket strapped to his back — Doso, Li Du guessed. The third person was speaking in loud, slow Chinese.

"Souls lost," Campo was saying, "as if abandoned by God."

"We share your concern." The speaker was indeed Doso. "But we must defer to the Chhöshe in matters of burial, and to the astrologer who will come from the village when the path is clear."

"But I do not trust —" Campo stopped at the sound of Li Du's approach and swung around to see who had come.

Doso greeted Li Du in Chinese. He sounded relieved. "You have come from the temple," he said. "We are going there now."

Rinzen gave a small bow. "Does the Chhöshe continue his prayers there?"

"He does," replied Li Du.

Doso shifted his ursine shoulders to redistribute the weight of the basket, which was so heavy that its straps had pressed deep grooves into his coat. Li Du saw that it contained iron tools and twine. "I will not keep you here in the snow," said Doso, addressing both Campo and Li Du. "Please go down to the kitchen, where food and drink await you at the hearth."

Campo looked as if he could not decide whether to resume his pontification or continue toward the promise of warmth.

Li Du hesitated. The idea that had occurred to him in the studio fluttered in his mind, uncertain yet insistent. "I do have one question," he said. "It is only the idle curiosity of a traveler. I carry with me a journal written by a scholar who once passed through this part of the world. He writes that in the mountains above Bathang, which I know is not far from here, he encountered pools of water heated by the earth. Even in winter, he writes, they steam like a pot over flame. I hope to encounter this marvel, and wonder if there are any such pools on your land."

Doso's eyebrows lifted in surprise. "There are."

"Well," Li Du said, as casually as he could, "then I am glad I thought to inquire."

Doso's face became serious. "But we do not visit them. The villagers consider it an unlucky place."

"Even so," Li Du said. "Unusual phenomena are always of interest to a traveler. Can you direct me to them?"

"They are not far," said Doso. "You might have perceived their odor from the path when you arrived yesterday. But are you certain you wish to visit them now? Such springs are not uncommon in these mountains."

Li Du nodded. "I would regret missing the opportunity."

Doso relented. "Then I will tell you the easiest way. Return to the bridge and retrace your steps on the path along which your caravan traveled. When you see a boulder with trees growing on top of it, leave the path. There is an old stone wall. Follow it, and you will come to the pools."

Campo coughed and, with a visible shiver, stamped his feet to warm them. "It is very cold," he said. "I will go to the hearth, as you suggested." He resumed his progress down the stairs, his breath clouding the air

117

around him.

Doso switched to the local tongue. "He is upset that our funeral customs are so different from his own."

Li Du nodded. "He is a devout man."

"I have no wish to burden my guests," said Doso. "But I know you have experience with his people. Perhaps you can talk to him. He believes that we intend to consume the flesh of the dead man. I told him that such a ritual has never existed in my family, that it is our custom to cremate the dead. I am not sure that he understood me."

"Of course I will speak to him," said Li Du. "He is unsettled by what occurred, and eager for the snow to melt."

Doso nodded and looked up at the sky. The clouds were so close that it felt as if they were descending slowly to engulf them. "There will be no thaw today."

Rinzen glanced over Li Du's shoulder. "Did you find the temple's collection of books?"

Li Du shook his head. "I did not wish to disturb the Chhöshe in his prayers," he said.

"What books?" Doso looked from Rinzen to Li Du.

Rinzen answered. "I remembered the charming collection of scrolls housed in the temple, and suggested to the scholar that he might examine them."

"There are no books in the temple," said Doso, gruffly.

Rinzen looked surprised. "Then my memory was incorrect."

"There were books once," amended Doso. "But they were destroyed years ago in a fire. The temple burned almost to the ground."

With a slight grimace, Doso again adjusted the heavy basket on his back. Li Du, observing that Doso was anxious to continue upward, stepped aside to let them pass.

Li Du found Hamza at the manor's hearth telling the children a story while helping them to hull walnuts. Hamza's hands, like the children's, were black from walnut oils. Today he looked young. He could have been the eldest brother of the other three, who were looking at him with worshipful expressions. The old woman sat watching and spinning her prayer wheel. Her eyes were blurred, like spreading ink drops, and she appeared to be smiling.

Hamza gestured for Li Du to sit down. "I have been teaching the children that not every tale requires bandits in order to be entertaining," he said, as he filled a bowl with butter tea and handed it to Li Du. "What did you think of the temple?"

"I went in search of books," said Li Du, "but I did not see them."

"Why not?"

Li Du blinked. "What was your question?"

Hamza raised his eyebrows. "My question was why you did not see the books, but now it has changed. What is it that preoccupies you?"

Li Du drained the bowl and stood up. "The books were lost in a fire. As for what preoccupies me, I will tell you, but perhaps it would be better to speak elsewhere." He directed a meaningful glance at the children, now lost in their own little conversation about the cave of thieves that only opened when a password was spoken, and that contained a carpet that could fly through the air.

With Hamza in tow, Li Du traversed the hallway away from the kitchen. They passed the door to a sewing room, through which Kamala could be seen seated at a loom, sending a shuttle deftly between panes of white threads. Li Du turned right into the adjoining wing. An open shutter allowed him a glimpse down to the courtyard brazier, where Campo's translator, Andruk, sat alone in front of the flames.

Li Du did not speak until they were in his room, the door shut behind them. Then he said: "I do not believe Dhamo went to the bridge to die."

Hamza moved a cushion from the bed to the floor and sat down on it, cross-legged, his back against a wall. "Perhaps not," he said, "but Death was waiting for him there. Death often waits on bridges. Sometimes he is dressed in black armor. Sometimes he sits atop a black steed and challenges those who wish to cross."

Li Du looked at his friend. "He did meet death there, but not the apparition you describe. I think there was another person on that bridge with him."

"Ah," said Hamza. "Then you think —" He stopped and waited for Li Du to complete the sentence.

"I think that Dhamo was murdered."

"The temple told you this?" Hamza did not appear surprised. He rarely did.

Li Du lowered his voice to a whisper. "I saw the room where he painted his thangkas."

"The room filled with color pots and brushes? I was there too."

"No," Li Du said. "There is a room behind that one. In it is a thangka that is incomplete."

"Yes?" Hamza waited expectantly for Li Du to continue.

Li Du drew in a breath. "There were three colors applied to it: white, blue, and green. Do you know what color follows?"

"I do know it," said Hamza. "The order is set by custom. Red follows blue and green."

Li Du nodded. "Dhamo needed red to continue the painting."

"And he had a room full of pigments ready to grind and mix with glue," said Hamza. "I saw the cotton soaked with lac dye."

"But he did not need lac dye," said Li Du. "Lac is a weak red. It is used to paint details. For the foundational color, he needed true vermilion. He needed cinnabar red."

Now Hamza was leaning forward. "How does this relate to his death?"

"I found a bowl in Dhamo's studio," Li Du said. "It is empty of all but a few granules of the vermilion Dhamo needed to continue his work. I think that Dhamo left his studio yesterday not to kill himself, but to renew his supply of cinnabar."

Hamza leaned back against the wall again. "That is not credible," he said. "You suggest that this eccentric painter set out in a storm on a journey to the nearest market town — which, my friend, is ten days' travel from here at least — to purchase cinnabar?

I am not a logical man, as you know, but even to me that seems unlikely."

"He did not need to go to the market for red pigment."

Hamza gave an exasperated huff. "But you just said that his supply was empty."

"It was. But according to *The Making of Pigments,* cinnabar grows on stone touched by the water of hot springs. And I have just learned that there are hot springs just on the other side of the bridge."

"Well, scholar, I could have told you about the hot springs if you had asked me."

Li Du stared at his friend. "But how do you know of them?"

Hamza, pleased with himself, pinched his beard to a finer point. "*Your* reason for traveling remains mysterious, but I have always been honest about mine. I am a collector of tales. I heard about the hot springs from an old man in the village who told me not to visit them."

"Doso said that the villagers do not visit them because they are unlucky."

"Unlucky." Hamza made a scoffing sound. "Simple answers like that allow important truths to be forgotten. Here is what the villager told me. There is a curse on the pools. When the dead journey through the realms between death and life, we cannot see them and they cannot see us. But these pools are enchanted. The dead can see them, and are drawn to them as snakes are drawn to woodpiles. So they go to the pools, and become trapped under the water. That is more interesting than simply 'unlucky,' I think you would agree."

"It is," said Li Du, "but there is no mention of cinnabar in this story."

"No," said Hamza. "But even if Dhamo went to the hot springs to collect pigments, as you say, what makes you think he did not kill himself on the way back? If the story of the pools is true, he might have seen a terrible vision there. He might have been pursued by ghosts that emerged from the dark waters."

Li Du began to pace the room. "Then where is the cinnabar he collected? There were a few shards of it near him on the bridge, but there should have been a basket or a pouch full of red rocks. What happened to it?"

Hamza's forehead creased. "And because of this you suspect that someone murdered him? It is a tenuous conclusion."

Li Du rubbed the back of his neck. Hamza was right. "I know," he said quietly. "Even so, I intend to visit the hot springs."

A speculative look settled on Hamza's

features. "What is it that you expect to find? Do you think Dhamo will be trapped in the pool waiting to explain to you how he met his end?" Hamza paused and reflected on his own words. "That is not such a bad thought — if he was murdered he may be there waiting to tell someone who it was that killed him."

When Li Du did not answer immediately, Hamza went on. "Red," he said thoughtfully, "from the stones of a hot spring. Did I ever tell you about the woman in a forest who once tried to sell me a pot of red paint from the Caspian Sea? She claimed that the sand used to make the paint came from the crushed skeletons of insects who lived in the fires that filled the earth's crevices before there were oceans. She told me that a certain kingdom of seafaring warriors used it to paint their faces, and that unknown to their enemies, the paint granted them invincibility in battle." Hamza paused expectantly, as if he was waiting for a question.

Li Du pulled himself from his own musings and looked at Hamza. "Did you buy the paint?"

"I did not," Hamza replied. "She wanted a lock of my hair, and nothing good could come of an exchange like that. You are determined, then, to search the cursed pools for crystals red as blood. Before you do, come with me to the caravan. Norbu is using the time we have here to experiment with spices he bought back in the Gyalthang market, and the fragrance of the smoke through the roof reminds me of the time I dined with the ghost of the sultan's own chef."

Avoiding the outdoor stairs to the courtyard, which had not been swept since the second snowfall and looked treacherous, they went to one of the interior staircases. It was dark and ladderlike, descending from a rectangular opening in the floor. The storage room below it smelled of barley, a wistful reminder of the sunshine that had dried it.

Hamza went first. Li Du was halfway down, his hat just level with the floor, when he heard footsteps. They came from the room in which he had glimpsed Kamala weaving. Li Du took one more step down and ducked his head into the shadows as someone stepped out of the room into the hallway. Looking up, Li Du could just see the embossed leather boots of the trader, Sonam. As he watched, they pivoted. Sonam had turned as if he meant to reenter the room.

"I have offended you," said Sonam, addressing someone inside.

Li Du looked down at Hamza, who appeared slightly blurred through a thin haze of flour in the air. He motioned for Li Du to stay quiet and listen.

Kamala's voice answered. "I cannot accept your gifts."

Sonam's tone became soft. "The women in the palace wore these jewels on golden chains as fine as the threads on your loom. They are considered the most beautiful women in the world, but their loveliness does not compare to yours. That is why I brought you the jewels — they should adorn a woman worthy of their luster."

Li Du heard a sound below him and glanced down to see Hamza looking disdainful.

The faint clatter of the loom had stopped. "Doso brings me jewels as fine as these."

Sonam gave a contemptuous laugh. "From the markets in Gyalthang and Dajianlu? Nothing fine passes through those rough villages, save a few bricks of good tea. Hold that blue stone to the light. Do you see the star inside it?"

Kamala's reply was sharp. "And I suppose you will tell me that you paid for these?"

"You wound me with your distrust,"

replied Sonam. "I only wanted to please you."

"It would please me if you left my house and never returned to it."

Sonam took a step forward into the room. "Is that really what you want? And what will happen if the lord of the manor, who for all his strength and honor, is not a young man, should join the ancestors that he speaks of so often, and at such length?"

Li Du heard wood scrape across the floor, followed by light footsteps. When Kamala spoke again, her voice was much closer. "Do you threaten my husband?"

"I would never threaten Doso," said Sonam. "Our families are as one."

Li Du heard faint rustling and clinks. "Take back your gifts," Kamala hissed. "Doso may be bound to his promises, but I will protect my children from thieves."

There was a silence. Then Li Du heard the heavy boots start purposefully in his direction. He ducked deeper into the shadows and began to descend the stairs as quietly as he could. Above, he heard Sonam's muted reply. "I wonder," he was saying, "if you will regret your words."

"I found his wooing unimpressive," said Hamza, once they were outside the manor walls and walking toward the caravan camp.

"I do not believe your opinion was the one that interested him," Li Du said, "but I do not think she was impressed either."

"Bad behavior, to try to seduce the wife of the manor lord while he is away honoring the dead."

Li Du nodded his agreement. He had seen Kalden and the muleteers in enough villages to know that flirtation with local wives and daughters was usual and, for the most part, harmless. But that was not the interaction they had witnessed. "I wonder what secures his welcome here," he said.

"Perhaps a life owed for a life," said Hamza. They were passing Yeshe's hut.

Li Du was still musing. "She called him a thief."

Hamza looked sideways at Li Du. "I interpreted that as a general insult. Are you saying now that you think Sonam killed Dhamo?"

"I do not see why he would have." Li Du thought for a moment. "I do not see why anyone would."

A voice hailed them, and they turned to see Andruk coming toward them through the snow. He reached them and stopped, slightly out of breath. "Have you seen Paolo Campo?" he asked.

"I met him on the stairs from the temple," Li Du said. "I believe he was heading for the kitchen hearth, but I did not see him there. He is not in his room?"

"I have just come from his room."

"Perhaps," said Hamza, "he is endeavoring to convert the Khampa."

Andruk looked doubtful. "He is a timid man, always fearful of bandits. I doubt he would approach the caravan alone. But if you are going there, I will come with you."

As they approached the hut, the sides of which bulged at the seams where blankets were piled within, they heard laughter. They went inside. Sera-tsering was sitting on a log that had been made into a semblance of a throne. She commanded the attention of the muleteers.

"And no one," she was saying, "knew that the land had been ruled for fourteen years by a man who was dead." This conclusion was greeted with murmurs of appreciation and interest.

Hamza came to a sudden halt. "First she interrupts me," he whispered, half to himself and half to Li Du, "and now she steals my occupation?"

Andruk glanced around the single room. Campo was not there. With a bow to Kalden and a nod to Li Du and Hamza, he turned and ducked back out into the snow.

Sera looked up. "Will you join us?"

Hamza crossed his arms over his chest. "So we are passing the afternoon with tales," he declared.

Sera tucked her hand into her long woolen sleeves. "That is what travelers do when the weather traps them together," she said. "Or perhaps someone has a set of dice to play the Game of Tigers, or pebbles for the Game of Many Eyes?" She looked around the circle expectantly.

Hamza's face was determined. "If one tells a story, another must follow. Let us see if I can amuse you, as you appear to have amused my companions." He circled the fire behind her to an available place, and sat down.

"This little scholar librarian," said Hamza, pointing to where Li Du stood, "whose coat is patched and who walks so quietly through the mountains beside his gentle mule, is, beneath his humble exterior, a truth-seeker and master of deduction. You look incredulous? I could tell you of our adventure in the market city under the mountain, where we met Death on the day the sun was stolen from the sky. Were it not for my assistance, we might never have solved that puzzle. It was I who told him the tale of a great detective, and so inspired him to action. I speak of Judge Dee, that tireless magistrate, who sometimes traveled to Bassorah to visit a distant cousin."

Li Du watched Hamza's posture change. It became straighter, more commanding, while at the same time he leaned forward just slightly, as if he were confiding in a friend. "In Bassorah there was a market that was also the center of revelry in the city."

Li Du pictured the slope of white snow outside that led down to the trees, but he did not move. Half lost in his own thoughts, he remained standing by the door. Hamza began.

"As the sun set and the torches and lanterns were lit, light shone through silk and tassels. Acrobats and dancers and puppeteers performed their art. Vendors sold perfume bottles crusted with filigree and jewels, and books with paintings of ships visible only when their pages were pressed together, and scarves that changed color to complement the thoughts of their wearers, and fruits and breads and savories that could turn ill humor to pleasure. Every evening the market was more beautiful and more alive than the evening before, and every morning it was gray and brown and befouled, piled with chewed bones and inhabited by yellow-eyed cats.

"One morning, just as the dawn was about to break and the market hovered between life and death, a guard from the palace glimpsed two figures in an alley, one in patchwork silk, the other in a dark cloak. He saw the cloaked finger turn and strike a mighty blow to the head of the other, who crumpled to the ground. The guard called to his men, and together they apprehended the culprit.

"Now, the man in the silk patchwork who lay dead in the alley was none other than the Sultan's favorite jester, a performer unmatched in wit and talent. He was adept at acrobatics, contortion, sword-swallowing, tightrope-walking, tumbling, juggling, and the telling of riddles. He could assume the mantle of the melancholy fool, the wise fool, or the fool of good spirits, as suited the mood of his audience.

"When his name was cried out through the streets, his wife came running from their home and cast herself upon the jester's body, crying out for justice against the drunkard who had slain him. The culprit, a courtier who had committed no offense before in his life, waited in tears for his execution, and could only say again and again that the jester had loomed at him from the shadows of the alley and would not speak when addressed, putting the courtier so in fear of his life that he struck the jester down, with no intention of killing him at all.

"In due course, the Sultan ordered the courtier executed. But just before he was to step onto the gallows, there came a cry from the square. It was the cook who lived near the market, and he stepped forward tearfully. 'You must not kill this man,' he said, 'for it was I, and I alone, who killed the jester.'

"The cook explained that when he came home the night before, he saw a man in the garden, believed him to be a thief, and in the dark he struck him. When he examined the stranger and found him dead, the cook was so afraid that he carried the body to the market and propped it up in an alley, where it looked as alive as a living man. But the cook could not bear to see another accused.

"The cook prepared to meet his death, but just as he was going to the gallows, there was a cry from the crowd. It was the doctor, who lived in the house next to the cook. 'You must not kill this man,' he said, 'for it was I, and I alone, who killed the jester.'

"He explained that he had come home that night very late. The jester must have come to see him about an ailment, and was sitting on the top of his stairs. But the doctor, not seeing him, tripped and sent the poor jester tumbling down. When he examined him and found him dead, the doctor was so afraid that he strung the body on a rope and lowered it from his balcony into the garden below, which he knew to be frequented by hungry dogs. 'And so,' he finished, 'he was dead already when the cook struck him.'

"Now the doctor prepared to meet his death, but just as he was about to be executed, another cry came from the crowd. Now two people stepped forward, a tailor with a weathered, kind face and his wife, a woman of vibrant beauty. They spoke in tones broken with grief. 'It was we, and we alone, who killed the jester,' said the tailor.

" 'As everyone knows I have been at sea a year and a day to sew a coat for a king in a distant kingdom. I returned only last night and my wife, overjoyed to see me, hired this jester to entertain us on the celebratory occasion, knowing him to be excellent company. Wanting to show him hospitality, we insisted that he eat and, though he said he had already eaten, prevailed upon him to share our dinner. And that is how he choked on a fishbone and died there at our table.

To our shame we were afraid. We carried him to the doctor and left him there in the hope that he might by some miracle be revived. So you see, we alone were responsible for this deed.' "

Hamza paused as if he had finished, and Sera, who was using a knife to shell walnuts and hand them around to the muleteers, said, "That is a good tale, but I have heard it before."

Hamza's smile was one of immense self-satisfaction. "Perhaps you have," he said, "but you see, there are few who know that Judge Dee was visiting the Sultan's court on that day." Hamza set his hands on his knees.

"So the tailor and his wife, who had been so happy to be reunited after many months, prepared for death. But just then another voice cried out from the crowd, 'Oh Sultan, stop the execution!'

"The Sultan looked and saw Judge Dee step forward out of the crowd.

" 'What,' said the Sultan, 'will you say that it was you, you and no other, who killed my jester?'

" 'No, Sultan,' replied Judge Dee, 'but all the same I do not think that the confession of the tailor and his wife is the final term in this series. I beg your forbearance to allow

136

me to offer an alternative explanation.'

" 'You may speak,' said the Sultan, much intrigued.

" 'Today we heard four confessions from four culprits who think they killed the jester, but not one of them wished him dead. It occurs to me to wonder, this being a violent and sudden death, whether there was anyone who did desire it. Sultan, was the wife of the jester a jealous woman?'

"The crowd began to whisper and the Sultan, after a moment's thought, nodded his head. 'She is known to be so.'

" 'If the tailor's wife, a woman of surpassing beauty who had for a year and a day lived without her husband at home, did several times hire the jester to perform for her, would it be in the character of the jester's wife to suspect that this evening's entertainment was in truth a romantic assignation?'

"The Sultan nodded again. 'She has many times said that she would kill her husband should he ever stray from her. But even if what you say is true, you forget that the jester was alive when he came to the house of the tailor, and that the tailor and his wife saw him choke upon a fishbone.'

"The tailor's wife, who was a very honest person, cried out, 'Alas, it is true. I saw the bone in the fish as he put it into his mouth.'

" 'Does it not strike you as strange,' said Judge Dee, 'that a man who has learned the secret art of opening his throat to swallow swords and nails should choke to death on a fishbone?'

"Judge Dee turned to the wife of the jester, who was as pale as the inside of an apple, and said, 'You did not know that the tailor had returned, and thought that your husband desired the tailor's wife. So you poisoned his dinner.' Judge Dee turned back to the Sultan. 'So you see, the jester was already dead when he came to the tailor's home, though only Death himself knew it. Death, and the jester's wife.'

"Seeing the accusing faces of the crowd, the wife cried out, 'Yes, yes it was I, and I alone, who killed the jester.'

"The Sultan, who was not without mercy, and who was much impressed by these strange events, declared that the jester's wife would be executed unless she could tell him a story stranger than the one he had just heard. And so she began . . ."

As Hamza started his next tale, Li Du slipped quietly out the door.

CHAPTER 9

He was not the first to cross the fields after the storm. Trails of footprints and hoof-prints connected to form cryptic constellations in the snow. The trees seemed to grow taller as Li Du approached them. Just before he entered the forest, he stopped and turned around. He had descended far enough that from his present angle he could no longer see the manor or the huts. He lifted his gaze higher to where the forest resumed. He thought he could almost see the hollow tree halfway up the stairs to the mountain temple. Higher still, there was an elusive suggestion of jagged peaks amid the clouds.

A short walk through pines and stubby oaks brought him to the bridge. Muddled footprints led across it. Icicles hung from its single leaning railing. Underneath, water flowed smooth as gray marble between banks cluttered with frozen filigrees of ice and leaves.

He crossed and started up the path, kicking the toes of his boots one at a time into the snow. When he could, he used the footprints that were already there to keep him from sliding down the steep incline. Glimpsing movement overhead, he looked up and saw the torn scrap of cloth from his own sleeve fluttering out of reach on a branch. For a moment he expected to see himself standing on the path, looking ruefully at the damage to his coat. He pushed through the specter, and continued up.

The boulder Doso had described was distinctive, and Li Du identified it easily. It was a hulking miniature mountain that wore a crown of tangled trees. Its craggy face, streaked with snow and lichen, observed Li Du with an expression of morose foreboding. He left the path and skirted the rock. On the other side, he found a crumbling old stone wall half covered by a rhododendron thicket.

With no path under the snow, it became difficult to navigate the dense brush and brambles. Li Du lost sight of the footprints that had preceded him, but he perceived an odor, and followed it. It was the smell of elemental movement beneath the earth, acrid and metallic, and it led him to a thin stream trickling through the snow.

He followed the stream until he came to a broad rock face, the lower half of which was interrupted by a series of loamy tiers. These were accessible by way of various small paths leading up through the trees and boulders that crowded both sides of the escarpment. Li Du counted three deep pools, each with a mantle of steam hovering just above its surface. He guessed that there were more of them hidden from view higher on the rocky face.

Squatting on a flat rock beside the nearest pool, Li Du dipped his fingers into the water. It was warm enough to sting his cold skin. He shifted, dislodging a clump of snow, which became transparent the instant it touched the water, then disappeared. With the sleeve of his coat pushed up to his elbow, Li Du extended his arm beneath the surface. The wall of the pool was coated in thick slime.

He stood and made his way carefully to the next pool. Again, he reached in. This time, his fingers caught on a section of the wall that was rough. He could feel score marks, and cavities where stones had been pried away. Using a knife drawn from a battered leather sheath at his belt, he scraped at the rough section until he felt a piece of it chip away. He caught the fragment and raised it out of the water to examine it. It glistened red. He put it in his pocket.

Leaning back on his heels, Li Du raised the knife to dry it on his sleeve. He was about to return the blade to its sheath when he paused. The silver that was inlaid into its wooden hilt had darkened. It gleamed opalescent purple and green. He recognized the effect of age on unpolished silver, but in this case, it was as if a hundred years had gone by under the surface of the water while an instant passed above it.

The words of the Kunming merchant came back to him. *You're in our territory now,* he had said, *where blackened silver will warn you when water is bad.*

Li Du stood up. His own reflection regarded him with an indistinct face. The wind had strengthened. The trees around him bobbed their limbs up and down and swayed from side to side.

A sudden clatter startled him, and he looked up to see a small cascade of pebbles clicking and bouncing down the face of the cliff. They struck the surfaces of several pools, which instantly clouded with sediment.

From above, Li Du heard a cry. It was thinned and warped by the wind, but it was human. Another cascade of stones fell, and

Li Du raised his arms to protect his face. Lowering them, he saw movement at the top of the precipice. It was a dark mass, contorted, unidentifiable. Then, with a piercing shriek, it plummeted from the edge.

Li Du stared in horror as the shape unfolded in the air. Before he could move, there was a great splash on the uppermost tier. Drops of water splattered over his face. Without stopping to wipe them away, he began to clamber upward, scrambling through the mud around the pools. Loose stones tilted and slid beneath his feet. When he reached an overhang he could not scale, he rushed into the snowy forest and continued upward until he emerged level with the uppermost pool.

There were dark robes suspended within it. Slick leather and sodden wool floated to the surface. Beneath the water he could see the back of a head and pale hands. He plunged his arms into the pool, hooked his hands under the shoulders of the figure, and hauled backward. The head emerged, lolling forward onto Li Du's chest. It was Paolo Campo.

Setting his heels hard against the stone, Li Du pulled with all his might. The body became heavier as it was dragged from the water. Finally, Li Du collapsed under its weight. He freed himself as carefully as he could, turning Campo onto his back as he did so, then knelt beside the supine man. He touched the wrists and neck in search of a heartbeat. Finding one, he spoke Campo's name, taking the man's hands and rubbing them between his own.

Gently, he turned Campo's head first to one side and then to the other. His fingers came away bloodied, but upon examination the wounds appeared minor. Li Du looked up at the cliff. Campo must have been cut by branches as he fell. Miraculously, it seemed that Campo had struck the water without crushing his head or limbs against the surrounding stone.

Campo's eyes fluttered open, and he drew in a panicked breath. He stared at Li Du without recognition. He opened and closed his mouth several times without speaking. When he did speak, the words that emerged were whispered in a language unintelligible to Li Du.

"You are safe," Li Du said. "You fell, but you are safe. Are you in pain?"

Campo registered the Latin slowly, then shook his head. His eyes were wide and terrified.

"I am cold," he said. His gaze traced the rock up to the looming edge of the precipice, and Li Du felt him shudder. "I struggled," he said. "I tried — but I was overpowered."

"Who was there?" Li Du followed Campo's gaze, but there was no sign of movement above them.

"I do not know. I could not see. It was — the light was fading. I do not know what happened. But I felt — I felt hands on my back. Did I fall?" Slowly he raised his hand to his head. When he saw the blood on his fingers, his eyes filled with tears. "Am I dying? Here, with no one to say the last rites? No one to ease me with prayer?"

Li Du looked down at Campo. He could not leave him here to search for the assailant. And even if Li Du managed to overtake the culprit in the forest, what would he do? He scanned the trees. They were falling into deep shadow. He thought he could hear steps. Or was it the cracking of branches in the wind?

"You are not dying," he said to Campo. "Your wounds are not severe. But we must get you to a warm place. Can you stand?"

With Li Du's help, Campo rose to his feet, water streaming from his coat. He leaned heavily on Li Du. "My legs are shaking beneath me," he said.

Li Du observed with trepidation the climb

down from the pools. He could not carry Campo the way he had come. "We will find an easier way down," he said, and led the limping, slumping Campo into the trees.

Twilight fell. As they struggled through snow up to their knees, Li Du supporting Paolo Campo's drenched weight on one shoulder, the trees around them became black cracks in the purple-gray sky. Beneath the snow, brambles and forest detritus caught at their feet and threw them off balance. Campo began to ramble, slipping between languages, repeating words and phrases in supplication to his god.

Li Du felt himself tiring. The boulder with its crown of trees was ahead of them, but Li Du was not sure that he could carry Campo to the manor should Campo lose consciousness. They still had to navigate the steep slope down to the river and the bridge across it.

Close to them, in a thicket of bamboo stalks, something moved. Li Du concentrated on the place. It was something round and black. Li Du had seen bears before, but only at a distance, bounding across open scree slopes from one patch of trees to another.

A deep bark rent the air. From behind the

146

bamboo stalks that clattered in the wind, a dog emerged, a mastiff with a wild mane and open jaws. It emitted another low bark that seemed to vibrate the tree trunks around them. Beside it, another shape appeared. This one was human.

"Who's there?" a thin voice called out in the language of the caravans.

Trying to catch his breath, Li Du managed to call out his name. "I am a guest at the manor house across the river. My companion fell into one of the pools. He needs help."

The shape came closer, and Li Du saw that it was an old woman bundled in fur. "If you are thieves," she said, "I will tell my dog to kill you. And if you are demons, you won't be able to cross my threshold. If you are neither of those, then you can come inside and sit by the fire."

Without waiting for an answer, she approached and, with a grunt, lowered herself under Campo's other arm and stood up, taking half his weight on her own shoulder. "This way," she said.

CHAPTER 10

The hut that materialized amid the trees was as small as a herder's refuge, but more solidly constructed. A path had been cleared from the door to a stack of firewood equal in size to the hut itself. Li Du and the woman carried Campo inside. Obeying her succinct instructions, he helped remove Campo's soaked coat and robe, wrap him in blankets, and arrange his clothes to dry near the hearth.

Campo endured their ministrations meekly at first, but as the heat began to revive him, he became agitated. His attention went first to the woman, then to the two dogs that dominated a corner of the room. The mastiff that had accompanied its mistress outside was one of a pair. As large as lions, their black manes tangled with twigs, they stared with open jowls at the scene before them.

Clutching Li Du's sleeve, Campo spoke

in a panicked voice. "A witch," he gasped. "You have brought us to the lair of a witch. We are not safe here."

"We are less exposed to danger here than we were outside," Li Du said. "You need warmth and rest. This woman risks her own safety to welcome us."

Campo released Li Du's sleeve with shaking fingers, but whimpered as one of the dogs emitted a low growl. At a sharp command from their mistress, they slid their enormous front legs forward to lie down, their heads resting on their paws, their eyes alert.

The woman spoke to Li Du. "Will you go outside and bring wood for the fire?"

Li Du turned and went to the door. As he opened it, he noticed a sword leaning against the wall. Its corroded hilt was shaped like the head of a serpent. After a quick glance behind him, he went out and made his way between piles of snow to the stacked wood. He selected as many logs as he could carry and brushed the snow from them. His arms full, he returned to the hut and used his shoulder to push the door open.

On reentering, he was able to form more of an impression of the hut's interior. Years of smoke and heat had imbued it with living warmth. Bundles of lacy snow tea hung beside garlic garlands and lily bulbs strung like necklaces from one corner of the ceiling to the other. Tables and shelves were piled with wooden bowls and black clay pots. Animal skulls cast creeping, fanged shadows on the walls.

Campo was murmuring, his eyes searching the flames. The woman, meanwhile, had stoked the fire and was using a mortar and pestle to grind something soft and sweet-smelling. She added water to it from a kettle that rested on three hearthstones, then handed the bowl to Li Du. "Give him this," she said. "It will quiet him."

Li Du took the mixture and inhaled the familiar sweet scent of buckthorn. He knelt in front of Campo, gently persuaded him to take it, then rose. The woman gestured for him to sit on the bench beside Campo. She added a log to the fire, then sat across from him, the dogs close behind her. She and Li Du regarded each other in mutual assessment.

She was older than he. Her long gray hair was braided and draped over one shoulder, where it mingled with the shaggy fur of a vest worn over a dark dress. Her small face seemed to recede from a pointed nose. She appeared tiny, with fragile bones and narrow shoulders that curved into a thin, concave chest. But Li Du knew that her size was misleading. She had supported Campo's weight easily across her shoulders. She was looking at Li Du now with frank, unafraid inquiry.

He told her who he was, where he had come from, and, briefly, how he had come to travel with Kalden's caravan.

"I am called Lumo," she said. She gave no indication that she intended to say more.

Li Du looked at the walls. "Have we come to the village?" he asked. "Perhaps I did not comprehend its location relative to the manor. I thought they were on the same side of the river."

Lumo leaned forward to stir a pot of soup that was suspended from blackened chains over the fire. "This is not the village," she said. Her accent was different from that of the family in the manor, and reminded Li Du of Kalden's voice.

Campo coughed as the smoke from the fire shifted toward him. He moved a little to the side and leaned back against the wall, drawing the blankets more closely around him.

"What happened to your friend?" asked Lumo.

"He fell from the precipice above the hot

springs," Li Du said. He recounted to her what had happened, attributing his own presence at the hot springs to the curiosity of a traveler. He did not mention the unidentified assailant.

Lumo clicked her tongue against her teeth. "Old Dhamo visited the pools yesterday, and now he is dead. Your friend visited them today, and he is lucky not to be dead. Perhaps you should take care where your idle curiosity leads you."

Li Du did not know whether he imagined her emphasis on *idle curiosity*, but the look she directed at him was shrewd. He suspected that she guessed more about his motivation for visiting the pools than he had revealed.

"Then — you know what happened to Dhamo," he said.

There was no change in her expression. "I saw him dead on the bridge."

"Why did you say he visited the hot springs?"

The question gave her an instant's pause. "I do not know that he visited them," she admitted. "But that was the only reason he ever came this way."

Li Du nodded. "To collect cinnabar."

Now she looked slightly surprised. "Yes."

"Did you know him well?"

Lumo exhaled sharply through her nose. "No one knew him well. Dhamo sustained himself on the company of his own mind."

"You do not seem upset that he is dead."

"As I just told you, I did not know him well. As for Death, that is a different matter. I have met Death often, often enough to exchange nods when we pass each other."

She looked at Campo. "I am not frightened by the sight of a mad monk who has cut out his own insides. But this man appeared very afraid for someone who simply lost his footing."

Li Du hesitated, unsure of what to say. Her direct look emboldened him to be frank. "Did you see anyone else in the forest during the last hour?"

She considered, then shook her head. "I did not see anyone until I met the two of you," she said. She reached behind her to pet one of the mastiffs. "But this one growled more than once. I thought she must have heard a bear nearby." She returned her gaze to Li Du.

Campo's head had fallen forward. His chin rested on his chest. Li Du heard his breathing become even.

"I urge you to be careful," he said.

Lumo appeared to search his face for the answer to a question. She frowned as if she was dissatisfied. "Careful of what?" she asked.

"I am not sure that Dhamo's death was what it seemed."

To his surprise, Lumo did not question him. She nodded. "This path is walked by many strange visitors," she said. "People with secrets. People who do not want to take the main road." She leaned forward. "But never so strange as the gathering who have come to Doso's manor now."

"Then you also suspect —"

Lumo interrupted him. "I know nothing of what happened to Dhamo. I have no wish to know, nor any wish to speak of it."

Suddenly both the dogs raised their heads. Their ears, almost lost in the black shaggy hair around them, perked.

Lumo looked at the door, then at the dogs. "Why don't you bark?" Her tone was scolding, but her expression was troubled.

The dogs emitted low whines, but did not stand up. The firelight shone in their dark eyes and wild fur.

"Are you in there, librarian?"

Li Du started. "That is Hamza," he said. "He is another traveler with the caravan."

Lumo shifted her gaze from the dogs and gestured a hand in the direction of the door. "You may let him in," she said.

154

Li Du moved quickly to the door and opened it. The icy air rushed in. It carried with it a thin flurry of snow that scattered and quickly melted on the floor.

Hamza stood holding up a guttering torch, puffing pale cold clouds of breath into the night air.

Inside, Hamza brushed the snow from his legs and straightened, taking in his surroundings with apparent interest. As usual, the visible signs of physical hardship retreated from him almost instantly. His beard looked carved and lacquered, his blue embroidered hat like new, and his bearing that of someone who had just begun the day after a good night's sleep.

He bowed to Lumo. Then he turned to Li Du. "I came looking for you, thinking you had been pulled under the water by a cursed ghost. Did you find the hot springs?"

"He did," said Lumo.

Hamza's gaze took in the sleeping Campo wrapped in blankets, and the drying clothes. "What has happened to Paolo Campo?"

"We do not know," Li Du said. "He fell from the cliff above the pools. He is not badly hurt, but he is unsteady. I was trying to bring him back to the manor when Lumo found us."

Hamza raised his eyebrows in surprise. He addressed Lumo. "Then you, grandmother of the forest, have saved these two men, one of whom is my dear friend, from a dire fate. You have my deepest gratitude." Hamza bowed again with an air of such unquestionable sincerity that her hard face crinkled in pleasure. She leaned forward to look in her pot. "There is food," she said, and gestured for Hamza to sit down.

As Lumo reached for three bowls on a nearby shelf, Hamza and Li Du exchanged looks. *Be cautious,* Li Du tried to indicate in his expression. Hamza gave the barest inclination of his head in response, and sat down.

Lumo had turned to the stew and was ladling it into the bowls. "And what kind of traveler are you?" she asked Hamza without looking up.

"I am a storyteller, grandmother," he replied. "I came to these mountains to tell a story to an emperor. That feat accomplished, I seek other adventures."

"And him?" she asked, extending the ladle in the direction of Paolo Campo.

"Paolo Campo is a religious man," Li Du answered. "From a country a year's journey to the west."

"What is he doing here, then? Seeking

enlightenment? Or fleeing some war?"

Li Du reached up and rubbed the back of his head thoughtfully. "He believes that there were once people of his faith in these mountains. He hopes to find them, and to convert those of other faiths to his own."

"And is his faith the superior one?"

"He believes it to be the only true belief."

"Well, maybe our lamas should listen to him. Corrupt charlatans, most of them. Not many good ones left. I once heard a dying lama speaking to his students. They asked him how they would recognize his reincarnation. He became enraged. 'Lies and falsehoods!' he cried out. He told them that if anyone claimed to find his reincarnation, they should stuff his lying throat full of ash. 'For,' he said, 'with the number of sins committed by lamas in this land, the only place I'll be going after death is hell.' " Lumo paused. "He was an honest man."

Hamza raised his eyes from his bowl. "We do not meet many people in this country who would speak so about monks and lamas."

Lumo shrugged. "I am too old to say other than what I think."

"I commend your honesty," said Hamza. "But are you not, perhaps, a little severe?"

Lumo gave Hamza a suspicious look. "You

mock me?"

"I do not."

"You are too young to understand."

Hamza's face was serious, but his eyes sparkled. "I am as old as the oldest grandfather in the stories I tell, and as young as the youngest prince or peasant."

"And who is the oldest character in your stories?"

"Well, grandmother, that is a difficult question and one it will take some time to answer. You see, there was once a turtle who fell asleep by a pool filled with tears of a goddess who —" He stopped to sip the soup broth.

Then he gave a sigh of appreciation. "I have not tasted such good soup since I was hosted by a giant who was setting a trap for a hunter and wished me to tell him if the food was enough to entice the most disciplined man. I was happy to help, for I was not his quarry, and was able to enjoy the food without danger."

Lumo looked at the dried meat hanging from the ceiling. "It is Doso's generosity that sustains me," she said.

"How did you come to live here?" asked Hamza. "Your accent is not from these mountains."

Lumo looked speculatively at her unexpected guests. Then, with a shrug, she settled back in her chair. "I was a traveler once," she said. "The circumstances of my life left me alone in the world with no wish to stay near the monastery where I was born. I left my home, and for many years I moved through the roads like a raindrop rolls down the veins of a leaf." She held up a finger and traced it through the air.

"You were a pilgrim?"

Her expression hardened. "I was no pilgrim," she said. She turned to the two dogs, and her face relaxed. "I was only a traveler. And one day, I became like a lamp that has no oil left to burn. And I stopped so that I could die." She delivered this statement without emotion. Then she began to count softly under her breath. "Fourteen years ago," she said. "That was when I could no longer go on. And that is when the lord of this manor found me and told me that his ancestors would not allow him to let someone die if he could help them."

She looked up with an enigmatic smile. "Fourteen years beyond my time, I am. So you see why it is difficult for me to be afraid."

"And you have lived here all those years?"

"In this cabin. Doso made it sturdy, and he sends the boy Pema to bring me what I need. Sometimes Kamala asks me to sew for her. A generous family. You have met Yeshe?"

"He greeted us when we came to the manor."

"Another of Doso's good deeds. Yeshe dragged himself over the pass a few years ago. A farmworker for hire, on his way to offer his services for the harvest, until he was set upon by thieves. They cut his ankles and left him to die in a ravine. He had the good luck to be discovered there by Doso before the wild animals got to him. Yeshe's injuries crippled him — Doso took him in and he has lived in that cottage ever since."

"Cruel thieves," said Li Du, "to assign their victim a lingering death." He repressed an involuntary shudder as a memory of the executioner's platform in the Forbidden City assailed him.

Hamza was looking at him inquiringly, but he was saved from having to explain his discomfiture by movement in the corner of the room. The dogs had stood up and begun to growl. Several minutes later, a knock announced the arrival of Doso himself, who, accompanied by Andruk, had come to retrieve his missing guests.

CHAPTER 11

"He is resting," said Andruk, as he entered the manor kitchen, where Li Du sat with Doso and Kamala. She held her baby while the other children slept bundled behind her on the wide bench.

"Could he give any description of his attacker?" Li Du asked.

Andruk accepted a cup of clear liquor from Doso and sat down. "He was not attacked," said Andruk. "Now that he has had time to recover and to recall what happened, he is certain that he merely lost his footing."

Doso's exhale was almost a sigh. His broad brow relaxed. "The snow is deceptive," he said. "It extends beyond where it is safe to step."

"He is not badly injured?" The question came from Kamala.

"He was fortunate," said Andruk, "to land where he did, and so near a rescuer."

They all turned to look at Li Du, who hesitated. "I am relieved that he is better," he said finally. "We both owe a debt of gratitude to Lumo."

Doso nodded. "We see very little of her. She comes to the manor for festivals, but usually she is content to be left alone. Pema brings her food and chops her wood."

Andruk spoke in a tone of polite curiosity. "Where did she come from?"

Doso and Kamala exchanged glances. "She was born to a religious family," Doso said, "but they followed an older tradition."

Li Du nodded his understanding. "They resisted the reforms?"

Doso hesitated, then gave a grunt of affirmation. "You understand that we do not harbor any criminals," he said. "The wars between the monks are resolved, and she is an old woman. But you are correct — her family was among those who rebelled against the Great Fifth Dalai Lama, to their sorrow. She was the only survivor."

Li Du had not yet been born when the Fifth Dalai Lama suppressed the rebellions. As a student, Li Du had read a copy of the Dalai Lama's edict, which had been conveyed to the imperial court by its spies in Lhasa. He remembered the words of the Great Fifth to his Mongol soldiers: *Regard-*

ing the adversaries, these oath breakers and legion of foes, see that the lines of their fathers become as trees with their roots cut, the lines of their mothers as streams dried up in winter, the lines of their sons and grandsons as eggs cast against stones, their attendants as dry grass consumed by flame. No wonder the Kangxi had been concerned about the growing power to China's west.

Kamala was looking at her children. She said nothing, but Li Du felt her emotion stronger than the heat radiating from the fire. Her expression was one of absolute conviction, empty of the small thoughts that usually play at the edges of a face. *If someone threatened her family,* thought Li Du, *she would strike him down, were he the Dalai Lama himself.*

Li Du addressed Doso again. "You are very generous to those who come to your land. Lumo told us that Yeshe also remained at your invitation. To the weary and injured, this valley offers unanticipated refuge."

Doso put up a hand in polite rejection of the compliment, but he seemed pleased. "To have left them to continue alone would have been the same as killing them. It was my duty to help."

Kamala was fiddling with a loose thread in the swaddling. "Yeshe is a sweet man who suffers but does not complain. When he first came here, we did not think he would live. And when his wounds healed, I feared the presence of a stranger so close, a man like that, with no family. But he is good. He is gentle with the children and watchful of their safety." She looked lovingly down at her three sons and daughter, their red-cheeked faces calm and asleep.

Then her mouth tensed. "There are others," she said, "who are less deserving."

"Promises cannot be broken," said Doso. His statement brooked no argument. It was infused with the physical strength of the man who uttered it. "I honor the vows I make, as I honor the traditions of my fathers."

Doso spoke with such unself-conscious assurance that Li Du felt a twinge of envy. Doso was a man who did not struggle to reconcile life's inconsistencies. He was secure in wealth, strength, and family. He had no concerns with advancement within a bureaucracy, and little awareness of the world outside his valley.

Li Du stood up and, with a bow to his hosts, announced his intention to retire for the night. Kamala set the baby beside her and used blackened iron tools to pull several stones from the fire, which she wrapped in two woolen packages. "Please take these to warm your feet," she said, carefully transferring both to his arms. "And these are for your friend, if he is still awake."

"Of course I am awake," whispered Hamza. He stepped aside for Li Du to enter. With a glance in each direction down the dark, silent hallway, he closed the door. "What is happening in this place?"

"According to Andruk," said Li Du, "Campo now claims he was not attacked, but simply lost his footing."

"By your tone," said Hamza, "I surmise that you do not believe it."

Li Du set the warmers down on the bed. "No. I heard Campo's words clearly. Someone was up on that precipice with him."

In a corner of the room was a table, on which a candle flickered unsteadily. Hamza crossed the room to it. "Why would Campo alter his account?"

"He must be protecting the identity of his attacker," said Li Du.

Hamza trimmed the candlewick with a pair of flat blades, then straightened. "But why? And who?"

Raising a finger to his lips, Li Du answered in a hushed voice. "Whom did you see while I was gone? Is there anyone you are sure was not here at the manor?"

Hamza raised his hands in a helpless gesture. "I cannot tell you. I stayed in the hut with the Khampa until it grew dark and I became concerned for your well-being."

Li Du cast his mind back to the scene in hut. "Did Sera-tsering remain there also?"

"No," Hamza replied. "She left not long after you did." He lapsed into speculative silence, then added, "If she is what she claims — a simple traveler going to visit her sister — then I will cease my storytelling and become a silent hermit. But I do not think she is a murderess."

Outside, the floorboards of the hallway groaned as someone passed by the closed door. When it was quiet again, Hamza continued. "What of Dhamo? Do you still believe that he was murdered?"

"I am certain of it," said Li Du.

Hamza nodded. "Because of the attempt on Paolo Campo?"

"The two events must be connected," said Li Du. "But Campo had not yet fallen when I came to the conclusion that Dhamo was murdered. I found cinnabar at the pools."

"My friend," said Hamza. "I confess I still do not see why the cinnabar is so important."

"It is important," replied Li Du, "because

someone who is in the middle of performing a mundane task does not suddenly commit suicide."

"He might," said Hamza. "If he was driven into a state of terror or despondency, as I suggested to you earlier today."

"Yes," Li Du agreed. "But in that case — if something happened to cast him into an agony so extreme that it overcame his reason — would he have taken the time to disguise his original errand?"

There was a silence. "No," said Hamza, finally.

Li Du took a deep breath. "A murderer, however, who wished to make a murder look like a suicide, would do exactly that."

"Explain this to me," said Hamza, with a gesture of invitation. He leaned against a wall and crossed his arms over his chest.

"Dhamo went to the hot springs to collect cinnabar," Li Du said, thinking as he spoke. "He intended to return with it to his studio and continue his work. When I examined the hot spring pool, I touched scoring where a blade had scraped and pried away the rock. Dhamo must have had a knife with him."

"He did," said Hamza. "A knife that was later buried in his body."

With a little shake of his head, Li Du went

on. "Dhamo was killed with a silver blade. I saw it this morning at the temple. It is an ornate weapon, and it was not the one that Dhamo used to chip at rocks."

"How can you be sure?"

"Because the water of the hot springs tarnishes silver. If Dhamo had used that blade, it would have turned black." Li Du withdrew his own knife from its sheath and handed it to Hamza, indicating the silver in its hilt.

Hamza looked impressed. "Then where is the knife Dhamo used to collect the cinnabar?"

"Exactly," replied Li Du. "There was no knife with Dhamo's body except for the one that killed him. So where is the prosaic tool to fit the prosaic task? My guess is that the murderer tossed it into the stream, along with the cinnabar Dhamo had collected. Without them, the scene appeared as the murderer wanted it to appear. Dhamo went to the bridge with paint and a knife, and submitted to his demons."

With a grave expression, Hamza handed Li Du's knife back to him. "Surely there are easier ways to kill a man," he said. "Why choose such an elaborate scheme?"

"I don't know," Li Du said. "And here is another question. What is the meaning of the painted mirror? It was not necessary to the appearance of suicide."

Hamza had no answer. "What will you do," he asked. "Will you tell Doso?"

Li Du let out a shaky breath, aware that he was exhausted. With an effort, he gathered his thoughts. "I do not think we should announce our suspicions yet," he said. "Whom can we trust?"

A crease appeared between Hamza's eyebrows. "We can trust Kalden."

"Are you sure? Why has he been so evasive about his reason for bringing us here?"

Hamza opened his mouth to speak, then closed it. "I don't know," he said.

Li Du picked up one of the warmers. It was still hot. "Tomorrow I will investigate the place from which Campo fell. Maybe something was left there."

"If you are going back to the hot springs," said Hamza, "this time you will not go alone."

CHAPTER 12

It had snowed a little more during the night, and Li Du and Hamza emerged from the manor to a smooth, featureless pasture. At the open door of Yeshe's hut, the old man was accepting buckets of water from Kamala's two eldest children. He hailed Li Du and Hamza, and they made their way over.

The two children stood close to Yeshe, their dark eyes conducting a wary assessment of the strangers. "Go back to the hearth," Yeshe said to them. His face when he looked at them was kind. "Your mother will praise you if you are quick in your chores."

They scampered back toward the manor, the empty buckets swinging in their hands. Yeshe's expression hardened as he looked up at Li Du and Hamza, and Li Du wondered how much of his apparent cantankerousness was indicative of the physical pain he suffered. Li Du doubted that the cold was kind to scarred and twisted joints.

"Wandering through the forest at night," said Yeshe. "You two are lucky you travel with those Khampa. You won't last long in these mountains making decisions like that. I hear that the foreign monk fell, but didn't break any of his bones." Yeshe glanced down at his own legs.

"It is true," Li Du said. "He was very lucky."

"Maybe his god let him sprout wings like one of the pictures in his book," Yeshe said.

"What book?"

Yeshe shrugged. "He came into my place to show pictures in a book to me and to the children. In his bad Chinese, he tried to tell them about his god. They didn't understand, and wouldn't pay attention to him." A hint of pride crossed Yeshe's features. "They like my stories better," he said.

Hamza looked interested. "What stories do you tell them?"

Yeshe shrugged again. "The kind of stories that children like. Stories that frighten them."

A short while later, Li Du and Hamza stood together on the ledge from which Campo had fallen. The fresh snow, in combination with the sweeping wind, had left only illusory suggestions of footprints. Several broken branches hanging askew near the edge testified to where Campo had clutched for balance. Below them were the pools, shining indistinctly through the vapors that eddied across their surfaces.

"I have seen pools like this before," said Hamza, "in the hills north of Kham. Those springs were near a monastery, and they were heated by a spirit who used to torment travelers. One day, the spirit led the wife of a soldier into a ravine so that she would be lost, only to fall in love with her when he saw her crying amid the thorns and rocks. He tried to lead her to safety, but she slipped and fell to her death. The repentant spirit went to a temple high on the mountain and asked the monks how he could atone for his actions. The clever monks told the spirit that he could atone by warming the water in the mountain. So the spirit kept their water hot for many years, and was grateful to the monks for their counsel."

"And the monks were grateful for the warmth," Li Du said.

"Just so," said Hamza. He scanned the snow around them again. "We have not learned much from coming to this place."

"No," Li Du agreed. His gaze was focused on the view through the trees. He pointed.

"You can see the bridge," he said, "if you stand just here."

Hamza moved closer and looked. "I can see it," he said. "From this distance, and with the the fresh snow, it has a tranquil look."

Li Du only half agreed. It was not hard to imagine death within that vista of wintry gray and white. What was difficult to picture were the colors: the crimson robe, the lurid splashes of blood and layers of paint. He retreated from the ledge and paced slowly in the direction of the woods, deep in thought.

In front of him was a tree that had fallen long ago, and was covered in an undisturbed layer of snow. He pulled his right hand free of its sleeve and considered. Several moments to untie the leather packets of paint, then . . . he dipped a finger into the snow and traced a circle into it. He pictured a gold bead like the one in the box at the temple, dampened and crushed and applied in a ring. Finally, a sweep of blue.

Hamza came and stood beside him. "The white mirror."

The shape looked up at them like a face with curving, outstretched arms.

"It was roughly done," Li Du said. "It would have taken only moments."

"Even moments risk discovery," said Hamza. "It must have been very important to the murderer."

A voice announced a presence in the trees. "So you have come back." They turned to see Lumo. She was bundled in furs that made her form appear larger than it was, and her face appear small and dainty as a squirrel's. Li Du noticed that her age gave her no trouble moving through the snow. She was not out of breath. Beside her stood one of the mastiffs.

"This is where Campo fell," Li Du said. "He says that he slipped."

"You do not believe him?"

"You yourself observed his fear last night."

Lumo considered this. "Let us be straightforward," she said. "You think that someone killed Dhamo. You think that the foreigner knows something about it, and that someone pushed him from this ledge. Is that so?"

Li Du and Hamza exchanged looks. "I am not satisfied with the explanations that seem acceptable to the family and guests at the manor," Li Du said finally.

"Well I don't know anything about it," said Lumo. "I told you last night — strange roads, and strange people that travel them. It has nothing to do with me. What is it that you have done?" She was looking at the outline Li Du had traced in the snow.

"It is the shape that was painted on Dhamo's body — we think it was a mirror."

"Is that what it was? It didn't look like any mirror to me."

Hamza nodded sagely. He was petting the mastiff, who had sat down in the snow. "After all, a mirror, by its nature, reflects. The painted mirror does not."

"Don't start talking like a monk," Lumo said. She sounded irritated.

Li Du changed the subject. "What brought you out of your hut — when you saw Dhamo on the bridge. Did you hear something?"

"Hear?" Lumo shook her head. "My hearing is not so keen as that. I was out in the snow because I was showing my guest the way to the path. It is easy to get lost in a storm, even when the distances are short. And the snow was falling heavily by then. We saw Doso and the others. Then we saw Dhamo."

"Who was your guest?"

"The woman called Sera-tsering."

"You know each other?"

"I met her on the path the day she arrived. We spoke, and I invited her to visit me. She came to my door very early that morning — the day Dhamo died — and we remained inside talking and drinking butter tea."

"What can you tell us of her?" Hamza asked the question.

"She is a good traveler," replied Lumo. "And she speaks entertainingly of cities I have not seen since I was young. Much has changed since I stepped off the trade route paths."

"One does not meet many women traveling alone," Li Du said.

"And so you assume," said Lumo, "that there are not many who do it. Consider instead that women who travel dangerous roads are clever enough to avoid being noticed by strangers unless they wish to be."

Li Du accepted the rebuke. "Then," he said, "I would guess that since you yourself traveled these paths once, as Sera-tsering does now, you are both adept at observing your surroundings. Did you see or hear anything unusual in the forest that day, or yesterday?"

Lumo's expression became set. "Only the bells of your own caravan," she said. "And I am tired of talking. If I were you, I would wait by the hearth fire until the snow melts and your caravan can be on its way. There's no use asking questions that won't be answered."

Paolo Campo called down to Li Du from an opened shutter in the courtyard's central tower. Li Du looked up at the painted woodwork, from which emerged a brown sleeve and pale hand, one finger pointed downward toward the entrance to the building.

Inside, a staircase slick with packed snow led up to the second floor. At the top of the staircase, Li Du turned left into a dark hallway crowded with crates, stained, misshapen saddlebags, blankets and furs piled almost to the ceiling. He squeezed through the clutter, which smelled of campfire smoke, into Campo's room.

It was a small but luxurious space. The floor was covered in thick layered rugs of many colors and patterns, on top of which stacks of padded coverlets and animal skins invited occupants to sit or recline comfortably. Chinese brocaded silks covered some of the pillows. Bright embroidered wool encased others. Two covered copper braziers were lit in the center of the room beside a heavy desk laden with piles of books and papers.

In one corner was a shrine that housed a

silver statue of a Buddha seated on the curling silver petals of a lotus flower, surrounded by tendrils of silver cloth molded to appear suspended in the air. Campo had reappointed the shrine by nestling a wooden crucifix into the arms of the statue.

"I am gratified to see you so recovered," said Li Du, watching Campo's face.

Campo's smile lifted his loose cheeks like cinched draperies. "I wish to convey to you my sincere gratitude. You pulled me from the very jaws of death."

"I am thankful that I happened to be so close," Li Du said. "But I did wish to inquire of you — were you alone there at the top of the escarpment?"

"Alone?" Campo's eyes did not meet Li Du's. "Ah. You refer, perhaps, to the words I spoke to you after you pulled me from the water. I was not in my right mind when I uttered them. Yes — I was alone. I simply stepped too near the edge, and the snow slipped away under my feet."

"But the rocks and pebbles that were dislodged — it seemed to me as if you struggled."

Campo shook his head vigorously. "I clung to the branches around me as I fell," he said. "But be assured — there was no one there but myself."

"And what brought you to that place?"

With a nervous little flutter of his hands, Campo made a vague gesture encompassing several opened crates in the corner. "My work," he said. "You perceived, I am sure, the heavy burden of equipment I carry."

Li Du glanced behind him. "Are the items in the hallways yours as well?"

Campo nodded. "It is an unwieldy load, but essential."

"Essential to . . ."

"To my surveys of the land," said Campo. "We cannot hope to locate the lost Christian kingdoms if we do not trace our route as we go." He went to one of the crates and removed an object from it. "The drum of a base box," he said, handing it to Li Du, who took it carefully. It was gilt brass, etched on both sides, with a compass set into its center.

Li Du raised it close to his eyes. "Boreas, Zephirus, Favonius, Corus," he read.

"The names of winds," said Campo. "In the Greek and the Roman systems."

Turning it over in his hands, Li Du marveled at the intricate calendrical and zodiacal scales etched in concentric circles on its face. "It is exquisite," he said. "I would be pleased to learn how it is used." He handed it carefully back to Campo.

"These instruments are all very advanced," said Campo, returning it to its box. "Designed in Lower Saxony by a master craftsman. It has required enormous effort to carry them such a great distance. These are barbaric lands — I am told that thieves will beat and strip even those with nothing but the clothes on their backs. But sit, please." He gestured to cushioned seats, then retrieved one of the braziers from its place beside the desk and set it near the window. They sat down opposite one another, Campo leaning forward into the transparent shimmer of heat.

"Did you travel here from Lhasa?" Li Du asked.

Campo nodded. "I left Rome five years ago. I was, for a time, in India. Brother Achille, who was in Lhasa already, requested that a companion be assigned to him for a journey of exploration. The Church sent me, and I met him there." Campo sighed. "If it were not for Brother Achille's indefatigable good humor, I do not know how I could have stayed in this country as long as I have — what hardships we have endured."

An almost imperceptible spasm crossed Campo's face, as if an insect had skittered across his cheek. "The high mountains are most terrible." He raised an index finger marked by a ragged scar. "I cut my finger and felt no pain. I would not have noticed the injury if I had not seen the blood in the snow. Your body could be torn to pieces and you would be too cold to know it until you turned your eyes to observe your own destruction. There are bridges made of snow that crumble away under your feet. Nothing grows, they burn the dung of the animals for heat, and you cannot sleep for the lice that bite you. You cannot remove your coat for a moment or your breath will freeze in your chest. It is a terrible place. Terrible. There were times —" Campo's eyes now focused on Li Du with a kind of plea. His voice became a whisper. "There were times I almost cursed out loud."

Li Du was about to respond, but Campo spoke again. "I did not call you here only to thank you."

"What was your other purpose?"

"To warn you." Campo's green eyes shone between pink, windbeaten lids. "Stay away from the lama at the temple," he said.

Li Du blinked in surprise. "You speak of the Chhöshe."

Campo nodded. "I believe that he is the devil's novice, and that the devil, speaking with the tongue of his servant, seeks to do us harm. I fear it was he who goaded the painter to perform such abhorrent and grotesque violations upon himself."

"What reason do you have to think so?"

Campo reached into a basket filled with pine tapers. He lifted the brazier's copper lid and piled them onto the little pile of embers. "I know all about them, these boys who are born and, before they can speak more than a few words, suddenly produce whole sentences about a previous life."

Seeing that Campo had paused only to draw in a breath, Li Du waited. Campo went on. "I have definite proof," he said, slowly, "that it is the devil who orchestrates this deception."

"Definite proof?" Li Du lifted his eyebrows.

Campo sat back. "I will explain it to you. A lama of some high status dies, and goes, as he must, to the pit of hell. You know of hell?"

"A place of fire and punishment." Li Du gave the answer distractedly. He was considering how he might turn Campo to the subject of his whereabouts on the morning of Dhamo's death.

"It is more complicated than that," said Campo, "but yes, a place of fire and punishment. And while this lama's soul is there, the devil has the opportunity to speak to him, to question him on the secrets of his life: a description of his favorite hat, or where he hid his copper pot. With this information the devil returns to the world, takes possession of a small child, and whispers the secrets to him. Then, when the lamas and emissaries come to question the boy, he answers in the words of the man who has died. And thus he is pronounced by the lamas to be a reincarnation, and evil is perpetuated under the guise of a miracle." Campo paused, slightly out of breath. "It is the only possible explanation."

Li Du pulled off his hat, studying it while he considered a response. "Your argument may merit discussion, but I suspect that there are ways to refute it. For those who believe in —"

Campo interrupted him. "My opinion does not come just from theorizing." Campo's fingers picked nervously at the calluses on his hands. "I saw it myself."

"What did you see?"

Campo lifted his gaze up in the direction of the mountain. "The young lama — this Chhöshe, as he is called — appeared very peaceful when you observed him yesterday, but I know otherwise. I heard him rail and cry in the unearthly howls of the tormented."

"What happened?"

"It was on the day he arrived. He came to the temple on the mountain, but he did not notice me in the shadows. He went to the altar and walked around it three times. Then he went to the door, and I heard him speaking to the boy who tends the goats. It was then that the fury took him."

"He was upset?"

Campo looked defensive. "He was more than upset. The other one, poor youth, was bewildered. I think he tried to speak soothingly, but the lama would not listen. He ran alone into the snow. I left before he returned."

"And what about the morning that Dhamo left the temple to go to the bridge? How did the Chhöshe behave then?"

Li Du thought he glimpsed wariness enter Campo's eyes. "You misunderstand," said Campo. "I was not at the temple on *that* day. I was here. The rigors of surveying work take place not only in the outdoors with octants and tapes, but at a desk, with complex mathematical equations. You see." He stood and led Li Du to the desk, on which were arranged papers covered in grids, circles, and rough outlines of what appeared to be mountains.

"Then you did not go to the village with

the family."

"No — I had seen it before and could make no connection with the people there, even with Andruk's help. I am afraid that out in these remote places the people are too uncivilized and rude to be receptive. They are not like you — a scholar's mind is better prepared to learn."

"You were in your room the whole morning?"

This time, Li Du was certain he saw suspicion on Campo's face. He thought that Campo might challenge him on his reason for asking, but Campo did not. "I visited the cottage of the cheese maker," he said. "But the children had been left to his care, and were riotous and unpleasant. I took some food and warmed my hands at the hearth, then returned, and was here until Andruk told me that the painter was dead. I hope never again to hear such a vile account."

"As do I," Li Du said. He stood up. "Again, I am relieved that you are unhurt." He moved to the door, and was about to step out of the room when Campo said, very quietly, "It is a terrible sin to take your own life. For that alone he burns. My failure to save him pains me. But the painter's heart was as a piece of stone, and on it was

185

engraved his own certain damnation. As it is written in the book of the all-virtuous wisdom of Sirach, *a hard heart shall have evils at the last.*"

The door to Sera-tsering's room was open, but she was not there. Li Du hesitated for a moment on the threshold. He looked to his right — his own room was two doors down — and to his left, past Hamza's room, to where the hallway angled sharply toward the kitchen. He checked the dark ladder stairs to the barley storage room. There was no one there. He paused for another instant, listening for sounds of someone approaching, then slipped inside.

Sera's room was similar to his own. A shrine occupied the corner behind a butter lamp with a white wick that had not been lit. Her possessions rested on the floor in another corner, twin leather saddlebags that had seen hard travel but were not old. Listening for steps outside and hearing none, he knelt in front of the bags and opened one.

Careful not to disarrange the contents, which were organized with precision, Li Du quickly ascertained that the bags contained nothing unusual. There were blankets and clothes rolled up tightly, tea bricks wrapped and tucked into clean pots, a heavy sack of rice or millet. He discovered a knife, a fine blade, heavier than it looked, with a sturdy hilt made for larger hands than Sera-tsering's.

He slipped the knife back into its place, and his fingers found the edge of a wooden box. He pulled it out gently and smiled in spite of himself when he undid the copper clasp and opened it to see an elegant writer's kit. It contained a cast-copper inkwell covered in leather, a delicate agate bowl for washing brushes, three bamboo brushes, ink sticks, needle and thread . . . The items were all familiar to Li Du. In one compartment was a red cylindrical seal tied in place with leather straps. He untied them and looked at the word on the seal. It was a Chinese name, a noble family, though not one that he knew personally. *Why is a woman from Lhasa carrying a Chinese seal?*

Li Du returned the seal to its place, careful to tie the straps around it just as they had been. He was fumbling with the clasp of the box when he heard steps in the hallway outside, and felt the shudder of floorboards under his own feet. He put the box away, flipped the leather covers back over the packs, and stood up, searching his mind for an excuse. Just as he thought Sera herself would walk into the door, he saw two figures pass by and continue on past the room without stopping or glancing inside.

They went into the room between Sera's and Li Du's own — Sonam's room. Li Du stepped quietly to the wall and put his ear close to it.

"— you should remind them that you are a son of this house, not some village boy. Doso made a blood oath to your father."

The voice that answered was Pema's. "But I could serve you —" The rest of his words were lost, but Li Du heard desperation in them.

"— honest with you. You are not built for it. The roads I travel are more difficult than you can imagine."

"But if I could only come with you for a year."

Sonam's voice became impatient. "If you stay here you will be lord of the manor when Doso dies. I will not permit you to risk your inheritance."

"Two years ago at the spring festival you said that when I was old enough I could go with you, that you would take me to the sea and to temples big as mountains and forests where the flowers are as big as goats."

Sonam laughed. "You overheard a conversation I was having with a woman. Women like to hear about colorful places. That was not meant for you. You belong here. Doso is a dull man. He will honor his promise to your father. He considers you his blood, even if he wishes —" Sonam stopped.

"I know what he wishes." Li Du heard pain constricting Pema's throat. "They don't want me here. No one ever wanted me here."

Li Du stepped back from the wall as a thump against it indicated an impatient fist striking the wood. "This is an easy life. Don't whine."

Li Du remembered the glint in Pema's eyes the day before. There had been desperation in those eyes.

The door of Sonam's room swung open and thudded against the hallway wall. Li Du heard Pema's light steps, followed by the strike of a flint and clatter of a brazier lid in Sonam's room.

Li Du emerged into the hallway just in time to see someone come out of a door at the other end of it, moving with quiet, deft confidence. It was Sera-tsering. The room was his own.

She looked up and saw him. For an instant her expression froze. Then she smiled and raised her hands in a helpless gesture. "I am unused to staying in grand homes," she said. "I walked into this room without thinking. Is it yours?"

Li Du looked over her shoulder at the door to his room, which she had pulled closed behind her. He saw her eyes flit briefly over his shoulder to her own door.

"Yes," he said. "That room is mine."

She looked away, brushing a speck of invisible dust from the sleeve of her coat. "You must be used to fine mansions — coming from the palace of the Chinese Emperor."

"I have been away from Beijing long enough that I don't think I would be used to anything there, should I return."

"And do you plan to return?"

"At present I am bound for Lhasa."

She nodded. "Your caravan is not traveling by the usual route. Do you know why?"

"I do not," said Li Du. "But I myself prefer remote paths to crowded ones."

"These isolated valleys can be hazardous to those who are not familiar with them," said Sera. "I heard about the foreigner's accident. He was not badly hurt, I hope."

"No," said Li Du. "But the shock of the fall debilitated him. We were fortunate to find help in the forest. From Lumo — I think you have met her."

"Yes," said Sera. "I visited her the day before yesterday."

"So she told us. You were there all morning?"

Li Du thought he detected the briefest hesitation before Sera replied. "Yes."

The sound of footsteps distracted her, and she turned her head to glance at the open door of Sonam's room. "Excuse me," she said to Li Du. "I promised to help the lady of the house. There are often tenants from the village here to assist her, but with the snow, there is no one."

Li Du watched Sera walk away down the hall, her dark coat blending with the shadows, until she turned the corner toward the kitchen and was lost to sight. He returned to his room and made a cursory inspection. Nothing was missing. He gathered his coat tightly around his shoulders, adjusted his hat, and exited, closing the door tight behind him.

As he went by Sonam's room, he glanced inside. Sonam was sitting on a chair, a saddlebag open in front of him and some of its contents scattered across the floor. He was holding a folded paper. As Li Du passed the door, Sonam raised his head and looked for a moment at Li Du. Without saying anything, he returned his attention to his possessions, thrusting the folded paper back into the bag. Li Du continued down the hallway, the imprint of Sonam's cold, speculative stare deep in his mind.

CHAPTER 13

The muleteers were amusing themselves by practicing archery. From his vantage point near the outer door of the manor, Li Du watched a black arrow cut through the white and gray landscape. It struck a log hung from a tree at the pasture's edge. The log swung slowly back and forth.

Li Du considered walking toward them, but decided that the answers to more pressing questions lay in the other direction. He skirted the manor's outer wall until he reached the back corner and the trail that led to the stone stairs. He was about to start up it when he heard a stifled thud followed by the melodic clatter of logs tossed onto a woodpile. Turning toward the sound, he made his way along the back wall of the manor.

About halfway along it, in the shadow of the central tower, he found Doso standing in front of an enormous supply of stacked firewood. Doso's belted coat was parted and bunched at his waist, his arms out of its sleeves, freeing him to swing an ax in a broad arc over an upright log.

The ax struck the log's pale face and wedged deep into its center. Doso raised a booted foot to lever the heavy blade free. He remained for a moment leaning his elbow on his knee. Then, with a grunt, he pried the ax out. Li Du waited to speak until Doso had swung again. This time the blade struck deeper, but the log did not split.

"Will there be more snow?" Li Du asked.

Doso pivoted. When he recognized Li Du, he released the handle of the ax and straightened, raising a hand in greeting. "I think not," he said, glancing up at the sky. "It will be warmer tomorrow. You are eager to continue on to the pass?"

"I know that Kalden is concerned about the arrival of winter," said Li Du, approaching Doso through snow scattered with wood splinters and curls of bark. "He wants to be in Lhasa before the paths close."

Doso nodded. "His decision to come this way surprises me. We rarely see caravans here — the road through Dajianlu is faster and easier." His eyes flicked past Li Du to the path up the mountain. "You are on your way to the temple?"

"Yes."

Doso turned his back to the forested slope. "I do not go there often," he said. "I make my offerings at the temple within my own walls. When I was a younger man, I used to visit the shrines scattered across the peaks. Now Pema is old enough now to take the yaks up on his own."

"He works hard," said Li Du. "You must be proud to have a son so committed to the health and success of your family home."

"Pema is a good boy," said Doso. "But he spent too much time in the painter's studio. It was not a place for impressionable children — my wife never allows our younger ones to go there."

"Why not?"

Doso reached an arm across his chest and pressed his hand to his opposite shoulder, grimacing at some ache. "I trust women to make these decisions. But Pema has a fascination with the place."

"It seems," said Li Du, cautiously, "that Pema was the only person with whom Dhamo associated."

"I admit that it worried me," said Doso. "I am a religious man, but the lord of a manor must pay attention to his land and to the people who live on it. He must marry a good woman and have sons with her. The life and duties of a man are different from those of a monk."

"Does Pema wish to be a monk?"

For a moment Doso looked disconcerted, but his reply was firm. "No," he said. "Pema is the eldest son and heir to this house. His responsibility is here, as mine was, as my father's was before me." Doso turned to the half-split log and pried the ax from it. "Pema is fortunate to have lived to be a man," he said. "You have seen the scar that marks his face?"

Li Du did not need to answer.

"Death almost took him," said Doso, "soon after he became my son. He was not yet two years old."

"That is very young to sustain such an injury," said Li Du. "It must have been a dangerous wound."

"Still a babe," said Doso. "My wife — my first wife — was out gathering mushrooms with women from the village. Our son —" Something flickered in Doso's face, and he hesitated. "Our first son was only a little older than Pema, though he was much bigger and stronger. The two of them lay sleeping side by side in the soft moss. My wife told me that she heard a cry so loud and inconsolable that it rang to the tops of the trees. It was my son — Tashi was the name we gave him. He was wailing because he had woken to find his brother gone from his side."

Li Du said nothing. He felt the tension of the other man's memory deep in his own stomach. Doso sighed and shook his head as if after many years he could still not believe what had happened. He continued. "The women rushed through the forest calling for Pema. It was my wife who found him in an outcrop of rocks. There he was, lying between two black bear cubs, his tiny face bloodied. His screams must have frightened the mother. The claw that rent his cheek left its permanent mark."

Doso hefted the heavy ax, testing his grip, preparing to swing it again. "If Tashi hadn't screamed so loud," he said, "we might never have found Pema alive. But my son was always that way. It was his self-appointed task to protect his brother from harm. We should have guessed, even before the delegation came, that Tashi was a holy child."

Crystalline in their new coat of snow, the stairs rose through the forest beneath jade-green lichen garlands spangled with ice. As before, Li Du was obliged to rest beside the old hollow tree at the top of a particularly steep and crooked ascent. He waited for his heart to slow and his breath to return, then continued up.

Emerging from the trees, he saw that there was a new structure between the prayer flags and the temple. In the center of a circle cleared of snow was a pyre, a metal grid supported by layered logs and bound kindling. A wide trail of overlapping footprints led away from it into the forest a little way from the top of the stairs, suggesting an alternate route down to the manor.

Li Du passed the prayer flags and the pyre, climbed the stairs to the temple, and stood under its overhanging roof, hesitating in front of the door to the chapel. Behind him he could hear prayer flags fluttering like the wings of a hundred birds. Li Du pushed the temple door open and stepped inside.

The flames in the butter lamps strained toward him in the dark, then away as the air currents shifted. In front of the altar, the body that yesterday had been supine was now sitting up. Its limbs were wrapped in layers of thick white cloth and bound in a stiff arrangement, cross-legged, the hands tied in place at the knees. There was only a suggestion of a face under the wrappings, but still Li Du felt its gaze on him.

The Chhöshe was standing in front of one of the thangkas hanging on the wall. He was leaning forward, his nose almost touching the painting. Absorbed in his contemplation, he did not notice Li Du.

"I am sorry to —"

Li Du's quiet interruption caused the Chhöshe to swing around, startled. For an instant, Li Du thought that he was looking at Doso. The young man before him was a duplicate of his father. He had the same oval face, the same high, lean cheeks and sturdy jaw, the same thick neck and broad shoulders. He towered over Li Du.

As he had seen the Khampa do when they met lamas on the path or in villages, Li Du knelt and prostrated himself. The Chhöshe watched impassively as Li Du performed the movements awkwardly. When Li Du had touched his face to the ground three times, he stood up and wiped the dust from his hands.

"I am sorry," he said, after he had introduced himself. "Is it wrong for me to be in the temple at this time?"

The Chhöshe shook his head. "I do not think it is wrong," he said. His voice was unexpectedly frank, and belied his somber bearing. "In my school at Drepung, we often discuss what to do when Right Action is not clear." His gaze shifted to the body at the altar. "Your presence here is a distraction for him, perhaps, but it is inconsequential compared to the others, the ones only he can see. He wanders in bardo. He does not know which of the six realms to enter."

"I must apologize for my ignorance," said Li Du.

The Chhöshe's eyes brightened with amusement. "It is said that here every district has its own dialect and every lama his own doctrine." After a pause, he stepped closer to Li Du. "I recognize your voice," he said. "Thank you for your help yesterday."

"My help?"

"The foreign monk would not have left if you had not drawn him away."

Li Du remembered Paolo Campo's zealous determination to interrupt the Chhöshe's prayers. "He was upset, as we all were, by the violent manner of Dhamo's death. The dictates of his own religion compel him to intervene."

"His god must be a powerful one," replied the Chhöshe, "to preserve him when he fell." He paused. "Did you come here to make offerings?"

"I came to speak to you."

"On what subject?"

"I — I have been preoccupied," said Li Du, "with the sign that was painted on Dhamo's body — the white circle framed in gold."

"The sign he painted on himself," said the Chhöshe. "The mirror."

"Yes. The mirror. Can you tell me what the symbol means?"

The Chhöshe hesitated, but when he spoke, it was with confidence that appeared natural to him. "The mirror is a symbol of the enlightened mind," he said. "It sees objects as they are, and it reflects them as they are. It does not alter or distort what passes before it, as we alter and distort what passes before our eyes. It does not react to what it sees, as we react to what we see." He paused, consulting his memory. "Ultimately, the mirror reveals objects as they truly are — illusions with no substance. The mirror shows us the truth. The mirror shows us emptiness."

Li Du allowed the words to sink into his mind. "But why would Dhamo have painted it on himself?"

The Chhöshe was looking at him curiously. "I do not know."

"Do you have memories of him?"

"What?" The question took the Chhöshe off guard.

"Do you have memories of Dhamo? You were a young child when he came to this valley and you left it."

"I do not remember him. I do not remember this valley at all. As you say, I was a small child when I left." The Chhöshe lapsed into silence. His gaze roved across the surface of the temple walls. "Drepung is very different. There are grand temples and golden prayer wheels, and hundreds of monks and pilgrims from every city. Not like this place, where there was only Dhamo."

In the silence that followed, Li Du turned to the painting the Chhöshe had been studying. It was a simple image depicted in precious materials. Its surface was covered in gold leaf that had been burnished smooth. Onto the gold, vermilion figures had been painted with a fine brush. They were faint shapes — heads and shoulders barely distinguishable from their golden background.

"Is this Dhamo's work?"

The Chhöshe turned to it. "I do not know — it might have been. The family is wealthy. There are treasures here, and at the manor, purchased from other places."

Li Du scanned the cluttered wall. "What will happen to the thangka that Dhamo left unfinished in his studio?"

The Chhöshe considered the question. "In

a monastery, thangka painters have many assistants. Dhamo painted alone — there is no one to complete the work. What is your interest in thangkas?"

Li Du searched for an answer. "At an earlier time in my life, I was a librarian. I have a habit of asking questions about anything that involves ink on paper, parchment, or silk."

The answer seemed to satisfy the young man. "If you wish to see the unfinished work, let us go and look at it together."

Li Du followed the Chhöshe across the chapel and into the studio. The door to the inner room was closed. The Chhöshe strode across the floor ahead of Li Du and opened it. He was still for a moment, his shoulders blocking Li Du's view. Then he stepped aside. Li Du saw the narrow cot, piled with dark furs, as before, and the bowl of dried blue paint. The pillow still rested in front of the easel.

But the ties that had held the thangka suspended in its frame had been cut. There was nothing there. The painting was gone.

Hamza found Li Du sitting on the edge of Dhamo's cot, staring at the empty frame where the thangka had been.

"You know there is no painting in that

frame," said Hamza.

Li Du looked up. "I do."

"I am relieved to hear it. Why are you looking at an empty frame?"

"Because this frame contained Dhamo's unfinished thangka. Someone has taken it."

Hamza stepped more completely into the room. "This place has the feel of a prison," he said. He knelt before the frame and examined one of the dangling threads. "The young Chhöshe is praying just on the other side of this wall," he said, tilting his head toward the chapel. "He must know who took it."

"I have spoken with him already," said Li Du. "He says he was here yesterday afternoon, praying as you see him doing now. But he says that he did not see or hear anyone go into or out of the studio."

Hamza was silent. He lowered his voice to a whisper. "And the Chhöshe? Could he have taken it?"

"Either he did, or someone else managed to enter and leave the studio carrying a thangka without him or anyone else noticing."

Hamza assessed the frame. "How large was the painting?"

Li Du held his hands shoulder-width apart. "The Chhöshe told me that after I left yesterday, Doso and Rinzen arrived. I saw them myself on the stairs. He says that Pema came after them with a pack animal, and that he and Doso built the funeral pyre while Rinzen assisted the Chhöshe in preparing the body. A little later, Kamala brought them food. Andruk came in search of Campo. Incidentally, not one of them was here consistently through the afternoon. Which means that any one of them might have followed Campo into the forest."

"The Chhöshe is sure that no one came into this room?"

"That is what he says. But he admits his attention was on his prayers."

Hamza turned to look at Li Du. "And why do you sit and study the empty frame?"

"I am trying to remember what it contained."

"And do you remember?"

Li Du sighed in frustration. "I did not take the time to study it. I retain only an impression of the charcoal sketch."

Hamza nodded. "And the only colors were blue and green."

"Yes. The central figure wore chains of pearls and severed heads across his chest. He had tusks like a boar and wore a crown of skulls. His many arms were stretched wide, and beneath his feet were tangled human forms. There were three figures above him, and three below, and so many details I could not possibly recall them." Li Du raised a hand and rubbed his eyes. "Shells and tongues and eyes and animals with jewels falling from their jaws . . . and flames. The figure at the center was surrounded by a ring of flames. When I described it to the Chhöshe, he told me it might have been a wrathful incarnation of the bodhisattva Manjusri."

Hamza had begun to traverse the periphery of the small room, his head lowered as he listened to Li Du. When Li Du finished, he stopped. "Let us go out into the air," he said. "I do not like these walls."

As they made their way through the outer room, Hamza stopped just long enough to pick up one of the little golden spheres from the bowl full of them. "Pilgrim beads," he said, and held it to the light with a look of appreciation. "I have always liked these. They are like the eggs of the hawk who flew to the sun and hunted with the firebirds." He handed it to Li Du.

"Gold powder," said Li Du, "that turns to gold paint in water."

"My description was better," Hamza said. "But yes — that is what they are."

"One of these must have been used to

paint the mirror's golden frame," Li Du said. "That is why there was no packet of gold paint. It was not needed."

Hamza took the bead back and set it in the bowl. "This murderer uses beautiful objects for ugly purposes."

Outside, they were instantly enveloped by shifting gray clouds. As they began their descent to the manor, Li Du gave Hamza a brief account of his search of Sera's room, of the conversation he had overheard between Pema and Sonam, and of his meeting with the Chhöshe. He concluded with a summary of Paolo Campo's insistence that tulkus were servants of the devil.

Hamza sighed. "When I die, please protect me from the actions of the faithful."

Li Du, who was used to such statements, was only faintly surprised. He asked Hamza what he meant.

Hamza looked over his shoulder toward the temple that was no longer in sight. "There are places," he said, "in this land and in others, where the wealthy are preserved in shrouds like the one that now wraps the painter. Instead of being released into the air by fire or offered to the creatures under the earth, they are kept preserved in hidden castles of the dead. Their faces are covered in masks painted to resemble the way they looked in life. But their skin is gold and their eyes do not move." Hamza frowned. "If you have any influence when the time comes, please do not permit me to be locked away like that."

Li Du considered Hamza's words. "In my opinion, you cannot be condemned to a fate after death unless it is within your own belief to be condemned to it."

Hamza stared moodily at a tree. "You do not have to believe in something to be consumed by it."

"What do you mean?"

"I have heard it said that gods are sustained by the belief of the people who worship them. If you think this is true, you might assume that gods are desperate to keep their believers. But that is not always so. I have met gods who are ready for death, but are not granted it. They want to dissolve, but their worshippers will not let them. For these gods, belief is a prison."

"But we all have the will to survive."

"Dhamo did not. Or so his murderer wished us to accept."

Li Du made a little sound acknowledging the truth of this, and Hamza continued. "I would not want to be a saint or a god. I might want to be a white bird, someday, who sings for the forest in trees as big as worlds, or skims the waves over rocks to comfort castaways on islands invisible to ships."

Li Du was lost for a moment in the current of Hamza's words. With an effort, he pulled himself out of it. "What have you been doing?"

"I had an illuminating conversation with the unhappy heir."

"Pema?"

"The very same. And I will tell you now what I learned. On the day Dhamo died, Pema says he was taking the goats out to graze. But he had another errand that morning — to bring to Lumo a round of fresh cheese."

"Did he see something in the forest?"

"It is what he did not see that is of interest to us. He told me that Lumo was there in her house, sound asleep by the hearth. She was there alone."

Li Du understood. "Which means that Sera-tsering was not at her cottage all morning."

"That is also what I deduced. According to Pema, he left the cheese by the door, returned to the manor, and took the goats out on this side of the river. He saw no one in the forest." Hamza paused dramatically. "It seems our next question is for Sera-tsering. I maintain that she does not give the impression of a murderess — at least, not a murderess of monks she does not know. At present, my suspicion is that she changes form between a woman and one of those golden beasts that climbs mountain cliffs on four hoofs, sure-footed where a person would fall."

CHAPTER 14

Li Du and Hamza entered the manor court-yard and saw Sonam across the snow in one of the open barns. He was standing beside an obsidian yak with snow-white patches on its sides. As they watched, Sonam knelt and pressed his hand to the animal's shoulder, assessing its musculature with practiced skill.

Hamza murmured under his breath, "I will go to look for Sera-tsering at the Khampa fire. You speak to this rogue who is likely deciding which of the manor lord's cows to steal."

Hamza turned away, leaving Li Du to cross the courtyard alone.

"The Chinese librarian," Sonam said. "You travel with the Khampa."

Once again, Li Du was struck by the familiarity of Sonam's voice. "Is it possible that we have met before?"

Sonam scrutinized Li Du's face, then

shrugged. "I do not think I know you."

"Then I must be mistaken," said Li Du.

"My business sometimes takes me to your Chinese cities," said Sonam, returning his attention to the animal, who submitted stoically to Sonam's inspection of its mouth.

"Your business?"

Sonam straightened and patted a dark flank. "Some trading, some work for hire." He looked at Li Du. "So you are going to Lhasa. Have you crossed mountains before?"

"In my own country, yes."

Sonam's mouth twisted in amusement. A lock of dark hair, weighted by turquoise beads, fell across his face. He raised a hand to smooth the strand back over his shoulder. "The mountains in your country are not mountains. They are hills."

"I know that the way to Lhasa is difficult."

"Let me offer you some advice," said Sonam. "Rub charcoal into a cloth and bind it across your eyes to protect them." He raised a finger and pointed to his own dark, sparkling eyes. "Up there, the snow reflects a thousand suns."

Li Du, a little taken aback, thanked him for the suggestion.

"I won't ask you to pay me for it," replied Sonam, "but if you hire me to be your guide, I'll get you to Lhasa a month ahead of Kalden Dorjee and his caravan. How much silver are you paying them to guide you?"

"I am in no hurry to reach Lhasa," Li Du said. "And I am happy in my present situation. But I thank you again for the advice."

Sonam shrugged. "Let me know if you reconsider," he said. "I know the routes better than anyone." He paused. "And if you speak again with the dignitary, tell him that I heard he was going to send his correspondence to Lhasa with your caravan. Tell him I could deliver it faster."

"You could tell it to him yourself."

"I will, but you noblemen listen more closely to each other than to people like me."

"You say that your business is in trade and work for hire. I am curious — what business brought you to this remote place?"

Sonam raised his eyes to the closed, painted shutters of the kitchen. "I came to visit my nephew. Pema's father — his birth father — was my brother."

Li Du absorbed this new information with interest. Sonam was Pema's uncle. This explained his connection to the family, and the welcome he had received at the manor. "Then Pema's father —"

"Taken by illness," said Sonam. "His mother, too." He gave a long sigh. "I would have raised my nephew myself, of course, but I was hardly more than a boy. Doso had fought beside my brother when they were young men, and there was an oath of loyalty between them. Doso insisted that he was honor-bound to adopt Pema."

"I understand," murmured Li Du.

"I come to visit my nephew as often as I can," said Sonam. "Adoption is binding as blood, and as the eldest, Pema is heir to this land. But a lord can become forgetful when his beautiful new wife gives him sons. I have a deep affection for Pema, and wish to ensure his happiness."

"If you are concerned for Pema," said Li Du, "you might make some effort to assuage his grief."

"His grief?" Sonam looked mystified.

"Over Dhamo's death," Li Du replied. "Of anyone at the manor, it was Pema who spent the most time in his company."

"Ah," said Sonam, seeming to lose interest. "I knew very little of the painter. He was a recluse."

Li Du persisted. "You knew nothing else about him?"

He thought he saw a sudden shrewdness enter Sonam's eyes, but he was not sure.

Sonam's tone was dismissive. "He's been in that temple a long time," he said. "I wasn't here when he arrived, but the villagers talked about that day for years."

"You mean the day he identified the Chhöshe."

Sonam nodded.

After a moment's thought, Li Du said, "It is a great honor to a house, is it not, when a tulku is found."

Sonam's lips curved in a smug smile. "An unexpected honor."

"What do you mean?"

"The Chhöshe was Doso's first son."

"Yes — I have seen the resemblance between them."

Sonam's smile widened to a self-satisfied leer. "You do not understand. He was his *first* son. In these lands, first sons are rarely called to a religious life. That is for second sons."

"And in this case —" Li Du stopped, hoping that Sonam's pride in his superior knowledge would lead him to continue his story.

"In the beginning, the proceedings went as they usually do," said Sonam. "The delegation came to the manor and said a boy in the house was a tulku."

Li Du was beginning to understand. "The

family expected it to be Pema."

Sonam nodded. "But in the end, it was not. It was the other son. The wheel turns as it turns."

"How did the identification happen?"

Sonam gestured vaguely. "I don't remember. It was something to do with a painting."

"A painting by Dhamo?"

"Yes. Some vision he had. But I told you — I wasn't even here. Why do you want to know about it?"

Li Du looked directly at Sonam. "I am curious about how he died."

Sonam returned the look. Then he retrieved a long blade from where he had set it in the straw. Its hilt was wrapped in red yarn. "A monk," he said, "who spent his days with demons painted his flesh and offered himself to death, clutching his beads in one hand and counting prayers all the way into the next realm. That is how Dhamo died. I will give you one more piece of free advice. Let that explanation be enough."

The courtyard fire, unattended, had burned to white ash in the brazier bowl. One thin core of a log remained, crusted with black and white scales. Li Du watched the wind catch a flake and carry it into the air, where it disintegrated.

In need of warmth and food, Li Du climbed the courtyard staircase to the hallway outside his own room. He was on his way to the kitchen when he heard a voice. It came from the sewing room, where he had previously overheard Sonam and Kamala. The voice he now heard belonged to Sera-tsering. He hesitated at the half-open door, listening.

"Our swords met," she was saying, "and I perceived that my attacker was not a man, but a woman. I promptly confessed my own deception. Once she realized that I, too, was a woman in disguise, she declared she would not rob me after all, and we shared a companionable meal."

"But would you not be safer traveling with a caravan?" Li Du recognized Kamala's high, clipped tones. "I met a woman in the Dajianlu market who tried to bargain me down to only twelve bricks of tea for one of our finest bulls. She traveled, but as the wife of the caravan cook, not alone."

"I have traveled in companies before," came Sera's reply. "But caravan mules are strung with bells and decorated with feathers. When I am alone I am more vulnerable, but it is easier for me to avoid attention."

"You must miss your sister," said Kamala,

"to risk so much for these visits. I would never go so far from my own house. When I go the market, I am unhappy from the day I leave until the day I return."

"Lumo traveled the width of Tibet alone," said Sera. "It is easier when you have no family to leave behind."

Li Du heard a faint rattle followed by a loud clack, then Kamala's voice. "If my children were taken from me, I would follow them into death to protect them during their journey through the shadowy realms. I would not let them face the fearful tests alone."

"Who is there?" Sera's voice startled Li Du.

He stepped in. "I was just going to the kitchen," he said.

Kamala sat at the loom. A colorful pane of intricate patterns extended in front of her, ending abruptly in a forest of white thread. Her daughter was beside her, watching, the infant cradled in her arms. The two boys played on the floor. Sera was carding yak wool between two brushes.

"There is butter tea and bread at the hearth," Kamala said.

Li Du was about to go when Sera spoke to him. "You were very quiet there at the door. Eavesdropping can be dangerous.

Consider the emperor who disguised himself as a commoner in order to hear what his soldiers really thought of him."

"I do not know that history," said Li Du.

"It did not end well," replied Sera.

"For the soldiers?"

Sera smiled. "For the emperor. And on the subject of emperors, I was about to recount a history to the children in which your own emperor plays a part. Will you stay to hear it?" She gestured for him to sit.

"I would be glad to." Li Du went to the chair she had indicated.

Sera turned her attention to Kamala and the children. "You have heard, perhaps, the legend that all of Tibet is built on the body of a defeated demoness. She is held down, imprisoned by temples like pins to fix her joints to the earth. The temple in Lhasa is the one that pins down her heart.

"Lhasa is a city where every object is multiplied a thousand times. A single temple has a thousand duplicates. For every sculpture there are a thousand like it. In Lhasa there are so many flags and scarves and butter lamps that they will never be gone, even when sand and wind and water scrape the city down to its foundations.

"At the time of my birth, Tibet was ruled by the Great Fifth Dalai Lama, who was so powerful that even the most fierce and war-like families, who live on horses in the northern mountain plains where there are no trees, swore allegiance to him."

"You mean," asked the elder of the two boys, "the ones that cut Yeshe's feet so that a tiger would eat him in the forest?"

"Not all of the northerners are bandits, but hard lives can make hard people. Many conquerors were born in places where death takes the weak away quickly. But even the northern clans, who have always followed their own laws and no others, pledged their loyalty to the Fifth. He lived beneath the golden roofs of two palaces, the White Palace and the Red Palace.

"With each year of his rule, Tibet and its people grew more prosperous, more power-ful, and more secure in the bonds between its clans and cities and monasteries. But one day, death came for the Fifth, as it had to do. And do you know what happens when the great lama dies?"

"He is reborn," said the boy, "and they find him wherever he has gone."

"Yes. But events did not unfold in the usual way when the Fifth died. You see, he had in his service a regent who had been his student since childhood and who loved him. The regent knew that with the death of the Fifth, families who were united only out of loyalty to him would renew old quarrels. And certain —" Sera paused her narrative and her eyes flickered to Li Du. "Certain other powers could turn their eyes to leaderless Lhasa.

"So the regent concealed the death of the Fifth. He proclaimed that his master had retired into solitary meditation and would no longer speak to anyone or see anyone. The body of the Fifth was hidden. The secret was kept. And it was kept for a very long time. For years, Tibet was ruled by a man who was dead."

The children stared at Sera, transfixed. She smiled and leaned forward. "But even though his deception was successful, the regent knew that his master was dead, and that somewhere in this land or another, his successor had been born. Somewhere, the Sixth Dalai Lama waited to be recognized and brought to his true home in Lhasa."

Li Du sensed a presence behind him and turned to see who had come. It was Hamza. He was watching Sera with a concentration and intensity that Li Du had not seen in him before. His eyes were narrowed in assessment, as if he was looking at her for an answer to a question that confounded him.

Sera herself was so caught up in her own

story and in the attention of Kamala and the children that she did not appear to notice Hamza's arrival. "The regent sent out emissaries in secret to search for the boy," she said. "They asked their questions very discreetly so that no one would guess what they wanted. They searched for signs described to them by the regent's most trusted lamas and astrologers. And soon, they found him, a little baby, born in a humble town in a land not quite Tibet, not quite China, not quite India, a land a bit like this one, a hidden place on the border of empires.

"But what could the regent do? He could not reveal the boy to the public. He could not raise the boy as the Sixth Dalai Lama when everyone believed the Fifth still to be alive, ruling from the shadows of his solitude in the palace. So what did the regent do?"

Sera paused, enjoying the silence. Then she drew in a breath and continued. "He hid the boy in a tower in a village that no one knew existed. The boy was kept there, not knowing why, and uncertain of who he was. For a time his family stayed with him, but then he was alone, and lived only in the company of tutors who came and went. At night, the boy could see the stars through his window.

"But I think that he did not always stay there. I think that he ran away for days and months at a time. He traveled on ships through storms and ate delicacies and fell in love and learned the names of animals and flowers from sight and not only from pictures in books."

Sera paused. She stretched her shoulders slightly, a leonine movement barely perceptible under her voluminous black wool travel clothes. "When the boy was sixteen years old, the regent revealed the truth to the city, and brought the boy to the palace to take his place as the Sixth Dalai Lama. But what do you think it was like, after all those years of not knowing who he was, to be suddenly surrounded by people expecting him to be a leader? He did not like it at all. So he would go into the city at night in disguise and dance and sing and drink with the common people."

"Was he punished?" asked the boy, with an apprehensive look at his mother.

There was a wistfulness in Sera's smile. "Not for that," she said. "The people loved him even though he did not spend his time making laws and strategies."

"Is he there now?" Kamala's daughter asked the question. Her fingers were netted in colored threads.

"No. He is not there." Sera's eyes were sad. "Just as the regent feared, the northern clans discovered that Tibet no longer had a strong leader. For them, Lhasa was like a bright pebble that your little brother has and that you want for yourself. It is easy to take. It was not long before Tibet had a new ruler."

"But what happened to the boy who was the Dalai Lama?"

"The new khan declared that the recognition of the Sixth had been a mistake, that he was a false incarnation and impostor. He was imprisoned and sent away to China, where the khan's ally, the Emperor of China, promised to keep him."

"Then he is in China now?"

"No. He never arrived in China. He became sick on the road and died."

There was an abrupt silence. Then the little girl began to cry. Sera leaned forward and touched the girl's cheek. Her low, assertive voice became very gentle. "Or maybe he did not. Some say that he escaped. So if you meet a man on the road, a pilgrim perhaps, and think to yourself, deep in your heart, that he is a prince, then maybe it is the lost Sixth. No one can say whether this is a true story or a false one — it is only one version of events."

■ ■ ■ ■

After the midday meal, the manor inhabitants spread throughout the compound, clustering around sources of heat or occupying themselves with chores. Li Du and Hamza found the door to Sera's room closed. Hamza knocked, and she opened it. She had taken off her coat, and now wore a voluminous shawl of red wool belted at the waist over a dress of supple leather. Behind her in the room, a ceiling brazier emitted tendrils of smoke that snaked toward the window.

Her expression was defiant. "Have you come to chastise me for incautious speech? I do not regret my words. One benefit of being so far from the hearts of empires is that I can speak freely on subjects of interest to me."

"On the contrary," said Li Du, mildly. "It is a freedom I, too, enjoy."

Sera's brows drew together. "Are you here to discuss my political allegiances?"

"Not at all," replied Li Du. "I appreciated your account. It was one I had not heard before."

This statement was met with silence. "I remember the uproar in Beijing," Li Du went on, "when we heard that the Great Fifth Dalai Lama had been secretly dead for fourteen years. It was an embarrassment to the Emperor that none of his spies had uncovered the deception sooner."

The furrow between Sera's brows disappeared as her eyes widened in surprise. "You speak of your Emperor as if he were a man. I did not think that was permitted."

Li Du gave a small smile. "As you say, we are a long way from the center of the empire."

Sera regarded him warily. "Then why have you come?"

Hamza had been examining the carved and painted animals that decorated the lintel above the door. "The day before yesterday was a dreary day to be wandering in the forest," he said.

Sera looked from one to the other of them. "I was not wandering in the forest."

Li Du looked at her. "You told me that you spent the morning with Lumo," he said.

"I did."

"But you were not there the whole time."

The furrow reappeared between Sera's brows. Her posture became tense. "Why do you care where I was?"

The time for disguising his inquiry as casual conversation was over. Li Du lifted his eyes to hers. "We are not certain that Dhamo killed himself," he said. He kept his voice just above a whisper.

Sera's expression was carefully blank. "Whatever happened to him," she said, lowering her voice also, "I had nothing to do with it."

"But it is true that you were not at Lumo's the whole morning," said Li Du.

"I have no reason to discuss this with you," she replied.

Hamza crossed his arms over his chest. "You do not know who we are. My friend may be a magistrate in disguise. I may be a prince. You should tell us the truth."

"I didn't kill the painter," said Sera.

Li Du spoke. "If we are correct, then someone did. Yesterday there was almost another death. Consider that if a killer is among us, no one is safe. I urge you to tell us what you know."

Sera did not answer.

Hamza renewed his efforts, his voice low and stern. "What secret errand took you from Lumo's while she slept?"

Sera met his eyes. "You think it is so important to know what I was doing during that time?"

"I think," said Hamza, "that you should stop treating us as fools and explain what you were doing in that snowy forest even as a man was meeting his doom amid those same trees."

"I was bathing."

There was sudden and complete silence. Hamza stared at her. "Bathing?"

"Yes," she said. "I was bathing in one of the hot pools. Lumo had showed them to me several days prior, and when she fell asleep I decided to go there and bathe."

"Bathing — without clothes?"

Sera's face was impassive. "It was very pleasant."

"But you were bathing."

Li Du looked at Hamza with exasperation. "I am surprised, my friend, to see you overcome, when you have told me so often of the many harems you have visited, where bathing women anoint themselves in rare perfumes while you tell them stories."

Hamza was instantly affronted. "I am not overcome."

Li Du turned to Sera. "Dhamo went to the hot springs that morning. Did you see him there?"

She hesitated. "I did not see him there."

"But you saw him somewhere else."

She nodded.

"Tell us what happened."

With a long exhale, she relented. "I was in

one of the higher pools," she said. "I thought I saw someone through the trees some distance away. I did not want to encounter a stranger, so I left as quickly as I could."

"Can you describe this person in any more detail?"

She shook her head. "It might have been a shadow." Her eyes went to Hamza. "I thought it might be you."

"If it had been me, I can assure you that I would have made my presence known."

Sera continued. "I was returning to Lumo's through the forest. It was getting colder. That was when I saw Dhamo. He was coming up the path from the bridge. He must have been going to the hot springs."

Somewhere in the hallway, the wind caught a shutter and rattled its hinges. "Is there nothing more you can tell us?" Li Du asked.

For a moment it seemed that she would say more. Then she shook her head and took a step back into her room. "Nothing," she said. "I have told you all I know."

CHAPTER 15

Pema sat by the courtyard brazier holding a bowl of butter tea. The barn behind him was swept, and a shovel leaned against the wall beside a wheelbarrow full of dung. A cow raised its head at Li Du's approach, watching him with the expression Li Du often saw in cows, as if it was seeing something different from what Li Du imagined himself to look like.

At the sight of Li Du, Pema seemed to emerge from a trance. He hastily offered Li Du tea, which Li Du accepted only in order to prevent Pema from becoming self-conscious about drinking his own.

"When I went to the hot springs yesterday," Li Du said, handing his bowl across the fire, "I found cinnabar rock."

Pema nodded and filled Li Du's bowl. "Dhamo used it to make red paint."

Li Du turned his bowl absently around in his hands. "It occurred to me that Dhamo might have gone to collect cinnabar on the morning of his death."

Pema's forehead creased beneath his matted hair. "Why do you think so?"

"I happened to notice that he had none left in his studio," said Li Du. "I found a bowl that contained only a few shards of it."

Pema shook his head. "That cannot be. The bowl in his studio was full of vermilion. I am certain that it was because he asked me very recently to make sure of it."

Li Du looked up. "What did he say?"

"He said that he needed red paint for the thangka he was painting — the one the pilgrim commissioned. He asked me to tell him if the bowl of vermilion was full. I checked, and it was."

Li Du set his bowl down on the stone beside him. "Are you speaking of the thangka that we saw tied to Dhamo's easel yesterday?"

"Yes."

"Where is the pilgrim who commissioned it?"

"He left nine days ago — maybe ten."

"Did he intend to return for the completed painting?"

"No — it was not for him. It was for his monastery. He was going on a pilgrimage to the holy mountain. I was going to take the painting to Dajianlu and send it with one of the merchant caravans. That is the usual way it is done."

Li Du nodded his understanding. A caravan could carry items from this remote location to a more central one, where they could be handed to couriers. "I assume," he said, "since the thangka is no longer in the easel, that you have packed it to be sent to the monastery in its unfinished state?"

Pema's confusion appeared genuine. "I did not take the thangka from the easel," he said.

"Do you know who did take it?"

"No. I — I do not understand how it can be gone. No one spoke of taking away the thangka." A look of fear crossed Pema's face. "Could it have been taken by — by a demon? If a demon drove Dhamo to — to do what he did, could the painting have been the source of the curse?"

"I suspect there is another explanation," said Li Du. "What makes you think the painting drove Dhamo to kill himself?"

Pema was looking increasingly uneasy. "I — I do not know. I do not know how other thangka painters complete their work, but Dhamo used to recite strange prayers while he painted. I could hear him through the door sometimes. 'I seal the mountain,' he would say. 'I seal the mountain against demons. The sword on fire, the three jewels, the skull-cup, the triple pennant . . .' " Pema stopped and looked up.

Sonam was coming down the exterior staircase into the courtyard. He wore a bright red sash around his coat, and had cleaned his boots. He greeted them both as he led his horse out from the stable.

"Where are you going, Uncle?" Pema's voice was polite and strained.

Sonam gestured vaguely up over the manor wall. "I am tired of sitting at the hearth." He patted his horse's neck. "And my horse is tired of the barn."

Pema lowered his gaze. "The caravan leader was looking for you," he said quietly.

Sonam glanced in the direction of the camp. "He wants advice on navigating the trails on the other side of the pass," he said, with a shrug.

Pema stood up and shouldered his woven basket. "I am to bring more wood for the hearth," he said. "May I walk out with you?"

A slight frown crossed Sonam's features, but he acquiesced. Li Du watched them go. Pema seemed like a frightened, lonely boy, but as he followed after his uncle, Li Du detected new resolution to the set of his shoulders. He wondered what it meant.

After they had gone, Li Du stayed watching the flames, listening to them hiss and crack. Blue and red tongues lapped the wood. A log had broken and formed a hollow in the fire, which now breathed heat too intensely on his face. He shifted his bench backward. *Fire is a source of comfort,* he thought, *and at the same time the inspiration for the worst torture imaginable in the afterlife.* He looked at the dark door of the family shrine across the courtyard, then up to Paolo Campo's window. For Campo, hell was an inferno. For the Chhöshe, a ground and sky made of copper glowing with the heat of a forge.

There had been no fire pits permitted near the imperial library in Beijing. The nearest one had been in a garden separated from the library by a high stone wall, a pond, and an expanse of tiled courtyard. No spark could survive long enough to float through one of the latticed windows and touch parchment.

Li Du's mind traveled to a day he had spent reordering the library's medicinal volumes. It had taken longer than it should have, because he had stopped so often to read the books. The authors of what he'd expected to be dry medical texts had expressed themselves with surprising personality. *The physician who cannot analyze a pulse is like a spy who is ignorant in the writing and sending of dispatches. He cannot pronounce a problem hot or cold.*

That day, Li Du had left the library, crossed the tile courtyard, skirted the pond, and passed through the keyhole door in the wall to join Shu at the fire pit. Shu had been waiting for him at the low stone table. When he saw Li Du, he began to slide chess pieces into place on the board that was etched into the stone surface.

"You know," Shu said without preamble, "that when the foreigners play their version of this game, they call this piece the king. What a dangerous idea, to let subjects entertain themselves with phrases like *The king is dead* or *I will use my queen to capture your king.* I am surprised any ruler would allow it. What ideas people would get!"

Li Du looked across the table at his teacher. "Or one might say that a king who does not allow his title to be used in a game reveals that he feels insecure of his power."

Shu gave him a chastising look. "A king must make his subjects respect him."

"Yes — by ruling well. Not by punishing them for playing games." Li Du pushed a piece halfheartedly into place.

235

Shu raised his eyebrows. "Something has distressed you?"

"The writer Tai Ming-shih has been arrested, and they say he will be put to death."

"Ah," said Shu. "But he has had many opportunities to change his ways, and he has behaved very unwisely. His decision to print the names of Ming claimants to the throne had nothing to do with his poetry. The Ming Dynasty is over and its princes are no longer princes. Tai Ming-shih brought about his own death."

"If all the poets are arrested except those who write on topics that please the Emperor, then our empire's poetry will be lifeless. No one who is afraid to put the right word into place can write good poetry."

"The Emperor will be merciful. He has always been merciful to scholars."

"Merciful. So it will be a beheading instead of a lingering death?"

Shu sighed. "Our Emperor is no tyrant. You are too young to remember when he came to power, but I can tell you from my own memory that he takes more care with life and death than any Emperor since Song Taizu. He reformed the Board of Punishments, and himself personally reviews lists of men condemned to death in the empire. He checks for administrative errors, a task that has always belonged to the lowest secretary. Last year when he put down the rebellion of his general in the south, he had every household in the rebel areas questioned so that he could spare those who were pressured into supporting the traitors against their will."

Li Du sighed and slid a piece absently across the board. Shu placed a finger on it to stop its movement and looked very seriously at his student. "The trouble with you young scholars is that you criticize everything without imagining what it would be like to have the power to make decisions about life and death. You *think* you have opinions, but in truth you lack conviction. Now, cheer up and let us find out if today will be the day that you finally start to understand the rules of this game."

And the writings of Tai Ming-shih were all burned, Li Du thought.

Then, as if the burnt writings of Tai Ming-shih had blown into the present, Li Du noticed a charred piece of paper caught in a crack in the wall of Doso's barn. He stood up and went over to it. Carefully, he pinched the brittle fragment between his thumb and forefinger and drew it out from where it had been trapped. It was blackened at the edges, but when he held it to the light, he could make out faint lines still visible on its surface.

It looked like a sketch of a flower. A lotus, he thought. Its petals opened upward, as they would to cradle a seated saint. Beside it, a line curved upward into a shape that was now lost. After a moment's consideration, he dismissed the possibility that the fragment had come from the missing thangka. This was certainly paper, whereas the thangka was being painted on fabric.

His librarian's mind moved through the possible uses of paper: a letter, a report, a note of permission, a receipt, a book, a drawing, a map . . . He frowned. Whatever it was, it had been destroyed recently. The scrap would not have remained in the wall for long before being dislodged by the wind or by the shifting flank of an animal. Further inspection yielded no more information. With a furrowed brow, the paper still pinched between his fingers, Li Du climbed the courtyard stairs and went inside.

Once he was back in his room, Li Du went to the table by his bed and opened one of his bound books. He placed the paper between its pages, and closed the cover. As he did so, his eyes fell on the traveler's writing set that rested beside the pile of books.

It was new. He had purchased it for himself at the market shortly before the caravan had left Gyalthang. He smiled slightly. *Of course,* he thought, *I bought ink instead of a new coat.*

There had been only one ink seller in Gyalthang. Li Du had walked into the shop to find its owner absorbed in the careful chiseling of a circular jade seal. The yellow jade was so pale it was almost translucent, like river water clouded with white sand in the sunshine. On thin shelves along one wall were more seals, some cylindrical, others with flat planes and edges. They were carved from jades and marbles of all colors.

Li Du had picked up a brush. The seller had indicated a sheet of stone and a bowl of water. Li Du had dipped the brush in the water and drawn a character onto the stone, watching the wet bristles spread and narrow as he pressed and lifted, observing the personality of the word produced. One brush had given him a confident hand, another a feminine one, another the neat precision of a scribe concealing his own unique temperament behind clipped, repetitive accuracy.

While Li Du had shopped for ink, the muleteers had spread through the market to purchase supplies. Once he had bought the modest travel case containing three brushes, ink sticks, an ink stone, and a sheaf of paper, he had set out in search of the others. Carrying his new possession under one arm, he had walked through the merchant stalls, enjoying the smells of broth and spice and savory steam and looking forward to dinner at the inn. He had stopped at the sound of Kalden's voice.

Kalden had been standing in an alley. Overhead, copper pots were silhouetted by the brilliant setting sun behind them. Li Du had squinted, unable to see. Kalden had been speaking to someone, a merchant or a traveler. Li Du had seen a glint of silver beads in long hair. He had heard a voice — heard it drawing out its syllables, pronouncing words with a confident, persuasive rhythm.

Li Du froze. The voice had been Sonam's.

The muleteers were playing a game of dice around the cabin fire. Bowls of butter tea were balanced on rocks and saddlebags and between them on benches. Norbu was finishing an account Li Du had heard him give several times of a violent company of bandits who had harassed travelers near his village for months.

"No respect for any authority," Norbu was saying, "not even the Dalai Lama. I heard they met a monk on the road and asked him to perform a miracle. When he could not, they killed him. And it was worse when they punished any of their own — slow deaths, those were."

Kalden took his turn to roll the dice. They scattered across the ash and dirt. Li Du reached down and picked up one that had stopped close to him. Kalden put out a hand to receive it, but Li Du did not offer it back. "I do not know," he said to Kalden, "whether your secret is yours alone, or whether you are all aware of something that I am not."

Kalden's close-set eyes revealed no emotion, but his jaw tensed. "What are you talking about?"

"You have not been straightforward about your reasons for coming to this place."

Hamza showed his support with an imperious nod. "As a guest of this caravan who has provided you entertainment and diplomatic services, I demand a description of the spider into whose web you have clearly led us. What are we doing in this valley, and how likely are we to die here?" The dramatic force of the statement was undercut by the unworried tone in which Hamza delivered it.

"We are in no danger," said Kalden. "I

have no obligation to explain my decisions to either of you, but in this case, I already have. All the caravans go through Dajianlu. We are finding a new way. The clever trader explores paths unknown to others."

Li Du looked down at the rough die, turning it over in his fingers. "Does the clever trader usually conduct these explorations so late in the season? When the snows have already begun to fall, does the clever trader still choose a route that is unfamiliar and indirect?"

Kalden's face was like stone. "There are no straight paths through the mountains," he said. "Every route has its risks."

As the muleteers murmured their agreement, Li Du slowly curled the fingers of one hand around the die until it disappeared into his closed fist. He looked up and met Kalden's gaze. "You came here to meet the man called Sonam. Why?"

A muscle twitched beside Kalden's eye. "I don't know what you are talking about," he said.

"I recognize him," said Li Du. "I saw you together in the Gyalthang market."

Kalden raised a hand and rubbed his jaw, delaying his answer.

"I know," Li Du said, "that on a high pass when the trail is crumbling and the wind threatens to blow the caravan from the mountain, there must be only one person who makes decisions. You are the leader of this caravan, and I would not challenge your actions without good reason. A man has died. Another man has been thrown almost to his death, and cannot, or will not, say who pushed him. If you think that we are not in danger here, then you are wrong."

While Li Du spoke, Kalden regarded him in silent assessment. When Li Du finished, Kalden leaned forward and adjusted a log on the fire. It split apart, filling the air with glowing red sparks. Kalden leaned back. "Tell me what you know," he said.

Li Du began with the cinnabar granules that he had seen beside the body in the snow. He explained how he had found the same granules in an empty bowl in Dhamo's studio. He gave a brief description of his journey to the hot springs — they had already heard the account of Campo's fall from Hamza — and of his discovery of cinnabar there. He told them of the water that changed the color of silver (a statement met with knowing nods from the experienced traders), and of the silver knife that had killed Dhamo. He described, finally, the thangka that had been cut from its frame.

"I ask you now again," he concluded, "to

explain to me how it is that we arrived in this valley to honor a secret assignation in the very hour that a knife was driven into a man's body?"

The muleteers looked at each other, then at Kalden, waiting for him to speak. It was clear from their expressions that they knew what he had to say. They were simply waiting to find out if their leader would choose to trust the scholar and the storyteller.

Kalden looked at the closed door of the cabin, and back at Li Du and Hamza. The fire spat and crackled. The wind whined through the open roof beams. Then he put his elbows on his knees and rubbed his jaw again. "My brother," he said, "told me that there are two kinds of men in the world. There is the brave man who goes into the mountains and makes a name for himself. And there is the dull man who stays home and quarrels with his mother. To be the brave man, it is necessary to take risks."

Li Du waited.

"We did come here to meet Sonam," Kalden continued. "But our business has nothing to do with murder."

"You may think it does not," Li Du said.

Hamza raised a finger and nodded wisely. "The man is a fox whose offers are full of tricks."

Kalden's expression became defensive. "I am not the fool in this," he said. "The fool is some corrupt official who is easily bought. Before I say anything more, do you swear you will not put my men in the way of harm?"

Hamza patted Li Du on the shoulder and gave Kalden a conspiratorial look. "If our patchwork scholar brings the officials down on your head for a simple case of smuggling, it will be the most remarkable event I have witnessed. And as you know, I have seen oceans catch fire, forests walk, and mice defeat lions in battle. Confess your mischief, old friend."

Kalden set his empty bowl down on the ground. "I am not a smuggler," he said. "I met Sonam for the first time in the market at Gyalthang. He impressed me with his knowledge of horses. I have become used to lowlanders who buy our horses in order to pretend they know how to ride them. But he spoke to me of the muleteers of Ponzera." The others around the fire nodded. Kalden, seeing that Li Du did not understand, added, "Those who know their horses know that the muleteers of Ponzera are unequaled. Their animals are the best."

Kalden went on. "We spoke. I said we were going to Dajianlu and he told me that the taxes there have become so high that a third of our profit will be taken from us. He advised me on which officials to seek out for better deals. It seemed to be good information."

"You trusted him?"

Li Du understood that Kalden was a man more used to describing the subtleties of a mountain's personality than a human's, and watched as Kalden shifted his shoulders uncomfortably. "He seemed a resourceful man, capable of accomplishing difficult tasks."

"I never trusted him," interjected Norbu. "He is the kind of swindler who leads a caravan to a remote place and has his bandit friends lie in wait to rob them."

"What offer did he make you?"

Kalden answered. "He said there was another way, a hidden pass that avoided the main road and Dajianlu. He described this place, and the family here."

"But why take a hidden route?" Li Du did not yet understand.

Kalden nodded. "That is what I asked him. He said he could help us protect our profits from the Chinese bureaucrats."

Hamza sighed. "Nothing is more disappointing in a story than the word 'taxes.' First because it puts the listeners off their good humor, and second because there is nothing interesting that can come of paying — or not paying — taxes."

Li Du ignored Hamza and kept his attention on Kalden. "But even I know that inspectors stop caravans at random from one end of the trade route to the other. If you don't pay at Dajianlu, you pay somewhere else."

"Yes," said Kalden. "But the evidence of payment is in itemized receipts that bear an official seal. If you show the receipts, you have paid your taxes."

"Ah," Li Du said, beginning to understand.

Kalden looked at Li Du. "Sonam told me that he knew an official in Dajianlu who would provide false receipts for our caravan. He told me that he could sell me these papers for half the price of the full taxes."

"But why here?" Li Du asked. "If the papers were in Dajianlu, why not buy them there?"

"Too risky to do it there," Kalden said, "with spies and officials in every inn and teahouse. He said he would go to Dajianlu, secure the false receipts, then double back and meet us at this pass. He said he could travel so fast on the familiar paths that he would arrive here at the same time as we."

Kalden shrugged. "So we decided to accept his proposal."

"And has he sold you the papers?"

"We will do it tomorrow." Kalden exhaled loudly. "Then the snow will melt and, with a bit of luck, we will get to Lhasa, then travel home with more coins to count than we anticipated. It is a simple agreement — we are not thieves."

Li Du's brow creased. "Most magistrates would say that avoiding taxes is theft."

Norbu glared at Li Du. "Kalden has put his trust in you."

"And I do not intend to break it," said Li Du.

"You understand now," said Kalden, "that this matter has nothing to do with the painter."

"Sonam said nothing of Dhamo when you spoke with him in Gyalthang?"

Kalden took his time to think. "I asked him how he knew of this place. He said that it was good luck for him." Kalden's expression tightened as a thought occurred to him. "He said that a mad old monk had helped ensure his fortune."

In the uneasy silence that followed, the specter of the dead man appeared in their shared memory, cold and painted on the bridge, blue skin and rent body waiting for them silently as the snow began to fall. His gray features conveyed a curse, a warning, a threat, an act of cruelty or insanity. Li Du took a deep breath and stood up.

"I told you all," Norbu said, "that we should have continued on. I'm still not convinced this wasn't a demon's work. If the sun comes up tomorrow, we should follow it out of this valley as soon as we can pack the tea on the mules. After that, the rest of them can murder each other without any distractions — it's not our business."

Kalden looked at Li Du and Hamza. "We can make room for you here. After what you've told us, I would not want to spend a night in that house, however fine its hearth or pretty its mistress."

It did feel safer here, in this leaning herder's hut fortified by tea and saddles. Li Du could almost pretend they were as they had been before, travelers whose only task was to move forward on the path. He drew in a breath and stood up.

Hamza gave an approving nod. "We remain at the manor," he said. "Our patchwork scholar has work to do."

CHAPTER 16

Hamza did not accompany Li Du to the manor immediately, but stayed behind at Kalden's request to answer questions about what he and Li Du had observed. As Li Du entered the manor courtyard alone, he glimpsed movement in the barn to his right. He turned just in time to see the Chhöshe move deeper into the corner of the barn where the animals crowded near Pema's little room. Li Du followed.

A woven basket with embroidered shoulder straps rested on the floor. It was filled with fresh cheese and butter wrapped loosely in cloth, a brick of tea, and bags dusted with traces of barley flour. The top of a wax-sealed bottle was visible under a stack of flat bread.

The Chhöshe stood near the back of the barn with his back to Li Du. His shaved head was covered in a stiff hat of yellow wool. One hand was raised, the red sleeve draped and fallen around his forearm. His palm rested on the shaggy, expansive neck of a black cow. It looked to Li Du like an old animal. Its gentle eyes were framed by long eyelashes. Loose skin hung down its chest in silky folds. The Chhöshe flattened his fingers against the cow's neck in a tentative, childlike movement.

"Did that animal travel with you?" asked Li Du.

The Chhöshe swung around in surprise, pulling his hand away. He looked embarrassed. "No — she belongs here."

"She seems a gentle creature."

"She always was," said the Chhöshe, absently. He pointed to the white blaze on her forehead. "When I was a child I thought the mark on her forehead was shaped like a fish."

Li Du looked at the mark and nodded. "I see the resemblance." He indicated the basket on the floor. "Are you preparing for departure?"

The Chhöshe glanced behind him. "I hope that the snow melts soon, but these are just supplies for the mountain temple."

"Did Dhamo come down to the manor for supplies also?"

The Chhöshe shifted uncomfortably. "Pema brought him his food." He looked down at Li Du with a touch of defiance in his strong features. "But I do not want to be served by —" He amended his statement. "I do not like to see others do work that I can do for myself."

"I understand," Li Du said. "You must encounter many people eager to demonstrate their devotion."

"There are many tulkus in the world, and my lineage is humble and little known," said the Chhöshe. "But I have had some encounters during my travels for which I was not prepared. At Drepung we are all monks and lamas. Our teachers instruct us and tell us what to do. But in these remote places, where harvests are uncertain and travelers are always afraid of avalanches and thieves, people are different. When they know that I am the Chhöshe they fall to the ground and will not stand up. We met a pilgrim on the road who spent so many hours making offerings to me and asking for advice and guidance that it grew dark and he had to share our campfire."

Li Du raised his own hand to the muzzle of his mule, who had ambled toward him and bent her head in a request for reassurance. "I have been warned to be careful of thieves," Li Du said. "The leader of my caravan says that one of their favorite tactics is to ask to share a fire, then steal from the caravan during the night."

The Chhöshe nodded. "I have heard the same warnings, but this man was alone and harmless. I drank wine with him, though I am not allowed to drink it at my school. And as I slept, Rinzen and the pilgrim exchanged news of Lhasa and of travels in the south. He was good company." The Chhöshe lapsed into thoughtful silence. "I hope he was not caught alone in the snow."

Andruk, the translator, was at the courtyard fire. His fingers were curled loosely around a stick that was charred at one end. Li Du took a place across from him and leaned forward toward the heat.

Andruk spoke first. "I have been thinking how fortunate it was that you were in the forest when my employer fell," he said. "How did you happen to be so close?" His Chinese was refined and confident, without studied formality. Li Du guessed that he had spoken it from childhood.

"I was out for a walk," Li Du said, vaguely, "to clear the troubles from my mind."

Using the stick, Andruk adjusted one of the logs. "I assume these troubles were inspired by the death of the painter."

Li Du nodded. "It was a gruesome sight

— his body waiting for us there on the bridge."

Andruk was looking at Li Du as if he was not entirely sure what to make of him. "My employer thinks that Dhamo was possessed by the devil."

"And you?"

"I do not believe in the Christian devil."

"Then Paolo Campo has not persuaded you to convert?" Li Du knew the answer according to Campo, but was curious to hear it from Andruk.

"He has tried," said Andruk, "but his faith does not attract me. He would perhaps have more success if he could learn the local languages himself, as his friend did."

"What is his companion like?"

"I have not met him. My family are tenants on the land of a monastery outside Zogong. Paolo Campo hired me after he had left his companion in that city." Andruk directed a dissatisfied look at the fire. "He is a difficult man to guide. He changes his mind. He forgets his own intentions. But perhaps you understand him better. You speak his tongue." Andruk paused. "You also speak the language of the trade routes. You must be a scholar of high rank."

Li Du waved a hand modestly. "The muleteers have been patient with me. I can speak their words, but I cannot write them."

A look of disdain crossed Andruk's face. "No one needs to write in these borderlands — the Khampa are rough people. And it is foolish to carry paper on paths where snow and rain soak everything before the end of a journey."

Li Du disagreed. He was often astonished by the fortitude of paper. Poems written by traveling scholars who lived and died centuries earlier had been found, crisp scrolls rolled neatly, aged but undamaged, in caves and huts and abandoned temple libraries. "There are ways to protect even the most fragile materials against snow and wind," he said. "I understand you wished to commission a thangka for your own monastery. It would have traveled on the back of a mule over snowy passes, across rivers, and reached its destination with each shape and line enduring as the painter intended."

Andruk's slim brows drew together, and he shook his head. "I commissioned no thangka," he said.

Li Du took a moment to question his memory, but found no fault in it. "Paolo Campo said that you were impressed by the paintings and intended to have one sent as a gift to your own monastery. I understand it was a common practice of pilgrims."

Andruk looked confused. "I did admire the paintings, but I had no intention of requesting one. My monastery is not wealthy, and I have no silver to purchase fine items for the temples in my own home. Paolo Campo must have misunderstood me. It happens often."

"I understand," Li Du said. "I have found that when a person is unsettled in his mind, command over a foreign language can weaken. I know that Paolo Campo has been upset by the death of the monk. His recent fall must have added to his distress."

Andruk's tone became tinged with exasperation. "I thought that he spoke often of the devil before we came to this place," he said. "Now he will speak of nothing else. He paces through his room and mutters to himself. It is as if he is afflicted with the same madness that struck the painter."

"Their hells are not so different," Li Du said quietly, his eyes drawn to the fire.

Andruk interlaced his long fingers and stretched his hands. "Both places of flame," he said, "and of mutilation. I have seen the paintings of the Christians. There are as many eviscerations and sharp-toothed monsters in their minds as there are in ours."

Li Du was struck by the similarity between Andruk's observation and his own only a little while earlier. "Perhaps there are more similarities between the worst fates we can imagine for ourselves than there are between the best," he said.

"I will be glad when we leave this place," said Andruk.

"How long have you been here?"

Andruk shrugged. "We arrived some days before you did."

"I hear that you have seen the village," said Li Du. "Is it a long way from the manor?"

"Not when the path is clear," said Andruk. "It is almost at the pass. The way is steep, but it is not far."

"You visited it two mornings ago," Li Du said. "With the family?"

"Doso and his wife had errands there, but we were not in company. I was merely curious to see the place."

"But Paolo Campo did not go with you."

It seemed to Li Du that Andruk lingered over his thoughts before answering. "No," he said finally. "Paolo Campo stayed at the manor."

"Except for when he went to Yeshe's hut."

Andruk looked up. "Yes — he was just leaving it when I came back from the village. I found him very upset."

Li Du nodded. "I understand that the

children were not receptive to his teachings," he said.

Andruk raised an eyebrow. "I did not think he would be so overcome by such a small offense," he said. "When I returned, I found Campo kneeling in the snow near Yeshe's cabin. His eyes were wet with tears and he clutched at his throat as if he could not breathe."

Li Du was startled. "Did he say what had so distressed him?"

"He was speechless. I had to help him to the manor. I settled him beside the hearth in the kitchen. He must have returned to his room not long after that — he was in his room when I went to inform him that Dhamo was dead."

"How did he react when you told him?"

"He was anxious to know what had occurred, and began soon after to speak of devilry." Andruk leaned forward. "The body — it was really painted?"

"Yes. I saw it myself."

"A white circle, banded in gold, with a handle wrapped in blue?"

"Yes."

"And no one knows why he painted it."

Li Du shook his head. "Do you?"

"How would I know? I did not know him. I have never heard of such an act."

Li Du was aware of a coldness in the way Andruk looked at him. It was not anger, or at least he did not think it was. It felt to him more as if the other man, the stranger on the other side of the fire, was asking him a silent question. Li Du just did not know what it was.

He had not gone far before he heard voices raised in anger. The words spun through the wind around him, unintelligible. At first he could not tell where they were coming from, but then a loud crash turned him around to face Yeshe's hut. As he hurried toward it, Li Du heard another crash, followed by the heavy thump of something hitting the wall inside.

Just as he reached the cabin, the door flew open and Sonam emerged, breathing hard and holding his hand to his face. As Li Du watched, Sonam pulled his fingers away and looked at them. His fingertips were bright with blood. He turned and spat red in the snow.

Li Du's attention was momentarily arrested by the drops of red against the white. "What has happened here?"

Sonam did not answer immediately. He had turned as if to reenter the hut. Then, slowly, he took a step to one side of the door, and gestured inside. "The old cripple attacked me," he said. "As if some madness took him."

Li Du stepped onto the threshold. In the dim, smoky cabin, overturned buckets gleamed, and the floor was covered in slick puddles of cheese and milk slowly spreading across the dirt. Yeshe was sitting down where he had fallen, his thin chest heaving, his face furious. Beside him, one of his canes lay cracked.

When he saw Li Du, he swallowed and pointed to Sonam. He opened his mouth to speak, but no sound came out. Remaining where he was, Sonam looked down at the fallen man and shook his head. He looked bewildered. "What came over you, grandfather?"

With a pained groan, Yeshe pulled himself up onto the bench beside the fire. A single log burned weakly over the hot coals. Ashes were drifting slowly into the puddles of half-strained cheese. He coughed. "There was a misunderstanding," he croaked. "I thought he had insulted me, but I was mistaken." Li Du saw his jaw clench. "I ask your pardon," he said to Sonam.

"And you have it, grandfather," Sonam replied. "But you should listen carefully to what you are told. For an old farmer, you have a quick temper."

Sonam turned to Li Du with a grimace. He reached up and touched his hand to the place where his jaw had begun to swell. "Be careful what you say to the man." Sonam spat again into the snow, and strode away toward the manor.

Li Du surveyed the mess. "Please let me help you."

Yeshe's eyes narrowed. "Why would you help me when I attacked him?"

Li Du gave a little smile. "If you attacked him, I suspect you had good reason. You are not the first person he has offended here."

While Yeshe rebuilt the fire, Li Du swept up the milk and cheese as best he could from the dirt floor into a bucket, which he took outside and emptied in the snow. He used snow to wash the bucket, and returned to find the hearth warm again and Yeshe sitting on the bench beside it. He was using a short knife, its handle wrapped in strips of hide, to cut the branches from a stick.

Li Du sat down across the fire from the old man. "What happened?"

"It was nothing. A misunderstanding only." Yeshe rubbed the knuckles of his right hand. "I have some strength still," he said. "There was a time when I won every fight." He looked down at his crooked feet. "Until that one."

"Lumo said that you were a farmer."

Yeshe did not look up. "I never owned land. I traveled and worked for pay at the autumn harvest and spring planting. I took the trade routes. Met caravans like yours. Caravans, pilgrims, and thieves." Li Du saw his hands tremble.

"Are you hurt?"

Yeshe shook his head. "Bad memories," he said. "Just bad memories." His shoulders rose and he heaved a sigh. "Let us speak of better ones. What was I saying? I was telling you about traveling the roads back when my feet were strong." He smiled reminiscently. "I remember a caravan like yours — a caravan from Kham. One of my last memories before I was attacked was a great feast that I shared with such a caravan under the stars."

Seeing that the memory cheered Yeshe, Li Du asked him to go on. Yeshe licked his dry lips. "That was years ago, on a road west of here — outside Bathang. I came upon them celebrating their good fortune. They had gone to Bathang and learned that the Chinese tax inspector had died unexpectedly that very day. Bad luck for the tax collector, but good luck for the caravan."

He drew in a deep breath and released it

slowly, looking at the fire. "You never know what will happen," he said, and shrugged. "Except Dhamo."

Li Du turned to Yeshe curiously. "Dhamo?"

Yeshe grunted. "He knew what was going to happen. Took his fate into his own hands, didn't he?"

Li Du was struck by a thought. "Your door opens to the path down to the pasture. Did you see Dhamo go to the bridge that morning?"

Yeshe gave a short nod. "I did. Surprised me. Didn't see him out of his temple often."

"Was he upset?"

"Upset? How would I know his state of mind? His head was down and he was talking to himself."

"And no one went after him?"

Yeshe looked up sharply. "After him?"

Li Du allowed himself to appear disoriented and a bit bewildered. "I do not know why I ask the question. It is only that I have been thinking about his death, and of how unfortunate it was that no one happened to go that way. He might have been stopped — taken perhaps to a lama who could ease the suffering in his mind."

"I wasn't looking out my door the whole time," said Yeshe, "but I did notice someone else go that way. Ahead of Dhamo, not behind."

Li Du leaned forward slightly. "Did you see who it was?"

Yeshe shrugged. "Looked like a man. It wasn't a coat I had seen." He paused, then added, "In the winter when the weather is bad you recognize coats, not faces. But why are you asking these questions?" Yeshe's eyes were narrowed, suspicious.

"It is just my habit," said Li Du. "This place is unfamiliar and the manner of his death is difficult for me to understand."

"Yes," said Yeshe. "Won't argue with you about that. But you can't live in solitude like that old monk did without getting lost." He tapped a finger to his head. "Lost in your mind." He looked again at his legs. "The injury is bad enough," he said. "But it's the family that saved me, not the medicines. A kind family."

"They are generous to share their home with so many travelers," Li Du said.

Yeshe nodded. "If I had to make a bargain with a demon, I would do it to protect them from harm." He paused, then added, "Dhamo was not a safe person. You ask the lady of the house. Kamala knew it. You should not talk about him so much. It keeps him here. And no good will come of that."

Li Du emerged from the hut and saw Hamza coming toward him from the direction of the caravan's encampment. Li Du tucked his hands deeper into his sleeves and waited, his shoulders tensed against the cold.

A sound drew his attention toward the back of the manor. Someone was standing by the supply of chopped firewood. He squinted, and recognized Sera-tsering. Two at a time, she pulled logs from the stack, clapped them together to rid them of snow, and tossed them into a small pile beside her.

By now, the snow was packed down into paths. Hamza traversed the pasture at a quick pace. "Kalden is uneasy," he said, when he reached Li Du. "I think he is regretting this adventure more with every hour."

"But you believe that he has told us everything?"

Hamza nodded. "I do not think he knows more than what he confessed to us. But Kalden does not like situations that he cannot judge. Put the man on a ridge with snow falling, and he will choose the safest action. But put him amid schemers and he will fall

265

into every trap."

When Li Du did not answer immediately, Hamza gave an exaggerated sigh. "You are thinking with such intensity that I am becoming exhausted. Speak your thoughts out loud. The fresh air will make them less dense."

Li Du smiled at this. "They exhaust me also." Briefly, he told Hamza of what Andruk had said, and of the quarrel in Yeshe's hut. "I cannot see clearly the intentions of the people gathered here," he said. He was about to say more, but stopped.

Hamza looked at him. "There is more," he said. "You are preoccupied with something else. I see your own memories on your face — you cast your mind into the past. Why?"

"I —"

But Li Du had no time to answer. He saw the arrow pierce the air, but did not recognize it for what it was until he heard the thud of its impact, followed by the hollow clatter of logs falling against one another.

Sera remained still for an instant, staring at the arrow that had struck not an arm's length from where she stood. Then she dropped down to the snow and Li Du saw her squeeze between the woodpile and the exterior of the manor wall.

Li Du glanced beside him. Hamza was scanning the trees on the mountainside above.

Another arrow hit the woodpile, sending a shower of kindling tumbling from the top and dusting Sera with snow.

"There!" Hamza pointed. Li Du followed the direction of his finger. He caught only a glimpse of a dark shape high above on a boulder. As Li Du watched, the figure scrambled down, and was gone.

"Did you see who it was?" Li Du asked Hamza, as they ran toward the woodpile.

"It was too far," said Hamza.

They reached the woodpile, where they found Sera huddled and out of breath, but unhurt. When they told her that the archer had fled, she stood up slowly and emerged from the protected alcove. Her face was tense, but Li Du observed with surprise that it was not from fear. She was angry.

Hamza immediately started up the stairs.

"Stop."

At Sera's command, Hamza halted. "But the arrows were loosed from up there," he said, pointing into the forest toward the mountain temple. "We can catch —"

"No." Sera brushed the snow from her dress. "Let the snake slither away." She pulled one of the arrows from the wood into which it had lodged, cracking the thin log apart to release it. It was an elegant shaft, feathered and wickedly pointed.

"One of Doso's," observed Li Du, "from the collection in the barn. Anyone could have taken it. We must go inside — if we are quick then we will at least know with certainty who could *not* have done this."

"No," said Sera, for a second time. "Do not alarm the family and scare the children. This was a message for me. I understand it clearly, and I know who sent it."

"Who?" Li Du asked the question. Hamza emphasized it with an expression of impatient inquiry.

She looked from one of them to the other. "It is a personal matter," she said. "I would prefer to address it myself."

"A personal matter?" Hamza's tone was incredulous. "Two arrows just flew through the trees with you as their mark, and you ask us to behave as if you had a visit from a tiresome neighbor?"

There was a stubborn set to Sera's chin. "Do not scold me. You know nothing of the circumstances." Still holding the arrow, she gestured with it toward the woodpile. "That was the target," she said. "The intent was to frighten me, not kill me."

Hamza scowled. "Who is trying to frighten you?"

She ignored the question. "Tomorrow the weather will be warmer and the snow will melt. When the way is clear, we will each of us carry our separate problems to our separate destinations."

"I urge you to reconsider," said Li Du, quiet and serious. "You yourself saw Dhamo on the bridge. If you know something —"

"I don't know anything about Dhamo," she said. "If you really think that he did not kill himself, then pursue the matter at your discretion. But from what I saw, he took his own life."

Li Du tried again. "What problems belong to a traveler on her way to visit her sister?"

Sera knelt and gathered the logs she had collected into a rough canvas sling, which she hefted onto her back. "Please do not pry into my business," she said, and left them there staring after her.

Li Du looked up at the trees. "I will go up," he said. "I am sure that whoever loosed the arrow will not be there, but perhaps something was left behind."

"I will go with you," said Hamza.

"No — you should go after her," Li Du said. "Whatever she is hiding, it is not a safe secret. We must assume now that she knows more of Dhamo's death than she has yet told us."

"But it is clear now that she is not the killer," said Hamza.

"We cannot be certain," Li Du replied.

"But we just saw —" Hamza stopped.

"We saw someone shoot two arrows at her. We do not know whether that was the same person who killed Dhamo."

Hamza looked ready to argue, but Li Du spoke first. "I am only encouraging you to be careful."

Hamza's expression cleared. "You are right," he said, "though I still do not believe that she is a murderess." He lifted his chin and added, with unself-conscious arrogance, "I am sure I can persuade her to reveal more of what she knows. I have been told many times that I have an aptitude with words."

CHAPTER 17

Li Du climbed to where he thought the arrow must have originated. It did not take him long to locate the boulder. The snow around it was trampled. A set of footprints led away into the forest and downward, suggesting a route roughly parallel to the stairs. The trees, with the exception of the old hollow oak, were relatively thin and sparse, which reassured Li Du that there was no attacker lurking nearby.

His gaze rested on the bulbous, decaying trunk, around which the stone stairs curved. It looked back as if to ask him why he had returned. *With questions,* he said to it silently. Then, struck by an idea, he circled around to the other side of the tree. Through a hole in the rotten wood, he looked into the hollow trunk. There, thrust down into the dry leaves and snow that had collected inside the tree, was a bow.

Li Du reached in and drew it out. It was

luxuriously made. The limb of the bow, he noticed, was coated with frost where moisture had condensed and frozen onto it. The grip, however, was darker, the frost interrupted by the print of a warm hand.

He looked inside the tree again. Beside the fissure from which he had pulled the bow, there was another place where the snow was broken. *Which means,* he thought, *that the bow was here already, ready to be used when an opportunity presented itself. An opportunity to do what?* Li Du looked at the bow. *An opportunity to kill Sera-tsering. Or, as she claims, to frighten her. But why? And why was she so quick to dismiss the attack?*

Could Sera have killed Dhamo, and drawn upon herself some private retribution for his death? It would explain her unwillingness to call attention to what had happened. Or, he thought, could she have conspired with someone else at the manor, someone who now wished to end the alliance?

He looked down at the manor walls visible below. It was clear that Sera had no intention of telling them any more than she had. It was equally clear that if Li Du did not discover the truth quickly, someone else was likely to die before the snow melted.

Li Du stretched his cold toes inside his boots and adjusted his hat. Unsure what else to do with it, he replaced the bow in the tree. Where could he begin to break the silences to which the manor and its guests clung so determinedly? What connected the events that had occurred?

It had begun with Dhamo, he thought. But what did he know about Dhamo? *Paint,* he thought. *Dhamo was a painter. Dhamo's body was painted.* Li Du looked up in the direction of the temple. *Paint,* he thought, *and paintings.*

He had encountered three paintings since he had come to this valley. One was the painting that he had seen in Dhamo's studio, the incomplete thangka that had been stolen. The second was the painting that, according to Campo, Andruk had intended to commission, an intention that Andruk denied. And there was a third painting — the one that Sonam had mentioned. He had been telling Li Du about Dhamo's identification of the Chhöshe thirteen years ago. *It was something to do with a painting.*

Well, Li Du thought, *that is a question, at least, that someone should be willing to answer.* The best person to ask about the identification of the Chhöshe was the Chhöshe himself. With a last look at the manor, and a fervent hope that Hamza was exercising caution, he turned and continued up the stairs.

Snow had slid from the roof of the mountain temple, pulling with it a scattering of wooden shingles and the stones that had held them in place. Shingles and stones now littered a small patch of snow in front of the right-hand door.

As Li Du approached, he perceived movement from somewhere higher on the mountain. He looked up. The wind caught at the deep red and saffron clothes of a monk, pulling at the cloth and blurring the figure into a bright saturated phantom, the ghost of the painter now a painted brushstroke against the snow.

The illusion faded quickly. These were not the thin shoulders and aged face of the dead man. As the monk came closer, sliding down the steep incline through the snow with youthful strength, Li Du recognized the height and bearing of the Chhöshe. They approached each other through the snow. The Chhöshe was breathing hard from exertion, and his cheeks were red, making him look even younger.

Li Du prepared for the three prostrations, but the Chhöshe put out a hand in a gesture of refusal. "Please," he said. "I am grateful for your respect. There is no need — not in the snow." He raised his eyes up the slope of the mountain, from which wet, heavy clouds were sinking steadily down toward them.

"Where were you?" Li Du asked.

The Chhöshe gestured behind him. "I have duties up at the high shrine."

Li Du was confused. "There is another shrine?"

"A simple monument — a chorten. It sits just above the mountain temple. It is the duty of the monk of the temple, if there is one, to pray there once daily and light incense."

"Did Dhamo perform the duty before his death?"

The Chhöshe nodded. "And now I perform the task."

"And when you leave?"

"If there is no lama, the duty cannot be fulfilled. When one comes to take Dhamo's place, if one comes, then the responsibility will be taken up once more." The Chhöshe turned and followed with his gaze his own footsteps up through the snow. "Now it is a place where the wind batters stone and you can hear the snow on the mountain like a tiger in the forest creeping closer. But when the sun comes out — if you are lucky, you will see it. From that place you can see the holy mountain, and it looks at you with the reassurance of a thousand gods who tell you in a thousand voices that you are home."

The Chhöshe's expression changed as he spoke. Li Du turned to see what had captured his attention. Coming toward them on the path to the temple, which zigzagged up the mountain for ease of travel with horses, were Doso and Pema. Doso was leading a mule with two baskets strapped across its back, and Pema was bent forward under the weight of another basket.

As they approached, Li Du looked from the Chhöshe to Doso and was struck again by the similarity in build and affect between father and son. The closer they came to each other, the more Li Du perceived the strength of the bond that still existed between them. The Chhöshe accepted their signs of respect in silence.

Doso raised an appraising eye to the damaged roof, then turned to Pema. "You said there is a ladder?"

Pema nodded. His old goatskin coat was flecked with wood dust and splinters, and his breath puffed clouds into the freezing wind. He greeted Li Du with the apprehensive, nervous bow that Li Du had already come to expect from the timid young man. "It is just behind the temple."

Li Du watched Doso trace the shape of the temple with his eyes. He noticed Doso's gaze linger on a patch of charred wood beneath the row of prayer wheels. Then Doso turned away and walked purposefully toward the corner of the building. Pema hurried after him.

While Doso and Pema went around to the back of the temple, Li Du followed the Chhöshe inside. Li Du stared at the golden Buddha. The butter lamps appeared fresh, their flames strong and reflected across the curving shins, knees, and fingers of the seated statue.

The Chhöshe turned to face Li Du. "You say you are not a religious man," he said, "and yet this is the second time today that you have come to the temple." The words were spoken lightly, and Li Du had a momentary glimpse of what he must have been like as a boy. From the back of the temple came the thump and scrape of the ladder being dragged along the outside wall. The levity vanished from the Chhöshe's face.

"You and Pema were children together," Li Du said.

"That was a long time ago," said the Chhöshe. He spoke with a weariness that did not match his age.

Li Du permitted himself a smile. The man

before him was an incarnated spirit, but he was also a young person and a student. "When I instructed scholars in double meanings and allusions, they often began to speak like the tired exiles of our classical period, just as students of medicine think themselves to be afflicted by whatever ailment they are currently studying. You are not old enough, I think, for anything to be a long time ago."

The Chhöshe raised his eyes to meet Li Du's. All the humor in them was gone. "I do not speak only of time," he said. "At home, thirteen years can pass like one season. But distance has its own effect on memory. At Drepung we wake up when the stars are still in the sky, but we do not know the animals there. We do not wake up to the wind coming down from the mountain or the low bells of the yaks. We wake up and we pray. We study the middle path, logic, the six perfections. We sit in lines like beads on a string."

"Rinzen says that you have excelled in your studies."

The Chhöshe looked down. "I have applied myself."

A hollow impact vibrated through the chapel as something, presumably the ladder, settled against the roof. Li Du heard

Doso's voice and a jingle of bells from the bridle of the mule.

"I was told," Li Du said to the Chhöshe, "that there was a painting associated with your identification here at this temple."

The Chhöshe's face became very still, and the stillness emanated from him as if he had commanded the whole room to hold its breath and turn its face away. His voice was very quiet. "Yes. There was a painting."

Li Du persevered. "A painting by Dhamo?"

The Chhöshe drew in a deep breath. When he raised his eyes to Li Du's again, Li Du saw that through great effort, they were now calm. "Dhamo painted his vision in Lhasa. The mountains were the mountains of this place, and I was the boy in the painting."

"That is a great miracle. Rinzen said that the painting is still here."

"It *was* here."

"What happened to it?" Li Du asked the question even though he had guessed the answer already.

"It was destroyed in a fire nine years ago."

Li Du remembered Doso's mention of the fire that had damaged the temple. He looked again at the traces of burnt wood on the statues and columns, and the smoke-blackened thangkas among the bright, new ones. "A sad loss," he said.

The Chhöshe cleared his throat. "I must return to the prayers," he said.

"Of course." Li Du bowed and left the temple. He made his way through the snow to where Pema was just descending the notched ladder.

"I heard your conversation," said Pema. "You wanted to see the painting?"

Li Du nodded. "Old habits of a librarian. I am always interested in records, and by all accounts this painting was very unusual. I have never seen a painting of a vision before."

Pema hesitated. "The painting is gone," he said. "But I saw it every day before it was destroyed. If you want to know what it looked like, I can draw it for you."

Pema smoothed a sheet of paper over a table. He pinned down the corners with heavy bowls to keep them from curling. As he chose a stick of charcoal already scraped and carved to a stylus point, he said, "The painting used to hang just beside the altar."

"I am surprised you can still remember it," said Li Du. "Nine years is a long time."

"I looked at it often," said Pema. He glanced at the closed door separating them from the room where the Chhöshe prayed. "I missed my brother."

Pema's slim fingers were steady as he began to draw. "The painting showed the fourth incarnation of the Chhöshe," he said, "just as Dhamo dreamed it far away in Lhasa."

Li Du followed the lines as they took the form of jagged mountains across the sheet. He noted the facility with which Pema produced the image. "You cannot see them through the clouds," said Pema, "but these are the mountains just as they appear around this temple. And here are the stairs. He painted them just as they are even though he had never seen them before." As Pema continued to sketch, Li Du recognized the stairs that began at the lower right corner of the page and continued up to the top left.

The drawing showed a different season. Pema shaded the stairs the texture of dark rock, and filled the trees with leaves. "And here is the temple," he said, sketching it at the top left. Li Du leaned closer. The architecture was exactly the same, from the two doors to the row of prayer wheels in front.

Pema's hand slid back down to the lower left and he traced the light outline of a figure. It was a child — a little boy. He wore a hat and a goatskin vest over his tunic. Between his hands he held a round basin.

"What is that?" Li Du asked, pointing to it.

"It is a bowl of milk," said Pema. "Dhamo's vision said that the Chhöshe would carry a bowl of milk to the temple and make an offering of it there — here — at the altar."

As Li Du watched, Pema's hand moved up the stairs and he drew the boy again, still holding the bowl. Li Du remembered the painting in the library of the women who turned to mountains. Like that painting, Dhamo's had shown progressing moments in time.

Pema sketched the old tree, cloven and curved as it still was, and a third depiction of the boy. He reached the top and drew the boy again, kneeling, surrounded by sketched villagers with reverent expressions. Above the villagers were divine figures, floating in clouds, watching the scene.

He finished, and together they looked down at the drawing. "They say it was just like that when my brother brought the bowl to the temple," Pema said. "The villagers were all gathered there, just as Dhamo painted it, just as he saw it in his dream."

CHAPTER 18

The courtyard was empty, but the manor's daily activities were now mapped in paths through the white drifts. Someone had lit new incense sticks outside the manor shrine. The sweet, woody fragrance mingled with the musky odors of the barn.

Hearing voices from the kitchen, Li Du climbed the steps. Kamala and the children had begun preparations for dinner. Li Du blinked against the sting of hot pepper oil in the hearth smoke that filled the room. The old woman, Mara, slept in a corner, her dark clothes gathered up to her nose and a gentle snore whispering in the air around her. There was no suggestion of panic, which Li Du took to mean that Sera had followed through on her intention not to reveal what had happened at the woodpile.

Close to the fire, Hamza and Sera-tsering sat on stools across from each other at a low wooden table, on which a simple grid was marked in charcoal. Across it, black stones and white stones were positioned at the intersections between lines. They were smooth and polished, with rounded tops.

Sera lifted her right hand and passed it over a line of black pieces, replacing them with white ones. When she came to the end of the line, she held her clenched hand over the board.

Hamza slowly reached out his own hand and opened it, palm up, beneath hers. She opened her fingers, and the collection of black pebbles fell with soft clicks into his palm. He deposited his defeated soldiers into a growing pile beside him. On the table between them, set to one side, were four small silver coins.

Hamza gestured for Li Du to join them. He took a seat at the table, his back to the fire.

"I had not expected to find you playing a game," he said, mildly.

"It seems the lady traveler likes to gamble," muttered Hamza. He sounded disgruntled. "But we knew that already."

Sera did not reply, but Li Du saw a corner of her mouth quirk before her face returned to its set, focused expression.

"I used to play this game," Li Du said,

examining the board. The grid was square, nine lines by nine. Most of the pebbles in its interior were white, while black stones dominated its perimeter.

"It is not the game you think it is," said Hamza. "Your empire has its own game of encirclement, but this is called the Game of Many Eyes, and it is more ancient than yours." He placed the tip of an index finger on one of the black pieces and slid it two places to his left.

As Sera leaned forward, silently analyzing the new configuration, Hamza looked up at Li Du. "It will please you to know," he went on, "that the man who taught me the rules was a librarian like yourself. But his library was underground, a library built for the dead in a stone tomb beneath the desert sands. This man, this librarian, learned it from a book that included, in its first section, the rules of play, and in its second, the spells to reanimate the dead so that they could play it with the living. It was an ancient way, he explained to me, for the living to match wits with their ancestors."

Sera spoke without taking her eyes from the board. "I have heard the same story," she said.

"That surprises me," said Hamza. "It is not commonly known."

Sera smiled. "Perhaps I, too, have traveled to those ancient tombs where the dead wait to play this game with the living." Her hand hovered over a white stone, her fingers moving almost imperceptibly, as if they were independently thinking through strategy.

"Move that one," Hamza said, "and you expose yourself to attack." He lowered his voice so that it was barely audible. "A habit of yours."

Sera skimmed her hand across the board to a different piece, and made her move. "I think," she said, ignoring Hamza's muttering, "that it would be unfortunate to leave good game boards in dusty tombs."

Hamza lifted his eyebrows. "Who raised you, that you were not taught to respect the resting places of the dead?"

"I think I have told you already that I was born in Lhasa," Sera said. "As for who raised me, I was taught this game by someone very important, a friend to my family. And I do respect the dead. But when you travel to distant places, sometimes what you learned at home begins to seem less certain. You are exposed to so many other explanations for the world that you find yourself able to believe all of them and none of them."

Hamza did not appear to have an immediate answer. He lowered his hand to the board and touched a piece to move it. Sera placed her fingers gently over his. "That is my piece you are about to move," she said, "or did you not see that I conquered that row?" Hamza opened his mouth to protest, then frowned when he saw that she was right. She took her hand away and he resumed his study of the board.

"Then again," Sera said, looking up and across the room, "sometimes travel strengthens the beliefs we carry from home. When the world is strange and lonely, it can be a comfort to cling to what we think is certain." Li Du followed her gaze and saw Campo and Andruk emerge from the stairwell and come forward through the smoke.

Campo's eyes rested for a moment on Sera, then shifted to the game board. With a frown, he went to the fire and sat down while Kamala gestured for her daughter to prepare more tea.

Andruk came to the table and stood staring down at it. "You are playing the Game of Many Eyes," he said. Li Du watched as Andruk assessed the board, then lifted his eyes to look, with intense curiosity, at Sera. Andruk spoke quietly. "She will win in either four moves or seven, depending on what he does next."

Hamza raised an affronted face to Andruk, then glanced at Sera. She met his gaze without expression. Hamza sat up straighter and lifted his chin. "The outcome of a battle is never certain until it is fought," he said. He made his move.

Sera smiled. "If you are indeed a storyteller, you know that is not true. Half the epic recitations I hear describe doomed men going to battle even though they know they are doomed."

Hamza shook his head. "An audience can be told that the fate of a character is determined, and still they wait in anticipation, hoping that fate can be altered."

Andruk reached down and picked up one of the white pieces clustered at the edge of the board with the other pebbles that were not yet in play. He rolled the stone between his thumb and forefinger. "In the market in Zogong I saw men arrested for playing this game. It is illegal."

Sera plucked the stone from his fingers and set it down in the place of the piece she had just captured from Hamza. "In the big cities it is outlawed," she said, "but those small, capricious laws don't apply out here."

"Why is it outlawed?" Li Du asked.

Andruk appeared to wait for Sera to answer. When she did not, he said, "Do you know of the death of the regent who served the Great Fifth?"

Li Du did. "He was beheaded after a failed attempt to assassinate the khan in Lhasa — Lhazang," he said.

Andruk nodded. "There is a rumor that Lhazang Khan told the regent that if he could defeat him at the Game of Many Eyes, the regent could keep his life. The regent lost. Now the game has a reputation for being unlucky, and so it is banned."

"By whom is it banned?" The question came from Hamza. "It was not unlucky for Lhazang."

Andruk shrugged. "Lhazang Khan's command over this country is not yet accepted by all families. His declaration that the Sixth Dalai Lama was a false incarnation did not convince everyone. And it was a strange alignment of omens that revealed the Khan's own son to be the true incarnation."

Sera looked at Andruk curiously. "Then you think that the Dalai Lama who now sits in the Potala Palace is not the true Dalai Lama?"

Andruk's expression became shuttered. "I am not the only one who thinks it. I am only reporting what I have heard on the trade routes," he said.

Hamza had taken a long time over his

289

move. He came to a decision, smiled, and claimed seven of Sera's pieces. Sera watched him to replace white with black. "Rumors, lies, truths, and stories. It becomes difficult to tell them apart. The way I heard it, the regent and Lhazang played the game years before the regent's death, and the wager was a woman they both desired."

"What is this game?" Campo's voice from the fire was vexed, and he rubbed the scar on his hand as if it irritated him. He stood up to hover uncomfortably over the game.

Andruk, who had not been translating, explained in slow Chinese. "When one player surrounds the pieces of the other, they change color from black to white or from white to black, until the whole board is one or the other and there is a winner."

"The board is almost white," Campo said.

"It is possible," said Hamza, stiffly, "for a player to win with only one piece remaining."

Campo's gaze went to the silver coins on the table. "When Moses came down from Mount Sinai," he said, "he saw that while he was gone the people had made a golden calf. In righteous anger he threw the stone tablets to the ground and smashed them, and he destroyed the idol." Campo raised a hand to his chest. He was becoming agitated. "My own heart is pierced with sadness when I see the infidels bind themselves to the world with jewelry and palaces and silver coins, when a little of that wealth put toward new missions here in these wastelands would slow thousands of souls in their headlong rush to eternal perdition."

As Campo concluded, the soft echo of Andruk's translation seemed to infuriate him. He strode forward as if he would up-end the table and scatter the pieces to the ground. Li Du put a hand gently on the other man's arm, and Campo stopped. He looked down at Li Du's hand, and his demeanor changed, became timid. "I — I am not feeling myself," he said. "It is only that I am much preoccupied. I will return to my room to rest awhile."

After casting a final restless glance around the kitchen, Campo retreated to the door. Li Du, after a quick exchange of looks with Hamza, followed.

Li Du caught up to Campo in the courtyard. Campo seemed relieved to see him, and instead of reiterating his intention to rest, invited Li Du to converse with him for a while.

Once inside his room, Campo performed a brief but adamant genuflection before his makeshift altar, then moved toward the brazier.

"You seemed upset," Li Du said, watching Campo closely. "I wondered if perhaps you had recalled something more about the night you fell."

This appeared to confuse Campo. "No," he said, after a long pause. "I have nothing more to say about that."

"Then what distressed you?"

Campo's hands shook as he bent down to light the brazier. "A suspicion has been growing in my mind," he said.

Li Du waited for him to continue.

"I fear," Campo said gravely, "that we are imprisoned here not by the natural variance of moisture and air, but by sorcery."

It was not what Li Du had hoped to hear, but he did his best not to show his frustration. "This is an early snowfall," he said. "It is not an unusual occurrence, and will not keep us here much longer."

"But what if the snow does not melt," whispered Campo. "What if we are trapped here in this valley forever. What if we are in —" He stopped. It was as if he could not bear to finish the sentence.

He appeared so genuinely frightened that Li Du, concerned, placed a hand on Campo's arm and guided him gently to the cushioned seat beside the brazier. "Rest here," he said. Campo sat down obediently, and Li Du took the place opposite him.

"For a long time," Li Du said, "I traveled alone. I was in the border regions of the empire where I could not speak or comprehend the languages around me, and where I did not know the customs. Sometimes, during those years, my home seemed so distant that it was as if clouds had closed around the memory of it. I knew that it was there, but I thought that I would never see it again, even in my imagination. I thought I had lost my own past."

He saw that Campo was listening, and continued. "I say this to you because I want you to know that I understand. Sometimes I, too, came close to despair. But I urge you not to allow your fears to control you."

Campo had been picking at his chapped knuckles. Now he separated his hands and placed them on his knees, and Li Du saw tiny drops of blood where the skin had broken. He made a last effort. "Is there anything you wish to tell me? Something to which you have not been allowed to give voice? Has someone threatened you?"

Campo's gaze flew up. "What do you mean?"

Li Du kept his tone gentle. "Andruk

mentioned to me that he found you very upset."

Recovering himself slightly, Campo nodded. "Of course I was upset. The death of the painter, and my own accident . . ."

"No," Li Du said firmly. "I am referring to the morning two days ago. It was before Dhamo's body was discovered. Something had distressed you. What was it?"

A pink color suffused Campo's face. "It was nothing," he said, stammering slightly. "I was aggravated, perhaps, by the children's mockery of the book of the Lord, and the cripple's rudeness. That was all. Once again, Andruk misunderstands me."

Li Du was about to speak, but Campo did not let him. "You do not believe me. You ignore my warnings. But listen to me now." Campo drew in an unsteady breath. "Some believe that Christ bound the devil. But they are incorrect. Christ did not imprison the devil in a sphere to prevent him from working his will upon the world. That is not how he protects us. Christ teaches us to build fortifications against the devil's onslaught. *In my name they shall cast out demons.*"

Campo's eyes were feverish. "But the demons are not contained. They are free, and we must be vigilant against them. There is evil here. Can you not perceive it? You ask what distressed me. Did you not look at the table?"

Li Du was startled. "The table?"

"Andruk told me of the pagan symbol that marked the body of the dead man. Now it spreads. The configuration of stones. Black turning to white. The snow that fills the valley. Do you not see it? It is the white mirror, and it has cursed us."

Li Du put all his effort into calming Campo, and eventually convinced him to return to the heat of the kitchen fire, where the others were gathering for dinner. Li Du walked with him through the barn to the stairs, but did not go up. He remained in the barn, uncertain of where to go. Feeling stifled by the incense and barley dust and enclosed smell of animals, he stepped into the courtyard and left the manor through the dark corridor of painted animals.

Outside the manor walls, Li Du drew in a deep breath and looked at the sky, which rather than flushing with sunset color was simply becoming a darker gray. A low, snapping sound made him turn. He was not alone. To his right, a little way farther along the manor wall, Rinzen stood looking down the pasture toward the black trees. The wind caught at his bright, voluminous robes, blowing them into uneven waves that rippled around him.

A gust blew the stiff red hat from Rinzen's head and whipped his long gray hair into tangles. Li Du picked up the hat where it had fallen at his feet. Its brim was made of sleek, long fur, its crown of bright red wool. Li Du brushed the snow from it, then walked to where Rinzen stood and offered it to him. Rinzen took it with thanks and settled it back on his head.

"There are mountains there in the clouds," Rinzen said, looking into the blank gray void above the trees. He pointed. "That way lies Beijing." He turned around, tracing a line across space with his finger. "And that way is Lhasa."

"And we stand between them," said Li Du.

Rinzen nodded. "How many hundreds of valleys like this one separate the two great cities? Or thousands? It is a vast distance."

Li Du did not answer immediately. They stood, a comfortable silence between them. It seemed to Li Du that Rinzen shared his enjoyment of the wind striking his cheeks and ears, sweeping away dusty thoughts and half-remembered worries.

Li Du put his hand on his hat to keep it from blowing away. "You have reminded me

— the trader, Sonam, asked me to tell you that he can deliver your letters to Lhasa, and it will take him only a single month."

Rinzen bent sideways toward Li Du and cupped his hand to his ear. Li Du raised his voice over the wind and repeated the message. Rinzen straightened up, his forehead wrinkled in thought. "That seems very fast. I am not sure it is possible to make the journey so quickly."

Li Du nodded. "I think you would be wise not to take him at his word."

Understanding settled into the deep lines that framed Rinzen's mouth and eyes like cracks through stone. "I share your opinion. In my position, it is essential to know who is trustworthy, and who is not."

The wind gusted again. Rinzen pulled his hands from his long sleeves to lift his fur collar higher around his neck. "I can smell the smoke of the kitchen fire. Shall we go inside?"

He turned his shoulder toward the manor entrance, but Li Du stood transfixed. "Your ring," he said.

Rinzen had just tucked his hands back into his long sleeves. He drew them out again and followed Li Du's gaze to the ring finger of his left hand. Bands of gold and cut gems shone even in the dim light. But among the fine rings, symbols of his distinction, was one that did not shine.

"The silver ring on your left hand is black," said Li Du. He caught the look of surprise on Rinzen's face before Rinzen could hide it.

Rinzen held up the hand. "It is an old ring," he said.

Li Du met the other man's eyes. "And if I ask the Chhöshe, who has traveled with you for some months, whether the ring was black a week ago, what will he say?"

Rinzen was silent.

"You touched the water of the hot springs," Li Du said. He searched the wizened features for the thoughts behind them, but Rinzen's eyes mirrored Li Du's own. They moved infinitesimally in wary inquiry over Li Du's face.

Rinzen tucked his hand slowly back into his sleeve. He looked behind him at the open gate of the manor, then down to Yeshe's cabin and beyond to the Khampa hut that was beginning to glow through the cracks in its beams like a lantern in the twilight. "Yes," he said, in a voice just loud enough for Li Du to hear. "I was there."

"Did you kill Dhamo?"

"Dhamo killed himself."

Li Du gave a brief shake of his head. To

Rinzen's credit, he did not attempt another denial. His shoulders lifted in a sigh Li Du could not hear. "I did not kill him."

"But someone did?"

"I do not know the answer to that question." The creak of a shutter above them made Rinzen pause and look behind him at the outer wall of the manor. His eyes lifted to the overhanging second story and its painted rills and layers, but there was no sign or sound of movement there. Rinzen turned back to Li Du. "It is not safe to talk here."

"Why is it not safe?"

There was another creak, this one from the heavy door to the manor. They both turned to see Kamala, the wind pulling her skirt into whirling dark shapes around her ankles. She cupped her hands around her mouth and spoke, but they could not hear her words over the wind.

"She is calling us to dinner," Li Du said. "Why were you at the hot springs? What do you know of Dhamo's death?"

"I cannot tell you here. We cannot be seen speaking in this furtive way. Even that is not safe. Come to my room after dinner. I will tell what I know." Observing Li Du's wariness, Rinzen came closer to him and spoke in an urgent, low voice. "We are both

299

men of empires," he said. "You know the danger of secrets, secrets that are kept, and secrets that are not kept. You must understand my hesitation in speaking to you at all. But I will confide in you because I sense that you are a man to be trusted."

Li Du turned around. Kamala still stood at the door, waiting for them. He turned back to Rinzen. "I want to understand what happened."

"You have my word," said Rinzen. "I will tell you all that I know."

CHAPTER 19

"I can tell you the names of my forefathers from the time of King Trisong Detsen, who made my family noble." Doso raised himself up off his seat and refilled cups around the hearth. The manor's guests were all there, with the exception of the Chhöshe, whose duties were to the mountain temple and the dead man inside it.

"The first patriarch of my family was called Kalsang Samten. He was a laborer without status or land. When he was a young man, the king traveled to the borderlands to visit the temples he had ordered to be built." Doso looked at Li Du. "You know of Trisong Detsen? He was a very great king."

Li Du nodded distractedly. *The Testament of Ba,* he thought vaguely, picturing the room of histories in the Beijing library. Trisong Detsen had taken Chang-an, the capital of Tang China. But that was more than a thousand years ago. Li Du's fingers tensed around his bowl and he wondered if Doso intended to recount, for a second time, a thousand years of family history while his guests sat around the fire.

"Kalsang Samten was among those who were charged with building a hearth for the king's camp. This was no rough caravan camp, but a king's camp, you understand."

Li Du looked across the fire at Rinzen, who was listening with apparent attentiveness. He started slightly as Sonam called out for the men in the room to empty their cups. Li Du turned and saw Sonam drain his full cup and set it down with a grunt of appreciation.

Doso drained his own cup and went on. "My ancestor searched the forest and came upon a stone that he recognized immediately as a stone that would bring good fortune and protection to the hearth. But that stone had rested for many years in its place. It was half buried in the earth, and as heavy as a full-grown man. But Kalsang Samten required no assistance to lift it. He carried it to the place where the hearth was to be built and set it down there. The king was watching. He said that he had never witnessed such a feat of strength before, and was so impressed that he granted my ancestor Kalsang Samten nobility at that moment. The sons of our house have always possessed superior physical strength."

Li Du glanced at Pema. The young man was staring down at his bowl, his shoulders curved over it. The scar on his cheek reflected the firelight differently than the skin around it, its smooth surface emitting a waxy gleam.

Sonam leaned forward and filled the cups once again. He was smiling, seeming to enjoy the way the turquoise and silver beads in his hair clicked when he moved and drew annoyed glares from Doso. Sonam turned to Sera-tsering, but her attention was elsewhere. There was a crease between her eyebrows, and she drummed her fingers against her cup. Her own wild hair twisted and tangled like a mansion built for tiny spirits, the braids like hidden staircases twining along inky paths.

Doso began again, seemingly unaware of the rising sense of anxiety and impatience around the hearth. "There was a time," he said, "when the family had troubles. That was three generations after Kalsang Samten. At that time, my ancestor Samten Lobsang was killed in a bandit raid, leaving only a widow and an infant son. The family was so weakened that the land was to be returned to the king. But my widow ancestor was a strong woman, and she cared for the land alone in her husband's name for many years until her son was old enough to become lord. My family has been very fortunate."

Paolo Campo sat uncomfortably at the table where Sera and Hamza had set the game pieces earlier. He watched the fire. Several times he started up as if to take a place in the circle, but he seemed intimidated by the space crowded with outstretched boots and serving bowls. He dipped his bread morosely into his stew, only half attentive to Andruk's fluid translations of the conversations around them.

"But we have heard little of your history," said Doso. Li Du looked up, startled. Doso was talking to him.

"I — I am also from an old family."

Doso nodded. "I know you are a noble in the court of the Chinese Emperor. But how did you come to be a librarian? Have your fathers kept the books of the Emperor for many generations?"

"They have not," Li Du said. He paused, hoping he would not be expected to offer more. But he was aware of the people around the fire shifting their focus to him. *Naturally,* he thought. *They attend to the one who does not wish to speak.*

Doso, apparently unaware of Li Du's impatience, leaned forward and refilled Li Du's cup, then his own. He gestured for Li Du to continue.

"My father was a calligrapher," Li Du said. "But my ancestors have traditionally been magistrates."

"Magistrates?" Doso looked impressed. "The position of magistrate is a highly coveted one in your land."

"Yes," Li Du said. "But —" He hesitated. "But you were about to speak of this house. Which of your ancestors oversaw its construction?"

Doso raised his cup to Li Du and bowed his head, pleased. "I will tell you," he said, "of how the location was chosen."

Outside it was growing dark. As Doso's voice droned on, Li Du waited, restless and uneasy, for the meal to end. Li Du and Hamza entered the tower and climbed the dark, narrow staircase to the second floor. The doors to Paolo Campo's and Andruk's rooms lay somewhere to their left amid the leaning, irregular stacks of Campo's possessions. From inside Campo's room came the sound of pacing footsteps.

Rinzen's room was to their right at the end of the hallway. It was an elegant chamber, luxuriously decorated. The walls were adorned with a border of painted blue flowers. Embroidered silk pillows and lacquered wood gleamed in the candlelight. In contrast to Campo's congeries of bags and boxes, Rinzen's baggage comprised a uniform collection of walnut-hued satchels neatly arranged beside the bed.

Rinzen was seated at a desk preparing ink. His sleeve of deep yellow silk was pushed up his arm, exposing a thin, veined wrist. Li Du could easily picture him among the courtiers in Beijing. In that setting he would be an elegant, serious dignitary carrying a petition from Lhasa, indistinguishable from all the other elegant, serious dignitaries carrying petitions.

With a nod at Li Du and a frown at Hamza, Rinzen stood up. He raised a finger to his mouth to indicate silence. From down the hallway they could hear the murmur of voices. Li Du recognized the cadences of Paolo Campo's Chinese, but the words were too faint to comprehend.

Rinzen picked up an unlit copper lantern. Then he crossed the room to a recess in the wall covered by a heavy silk curtain. He pulled the curtain aside, revealing a staircase leading upward. With a gesture for them to follow, he disappeared into the darkness. After quickly exchanging glances, Li Du

306

and Hamza went after him.

The staircase led to a third floor, then to a fourth — a single, spacious room beneath the tower's roof. Rinzen set the copper lantern down on the table. He lit a pine taper, the light of which fell weakly across assorted objects arranged haphazardly across the floor. Li Du surveyed the collection of broken saddles, barrels, strings of bells, and rusted weapons. This was the discarded excess of a wealthy household.

Rinzen placed the taper into the lantern. Around it spread a starlike pattern of light. Rinzen studied the lambent diamonds and triangles for a moment before he spoke. "I expected you to come alone," he said, lifting grave eyes to Li Du.

Li Du met his look. "Hamza has my complete trust."

Light flickered on Hamza's stern, sculpted features. His oiled beard and black eyes gleamed. He addressed Rinzen. "Under the circumstances, you must agree my friend would have been foolish to come here by himself."

With the barest incline of his head, Rinzen acknowledged Hamza's words. "I will not deny that I am a dangerous man," he said. "But I pose no threat to you."

Li Du took a moment to absorb this statement. "And what of Dhamo?"

Rinzen shook his head. "I did not kill him."

"But you know something about his death," said Li Du, his eyes still on Rinzen's face. "Something you have kept secret."

"I know nothing about his death," said Rinzen. "I did see him on that day, but I had good reason not to speak of it."

"And we have good reason to think that someone else will die if we do not uncover the truth," said Hamza.

Apprehension momentarily distorted Rinzen's poise. He looked suddenly older, more careworn. "Please understand my hesitation," he said. "It is against my instinct to speak openly, however inclined I am to trust you, of all people." The comment was addressed to Li Du.

"What do you mean?" Li Du was puzzled.

Rinzen's eyes moved to the dark stairway. He picked up the lantern and held it aloft, illuminating the passage. Satisfied that no one was there, he returned the lantern to the table. He drew in a deep breath and exhaled slowly. "I am inclined to trust you," he said, "because it is known, in the innermost circles, that your actions in service to the Kangxi Emperor not only earned you a pardon from your exile, but elevated you to a position of trusted confidant and advisor to the Celestial Dragon."

Standing in the dusty attic of a manor hidden on a mountain far from Beijing, Rinzen pronounced the Chinese Emperor's honorific in a tone filled with reverence. It was a voice from a different world. Li Du blinked. "How do you know who I am?"

"Word of your actions in Dayan has traveled through the networks."

Suddenly Li Du understood. "You are a spy," he said, reading affirmation in Rinzen's face as he pronounced the words. "You are a spy for the Kangxi Emperor."

Rinzen nodded. "I never thought I would meet you, the librarian about whom so much has been said. What assignment brings you to this insignificant place?"

Hamza interjected smoothly. "We cannot reveal the private words that passed between the scholar and the Emperor."

Rinzen lowered his voice to a whisper. "I occupy a position close to the throne of the king — of Lhazang Khan himself. If it was known that I serve the Kangxi —" Rinzen did not finish the sentence.

"But the Kangxi Emperor and Lhazang Khan are allies," said Li Du. "The Kangxi facilitated Lhazang Khan's rise to power in Lhasa."

Rinzen's eyes narrowed. "There is no need to test me. We both know that our Emperor has been positioning the pieces for many years. Lhasa is his manifest destiny, and he will acquire it. Lhazang Khan is a blunderer and a fool."

In the silence that followed, Hamza lit another taper. Holding it in one hand, he began to pass the index finger of his other hand absently through its flame. "A dangerous position," he said, "to be a spy in Lhasa, where the mosaic tiles are polished so bright that it is like a city of mirrors. There is always someone watching. I was once told by a blind magician that the walls of Lhasa are under an enchantment. They are empowered to listen, and to whisper their reports in cold stone voices to those who know the spells. The best way to keep a secret in Lhasa is to hope it goes unnoticed among all the other secrets."

Li Du thought of the words Rinzen had uttered on the previous day as the wind pulled the ashes from the fire. *An invisible force may be inferred from the movement of the objects it manipulates.* Was it the Kangxi's hand that had reached across an empire to crush the life of a lone monk?

He addressed Rinzen again. "How is this connected to the hot springs, and to the day

Dhamo died?"

Rinzen paused, appearing to gather his thoughts. "To explain to you why I needed to speak with Dhamo alone that day," he said, "I must explain to you why I am here." He watched Hamza place the fresh taper into the lantern. "There is a rumor moving through the trade routes," he said. "It is being spread by pilgrims and spies. They say that the monks of Litang, a place almost as remote and difficult to find as this one, have recognized a child."

"An incarnation?" Li Du's brow furrowed.

"The greatest incarnation. They are saying that they have recognized the seventh incarnation of the Dalai Lama."

Li Du did not immediately understand. "But there is a living Sixth Dalai Lama in Lhasa."

Rinzen nodded. "Lhazang Khan's puppet Dalai Lama. The deposed Sixth who came before may have flouted decorum, but the people were devoted to him. Most feel no loyalty toward his replacement. Many claim that the first Sixth was the true incarnation, betrayed and treacherously deposed."

Here Rinzen paused, and waited as if in expectation of a response.

Li Du spoke slowly, remembering Sera's account. "The deposed Sixth died during his journey to captivity in the Forbidden City. If he *was* the true Dalai Lama, then he has been reborn." Li Du raised his eyes to Rinzen's. "There is a Seventh."

Rinzen gave a single nod that was tense with repressed excitement. "I am on my way to Litang to investigate this rumor."

"And if it is true?" Li Du was still considering the implications.

"If the rumor is true," said Rinzen, "then whoever has control of the boy born in Litang will be the most powerful person in Tibet. So you understand that my mission must be accomplished in absolute secrecy." Rinzen's tone became more urgent. "Lhazang Khan and the Kangxi are not the only contenders for power in Lhasa. There are others. The Dzungar Mongols in the north want the city. They have not forgotten their humiliation when the Kangxi defeated Galdan. There are also the foreign monks and traders from the West, whose agenda remains mysterious. Every power has its own spies on these roads — each one looking for an advantage."

"And Dhamo was involved in these conspiracies?"

For an instant Rinzen did not seem to comprehend the question. Then he shook his head. "Litang lies on the same path that runs through this valley," he said. "When I heard that the Chhöshe intended to visit the place of his birth, I seized the opportunity to make the journey to Litang without raising suspicion. I have overseen the Chhöshe's progress for many years. It is natural that I would accompany him." He paused and drew in a deep breath. "After so many years, I admit that I had forgotten about Dhamo. It was only when we arrived here that I remembered his identification of the Chhöshe, and his visionary powers."

Li Du waited for Rinzen to continue.

"It occurred to me," said Rinzen, "that if I could speak to Dhamo, he might produce a new vision that would guide me when I arrived in Litang."

Li Du glanced at Hamza, but the storyteller's expression was shuttered. Li Du returned his attention to Rinzen. "Did you speak to Dhamo?"

Rinzen opened his hands palms upward and studied the wrinkles etched on them as if they held an answer. "Yes," he said. "On the day of his death. I did not want to speak to him at the temple where I might be overheard. I glimpsed him crossing the pasture toward the forest, and I saw a chance to speak to him alone."

"What happened then?"

"I joined him at the hot springs. I asked him questions. I asked him if he had dreamed of a child in Litang. But in the years since I had last seen him he had withdrawn more completely into his own mind. He would not speak to me. When I had said all I could to persuade him to help me, I left. And I swear to you — he was well when I left him."

Li Du was keenly aware of his own disappointment. "But you must have seen or heard something."

Rinzen raised his hands in a gesture of apology. "I did not. I was intent on my own errand. I noticed nothing unusual in the forest."

"You saw no one?"

"I saw the woman — the traveler — as I passed near a small hut amid the trees."

"Before you spoke to Dhamo, or after?"

"Before."

"When you heard that Dhamo was dead, did you believe that he had killed himself?"

Rinzen looked down at his hands again. "When I spoke to him at the hot springs, Dhamo was not behaving like a man about to perform such horror upon his own person." His gaze moved to the light that pooled across the table as if he was searching for a memory within it. "But as I have told you already, he had changed since last I saw him. Perhaps he was in the grip of madness, and I was simply unable to detect it."

The pine tapers were burning low in the lantern. The room was becoming darker. Rinzen spoke again. "And yet," he said, "when I heard what happened to the foreign monk, I became afraid. I do not know what danger threatens us here, but no one who travels these roads can be trusted." He paused. "For my safety," he said, "as well as for your own, I ask you to keep my secret."

Rinzen picked up the copper lamp, now barely lit. As he started down the stairs, he turned, already lost in darkness. "Do what you can to pursue the truth of Dhamo's death, if the truth is what you want, but I urge you to be careful. In my life, I have learned to recognize danger. There is something dark here, something that existed before we arrived, something in this house."

"Wait." Li Du spoke the word quietly, still sensing Rinzen's presence though he could no longer see him. "What is the meaning of the white mirror?"

The silence was so deep that for a moment Li Du thought Rinzen was gone. Then the darkness answered in Rinzen's voice. "I think it wisest to see it as a warning."

■ ■ ■ ■

"For a broker of information, he had little to offer on the matter of Dhamo's death." Hamza's voice was hushed. They stood in the barn beneath the guest rooms, toward the back wall, where the shadows were deepest. Across the courtyard, firelight still glowed through the windows of the kitchen. The animals, who did not seem to mind Hamza and Li Du's presence, shifted in the dark around them.

"Very little," agreed Li Du. "He seems preoccupied with his efforts on behalf of the Emperor." Li Du tried to imagine what it would be like to be the Kangxi's spy in Lhasa. For how many years had Rinzen served as the Emperor's eyes and ears in that city, seeking out faces the Kangxi would want to recognize and conversations the Kangxi would want to hear?

"True," said Hamza. "For him, visiting this valley is only an excuse to go to Litang."

"On a secret errand to find the Dalai Lama's seventh incarnation," said Li Du. He paused. "It is interesting," he said, "to contrast Sera's account with his. She allows for the possibility that the Dalai Lama who was deposed and sent to be imprisoned in

China did not die. If there are others who believe as she does, that the Sixth is still alive, they will not believe that the infant in Litang is his reincarnation."

"You are wise," said Hamza.

"Am I?" Li Du raised his eyebrows, unsure how he had earned the compliment.

Hamza nodded. "To speak of belief, not of truth. These games are won not by the king who knows the truth, but by the king who controls the currents of belief."

And kills those who resist, Li Du thought. His mind went to Lumo. She had watched monks in crimson and saffron robes slaughter her family. Could she have carved out her pain on a member of the brotherhood responsible for that cruelty? "We have not considered Lumo," he said.

Hamza tapped his fingers thoughtfully on the back of a mule. "That is true," he said. "We know that Sera was not in Lumo's hut all morning. That means we do not know what Lumo was doing. She might have slipped out and waited for Dhamo at the bridge."

Li Du thought it through, then shook his head. "The timing does not follow. If Rinzen glimpsed Sera returning to Lumo's hut, then Dhamo must have only just reached the hot springs. She and Lumo were together after that until they saw Dhamo's body."

"They say they were," said Hamza. "But we still do not know what secret Sera carries that led to someone shooting arrows at her."

"I doubt it was Lumo scrambling down from the boulder this afternoon carrying one of Doso's bows," said Li Du.

Hamza closed his eyes. "Perhaps she has inhuman strength," he muttered, then sighed. "What of all the others?"

Li Du drew in a breath. "Let us think again of the day Dhamo died. Kamala, Doso, and Andruk were at the village that morning, but they did not remain together while they were there. The village is not far from the manor or from the stream. Any one of them might have gone to the bridge. We must also consider Pema, who claims that he went into the forest to bring food to Lumo, then took the goats out to graze alone. The Chhöshe also was alone except for when you yourself saw him praying at the temple. As for Yeshe — he was with the children at the time of Dhamo's death. And with his infirmity, he could not have climbed the boulder to shoot at Sera or overcome Paolo Campo."

Hamza sighed. "Then there is Paolo

Campo. We don't know who tried to kill him or why he refuses to speak of it. Is it possible that he is also a spy?"

Above them, footsteps thumped across the hallway floor. Li Du lowered his voice almost to a whisper. "It seems unlikely."

"Likelihood," said Hamza, "has not been a reliable restriction on what has happened in this valley since the snow began to fall. I begin to wonder if it is I, and not you, who is better suited to explain all that has occurred."

Li Du drew himself up a little taller. "I have not found the answers yet, but I have not given up."

"Humble librarian, I have every confidence in your ability. You misunderstand. What I meant was that perhaps this problem cannot be solved by a scholar in search of the truth. You seek an answer within the confines of certain rules. What if those rules have been broken?"

Hamza's expression was impossible to read in the dark, but Li Du understood. "You are suggesting that spirits and demons and ghosts may be to blame after all."

"It is possible, scholar. They weave illusions. Perhaps a demon can renew silver that has been tarnished in the springs?"

"There was an impression of a fingertip in

the paint."

Hamza's reply was almost instant. "Or animate the hand of a dead man to paint his own flesh."

"I do not know whether such demons exist," Li Du said. "But what of the thangka that was stolen? And the paper that was burned in the courtyard fire? These are the actions of people."

Above them, a door scraped the floor as someone pulled it shut. Hamza sighed. "I once met a princess who was waiting for her husband to rescue her from the castle of a sorcerer. It was the fault of the husband that she was there at all. She had been cursed to appear as a frog in the day and a woman at night. Her husband thought he could cure her of the curse by tossing her frog's skin into the fire one night after she had cast it off. She was instantly transported to the castle of the sorcerer. I offered to rescue her myself, but she preferred to wait and give her husband the scolding he merited. And of course — she loved him. But we enjoyed a pleasant conversation under the orange trees. It was she who told me that the morning is wiser than the evening. When it is light again, we will renew our efforts."

■ ■ ■ ■

Beneath the heavy furs and wool blankets Li Du thrashed fitfully. His thoughts were broken shards. Memories, suspicions, and inconsistences chipped against each other. He saw the vaporous forest pools framed in earth and snow. The villagers thought that the water held dead souls.

He dreamed.

He was in the library, lingering over a volume of forgotten poems. Behind him, a book fell to the ground. He turned and saw a woman sitting in a chair. He did not recognize her. As he watched, the hue of her skin changed as if she was illuminated through colored glass, blue shifting to green, then to golden orange. Her silk robes were suspended around her on invisible currents in the air.

The woman raised her left hand, and Li Du saw that she held a mirror by its golden handle. Looped through her fingers was a blue scarf like a wisp of sky. He saw the library reflected in the round face of the mirror, its shelves warped and curved. Moving closer, he saw his own face beneath a hat that was not faded. He took another step toward her, and the reflection in the mirror vanished. Its surface was white.

As Li Du took a step back in surprise, the woman also began to change. Her living eyes became flat and still. The silk printed with flowers and shells ceased its eddying movement and froze. Li Du raised his hand and passed it in front of the mirror. He looked for his hand reflected in its surface, but it was not there. He shifted his eyes to his fingers. They began to fade, becoming insubstantial and ghostly before his eyes.

He heard a sound. Someone was outside the library. Someone was banging on the door. Li Du hurried to the entrance hall.

Shu was there. He stood at a shelf, brush and bowl in hand, applying jewelvine to a corner where a worm had been spotted earlier in the day. The banging became louder. Li Du's chest constricted. There was no rattle of steel, no murmur of voices, and yet he knew with certainty that it was not just one person outside.

Li Du's own words formed a litany in his mind. *The Emperor should not have . . . the Emperor was wrong to . . . perhaps the poet was right . . . policy in the south is wrong and cruel . . .* He looked at Shu, but he could not hear what his teacher was saying above the banging.

Regret squeezed his throat and chest. He

closed his eyes tightly, trying to undo time and unsay words. He opened the door. There were the soldiers, identical to each other in bright studded armor. He saw an order and a red seal. He heard the voice. *You are under arrest and will be tried for treason.*

But he was thrust aside like a stray dog as they strode past him. The words were not for him. *Shu Tong jian, you have conspired against the life of the Emperor. You will be imprisoned until your case can be heard.*

CHAPTER 20

Li Du woke up the next morning to a crash. It came from the room beside his own — Sonam's room. As he struggled into consciousness, he heard a clatter, followed by the metallic drone of rings or coins spinning across wood. This was accompanied by a string of unintelligible words. A door slammed. Footsteps vibrated the floor as someone strode away down the hall.

Li Du rose quickly and went to the kitchen, where he found Sonam sitting at the hearth tapping a booted toe against the floor. His fists were clenched. The muscles in his neck were taut.

Kamala handed Sonam a bowl of butter tea. He snatched it from her, spilling the steaming liquid, which sizzled on the hot mudstone of the hearth. With deft movements, Kamala took the bowl back and refilled it.

"Is something the matter?" The question

came from Doso, who was ensconced comfortably by the fire. He regarded Sonam
with patronizing concern.

"No," muttered Sonam. "It is nothing. I
am not feeling well."

"Perhaps you should not drink so much
liquor," said Doso. "The men in my family
are never felled by it, but we have always
enjoyed strong constitutions."

"Do not accuse me of being a drunken
fool," snapped Sonam. "I have journeyed
across deserts and through jungles. I have
survived blizzards and hurricanes. I have
killed those who would have killed me. Do
not call me a weak man."

Doso lifted his own bowl and drank. He
raised a hand and gestured for Li Du to join
them. His glance flitted to Sonam, then
back to Li Du. It held an apology.

"If you are uncomfortable in our house,"
said Kamala, handing him the full bowl,
"then perhaps you would prefer not to visit
us here so often."

"Peace, Kamala," said Doso. "He is our
guest."

Sonam sneered. "And it is your duty to be
hospitable," he said. "It has always been so
easy for you. You make your offerings and
you congratulate yourself. Your ancestors
are so impressed with you. But you are a

line of ignorant country men with yaks and barley. You bring your wife dull jewels from a provincial market. Soon I will be a rich man, and you will not be so complacent." Sonam drained his bowl and stood up. "The butter tastes rancid," he said. Then he swung his heavy coat over his shoulders and strode to the door.

When he had gone, Doso put another log on the fire and urged Li Du to take fresh bread from where it rested on a flat stone laid over the embers. "I apologize," he said. "Rude guests do no honor to anyone."

Li Du inclined his head and offered a murmured compliment on the bread. Kamala brought a bowl of fresh, creamy cheese.

Doso finished his butter tea. "The sky is lighter today and the air is warmer. I have sent Pema to the village. He will assess the depth of snow on the pass. You and your caravan will be happy, I think, to be on your way." He set down the empty bowl and stood up with a slight grimace. "Please take your time to eat," he said. "I have work to do."

Left alone with Kamala, Li Du sipped his tea and ate quietly, listening to the fire, the hushed voices of the children, and the steady drone of the old woman's spinning prayer wheel. Suddenly, an unfamiliar voice interrupted the ambient noise. It quavered and scratched like the sound of a bow drawn across a single-stringed fiddle. "Karma," said the old woman. "Karma, are you bringing more tea?"

Kamala sighed and moved over to the grandmother. She rested her hand lightly on the dark, woolen shoulder and bent to the old woman's ear. "I am not Karma," she said. "I am Kamala. Do you remember?"

Mara turned her head, apparently unsure of where the voice had come from. Then her cloudy eyes settled on Kamala. "Thank you," she said. "You keep my son's home well."

Kamala filled Mara's bowl and helped the old woman to cup her hands around it. Their fingers overlapped like new roots growing over old ones. Kamala released the bowl and moved to stand over the children, who were cleaning and peeling tubers that would be added to stew. She chastised the younger boy for splashing water from the bucket onto the floor. Then she sat down to tend the fire.

"Does Karma live in the village?" Li Du asked.

Kamala looked up, momentarily confused.

Then she shook her head. "Karma was Doso's first wife," she said.

"I did not know that was her name," said Li Du. "Doso mentioned her when he told me the story of how Pema was almost lost to a bear in the forest."

Kamala sat back on the bench and rested her elbows on her knees. Li Du realized that it was the first time he had seen her not engaged in a task. He also noted that, even resting, she was acutely aware of her surroundings. Every sound drew a part of her attention — the movements of the children, the thud of a door, the ring of a yak's bell. He watched her silently put each isolated disturbance into place, building in her mind a model of all that was happening in her home.

"It is a miracle that Pema survived," she said. She was silent for a long moment. "I worry that, at his birth, some mistake was made by the astrologer. He has never seemed to fit in to this household. He is always out alone. He asks to sleep in the barn with the animals. Odd events seem to happen around him."

"What kind of events?"

"Doso told you of the bear in the forest. But there was also the death of Karma."

"How did Karma die?"

Kamala did not answer immediately. Then she adjusted her sleeve, pushing it away from her wrist as she shifted a burning log. "She died in a fire nine years ago. It was a dry autumn. She was praying in the temple and fell asleep. The wind through an open window caught the flame and set the scarves around the altar on fire. The building burned."

"Karma died in the fire that burned down the mountain temple?"

"Yes." Kamala reached out her hand for Li Du's bowl. He handed it to her. She filled it, then stood and passed it back with a hand so steady that the liquid did not splash, but remained as still as the hardened glue in Dhamo's pot. Li Du accepted it with a nod, but kept silent, sensing that she would continue talking. She did.

"I did not know Karma. We came from different villages. But they told me she was a good mistress of this house until her little boy was taken away."

"The boy who was recognized as the Chhöshe."

Kamala nodded. "He was very young to be taken from his mother."

Li Du had seen a child tulku once before, only from a distance, leaving Gyalthang with an official escort. The boy had been tiny enough to fit in a basket on one side of a hornless white yak. The other side had been weighted with tea to keep the saddle balanced. The child had barely been discernible amid the feathers and bells.

Kamala sighed. "But you cannot change what is, and it is a great honor to the family. Still, for some mothers, the situation is different." She stood up and went to the corner of the kitchen where several empty water buckets waited. The three children stood up without being told. While the girl helped secure the infant to Kamala's back with an embroidered wool sling, the eldest boy picked up two buckets. His younger brother tried to pick up a bucket, but it was too big for him. He dragged it along the floor until Kamala straightened up, the baby cooing on her back, and took it from him.

Kamala and the children left the room in a tangle of wool and fur. Li Du had finished his tea and was about to go himself when he noticed that the steady drone of Mara's prayer wheel had stopped. He turned to look at her.

Mara stretched open one of her hands and curled her fingers, lengthened by long, yellow nails, over her palm. She repeated the gesture. Understanding it to be a summons,

Li Du shifted to the place beside her on the bench.

"Can I bring you something, grandmother?" he asked.

She nodded and pointed at one of the embroidered wool blankets in another corner of the room. Li Du brought it to her, then helped her arrange it around her shoulders. She held its edges, fingering the embroidery idly, tracing the petals and patterns.

Her lips moved in almost silent speech. Li Du leaned a little closer. "I am sorry, grandmother," he said. "I did not hear you."

She frowned, an expression that was hard to recognize amid the ridges and draperies of her face. She tried to speak, but no sound came from her lips. Sensing her frustration, Li Du said, "It is my fault. My hearing is not what it once was."

She relaxed slightly. Encouraged, he gave a self-deprecating smile. "You have all been quite patient with me. I know that I speak your language very poorly."

Her eyes moved to his, searching for mockery or impatience, and not finding it. She picked up her prayer wheel, but did not begin to spin it. Then she brought her head close to his, and he heard her words as she breathed them into his ear. A strand of white hair that had curled away from her forehead touched his cheek.

"The painting," she whispered. "It was the painting that killed Karma. There was something wrong with the painting."

CHAPTER 21

"The painting?" Hamza rubbed his forehead. "Which painting do we speak of now?" He and Li Du sat at the hearth in the caravan hut. They could hear the muleteers occupied with various tasks outside.

The fire shifted, sending smoke flecked with glowing sparks whirling toward Li Du. He coughed and moved sideways on the bench, brushing ash from his coat. "She did not say."

Hamza adjusted the logs, and the flame settled. He withdrew a long stick and, with a quick puff, extinguished the flame at its tip, leaving it black and smoking. "What were her precise words?"

Li Du concentrated. "She said, 'It was the painting that killed Karma. There was something wrong with the painting.'"

"I have heard of paintings coming to life," said Hamza. "They say the serpent spirits of an ancient school had a method of imbuing painted figures with magic to make them appear alive. Those who saw the paintings would carry on conversations with the painted people. But they were only illusions."

"Like Granny Liu and the mirror," Li Du murmured.

"Who is Granny Liu?"

Li Du smiled at the memory. "She is a character in a book who becomes lost in a grand mansion after drinking too much. She enters a room and, in looking for a door to get out, encounters a friend of hers. But the friend does not answer. Granny Liu does not realize that she is speaking to a mirror."

Hamza shuddered. "The poor woman."

"Most of the courtiers who read it considered it an amusing anecdote," said Li Du.

"But how terrible," said Hamza, "to be trapped in a room with no door and only a mirror containing a stranger who will not speak."

Li Du was about to dismiss Hamza's words, but after a moment's thought, he stopped himself, acknowledging the terror of the situation Hamza described. "Fortunately for Granny Liu," he said, "she realized that what she saw was not reality, but illusion. And once she understood that the object in front of her was a flat piece of glass, she perceived that its shape was very similar to a door."

"And was it a door?"

Li Du nodded. "Yes. She found a hidden spring to open it, and it led her into a secret passage."

"Ah," said Hamza, relieved. "That is a good start to a tale."

Li Du nodded. "But let us assume that we are not looking for a painting that came to life. We are left with the question of how a painting might kill someone, or, stated in a way that is perhaps more useful, how an old woman might come to *believe* that a painting killed someone."

"How did Doso's first wife die?"

"In the fire at the mountain temple. Kamala says that it was an accident. As for paintings, the fire that killed Karma was the same fire that destroyed the painting Dhamo made — his vision of how the Chhöshe's reincarnation would be recognized."

Hamza handed the charred stick to Li Du and brushed the grit from the flat surface of a rock embedded in the dirt floor. "Show me what this painting looked like."

Using the burnt end of the stick, Li Du began to reproduce the sketch Pema had made in the temple.

Hamza watched him. "I see you are not

an artist," he said.

"It is a rough approximation," replied Li Du, continuing to draw.

When he had finished, Hamza squinted down at the dark lines. "Those are the stairs set into the mountain," he said.

"Yes," replied Li Du. "In Pema's drawing, even the hollow tree was identifiable." He pointed.

"And the mountains behind the temple," said Hamza. "You have drawn this one in the shape of bird's wing even though you have never seen it. The sun was out on the day I arrived — I can confirm its shape."

Li Du lifted his shoulders. "We will never see the original painting. But Pema sketched his memory of it with a sure hand."

"Miraculous," said Hamza, "that Dhamo should paint with such accuracy a valley he had seen only in a vision." He pulled a handful of black and white pebbles from his pocket and began to drop them one at a time from one hand to another as he lapsed into silent reflection. Glancing at him, Li Du was struck again by the difficulty of guessing his age. Most people, thought Li Du, have clues to their lives written on their faces. It is possible to perceive age and, even if it cannot be interpreted, an implied unique trajectory of suffering and pleasure and relationship to the air and the food that has nourished them to their current state. With Hamza, this was not the case.

"Prophecies are a complicated business," said Hamza. "Some say that a person must be mad to make prophecies. Others say that the gift of prophecy makes a person mad."

Movement at the door made them both look up. Kalden stood in silhouette. His shadow, cast by bright sunshine, cut through the room.

"Have you seen Sonam?" Kalden's voice dropped to a murmur. "We have yet to complete our transaction."

"I saw him at the manor hearth not long after sunrise," Li Du said. "But I do not know where he is now."

Kalden grunted, impatient, and stepped away from the door. "If you see him, tell him that I am waiting for him here."

Outside the hut, the sky had changed. The clouds were breaking apart, revealing an expanse of blue. Beyond the pasture, the high mountain peaks were still obscured, but the sun was warm on Li Du's face.

He turned to Hamza. Kalden had reminded him of something else. "I heard Sonam in his room this morning. It sounded as if he was ransacking his own possessions. When I saw him at the hearth, it was obvious that he was infuriated."

Hamza raised his eyebrows. "Did he say what angered him?"

"No, but he treated Doso with more insolence than usual."

Hamza drew in a deep breath and let it out in a sigh. "You look like you had bad dreams. I remind you of what I said last night, scholar. Cursed paintings, haunted pools, enchantments. Consider that all these events are games of the mountains and clouds."

"Perhaps they are, but I cannot pose questions to the mountains or the clouds. I will visit Yeshe in his cabin. I want to ask him again about his quarrel with Sonam. Perhaps he will reveal something that he did not tell me before."

Yeshe's gruff, raspy voice bade him enter, and Li Du pushed open the door. Yeshe sat cross-legged among his buckets. Andruk stood with his back against the wall and his arms crossed over his chest.

Li Du glanced around the hut cluttered with worn blankets, buckets, and churns. It smelled of old butter and fresh milk. "Paolo Campo is not here?"

Andruk shook his head. "My employer has not asked for me today. I do not know where he is."

"It seems he is often on his own," said Li Du. "Is his command of the local language improving?"

Andruk's wide mouth stretched wider in a humorless smile. "No — the man can neither speak nor hear. He occupies himself with his maps and prayers. Each day he seems more content to pass the hours conversing in his own language with his own god."

"What of his determination to win converts?" Li Du asked.

"He has not given up on his efforts," said Andruk, with a glance at Yeshe. "But our visit to the village when we first arrived seemed to discourage him. He declared the villagers beyond saving, and did not want to return. In my opinion, the locals found it entertaining to provoke him."

"How did they provoke him?"

Andruk shrugged. "He does not like to hear what he calls superstitious stories about demons and ghosts in the forests and mountains. The villagers perceived his discomfort, and enjoyed watching his face change color as I translated their tales."

"Stories about the forests," said Li Du. "Then they must have told him about the hot springs."

Andruk was faintly surprised. "Yes," he said. "They told him. He replied that the fires of hell must heat the water."

Yeshe dipped his ladle into a bucket, pressing it gently down until it was submerged beneath a layer of curds. "So you came here looking for the foreigner?"

Li Du shook his head. "No," he said. "I came to speak to you."

"About what?"

Li Du had prepared his story on the way to Yeshe's hut. He took a seat on a bench across the hearth from Yeshe and leaned forward confidingly. "My friend the storyteller has business in Lhasa," he said, "and wishes to speed his travel. He is considering leaving the caravan and hiring Sonam as his guide."

The ladle slipped from Yeshe's hand and sank down into the bucket. He ignored it and looked up at Li Du. "Tell your friend that would be a foolish decision."

"I have told him," said Li Du. "To me it is clear that Sonam is untrustworthy. But Hamza insists that there is no reason to doubt him." Li Du lifted his eyes to Yeshe. "I witnessed your quarrel," he said. "Is there nothing you can tell me that would help me dissuade my friend?"

Yeshe grunted. "I'll tell you this — Sonam's a thief. He'll cut your friend's throat and be off with his silver and his fine clothes before they reach Bathang. I guarantee it."

"How do you know?"

Yeshe's lips compressed. He retrieved his ladle and wiped its handle on his sleeve. "My argument with him is my own business."

As he spoke, the light in the cabin changed. The seams in the walls were suddenly visible, and the dirt floor was striped with pale spears of sunshine. Li Du swiveled on the bench to look outside through the open door. The snow on the pasture glittered. The icicles that hung from the edge of Yeshe's roof were watery and had begun to drip, making holes in the snow beneath them.

He saw Doso crossing the pasture toward the manor, and a thought occurred to him. He turned back to Yeshe. "Could it have been Doso you saw the day Dhamo died?"

"Eh?" Yeshe cocked his head.

"The person you saw and did not recognize," said Li Du.

Yeshe chewed his lower lip. "I don't think it was Doso," he said. "I told you — it wasn't a coat I'd seen. It was a great, black coat with tufts at the shoulders. Haven't seen it before or since."

Li Du heard a quick intake of breath and turned to see Andruk hesitating, about to speak. "I also saw that person," Andruk said after a moment.

"But you don't know who it was?"

"No. I could not see the face or form."

Li Du addressed Yeshe. "You saw this person precede Dhamo," he said. Yeshe nodded. Li Du looked at Andruk. "Is that also what you saw?"

Andruk appeared to consider the question. "Must have been," he said. "I did not see Dhamo, but I saw the person in the dark coat go into the forest. I was on my way to the village."

"Was this before or after Paolo Campo came here?"

Yeshe answered. "Paolo Campo came later."

He and Andruk were both staring at Li Du. Yeshe was the first to speak. "What's this about?"

Li Du did his best to look tired and addled. "I confess that I have not been sleeping well," he said. "My friend the storyteller speaks to me of curses and ghosts, and now I am afraid when I see my own shadow —" He paused. "Or my own reflection in a mirror."

Andruk's expression was wary. "A mirror," he said. "Like the one that Dhamo painted on his body."

Li Du did not answer. Yeshe began to wring out a cloth, squeezing moisture from it with strong, sinewy hands. "Talking about death brings it closer," he said.

Andruk ignored Yeshe. His attention remained on Li Du. "Have you found the thangka that was missing?"

Li Du looked at Andruk, slightly startled. "How did you know about the missing thangka?"

"Your friend told me. I believe he intended to ask me if I had taken it. But he became distracted by an explanation of his own invention — he suggested it had folded itself into a tortoise and crawled into the forest to grant the wishes of birds."

Li Du remained serious. "Did you take it?"

"I did not," said Andruk. "What did it look like?"

"It was incomplete. The Chhöshe believes it was a wrathful incarnation of Manjusri."

Andruk stretched his fingers, cracked his knuckles, and lifted impatient eyes to the ceiling. "I do not like being trapped so long in this valley," he said.

Yeshe picked up one of his canes and gestured with it at Andruk. "You think it is bad for a few days. I am here through all the seasons of all the years. When my legs were well, snow never stopped me from crossing a pass when I wanted to cross it."

Li Du watched Yeshe hobble to the door and look out into the glaring sunshine. Beyond Yeshe, Li Du recognized Pema trudging through the snow, bundled in his gray and brown coat.

"That boy," said Yeshe. "He always has a defeated look to him. Where's he going?"

Li Du stood up and brushed the ash dust from his coat. "Doso sent him to the village to see if the path is clear."

Yeshe squinted. "Well," he said, "that isn't where he's going."

"What do you mean?"

"I mean that's not the way to the village."

"Is he going to the temple?"

Yeshe considered. "Might be, but he's not taking the quick way there. Seems to me he's heading toward the old landslide. It's impossible to get to the village that way."

Li Du looked out after Pema, who was almost lost among the trees. Murmuring a hasty excuse, Li Du set out after him.

CHAPTER 22

Pema's trail was easy to follow, but Li Du's progress was slowed by the melting snow. With every step, his boots broke through the icy surface and sank into slush. His coat and robes grew heavier as their hems soaked up water. Clumps of snow slid from bowed branches. Sun alternated with shadow as clouds skimmed restlessly across the sky.

He was behind the manor on a path he guessed ran roughly parallel to the stone stairs. To his left, he saw for the first time the rooftops of the village, but he was separated from it by a deep chasm. The footprints continued up, tracing the edge of the ravine. Li Du was so intent on searching the forest ahead of him for a glimpse of Pema that he did not immediately notice the additional footprints running roughly parallel to Pema's. When he did notice them, he stopped. Their edges were beginning to melt, but they were recent.

He increased his pace and soon caught sight of Pema standing in a dense thicket of rhododendron trees decorated with the last blossoms of the year, vivid pink against a background of snow and stone. Pema hesitated. Then he was gone.

Li Du struggled through the snow as fast as he could until he came to where the several sets of footprints converged at the edge of the ravine. The cliff across the chasm was a sheer wall. He inched forward carefully, with tiny steps, until he could see over the side. The wind pulled at his coat. He leaned forward as far as he dared.

Just below him, a narrow path, cleared of snow, sloped down to a ledge on the side of the cliff. Pema was standing on it, looking out over the precipice. The sun on his face was so bright that it erased the scar on his cheek.

Fearful of startling him, Li Du hesitated. But when he saw Pema move another step closer to the edge, he could not stop himself from calling out to him.

At the sound of Li Du's voice, Pema raised a hand, covered by the long sleeve of his cuff, to shade his eyes as he searched for the speaker. When he saw Li Du, he dropped his arm and scrambled up to join him.

"Did you already go inside?" he asked Li

Du, pointing behind him at the snowy ledge muddled with footprints.

Li Du's brow furrowed. "I do not know what you mean. I have only just come here."

Pema scanned the forest around them with nervous eyes. "Why did you follow me?"

Li Du was honest. "Because I saw you leave the manor as if you were carrying away a secret."

Pema turned hesitantly toward the platform cut in the face of the stone. "It is not really a secret. I don't think that you can call something a secret when it has no value. If you want to see it, I will show you."

Ignoring an instinct that warned him to be cautious, Li Du followed Pema down the ledge. As he clung to roots and scrubby branches to keep from falling, he was aware of the vast space surrounding him. Far below them in the ravine, an eagle glided silently, just ahead of its shadow on the face of the canyon wall.

They reached the ledge. A curtain of old dry vines fell across the cliff wall. Pema pulled them to one side and secured them in a wooden hook wedged in a crack in the rock. Light poured through, illuminating the inside of a cave. Pools of melted snow and mud reflected light up from its floor.

Pema stood to the side in silent invitation for Li Du to go in.

His first thought was that he had stepped into the nest of a bird from one of Hamza's tales. There was not a single patch of bare stone visible on the wall. Its surface was uninterrupted color. A pack of wolves ran silvery gray through an emerald field. A bear sat under a tree, its shoulders hunched over a beehive surrounded by flecks of yellow so bright Li Du could almost hear them buzzing. There were chipmunks and ravens and deer and foxes and a creature with a golden coat as pale as corn silk around a long, somber face. Birds swept the tips of their red and orange wings across the surface of a pond, sending ripples through a path of moonlight.

Teetering shelves were stacked with cracked pots and bowls filled with minerals and pigments just like the ones in Dhamo's studio. Glue strips hung from crags on the stone ceiling. Rolls of silk and parchment were stacked on top of each other.

"This is your work," Li Du said. "You used Dhamo's paints."

"I — yes. When I bought them, I always kept a little for myself. Not the expensive ones."

"And this cave?"

Pema reached out and touched a portion of the wall, tracing his finger around a rectangle of blue, then connecting one by one the stars surrounding it. "I used to come here with my brother," he said. "I have no memory of the day he left, but I remember playing here. We watched the ravens fly through the ravine and pretended that we could speak to them and that they could warn us of danger with their caws. After he left I came here alone. No one ever noticed."

"Dhamo did not know about your painting?"

Pema hesitated. "He might have known. He would not have given me paints if I had asked, but I do not think he would have cared about me taking them."

"That seems a contradiction."

"It is difficult to explain. Dhamo only cared about completing his commissions. When he was not painting, he was praying or meditating."

"You mean the commissions he received from pilgrims."

"Yes."

"He painted nothing else?"

"No. For him, the commissions were like —" Pema struggled for the right word. "— like commands."

"Commands from whom?"

"I don't know what I mean," said Pema, seeming frustrated. "Dhamo rarely spoke, but a few years ago at the harvest festival someone gave him wine to drink. He told me that night that the pilgrims were not pilgrims. He told me that they only pretended to be pilgrims, but that they were really bodhisattvas who knew spells to ward off demons. They needed a painter to paint their spells. That was his task. That was why he painted."

"Did he say anything more?"

"No. He never spoke of it again."

Li Du was silent, absorbing the information. He allowed his gaze to wander over the walls of the cave as he thought. "I have seen many paintings," he said. "I was a librarian in an emperor's library. Its walls were decorated with the works of the old masters, painters whose secrets will never be known and whose paintings will never be duplicated. Li Shan's *Wind and Snow in the Fir Pines* and Xia Gui's *Autumn Moon on Dongting Lake* greeted me every day when I was a student." He peered closer at the line of a doe's neck, which sloped down to meet the upturned nose of her fawn. "Seeing your painting is like looking at the old masters again. They did not paint on stone or in the sunlight through branches. They had never seen the golden beast that lives only in these mountains. Your work is exquisite. I have never seen its like before."

Pema touched the cold color on the wall closest to him. "When I come here, I feel as if I am far away from the valley, as if I have disappeared from it." His face became anxious and he glanced down at the wet, muddy floor. "But someone else has been here today."

Li Du felt suddenly cold. A cloud had covered the sun, and the back of the cave emanated a chill where the light had not touched it. "Does this cave continue deep into the mountain?" he asked.

Pema gestured toward the shadows. "It does not go far. There is an alcove there at the back, but water drips down the wall and it is cold and dark."

Li Du stepped deeper into the cave. He looked to the right and sensed more than saw the dark opening into another chamber. "Who do you think was here?"

"I — I don't know," said Pema. "Maybe it was the Chhöshe. The mountain temple is not far. Maybe he remembered. Or it could have been —" Pema didn't complete the sentence. Li Du heard the sharp clicks as Pema tried to strike a flint.

Li Du did not wait for Pema, but continued around a jutting outcrop of stone. Behind him, he heard the whisper and crack of flame catching pine needles. He stepped forward, deeper into the darkness, and paused. There was a presence in the back of the cave, a presence that was not as cold as the stone and the seeping water. He shivered and reached out, searching for the back wall. His fingers found nothing. He took a step and stumbled over something soft.

He heard Pema's step behind him. Torchlight poured over his shoulder and illuminated the back of the cave. Pema made a choking sound. The light danced wildly. Li Du saw the sheen of wet skin, eyes open and staring upward, lips slack and speckled with blood. A fan of black hair and turquoise beads spread over the shoulder and onto the darkly glistening floor. It was Sonam.

CHAPTER 23

Doso stood close to a group of grazing mules in the pasture just beside the manor. Even at a distance he was imposing, his physical power evident in his stance. The red tassels tied to the hilt of his knife were bright against his black coat.

He was aware of Li Du and Pema's approach. When he saw that they did not turn toward the manor gate, but continued down the slope in his direction, he strode to meet them.

"Is the way to the village open?" he asked Pema, with a curious look at Li Du.

"I — I did not go to the village," Pema said.

With a frown, Doso looked over their shoulders. "Our home is full of guests," he said. "You have responsibilities. I hoped you would bring the lama from the village to assist the Chhöshe at the temple, and the tanner's son to perform his service to the family and help Kamala in the house. This is an inconvenient time for you to disappear into the forest."

Li Du stepped forward. "Sonam is dead."

Doso swung to face Li Du. His look changed to one of complete incomprehension.

"We found Sonam's body," said Li Du. "He was murdered."

Doso raised his eyes again to look in the direction from which they had come. "You are saying," he said slowly, "that Sonam has been killed."

"Yes," said Li Du. "He was stabbed. His body lies in a cave in the ravine."

"Stabbed? But that is —" Doso paused. "What is this cave?"

Pema tried to meet Doso's eyes, but his own fell. "It is the cave where I used to play with Tashi," he said. "I — I don't know why my uncle went there." He turned to Li Du, as if it was easier to speak to him.

"I showed it to my uncle yesterday," he explained, haltingly. "I — I hoped that I could persuade him to take me with him if he thought someone might pay him for my paintings. But he — he laughed at me. I didn't think he would go back there. I —" Pema stammered into silence.

Doso appeared to be struggling to master

his emotions. "An angry ghost," he said in a hoarse voice. "Only a malevolent spirit can have inspired two violent deaths, one so close upon the other." As he spoke, he pulled a loop of black prayer beads from his wrist and began to shift the beads one by one along the string between his thumb and forefinger.

"Whatever power might have guided the blade," said Li Du, "it was a human hand that dealt the blow."

Doso's arm dropped to his side, but his fingers continued to count the beads. "You speak as if you have specific knowledge of what has occurred," he said.

"I do not know who killed Sonam," Li Du said. "But since the night I returned from Lumo's cabin, I have known that Dhamo did not kill himself."

Li Du explained how he had deduced that Dhamo had gone to the hot springs to collect cinnabar and been attacked and killed on the bridge. He repeated Campo's original account of being pushed from the escarpment. Finally, he described his discovery that the thangka was missing. He said nothing of his conversation with Rinzen in the tower, of Kalden's deal with Sonam, or of the attack on Sera.

Doso listened, his face set like carved

stone. "Now you will tell me that Sonam's death was connected to Dhamo's."

"It must be," Li Du said.

Suppressed anger slowed Doso's voice. "This valley is not a haven for thieves and murderers. My ancestors have always offered protection and care to those in need of it. Now you tell me that someone I have welcomed into my home, someone who is even now within the manor walls, has killed two people."

With clenched fists, Doso directed his gaze again at the manor. "I cannot hold court in my home like some magistrate," he said. "I can only protect the innocent from harm."

Watching him, Li Du reflected that Doso had forged his surroundings with steadfast determination. He had fashioned himself in the likeness of the ancestors whose names and histories he so often recited, easy, unexciting histories. Nothing in Doso's construction of his own character had prepared him for this eventuality.

"I understand that you are in a difficult position," Li Du said.

Doso did not seem to have heard him. "The strangers in my home must leave," he said. "Whoever brought this contagion must take it away."

Li Du's eyes moved to the fortified, self-assured manor. "You will have to communicate what has happened."

The furrows in Doso's forehead deepened. "Yes," he said. "I will do it now."

Li Du turned to look at Pema, whose drawn face was pale and upset. Doso appeared to have forgotten the young man — his son, Li Du had to remind himself — entirely.

"Tomorrow the pass will be clear," said Doso. "Your caravan, and all the other travelers, will continue away from here. I will provide whatever food and supplies are needed to facilitate a hasty departure. You understand that I do not wish to be inhospitable. But I see no other option. Tonight I will make offerings to appease the spirits and" — he looked up in the direction of the ravine — "to keep him from remaining here among us."

Li Du spoke quietly. "Sonam was rude to you this morning."

Doso shifted his broad shoulders. He stepped closer to Li Du, towering over him. "Sonam was a dishonorable man. It is no surprise that his end was violent. But his death has no connection to me, or to my family."

"And Dhamo?"

For an instant Li Du thought that Doso might strike him. "Dhamo may have occupied the mountain temple," said Doso in a strained voice. "But he was always a stranger here." He shifted his attention to Pema. "The animals are in your care now," he said, and without waiting for a response, strode away toward the 'manor gate.

Li Du watched him go. The tasseled prayer beads, black and silver, swung from his hand. Li Du's mind returned suddenly to the bridge. He pictured Dhamo, hands smeared with paint and blood, the string of prayer beads hanging on the tips of his fingers, bobbing on the water for an instant before the current pulled them away.

At the manor, it was Kamala who appeared to care most that death had visited the valley for a second time. She refused to participate in any discussion of how to move the body from the cave, or where to take it. Wild energy radiated from her as she gripped her children by the folds of cloth at their shoulders and napes, her fingers straining so tightly to hold them that it seemed to Li Du her whole strength was concentrated in the rigid tendons of her hands. She took them to the kitchen hearth, leaving Doso to attend to his guests.

Li Du and Hamza slipped quietly away to Sonam's room. It was furnished with a bed, heavy furs, a copper brazier, and a shrine. Sonam's saddlebags were open, their contents scattered across the floor. Li Du knelt and picked up a coin. He recalled hearing the clatter of coins on the floor that morning through the walls separating their rooms.

Hamza leaned against a wall and crossed his arms over his chest. "A painter dies with a mirror painted on his chest," he said. "And a thief dies in a painted cave. This is too much paint. What is the meaning of it?"

"I do not know the meaning of the paint," Li Du replied. "But I know why Sonam is dead."

Hamza stepped forward from the wall and reached for the coin. "This is an Indian rupee," he said. "Accepted in most of the trade route towns." He knelt beside Li Du and set the coin down. "Why is Sonam dead?"

"Because he knew who killed Dhamo."

Hamza raised his eyebrows. "Did he? How?"

Li Du closed his eyes, silently chastising himself. "I realized it when I saw Doso counting his prayer beads, but I should have seen it earlier. If I had, we might have stopped —" He paused. "We could have prevented his death."

Hamza placed a hand on Li Du's shoulder. "I do not understand your words, scholar," he said. "How did Sonam discover the identity of the killer when he spent all of his time insulting the mistress of the house, taunting his nephew, drinking his host's wine, and making crooked deals with our own caravan? He was not interested in looking for Dhamo's murderer."

"He did not have to look. He saw the murder happen."

Hamza picked up a leather pouch and began to loosen its ties. "But Sonam crossed the pass in the storm. By the time he arrived at the manor, Dhamo's body was already up at the temple."

Li Du shook his head. "Sonam lied. He crossed the pass hours earlier. I propose that he was in the forest. Do you remember what we saw when we investigated the scene of Campo's fall?"

"The bridge," said Hamza. "We could see the bridge."

"Yes," said Li Du. "There was a clear view of it. If Sonam was there, about to descend to the bridge himself, he would have seen Dhamo's killer. He would have seen everything. He did see everything."

"I do not understand," said Hamza. "How

can you be sure?"

"The prayer beads," replied Li Du. "When I spoke with Sonam about Dhamo's death, he described Dhamo's body. Most of what he said was the same as what everyone at the manor knew. The bridge, the torn robes, the paint, the wound that appeared self-inflicted . . . But Sonam included another detail in his description. He said that when Dhamo died, he was clutching his prayer beads."

"Ah," said Hamza. "A man who expects to die alone pays close attention to others who die alone. It is not surprising that Sonam mentioned the beads."

"It *is* surprising," said Li Du, "because Sonam received his description of the body from Doso, and Doso did not see the prayer beads. I saw them slip from Dhamo's fingers and be swept away by the current. Doso, the Chhöshe, Pema, Sera . . . no one who saw the body *after* we did can have known about the beads."

A crease appeared between Hamza's brows. "Then Sonam saw the body before you did."

Li Du nodded. "He witnessed the murder, then waited to observe what followed. He saw our caravan arrive. He saw Doso and Kalden return. He saw the body taken away.

Only then did he descend to the clearing and climb the pasture to the manor."

Hamza raised a hand. "If he saw everything that you say, he would have seen the beads fall from Dhamo's hand. He would not have been so foolish as to mention them to you."

"No, by that time, the snow was coming down heavily. It would have been impossible for him to discern that the beads were gone."

Hamza's hand remained raised, silencing Li Du while he considered what he had been told. "If all of that is true," he said finally, lowering his hand, "then why did Sonam not reveal the murderer's identity?"

"Because he realized that he could benefit from what he had seen."

Understanding dawned on Hamza's face. "He threatened the killer."

"Yes. And I think they met in the cave this morning."

"And instead of being paid," said Hamza, "Sonam was killed." He looked thoughtful. "It would have been easier and less of a risk to pay him to keep the secret."

Li Du shook his head. "I do not think anyone would trust Sonam to keep a secret."

Hamza raised an eyebrow. "Now you know the thoughts of a killer?"

362

"If I knew the killer's thoughts, I would know the killer's identity."

Hamza reached into the leather pouch and pulled out a long necklace of coral beads. He set it on the floor, reached in again, and withdrew a diaphanous silk scarf, golden as the inside of a plum. "You remember what I said to you when you arrived? I said that a traveler usually brings gifts. Trinkets and baubles — that is what traveling traders carry. He hoped to seduce women with these treasures."

Li Du scanned the little collection. There was something desolate about the finery. The objects were scattered across the floor, chipped pieces of a fantasy of wealth. He looked at the jeweled brooch. The depth of its blue and green stones reminded him of the colors in Pema's cave.

"Sonam boasted that he could travel from here to Lhasa in a month," Li Du said. "He won't deliver a letter or guide anyone there again."

Hamza's look became reflective. "I met a witch once who loved a sailor. She had no patience with the time it took for their letters to cross great distances, so she gave him an enchanted book and kept its twin. When she wrote in the pages of her book, the words appeared in the pages of his. It was a good idea, but it was not so good for him when he gave the book to —" Hamza stopped. "Wait," he said. "Where are the receipts?"

They had examined everything in the room. "They are not here," Li Du said.

Hamza looked puzzled. "They must be. Kalden said that Sonam hadn't given them to him yet."

Li Du raised his eyes to the door, where a figure now stood, watching them quietly. "The papers are not here," he said, "because someone took them."

Hamza's back was to the door. He frowned at Li Du. "But who took them?"

Li Du lifted his eyes over Hamza's shoulder to the door. "She did."

Hamza stood up and turned to see Seratsering step inside and pull the door closed behind her. She was looking at Li Du with open curiosity.

"Why did you —" Hamza started to speak, then stopped. He directed an accusatory look at Li Du. "Who is —" He stopped again and addressed Sera directly. "Who are you?"

Sera's eyes rested on Li Du. "Do you have the answer to his question?"

Li Du stood up and bowed his head in polite deference. "You are a tax official working under the auspices of the Board of Revenue, and you have come here as part of your investigation into forged tax receipts."

Hamza looked from Li Du to Sera. "The Board of Revenue? But that is an office of the Chinese imperial — you are an official appointed by the Kangxi Emperor?"

"No, but my husband was."

"Your husband?"

"I am the widow of the man who received that appointment." Sera addressed Li Du. "How did you know?"

"I apologize for the intrusion," he said, "but while you were searching my room for illegal receipts, I was searching yours for evidence that might have led me to Dhamo's murderer. I saw the seal that you carry with you — the seal of a noble family of my own empire."

Sera's serious expression warmed into a smile. "You cannot have guessed all that about me because of a seal," she said. "I did not find out anything about you from your room except that you value books."

"It was not only the seal," said Li Du. "I noticed your interest in the caravan when you came to purchase tea. Later, Yeshe mentioned to me that a tax inspector died some years ago in Bathang. And when Doso regaled us with his family history, including his ancestor who assumed responsibility for the manor and the village after her husband's death, I thought perhaps —"

Sera finished his sentence. "Perhaps there was another woman nearby who had taken up her husband's duty."

"The pieces fit together," said Li Du. "I was correct?"

"Yes," Sera said. "I am from Lhasa, as I told you, but I was married to the Chinese tax official in Bathang."

"It is not common for a woman to occupy such a position," said Li Du.

"No," Sera replied. "It is not. But rules are very flexible here in the borderlands. A woman who asserts herself can have more than she is commonly given reason to expect. I said that I would continue his work, and I showed myself capable of doing it. Until the ledgers began to contain discrepancies."

"And that is when you decided to search for the solution to the problem yourself."

"No one else could discover it. I left my secretary to run the office in Bathang, and I began to ask questions. My questions led me here."

"A moment, please." Hamza faced Sera. "You claim that you traveled here alone in pursuit of a criminal who had been selling falsified tax receipts to caravans. What did you plan to do? Challenge him to physical combat? Tie him up and throw him over your horse?"

Sera's face remained serious, but her eyes revealed her amusement. "I was not interested in the man who was selling the receipts —" She paused. "Until, of course, he sent two arrows in my direction."

"It was Sonam who tried to kill you," said Hamza.

"He was trying to frighten me," replied Sera. "He had guessed who I was." Sera glanced at Li Du, who nodded.

"Yes," Li Du said. "He saw you search my room, and he knew that you were asking questions about the caravan. Experienced criminals are adept at sensing when an officer of the law is near."

"He wanted to warn me away," Sera said. "But whatever doubt I had about who was here to meet Kalden left me when those arrows struck the woodpile. You don't need to spend much time with a man like Sonam before you know he is the type to shoot arrows at a woman collecting firewood."

"But I ask you again," demanded Hamza. "What were you going to do? Why didn't you announce to the household that Sonam was a criminal?"

"Like you," Sera said, "I did not know whom to trust. I knew that there was more happening here than petty thieving. I didn't know what else Sonam might have involved himself in."

"So you pursued a more subtle strategy," Li Du said.

She nodded. "As I said, I was not interested in the man selling the papers. I expect people like that to meet a violent end sooner or later." She paused, realizing the import of her words, then went on. "I was not even interested in the caravan buying the papers. What I wanted was the name of the official who had been bribed or threatened into placing his seal on them. Yesterday, after our game at the hearth, I snuck into this room and found the papers among his possessions. I have them now, and I know that it is the official called Fang Tong in Dajianlu who sealed them. I will ensure that he is removed from his position." She paused. "I should have guessed. My husband never liked him."

The gaze she then turned to Li Du was clear and focused. "I did not kill Sonam. Do you know who did?"

Li Du shook his head. "No. Not yet."

"But you intend to discover it?"

"I do."

Accepting his answer, Sera took a breath and drew her shoulders back. "That is reassuring. But I am concerned for Lumo, who lives alone in the forest. I want to bring her here, if I can persuade her to come."

Hamza stepped forward. "I will go with you."

"I do not need your protection," Sera said, and then softened. "But if the scholar can spare you, I will accept your company."

The manor's dark interior remained cold, unaware that the sun had come out. But outside, the snow was releasing its grip. Icicles dripped bright tears from the overhanging eaves into the courtyard. Islands of mud and grass expanded, flecked with blue and yellow gentians, autumn's flowers.

Paolo Campo was pacing through the mud in the courtyard. He took one of Li Du's hands and pressed it between his own. "Andruk told me what happened. Another man is dead. In a painted cave. It is a doorway to hell and it will swallow us all."

"It was not a doorway to hell," Li Du said. "Soon we will know the truth, and then we will be safe."

"Safe? How can you say that we are safe? We must leave this place. I will not die here and leave Brother Achille to travel alone. It is a terrible thing to be alone and so far from home. He will not know what has happened to me." Campo looked up at the sun and blinked as tears welled in his eyes. "I do not want to spend another night in this house."

Li Du looked down at the hands that gripped his own. Campo's fingers were bloodless white, the scar on his ring finger livid purple. "Perhaps we should go sit by the fire," Li Du said. "Your hands are very cold."

Paolo Campo nodded meekly. "Yes. Yes, they are very cold." He followed Li Du to the brazier and sank down onto one of the stools. Li Du sat across from him.

Li Du was aware of the group at the other side of the courtyard. Doso and Pema were saddling a mule to go to the cave, where they would remove the body and convey it to the mountain temple. The Chhöshe stood silently beside Rinzen, who was watching the preparations. Li Du could not see his expression. Now that the snow was melting and the manor's painted exterior walls were more visible, the contrast between Rinzen's yellow silk and his surroundings was less stark than it had been when the snow had made everything white.

Li Du drew a small package from his pocket. He ascertained that the kettle on the brazier was full of boiling water. Then he opened the package, careful not to lose a single leaf.

"I — I do not need tea," said Campo. "One must deny oneself comforts."

Li Du picked up a bowl resting beside the brazier and rinsed it with water from the kettle. "This is my own personal supply of tea," he said. "Are you sure that you do not wish to try it?"

Campo leaned forward and sniffed the leaves. His face brightened. "Brother Achille di Spiritu and I drank tea in Kathmandu that exuded this same sweet fragrance. In that case, I will for an instant indulge."

Li Du rinsed the dust from the leaves. His slow movements appeared to have a calming effect on Campo. When he handed Campo a bowl of pale green dragonwell tea, Campo took it and clutched it as he had clutched Li Du's hand. For a few moments, his whole body curved around its warmth. Then he looked up.

"I cannot stop thinking about the mirror," he said in a ragged whisper. "It is like the snow, the endless snow filling the air around us."

"Do you speak of storms on the mountain?"

Campo nodded. "Of storms, yes." His gaze became distant. "Did I tell you of the mule?"

Li Du was puzzled. "I do not think so."

"We lost a mule," said Campo. "Not long before we came to Zogong. The snow was deep. Our path lay along the side of the mountain, which sloped at an angle so extreme that I had only to reach out with my right hand to touch the mountain above me." Campo extended his arm. A drop of water from a melting icicle struck his open palm, and he pulled his hand away, tucking his arm against his body. "But below . . . The wind fell down onto us, dragging our packs and our clothes. Ahead of me through the snow I saw — I saw the mule slip. It began to tumble. There was no power in earth or heaven that could stop its fall. We heard the pots — the pots it carried, clinking and crashing. And then it was gone. The next day we searched but could not find the animal."

Paolo Campo looked fevered. In spite of the cold there was a sheen of sweat on his forehead and his eyes were like green glass. He blinked, and Li Du saw the memory vanish. Campo's look became urgent. "Who is the murderer among us?"

"I do not yet know," Li Du said. He waited for Campo to take a sip of tea before he spoke again. "Andruk said that he did not see you this morning. Were you here at the manor?"

Campo straightened. "I? Why do you want to know where I was?"

Li Du's voice was gentle. "I hoped you might have seen something that could help us discover the truth. Did you see anyone go that way?" He pointed in the direction of the ravine.

Campo twisted around. "No — I couldn't have seen anyone. I have been in the temple here at the manor all morning." He nodded toward it.

Li Du looked across the courtyard at the little building with the incense cauldron in front of it. "Why were you there?"

"It is essential to study the shrines of the infidel," said Campo. "I seek ways to convert them into houses of God."

"Was there anyone else there in the temple with you?"

Campo shivered. "The mistress of the house came to pray and to light the flames. She blew them out when she left — to leave them burning risks fire. She did not see me, and I was left alone in the dark."

Campo's eyes moved down to his own hands, and he twisted his fingers together. "At home," he said, "I lived in a monastery. During the day the sun was warm and I could smell the sea in the air that whispered gently through the boxwoods." He looked at Li Du as if there was nothing more important than for Li Du to see what he saw and hear what he heard.

"At night we woke in the dark to pray together, and the sound of our prayers was like the candle flame that lit the dark places. In our reverence we sang together as if we were one soul offering itself to the Lord, and for a moment we joined the angels in their heavenly chorus. There was no loneliness. There was no fear. Our weak bodies that suffered cold and fatigue were gone, and our whole selves were expressed as one."

Campo sighed. "When I hear the monks of this land sing together, I envy them. They are as we were." His face hardened. "But the notes they sing are out of tune. And the sound of those terrible horns is like that of a creature rising from the dark flames to destroy the world." Campo stopped. He seemed utterly depleted.

Li Du spoke softly. "I must ask you once more," he said, "to tell me what happened to you on the precipice."

Campo stammered. "I — I have told you everything. There is nothing else to tell."

Li Du exhaled in frustration. "I cannot help you if you do not confide in me."

Campo's eyes widened. "You — you wish to help me?"

Li Du nodded. For a moment Campo looked as if he would relent. Moments passed, but he said nothing.

"I will ask you a different question," said Li Du. "On the day Dhamo died, did you see someone in a black coat tufted at the shoulders?"

The effect of Li Du's words was instant. Campo's pallor became ghastly. He stood up, knocking the stool over behind him. "No," he said. "I did not see him. Please do not ask me any more questions. I beg you to leave me alone."

Li Du looked up and saw Rinzen and Andruk crossing the courtyard toward them. Rinzen's brows were drawn close together in his grooved forehead. As Li Du met Rinzen's eyes, he asked a silent question with his own. Rinzen responded with an almost imperceptible shake of his head and lift of his shoulders, which Li Du interpreted to mean that Rinzen, despite who he was, had no privileged information to offer on the matter of Sonam's death.

Andruk, Li Du saw, carried a knife at his hip that had not been there before. The look he gave Li Du was taut with suspicion. He spoke curtly. "We have been told that you believed Dhamo was murdered, but that you told no one. Why did you give us no warning?"

Li Du met Andruk's gaze without flinching. "Because there was no one I could trust."

"A fair answer," said Andruk, taking Li Du by surprise. The nervous affect that Li Du remembered from the night of Dhamo's death had been replaced by alert self-assurance. Andruk twisted his neck to relieve the pressure in his bones. "None of us can trust the others now," he continued. "But the snow is melting and we are leaving tomorrow. As always, our host was solicitous, but he made his wishes clear. He wants our saddlebags packed and ready by the mules before dinner."

Rinzen looked over his shoulder. Pema and the Chhöshe were just leaving the manor gate, one on each side of the mule. Li Du glimpsed new white shrouds in the baskets strapped to its saddle. "Doso is not with them," he said.

"Doso's wife will not allow him to leave the manor," said Rinzen. "My sympathies are with the woman. We are all confused and afraid — all but the one who is guilty of these crimes. Some of us come from places visited more often by violence. In Lhasa, horrors coexist with splendor. But this place — this valley — is quiet and peaceful. We must hope the family can cleanse the land with offerings, and that by spring this will all be forgotten."

"Not forgotten," Andruk said.

Li Du looked at him. "What do you mean?"

"The pilgrims will still come for their paintings, but there will be no painter here to paint them."

"That is true," Rinzen agreed. "I will speak to the monasteries in Lhasa. Perhaps a new painter can be sent here to continue the temple's tradition — to replace what is lost."

Campo was still standing. He looked dazed. "Where will we go now?" he asked Andruk. "Are we a long journey from Zogong?"

Andruk frowned. "Not so far. If you are ready to return, then you need only command me to guide you there."

"Yes," said Campo quietly. "I wish to

rejoin Brother Achille. I will consult the maps."

"You should be preparing to go also," said Rinzen, turning to Li Du. "Your caravan has already begun to pack its mules."

"The caravan is leaving?"

"They say they will attempt the pass before the sun sets today," said Andruk.

Li Du stood up quickly. With a final look at the faces around him, he turned and hurried across the courtyard and out into the pasture, his feet splashing through puddles that sent sunlit drops of water sparkling around his boots like jewels.

CHAPTER 24

Li Du arrived at the caravan camp to find that the fire inside the hut had been extinguished, and a new one built outside. There were no pots or pans propped over its embers. Instead, it was piled high with juniper branches, which were sending up clouds of pungent smoke as they burned. The muleteers were rolling blankets and stacking saddlebags on the woodpile and on the roof of the hut, out of the mud, while the grazing mules sought out gaps in the snow.

"We're leaving today," said Kalden when he saw Li Du.

"But it is already afternoon."

Kalden's face was grim. "We may not get far before we camp for the night, but we're not staying here."

"You don't have what you came for."

Kalden tossed a pebble into the fire with a sharp flick of his wrist. It struck a weakened branch, which burst apart in a flurry of sparks and smoke. "I want nothing more to do with those papers," he said. "Or this place." He picked up another pebble and rubbed it between his thumb and forefinger. "I'd rather pay the taxes than carry bad fortune with us out of this valley."

"I am close to discovering the identity of the murderer," Li Du said. "If you will delay our departure until the morning, I can reveal the truth."

There was no change in Kalden's stony expression. "Someone else could die tonight," he said. "I will not risk the safety of my caravan."

Li Du squared his shoulders and faced the taller man. "I have traveled with you for some time. I have listened to the stories you and your muleteers tell. You have faced wild animals and whole companies of armed bandits. Surely you can face one more night in this valley."

Kalden stiffened. "We have no reason to stay. The murders have nothing to do with us."

With a shake of his head, Li Du persisted. "Sonam came here to meet you."

Anger tightened Kalden's face. "Do you accuse me of killing him?"

"Did you kill him?"

"No."

"But his business with you brought him here," Li Du said. "It led him to his death. You claim that you don't want to carry bad fortune with you out of this valley. I suggest that helping me catch the person who killed Sonam would do more to protect you than burning juniper or making offerings."

Li Du thought he perceived a glimmer of uncertainty in Kalden's youthful yet weathered features. That, in combination with the sounds of imminent departure — squeaks of leather and wood, shifting horses and jangling bells — inspired in Li Du a calm determination.

"If you will not wait for me," Li Du said, "then I will remain behind. I will catch up to you if I can."

Kalden cast an appraising look over Li Du's resolute expression, tattered clothes, and threadbare hat. "These mountains are not like the southern hills that you navigated with your guidebooks," he said. "Are you really so determined?"

"Yes."

Kalden let out a long exhale. "My brother would leave you," he said.

"You are not your brother."

Norbu approached through the billowing smoke. He carried a wooden saddle. "This needs adjusting," he said. "Is there time?"

There was a silence. Then Kalden turned to Norbu. "There is time," he said. "We are staying here tonight."

Norbu opened his mouth to protest, but Kalden silenced him with a look. "We leave in the morning," he said.

After only a brief hesitation, Norbu nodded, then began to bark orders at the others.

Kalden returned his attention to Li Du. "One more night," he said. "You will not delay us longer than that."

"I won't try to," Li Du replied.

"You misunderstand," said Kalden. "It is not up to you or to me. It seems the manor lord's welcome has finally ended — he wants all of us off his land at sunrise." He shifted his gaze to the manor. "You don't have many hours left to find your answer. I hope you are close to it."

Li Du watched three figures, indistinct through the smoke, detach themselves from the forest. He recognized Hamza's blue hat, and surmised that the two accompanying him were Sera and Lumo. Hamza raised a hand in greeting. Leaving the other two to continue directly to the manor, Hamza strode across the field and met Li Du not far from the fire.

"Lumo agreed to come," said Li Du.

Hamza nodded. "She scoffed at Sera's concern for her safety, but admitted she was curious to see the strangers about whom she'd been told. She says she knew Sonam by sight, and didn't like him."

Li Du gave Hamza an account of his conversations in the courtyard, and of Kalden's capitulation. As he concluded, he began to walk back in the direction of the manor through the golden-green stubs of barley poking out through the snow. He had taken only a few steps when he realized that Hamza was not with him. He turned around.

Hamza was standing still, apparently deep in thought.

"We should return to the manor," Li Du said. "There is not much time."

"You would have stayed behind," said Hamza. "You would have renounced the protection of the caravan and stayed alone in that dark manor to search for a murderer who would likely not hesitate to kill you?"

"Yes," said Li Du. He started to turn away, but Hamza spoke again.

"My friend," said Hamza. "I have never asked you why you did not accept the invitation of the Emperor to return to his court."

Li Du was startled. "It is no longer my home."

"And yet," said Hamza, "I know that you think of it. I see memories in your face. You return home in your mind as if you are opening boxes and looking at the treasures inside. Then you close them again. And you walk farther and farther away from them. Why?"

"I have told you why," Li Du answered. "I wish to travel."

"Travelers talk about where they came from," said Hamza. "You do not."

"I was exiled. I prefer not to talk about it."

"But you are not an exile anymore."

Li Du looked away. Beyond the forest, wisps of cloud rested on distant mountain peaks like parchments draped over string in the sunshine outside the library. He could almost hear the pages fluttering in the wind. He drew in a deep breath.

"There was a librarian in Beijing," he said. "A man of refinement and wisdom. He was my mentor and my closest friend. I was young and full of ideas about what was wrong with the empire. I thought my criticisms were very clever. Shu never chastised me, but he always defended the Emperor. He countered my vanity and my heedless irreverence with eloquence and patience."

Li Du paused. "Others were executed for voicing opinions far less subversive than my own, but I was arrogant, and I trusted Shu."

Li Du looked up. Hamza was scrutinizing his face. "And he betrayed you," said Hamza.

"No. I — I don't know what happened."

"You don't know?"

Withdrawing one hand from its long sleeve, Li Du rubbed the nape of his neck and addressed his words in the direction of the mountains. "One afternoon, six years ago, the door to the library opened and the Emperor's bannermen were there. I thought they had come to arrest me. I was — I was very afraid. But they were not there for me. They were there for Shu."

Hamza's eyes widened. "Why?"

"He was accused of conspiring against the Emperor," Li Du said. "I was convinced that there was a mistake. I knew he was loyal. But then he asked to see me, and he told me that the accusation was true." Li Du closed his eyes. "I didn't believe him. Irrefutable evidence was offered at his trial. I searched for a piece that was missing, but I found nothing." Li Du opened his eyes and stared unseeingly at the mountains. "And then he was gone."

"And you received a sentence of exile."

Li Du nodded. "Because of my close association with him."

There was a silence between them. Then Li Du spoke again. "My family renounced me, and my wife remarried years ago. The Emperor's pardon does not change that."

"And your wandering path brought you here," said Hamza, "to number among the motley congregation drawn to this valley cradled by stone. This was a place unused to travelers until fate drew all of us here. Only Dhamo's paintings journeyed as we have, across mountains and through forests, to be revered by earnest novices in distant monasteries."

Li Du did not answer.

Hamza, noticing his abstraction, peered at his face. "Librarian," he said. "What preoccupies you?"

"Flowers," answered Li Du.

Hamza's expression turned to concern. "I know that you Chinese scholars have inclinations toward poetry, but I am surprised that now, of all times, you should be inspired to composition."

Li Du smiled. He put his hand on his hat as a gust of wind threatened to blow it away, and began to walk in the direction of the manor. "I was just remembering something that Pema said."

"About flowers?"

Li Du nodded. "Yes," he said. "About wildflowers in the fields."

Kamala was at the hearth ladling circles of smooth batter onto a griddle that rested on a pile of coals. The soft white edges bubbled and began to turn gold. The younger of the two boys stood beside her — the other children were picking walnut meat from a bucket of cracked shells. Kamala's face was calm.

Hamza and Sera sat at the low table. Lumo sat at the hearth. Her shoulders were draped in a wool blanket. She looked uncomfortable, holding the edges of her blanket with her fingertips and shifting her gaze to and away from Kamala and the children. She glanced up up when Li Du came in.

"I am told that you found Sonam dead in a cave," she said. "That man was always walking toward a violent fate. My sister married one like him. He took up with bandits and did not meet a good end. Of course, neither did she."

Li Du saw Lumo's glance move again to the children. She let the blanket fall away from her shoulders. "You keep your kitchen very hot," she said to Kamala.

"I am sorry, grandmother," Kamala said. Li Du heard the forced patience in her voice. "Can I help you to the seat on the other side of Mara? The wind comes down through the eaves there and it is cooler."

Lumo shook her head. "I'll be back in my own place soon enough — where I can keep my own hearth." Her eyes slid to Mara. "She does not talk anymore?"

Mara was awake, but did not seem to hear Lumo. Kamala rose and went to her. "Can I bring you anything, grandmother?" Mara raised her fingers in a dismissive gesture, but said nothing.

"She speaks sometimes," said Kamala. "But not often these days."

"She said something to me," Li Du said. "I hoped that one among you would help me understand what she meant. She told me that Karma was killed by a painting. She said that there was something wrong with a painting." He looked to Lumo, who was staring into the fire. "I thought that she might have been speaking of the painting that Dhamo made in Lhasa thirteen years ago — the painting of the Fourth Chhöshe climbing the mountain stairs. You said you came to this valley fourteen years ago. Did you see that painting?"

"Of course I saw it. I climbed the stairs to the temple on the day the boy was recognized. It was a very grand occasion." Lumo's eyes, bright beneath papery eyelids, observed the memory. "The whole village was there — waiting and praying. We all saw the painting framed in silk and flowers. It was of a little boy carrying a basin of milk up the mountain stairs and offering it at the temple."

"What happened then?"

"It was just as in the painting. The boy — Tashi his name was then — came up the stairs, the mountains around him, the sun shining on him, and the basin of milk held steady in his strong little hands. He carried it very solemnly to the temple, and knelt, and made the offering. The same as the painting in every detail."

Lumo paused and became thoughtful. "Something wrong with the painting?" she mused. "Something wrong with the painting? No. I would have said there was something wrong with the family. Karma was very upset. There was a celebration — a great feast. The village spoke of how fortunate the family was. But Karma's face — I haven't forgotten it."

No one said anything. The only sounds in the room were the sizzle and flap of Kamala frying bread, the snapping of the fire, and the plink of walnut morsels tossed into a bowl.

Lumo sat back and drew the blanket back over her shoulders. "Doso, too. On that night, Doso drank barley wine until he could not walk without swaying like a pine tree in a storm. I was going home with my lantern, and I saw him — the manor lord. He was outside the wall, and he was holding a man by the throat. I heard him weeping and railing. I held up my light and I saw that the man there against the wall was a monk. It was Dhamo. I think if I had not come, Doso would have choked the life from him."

Li Du did not have a chance to reply before Kamala spoke. "My husband would never harm a religious man."

Lumo gave a snort. "Anyone can harm anyone else."

Li Du saw Kamala's hands shake. "Doso took you in when you fell to the ground on the path and would have died."

"He did," said Lumo. "But I won't grovel to him because of that. I fell because I was ready to fall. I'd left Kham with no purpose but to walk until I walked right into the next life. Now fourteen years have gone by and I am still alive. I am grateful to Doso, but that is not what I intended."

Kamala took a wooden plate from the shelf and put the flat cakes, now golden and crusted, one by one in a pile. "Doso is in the shrine making offerings to protect all of us."

She lifted the lid of the kettle. "There is just enough boiling water left for tea," she said, and stood up. She picked up two empty buckets. As Li Du had seen them do before, the children stood, huddled so close they looked as if they were attached to her skirts, and followed her out of the kitchen.

Li Du caught up to Kamala as she headed toward the stream behind the manor, the children now trailing after her like ducklings, the little girl carrying the infant. When he offered to carry the buckets, Kamala handed them to him wordlessly.

"I must ask you a question," he said.

"What question?"

"You have mentioned your visits to the market at Dajianlu. Are you always among the party that travels there from this valley?"

"Yes," she said. "I go as long as the children are well."

They had reached the stream. Li Du filled the buckets. "Were you with Pema when he took Dhamo's thangkas to Dajianlu?"

She nodded. "That was his task while I bargained on behalf of the manor."

"I know that very little escapes you," said Li Du. "And that you recall details others would forget. Did you hear Pema say where the thangkas were going? Did he tell you their destinations?"

Kamala blinked in surprise. "They were for monasteries."

"Do you remember their names?"

She appeared to consult her memory. "They were not familiar to me," she said. "But Pema asked me to help him remember." After a short silence, Kamala spoke three names. She searched Li Du's face as if she was trying to ascertain the meaning they held for him.

The words swept through Li Du's mind with a rush of color, fragrance, and sound. He saw an old mosaic with a tile missing in the dragon's tail, smelled fresh sweet rice wrapped in leaves for a festival, heard voices chattering in the accent of the north — monks debating scholars to the cheers of students who had escaped class to watch. He knew these places.

To Li Du they were part of the landscape of knowledge ingrained in his memory. He knew the monasteries. They were all within a day's journey of the Forbidden City.

CHAPTER 25

The courtyard was in shadow when Li Du climbed the stairs to Rinzen's apartments and found him pacing slowly in his room. Rinzen ushered him inside and closed the door. "What is the matter? I hope that there has been no further violence."

"There has not, but I have come to warn you."

"To warn me of what?" Rinzen's face was grave.

"I believe that you are in danger."

Rinzen pulled one of his hands out from his sleeve and indicated that Li Du should sit. "Of course I am in danger," he said. "I have told you already who I am, and what secret I carry."

"But you did not tell me everything." Li Du sat at the edge of the painted wooden chair. Rinzen sat opposite him.

"Of course not," Rinzen said. "We both serve the Emperor, but to share all the secrets I have would be —"

"That is not what I mean." Li Du drew in a deep breath. "I believe that you are on your way to Litang, as you say. I believe that there is a rumor of a seventh incarnation. And I believe that you went to the hot springs to speak to Dhamo of what he might know."

"Then on what point do you accuse me of withholding information?" Rinzen's eyes were focused intently on Li Du.

"On the point of why you thought Dhamo might help you. You were not interested in his visions. You were interested in what he might have learned from the spies whose messages to the Kangxi Emperor are encoded in Dhamo's paintings."

Rinzen did not answer immediately. To Li Du's surprise, he closed his eyes. For several moments, Rinzen's silent cogitation dominated the room. The force of it was so intense that Li Du felt his own thoughts become weak and confused.

Rinzen opened his eyes. He nodded. "It seems I must place more trust in you than I was initially prepared to do. You understand why I did not confide everything to you. Even with your reputation, I would have been foolish to say more than was necessary. But who told you of this?"

"I was not told."

Rinzen looked at the door. "We must speak quickly and quietly. Explain to me, please, how you came to know, and why you have come here now."

Li Du bowed his head and began to speak in a voice just above a whisper. "I did not know it until today, when I was reminded of my first conversation with Pema. When he spoke of Dhamo's paintings, he compared them to the wildflowers that grow in mountain meadows."

"I do not understand," Rinzen said, frowning. "Did Dhamo share secrets with him?"

"No," Li Du said. "Pema was telling me that he wanted to visit places he had never seen. He said that Dhamo's paintings offered no escape because, like the wildflowers, they were always the same. The same flowers every year, he said, only in different patterns. I did not realize at the time that Pema was describing a quality unique to Dhamo's paintings."

Li Du paused to gather his thoughts, noting Rinzen's impatience. He continued. "Today, Hamza happened to mention that Dhamo's paintings traveled to distant places. His words made me think again of what Pema had said. I considered Dhamo's paintings once more. I asked myself what they were — silk panels filled with symbols repeated in varying orders, commissioned by pilgrims, and sent to specific locations. As a librarian, I am not unfamiliar with codes. I have seen many of them before. It occurred to me that Dhamo's paintings might have contained hidden messages. The more I considered it, the more convinced of it I became.

"Dhamo's thangkas would not be intercepted and read and recorded as they traveled. They were gifts to monasteries — a sacrosanct delivery that even thieves on the road would honor, for fear of supernatural reprisal. I thought of what you told me — of the networks of spies that run through the trade routes between China and Lhasa. When I asked for the names of monasteries where thangkas were sent, they were all familiar to me. They are monasteries near the Kangxi's palaces."

"And this led you to me."

"Yes. Where there are codes, there are spies. You had admitted to me already that you are an agent for the Kangxi Emperor. You were also the person who brought Dhamo to this place. I think that you brought him here to be a hidden transcriber of secret reports. They were commissioned by spies who wished to convey their messages to the Emperor. He turned the messages into paintings and directed them to their destinations." Li Du hesitated, then concluded, "A lonely life — he must have been offered a great reward."

Admiration competed with concern on Rinzen's features. He bowed his head in a suggestion of deference, then raised it. "You are correct in all but one point. Dhamo was not, himself, a spy."

"What do you mean?"

"I mean that there was no pretense in his work. He was a gift to us, a man of visions, a devout man. He believed, and believed willingly, that the messengers who came and commissioned paintings from him were trying to seal the mountains and monasteries against demons. He was not given messages. He was given a sequence of symbols — that is all. Fulfilling their requests was what he desired to do. He wanted no other reward. He did great service to the Emperor for thirteen years without realizing it."

Li Du nodded his understanding. "Until someone killed him."

Rinzen raised a hand and pressed his fingers to his temples. Again, he squeezed his eyes shut as if in the effort of thought. Li Du wondered at the weight and volume of secrets in the man's mind. "Yes," said

Rinzen. "Someone killed him cruelly."

"And with his death," said Li Du, "this point of communication is silenced."

Rinzen nodded. "I do not think another such person could be found. There will have to be new strategies."

A sound at the far end of the hallway caused them both to look up. Rinzen leaned forward. His voice became urgent. "What danger threatens me?"

"I believe that someone else knows the true reason that Dhamo was here. There is someone here in the manor who wants your network destroyed."

Rinzen looked uncertain. "I have considered it," he said, "but are you sure? Dhamo lived here for many years. He could have made an enemy. This could have nothing to do with his paintings."

Li Du nodded. "Nothing is certain. But the thangka that Dhamo was painting — a thangka recently commissioned — is missing. I saw it on the morning after Dhamo's death. On the following day, it was gone. I suspect that whatever message it contained was something very important — something that would have been of value to the Kangxi Emperor."

Rinzen appeared dazed. "A thangka is missing? Why did you not tell me before? I had no idea that Dhamo had received a recent commission." His voice became a murmur. "Is it possible?" he said, half to himself.

Li Du leaned forward. "Is there someone you suspect?"

Rinzen's expression became wary. "I do not know if I can trust you," he said. "The circumstances are not what I thought them to be."

"You have already trusted me with the purpose of your journey to Litang. Please trust me also with your suspicions. I feel that I am close to the truth."

Rinzen did not answer immediately. Then he gave a single, stiff nod. "The foreigner," he said. "It has occurred to me that he is not what he pretends to be."

"Why do you think so?"

"Because of Zogong."

"I do not understand."

Rinzen dropped his voice to a whisper. "The foreigner, Paolo Campo, says that his friend is a guest of the lord in Zogong, who has expressed interested in converting to the Christian faith. You understand that in Lhasa I am apprised of all the personalities and leanings of the nobility. The lord of Zogong is a devout man. One of his younger sons was recognized as a tulku from a

400

wealthy lineage. He benefits from the income of an estate and a monastery. He would never propose to entertain a foreign faith. In the past, perhaps. There was a lord in Zogong who did show hospitality to Capuchins when last they traveled across the country. But that was almost a hundred years ago. Paolo Campo's story — it does not make sense."

Li Du listened until Rinzen had finished speaking. "I see," he said.

Rinzen studied him. "You appear not to agree with me."

"Paolo Campo certainly has a secret," said Li Du. "But I do not think it has anything to do with codes or empires."

"What, then?"

"On that," said Li Du, "I will keep my own counsel."

Rinzen's posture was suddenly weary. He looked frail and nervous. "I do not know," he said. "There is a knot here that I cannot untie. I hope you can find the truth, but I urge you not to forget what I said before. The white mirror is a warning. I am sure that it is."

The door to Yeshe's hut stood slightly open. Li Du announced himself and, after a short silence, was told to enter. Inside, Yeshe was

401

crouched beside the hearth, which was smoking. "Wet wood," he said. "All of it is wet." With his weight on his arms, he lowered his head and blew on the coals. They glowed red. Another breath, and the kindling burst into flame. Yeshe grunted in satisfaction, then coughed and pulled himself onto the cushioned bench.

"The water won't boil right away," Yeshe said. "Sit down, if you want."

Li Du remained standing. "Thank you, but I am on my way to the temple."

Yeshe did not quite meet Li Du's eyes. "You are going to make offerings for Sonam?"

"I want to discover who killed him."

Yeshe gestured in the direction of the caravan cabin. "I'd say it was one of your friends. He probably made some crooked deal. Disagreements happen."

"What of your disagreement with him?" asked Li Du. "Will you tell me now what it was?"

To Li Du's surprise, Yeshe laughed. "You think I killed him? It would have taken me a whole day to get to that ravine. I can't travel through a forest in the snow, not without everyone seeing me." He paused. "Our quarrel had nothing to do with his death."

Li Du's gaze moved around the hut, humble and warm, the table stacked neatly with fresh cheese and rounds of butter pressed carefully into shape. "Then I will tell you what you will not tell me. I think that Sonam knew you before you came to this valley."

Li Du saw the start in Yeshe's shoulders, but Yeshe did not look up from the fire. Li Du went on. "He knew you were not a peaceful farmworker set upon by thieves."

Yeshe's voice was low, almost a growl. His chin jutted forward. "You lie."

Li Du continued. "You knew that Sonam was a thief — you warned me of it. What he knew was that you were one also. You both kept bad company. Maybe the two of you rode together through the mountains. Sonam liked to taunt you with the truth, a truth that might have cut your relationship with a family you have grown to love."

"No," said Yeshe. "I deny it. Why do you accuse me of being anything different from what I have proclaimed myself to be? I am a cripple — I'm no threat to anyone."

"When I learned the nature of your injuries," Li Du said, "I was reminded of a sentence given to traitors in my own empire. Later, I heard Norbu describe certain bandits whose cruelest acts were reserved for their own as punishment for betrayal. Your wounds did not come from an attack on an innocent traveler. They were inflicted by your former companions. When Doso found you, you passed yourself off as a farmworker and received hospitality that would never have been offered to a thief."

Yeshe's fingers twitched in his lap. He clasped his hands together. "Please," he said, "this family is —" He paused, overcome. "Doso took me in, but Kamala is — she is —" He stopped, and Li Du read Yeshe's feelings clearly on his face.

Yeshe raised his eyes to meet Li Du's. "I would do anything for her and for her children. With my broken feet I cannot protect them, or this valley, as Doso can. But I would never bring harm to them."

Li Du nodded. "I believe you. And more than that, I defer to Kamala, who knows more than anyone what is dangerous to her family and what is not."

Yeshe's shoulders slumped. "Then you are not going to speak of this? Threaten to have me cast away?"

"No," Li Du said. "Your former life exists now in the stories of bandits and adventurers that so engross the children from the manor. I would encourage you perhaps to vary your dark tales on occasion, but I will not betray your secret."

With a deep exhale of breath, Yeshe let his head drop to his chest, temporarily overcome. When he looked up, he met Li Du's eyes directly. "I understand that you are determined to find Sonam's killer," he said. "Sonam was not a trustworthy man or a kind one, but I would help you if I could."

"Did you see him this morning?"

"Yes — I saw him. I assumed he was going to the village but had taken the wrong path to the ravine. I was not about to call out and assist him."

"And did you see anyone go that way before or after him?"

"No one," said Yeshe. "My door was closed. The next person I saw going that way was Pema, and you yourself followed."

The sun was setting and the forest was melting in rivulets of color. Free of snow, the stairs were a wet, living gray, veined with moss and lichen. When Li Du reached the prayer flags, he caught a glimpse of movement to his left. Descending from a higher path, Pema and the Chhöshe walked on either side of a mule, over which a wrapped body was loosely bound.

They stopped. The Chhöshe, a brilliant spot of red and yellow on the slope, walked around the front of the mule and dropped to his knees in front of Pema. His arms were raised, as if in supplication. Pema stepped backward away from him, shaking his head. Li Du could hear their voices, but he could not discern the words.

There was a clatter of displaced rocks as the mule stepped forward, shifting the weight of its burden. Slowly, the white-shrouded form began to slip. With a cry, Pema lunged for the body. As he struggled to keep it in place, the Chhöshe sprang up and moved to help him. Together, they lifted the slumped form back onto the mule. They resumed their progress, and reached the temple door at the same time as Li Du.

"I thought that your caravan was leaving," Pema said.

"Tomorrow morning."

Pema looked over Li Du's shoulder at the sinking sun. He raised a hand, casting a shadow like a mask over his eyes.

"Why have you come?" The Chhöshe's voice did not conceal his distrust. "We must take him into the temple."

"I know," Li Du said. "And I would not distract you from your task unless it was necessary that I speak with you. Let me help you carry him inside."

The Chhöshe hesitated. "You will forgive

me, scholar, but you are a stranger to this valley, and the circumstances of his death—"

"I cannot help you unless you place a small amount of trust in me."

"How would you help him?" The question came from Pema.

Li Du looked at them. The Chhöshe, broad-shouldered and confident, stood ready to act. Beside him, Pema trembled visibly.

"Because," Li Du said, raising his eyes to meet the Chhöshe's, "I can give you the answer to the question that drew you back to your home."

CHAPTER 26

As twilight fell, the wind grew stronger. It pushed at the temple wall and slipped through cracks, catching the butter lamp flames and sending them into frantic agitation.

Li Du sat facing Pema and the Chhöshe. "Since coming to this valley, I have received several accounts of the day you were recognized as the Fourth Chhöshe. It was Rinzen who spoke of it first. He told me that thirteen years ago, emissaries from Lhasa came here in search of the Chhöshe. They were led by a vision — Dhamo's vision — of a boy at a temple surrounded by these very mountains."

Li Du made a small gesture of self-deprecation. "The customs of your land are not my own, but I know enough to understand that signs — in this case, the enactment of the scene in Dhamo's vision — are used to confirm the identity of a tulku. I know that it is considered an honor to a family when a tulku is born to them. But I also know that, by the laws of your school, the lama, once recognized, is no longer a part of his father's bloodline. His rights and his duties are those associated with the lineage of the lama he embodies."

The Chhöshe gave no sign of affirmation or denial, and Li Du went on. "I next heard of that day from Sonam." Li Du saw Pema flinch at the mention of the dead man's name. "Sonam used the phrase *an unexpected honor.* When I asked him what he meant, he told me that you —" Li Du looked at the Chhöshe. "— that you were the eldest son, and that it was unusual for an heir to be recognized as a tulku. It almost never occurs. He said that when the emissaries arrived and announced that their auguries had led them here in search of the Chhöshe, everyone believed that the boy chosen would be Pema. It was a surprise when the boy recognized was the other boy — Doso's heir." Li Du's glance slid to Sonam's body. "Sonam said that he had good fortune here. He meant, I think, that with Doso's eldest son removed from the bloodline, it was Pema, Doso's adopted son, who would inherit first. And as Sonam's nephew, you, Pema, were his connection to the family. If he could assert power over you, he could take advantage of the wealth and land that you would control."

Pema looked down at the matted fur of his worn sleeve. "I hope that I would not have let him. But please explain — why are you telling this to us?"

"It will be clear very soon," Li Du said. "What I learned next, I learned from you yourself. You duplicated the painting that had been destroyed. You showed me Dhamo's vision — the vision that came to pass on that morning thirteen years ago. I discovered later — from Lumo — other curious details of that day. She told me that neither Doso nor his wife were happy at the honor that had visited their home. Doso was so grief-stricken that he threatened to harm Dhamo for what he had done."

The temple seemed to hold its breath. Li Du went on. "That is what I was told. I will share with you now what I have observed. I have seen estrangement between two brothers who were inseparable." He addressed Pema. "I have seen your isolation from the man who acknowledges you as his heir. And I have observed you —" He turned to the Chhöshe. "I have observed you lie and say that you do not remember this valley when in fact you remember every detail of it."

The Chhöshe's face tensed. "I have not lied."

"You recognized an animal you had not seen since you were a child."

"I —"

"Pema does not remember the day you were recognized, but you do. It was that memory that brought you home. You remember that it was your brother, Pema, not you, who was given the bowl to carry up the mountain stairs that day. You remember finding him, afraid of the crowd and the strangers, his arms too tired to carry the heavy basin. You remember lifting the basin and carrying it to the temple yourself. And you remember being taken from your home for reasons you did not understand."

Pema was looking at the Chhöshe, who was staring unseeingly at the altar. Li Du continued. "You came back here because you have never believed yourself to be the Chhöshe. You came back because you wanted to see the painting again — to search it for the truth. And when you learned that it had been destroyed, you despaired of ever knowing whether it contained some clue, some assurance, that what happened that day, what took you from your home and your family, was not a mistake."

The flames on the altar continued to

flicker. A gust of wind beat softly at the door and whispered through its seams. "But how could it have been a mistake?" Pema asked. "The painting showed —" He stopped.

"The painting showed three moments in time," Li Du said. "The boy at the base of the stairs, the boy at the top of the stairs, and the boy making the offering at the temple. But what if the boy at the base of the stairs was not the same as the one at the top?"

The Chhöshe gave a shuddering sigh. "It happened at the hollow tree." He turned to Pema. "You were frightened. You said that you had been told to take the bowl to the temple and offer it there, but you were afraid. You hid in the tree."

Pema's eyes were wide and uncomprehending. "I don't remember," he whispered.

Li Du spoke to the Chhöshe. "You found him there, and you were determined to help him because he was weak and you were strong. You wanted to protect him as you always had done. Neither of you knew that the task given to Pema was an important one. Neither of you understood what would happen."

The Chhöshe cupped his face in his hands, then slowly drew them away. Tears glistened on his fingertips. "I tried to be who they said I was. I studied hard. But I could never stop thinking of my home. When I heard that my mother had died, I thought that it was my fault, that if I had been at home, she would not have — the fire might not have — and when I came back, I learned that it was — that it was the painting . . ." He trailed off, overcome.

Li Du turned to Pema. "Do you remember the day Karma died?"

Pema nodded solemnly. "She was here in the temple. She was often here. She fell asleep, but she had lighted many candles. And the dry wind blew through the walls and billowed the curtains to the flame." Pema bowed his head.

Li Du spoke quietly. "Your grandmother, Mara, told me that there was something wrong with the painting. Karma never believed that Tashi was the Chhöshe. She returned again and again to the temple, searching the painting just as you intended to search it, for some sign that was overlooked. My guess is that she looked for a scar on the cheek of the painted face that would identify the boy as Pema, not Tashi. Perhaps it was there. Perhaps it was just a fiber in the silk or a ridge of uneven paint. Her confusion tormented her."

"But who was it?" the Chhöshe whispered.

"Which of us did he intend to paint?"

Pity for both of them welled up in Li Du's chest, pity for the cracks that had broken their paths and confused the directions of their lives. "There was no misinterpretation of the painting," he said.

The young man who had carried the title of the Chhöshe like a burden ever since he was a child looked at Li Du in bewildered frustration. "But I have searched my mind. I can find in myself no other person than Tashi, no other home but this one, and no other family but my own." His expression twisted, approaching anger. "You cannot tell me the truth. You are not a teacher. You are not a monk. You have not studied our way or our texts. How can you say that you know?"

Li Du shook his head. "You misunderstand me. I am not telling you that you are the Chhöshe."

"Then what do you mean?"

"I mean that the painting was not real. There was never any vision of the Chhöshe in this valley. The details of this setting, the temple, a boy, and a basin of milk were supplied to Dhamo in Lhasa, not by visions, but by men. Dhamo thought that he was doing a service, but he was being used. The delegation that came to identify the

Chhöshe here thirteen years ago had a purpose that had nothing to do with incarnations."

"What purpose?" The Chhöshe's voice was hoarse, but it gained strength as he repeated the question. "What purpose brought them here?"

"The search for the Chhöshe was a ruse to disguise the real object of the mission, which was to place Dhamo in this temple, and to keep him here."

"W— why?" Pema stumbled over the single word.

Briefly, without embellishment, Li Du told the two young men what Rinzen had confirmed. He did his best to impress upon them the gravity of the information, but he could see that they were hardly listening.

"Then I am not the Chhöshe. I am Tashi, as I always was." Even as he spoke the name, it seemed to align with the young man's features.

"It is not within my power to tell you who you are," Li Du answered quickly. "As you said, I am not a scholar or priest. I can only tell you that the identification thirteen years ago was contrived for a hidden motive. Any deeper truths — those are not mine to reveal."

"And I —" Pema's voice shook. "I lost my

brother."

Tashi stood up. There was an eagerness to him, an energy that had not been there before. "There is so much that I do not understand," he said.

"And I hope very soon to explain it to you," Li Du said quickly. "But first I must ask for your help. I believe that the answer to the murders that took place here can be found in something that is missing."

Tashi answered immediately. "The thangka that Dhamo was painting."

"Yes. Pema, did you see it closely enough to be able to do as you did for the other painting? Can you draw it for me?"

Pema looked slightly startled. After a moment's thought he shook his head. "I cannot. I did not look at it closely. I am sorry."

Li Du reassured him. "It was an outside hope. But now I will ask you this — do you remember anything that was said by the pilgrim who commissioned it? You told me Dhamo spoke words as he painted, that he recited the symbols that were to appear in the thangka. Do you remember them?"

Pema concentrated. "I — I remember the pilgrim. He said, 'I come to seek the services of the painter they call Dhamo — the man of visions whose paintings recall the magic of the serpent spirits.' They kept the door of the studio closed. He — he had a very low voice and his hair was strange. It was black with a white patch in it. But I can't remember the words, not all of them. The lotus, the jewel-spitting mongoose, the knot . . ."

Tashi stopped his pacing. "I have seen that man," he said. "He was the pilgrim on the road. His hair — black with a tuft of white like a blaze on a black yak. He carried a walking stick. He had little else with him. A blanket, a bowl, a book and a meager supply of food."

"Yes," said Pema. "That was him."

Li Du looked from one to the other. They returned his look curiously. "You mean," Li Du said, "that the pilgrim Pema met here, the pilgrim who commissioned the thangka, was the same pilgrim you met on the road?"

"He must have been," said Tashi. He and Pema exchanged uncomprehending glances.

The pilgrim, Li Du thought. He closed his eyes. He had been mistaken. But if that was the case, if what they said was true, then —

He rose abruptly to his feet, strode to the door that connected the chapel to the studio, and opened it. The room was almost completely dark. The light from the butter lamps barely reached the threshold. He scanned the inky shadows, furnishing the room from memory. Shelves cluttered with pots and brushes, a table, a cold hearth . . . His thoughts caught on themselves. *A cold hearth.* He swung around and faced the chapel. His gaze moved to the eight tongues of flame suspended on the altar, then down to the bodies in front of them. Beside the recumbent Sonam sat the white form of Dhamo, bound upright, waiting.

Slowly, Li Du approached the stiff, wrapped form. He stepped carefully around Sonam's feet and knelt beside Dhamo's body. Even in the cold, the odor of death had begun to hover around the corpse. Li Du reached for the place where the end of the cloth tied the right hand to the knee. He untied it, and began carefully to unwrap the rough white material from the limb.

"What are you doing?" Horror distorted Tashi's features as he moved forward to stop Li Du. "The body was washed. The symbol is not there."

"I am not looking for the symbol," Li Du said. Tashi obeyed the authority in his voice and halted.

The cloth came away easily — it had been wrapped loosely, and as Li Du guided it from the body he saw Tashi's eyes narrow. "That is not how I wrapped him," Tashi said.

Li Du continued to unwind the outermost layer of the shroud. He moved up the body's left arm to the shoulder, gathering loops of material in one hand. He passed the bunched cloth across the front of the torso, exposing a deeper layer of shroud, and stopped.

Behind him, he heard a sharp intake of breath.

"Is that —" Pema moved closer, Tashi beside him.

"It is Dhamo's final painting," Li Du said.

He looped the length of cloth once more around the body, revealing what was hidden beneath it. Charcoal outlines spread across a background of clean white. Green fields and blue sky cast an oily gleam in the light of the butter lamps. Careful not to disarrange the final layer of shroud that clung to the dead man's skin, Li Du freed the thangka from the wrappings that had obscured it.

"We must return to the manor," he said. "I need your help, if you will give it to me."

Tashi's reply was instant. "What can we do?" Pema did not need to speak. He stood solemnly beside his brother, awaiting instruction.

"Hamza will be at the kitchen hearth," said Li Du. "You must send him to me without drawing attention. I will wait for him at the manor door."

"You know who killed Dhamo," said Pema. His voice, though quiet, did not shake. "And my uncle?"

Li Du nodded. "There is only one thing left to do to be certain. If I am correct, then I will be able to explain the circle bound in gold and blue. I will tell you the meaning of the white mirror."

CHAPTER 27

Li Du did not see the first star take its place in the sky, but he found it there when he looked up. The sight of it led him to look for others. Wherever his gaze rested, stars appeared, as if ignited by his search for them. Before long, the sky was filled with scattered light.

Hamza appeared beside him in the dark. "The two young men are changed," he said, "especially the taller one. Some transformation has occurred. Did they retrieve a butter lamp that was burning at the bottom of a well?"

Li Du kept his eyes on the stars. "It is you who are always telling me that names are important," he said. "Names can bind, or liberate."

"Do not speak to me as I speak to you, librarian. It is very disconcerting."

Li Du turned to him. "There is something I must do," he said quietly. "And there is someone in particular who would wish to prevent me from doing it. I need time. Can you keep everyone around the kitchen fire?"

Hamza's eyes glittered. "That is a service I am delighted to perform. What is it that you must do?"

"Find a book."

Li Du could hear Hamza's smile in his voice. "My dear librarian — I have come to appreciate your regard for all that is inked and bound. But in this moment, I question your priorities."

"It is an important book."

"And what is it that you carry with you?"

Li Du took the rolled silk from under his arm. "It is the thangka that was missing."

"It smells of death."

They were both startled by a light tread behind them. Sera-tsering emerged from the corridor and joined them. She tightened the belt around her long coat and slipped her hands into her sleeves. She looked at the rolled cloth Li Du held. He tucked it back under his arm.

"I have been given a task," Hamza said to Sera. "If you would condescend to help me, you must allow me to practice my craft without criticism or interruption."

"If it is important to the scholar, I will try," she said.

"I thank you for it," said Hamza.

As they turned to go, Li Du asked Sera to remain behind a moment. Hamza hesitated, nodded, and disappeared into the passage. Sera stepped forward to stand beside Li Du. They looked out at the brilliant expanse of night. Behind and above them came the sounds of footsteps, the lowing of barn animals, and the clack of Lumo's cane on the kitchen floor.

"You know who the killer is," she said.

"I am almost certain that I do." He turned to her. "Rinzen has the authority of the Lhasa throne, but we are very far from Lhasa. Doso has authority over this valley, but he will not act as judge. You are an official of Bathang. Will you claim this matter as yours to resolve?"

She smiled and shook her head. "No. I took my husband's position when he died because I did not want to be idle and because, at the time, it pleased me to do it. I did not want to marry again. And I did not want to go back to Lhasa."

"Why not?"

She looked at him. "Have you not guessed already? I do not keep it a close secret."

Li Du nodded. "Indeed I have guessed. Your family was allied with the regent who served the Great Fifth Dalai Lama," he said.

"Closer than allied." Sera's low voice was soft and controlled. She tilted her head back and searched the stars as if each were a memory and she was choosing from among them. "When I was a little girl, my uncle was trusted with a task. My mother and her sisters spoke of it in hushed voices. They whispered of a boy. I knew he was important, but I did not know why. They said he lived in a tower, and that my uncle guarded him, keeping him safe."

"The hidden child."

"By the time the boy came to Lhasa he was a young man, and I was almost a woman. My family had arranged a marriage for me to a Chinese official far from home. But I never forgot the boy in the tower. I hope —" She stopped and steadied her voice. "I hope that he did have adventures." She shivered, and stretched her shoulders under her heavy coat. "But you asked me a question," she said. "And I will answer. I am tired of being an official. There will be another to take my place. I will not go back. It is time for something new."

There was no source of light in the barn. Around Li Du the animals stirred, warm shadows under the creaking ceiling. He stood just outside the pale glow that rolled down the kitchen stairs along with Hamza's voice, faint but audible. "Tales," Hamza was saying, "to distract us from the evil that has visited this place, and help us pass the night until the sun comes to warm our thoughts."

His words were met with unintelligible murmurs and questions posed in hesitant, uncertain voices. Li Du heard footsteps above and blinked as a fine cloud of dust fell from the ceiling, stinging his eyes. He waited until Hamza spoke again.

". . . King Noe, one of the four fire-born kings and descendant of the destroyer of adversaries, who was brought into being by the prayer of a hermit in the mountains of Arbuda . . ."

The murmurs quieted and the footsteps returned to the fire. Li Du stepped lightly to a corner of the barn where three mules stood beside a pile of saddlebags neatly arranged against the wall, ready to be loaded onto the animals at dawn. He retrieved a copper lantern from a hook and set it on the floor. Then he crouched down, lit three pine tapers, and slipped them inside the lantern. A glow spread over trampled straw and oiled leather.

Quietly and carefully, he selected two bags and dragged them away from the wall into the lantern light. He untied the straps of

425

the larger bag and reached inside, where his hand encountered silk so smooth and soft that his fingertips lingered of their own volition. He identified various sundry items, among them metal cups, wrapped ink sticks, and a roll of parchment, which he examined and discovered to be blank. He set the bag aside, and pulled the smaller one toward him.

". . . city at the edge of the ocean. Near the port where the ships' sails gleamed was a beach where the children of merchants and sailors and servants played. Their favorite game was to race up the sliding sands of the tallest dune. Each day, the child who reached the top first was hailed by the others as the ruler of all the lands and all the oceans. And each day, the child who won the race appointed magistrates and ambassadors and storytellers and alchemists . . ."

Li Du's fingers cramped with tension. Every scrape of a boot on the floor above sounded like a footstep toward the stairs. He opened the second bag. He felt coarse wool and traced the curving, raised lines of embroidered flowers. There seemed to be nothing inside but cloth. Then his fingers found the hard corner of an object. It was not in the main compartment of the bag, but sewn loosely into its leather base. With some difficulty, he pulled out the stitches and drew the object free. It was a book.

". . . a jewel with the property of attracting other jewels to it. The ship's captain took this jewel into a deep stone cave, and with it found so many treasures that he lost his reason and stayed too long. The tide rose and the cave filled with water. When the sailors returned for their captain, they found a man identical to him in appearance, voice, and manner. They brought him onto their ship, not knowing that he was a prince of the lower world who meant to pilot them to his kingdom of shipwrecks beneath the sea . . ."

Li Du held the book to the light. It was sturdily constructed with a stitched binding of doubled thread. The cover was made of durable paper, three sheets thick, its corners wrapped in rough silk. He opened it. Inside, there was no title slip or author's seal. As he flipped through the pages, he felt the displaced air on his face as if the book were breathing. The contents were not printed, but drawn.

He placed the book open on the ground and blinked down at the inked lines. Then he reached behind him for the thangka, and unrolled it. He set the lantern on the upper edge and his knee on the lower. The swaths of blue and green were muted in the dim light. The charcoal outlines were faint, but discernible.

". . . and from the top of the highest dune the girl who was that day endowed with majesty saw the ship's tattered sails . . ."

Li Du turned to the first page of the book. There were five pictures, one below another, and beside each were one or more Chinese characters. He looked at the first picture. A bird with three legs. Beside it, the message *size and location of military forces.* Li Du scanned the sketched outlines on the thangka. There was no three-legged bird there. He looked at the second picture in the book. A frog impaled on a stick. Beside it, *notable deaths and their causes.* Again he searched the thangka, but the impaled frog was not there. Neither was the treasure box, which was drawn next to the word *strategies,* nor the trident with serpents wound around it, which appeared beside *names and roles.*

He looked at the fifth picture. It was a scorpion. In its mouth was a flaming sword. Beside it was the word *warning.* Li Du looked at the thangka. The creature was there. He fanned the pages of the book until he reached the section titled *Warnings.* Then he set to work.

". . . commanded the boy to bring her a water jug. When he had brought it, she turned to the sailors. 'Whoever can fit into this jug,' she said, 'is certainly not a prince of the underworld.' At once the false captain jumped into the jug, which she stoppered with a diamond seal . . ."

Li Du's task so absorbed him that he retained only a dim awareness of the shifting animals and the cadence of Hamza's voice. He labored on until finally, his fingers numb with cold, he closed the book and looked at the light from the kitchen. Silently he stood, adjusted his hat on his head, and returned the lantern, its flame extinguished, to its hook.

Holding the thangka and the book under one arm, he climbed the stairs up toward the kitchen. Just before he reached the top, he paused and set the two objects down carefully on a step, where, from the vantage point of the hearth, they would remain out of sight.

The guests and residents of the manor, including Yeshe and Lumo, were all gathered around the fire. While Rinzen occupied the place of honor and Doso controlled the most space with his height and broad shoulders, it was Hamza, sitting alone on a painted chair, who commanded the room.

Doso was speaking to Hamza. "— a welcome distraction. Will you continue? I expect most of us here would rather sit late by the fire than disperse into the dark."

Hamza bowed his head to accept the compliment, the point of his gleaming beard barely touching his silk tunic. "It would be my honor to continue," he said. "But my friend the librarian has just come in, and his expression suggests that, at this moment, his words are more valuable than mine."

Attention turned to Li Du, and he felt the force of their thoughts and feelings stretching toward him. He nestled his hands into his sleeves, an action that settled his thoughts and slowed the rapid beat of his heart.

"When I came to this valley three days ago," he said, "I saw a red-robed figure on the bridge. I thought that a monk had come to meet us. But he did not move or speak. When I went closer to him, I saw that he was dead. His posture was tranquil. The sheath at his side was empty, and he held the knife that had killed him as if he himself had delivered the blow. His fingers were coated in the same paint that marked his body. This lifeless man, it seemed, had not come to the bridge to meet us. He had not intended to meet anyone again in this world. He had come to take his own life."

There were murmurs and stirrings from the people around the fire. Andruk finished his quiet translation.

"I understand now that it was my first impression," Li Du continued, "and not my second, that was correct. Dhamo — that is, Dhamo's body — *was* on the bridge to greet travelers. It was there to be seen and to be remembered. But this was not by his own choice, and he did not go willingly to his death."

The atmosphere of the room was heavy with an uneasy, expectant silence. Li Du took a breath and continued. "Dhamo was lured to the bridge, where he was murdered, painted, and arranged into the position in which he was found." Li Du was aware of his own anger. It moved up his spine and shook his voice. "Dhamo's body was employed like a piece of parchment painted and mounted on a wall. It was used to convey a message."

"What message?" The question was Doso's.

It was Hamza who answered. "The white mirror."

Li Du nodded once. "Yes. But even as I

431

began to discover what happened on the day Dhamo died, I could attach no definite meaning to that symbol. For Kalden and the muleteers, the painted mirror was the act of a man pursued by demons, a final, desperate token of protection. The Chhöshe spoke of the significance of the mirror in the context of his studies: the mirror teaches that objects are illusions. Paolo Campo called the mirror a demonic mark, a curse indicative of evil. Doso claimed that, while the action was inexplicable, it was easily attributable to Dhamo, a man unlike other men."

Impatience resonated in Doso's voice. "If you know what happened that day, then tell us."

Li Du raised his eyes to meet Doso's. "On the day he died, Dhamo rose at first light to continue his work. He was fulfilling a commission for a thangka. As with every commission he received, it was a task that occupied his whole mind. He had applied a foundation of white, blue, and green to the sketched drawing. By established rule, the next color to be added was red.

"But when Dhamo located the bowl of vermilion in his workroom, he found it empty of all but a few granules. This surprised him, for when he had asked Pema to check his supply of vermilion, Pema had reported the bowl to be full. Dhamo did not wait. His determination to continue his work consumed him, and he took immediate steps to obtain what he needed. There was, not far from the temple, a natural source of cinnabar."

"The hot springs." Pema spoke quickly, then flinched as eyes turned to him.

"Yes. Dhamo gathered what he needed, and left the temple. What he did not know was that someone, anticipating Dhamo's need for vermilion, had emptied the bowl. When Dhamo departed the temple that morning, he was following a course that had been determined by his killer. He was walking to his death."

There were no questions now. The listeners waited, each seeing in their own way the scene that was being conjured for them.

"We know that Dhamo went to the hot springs," Li Du went on. "In his crimson robes, he was conspicuous, and easily recognized. Yeshe witnessed him go down to the forest. Sera saw him climbing the path in the direction of the pools. Later, I myself felt the scoring on the stone where he had pried the cinnabar rocks away. Dhamo intended to return with them to his studio, but he never reached it. He died on the bridge."

Li Du studied the faces of the people around the hearth. "Almost all of you had the opportunity to kill him," he said. "That morning, Doso and Kamala both went to the village, but on separate errands. Andruk also went to the village, but there is no one to account for what he did during the time he said he was there." Li Du addressed the three of them. "Any one of you could have gone to the bridge, returned to the village, and strode back to the manor in the falling snow as if you had been at the village the whole time you were gone."

Li Du shifted his attention to Paolo Campo. He did not change his language, instead allowing Andruk to continue to translate. "You visited Yeshe's hut," he said, "but you were not there all morning. And Sera —" Li Du turned to her. "— you left Lumo's home while she slept, and were for some time alone in the forest. You say that you saw Dhamo as he was approaching the hot springs. You could have stayed nearby, waiting, and followed him to the bridge."

There was a chorus of protests. Yeshe tapped one of his walking sticks on the floor in a demand for attention. "It wasn't one of the family who did this," he said. "You listen to me."

Doso's voice rose above the others, silencing them. "I cannot accept this," he said, with a gesture that encompassed himself and Kamala. "If one of us had crossed the pastures and fields to the forest with the intention of killing Dhamo, someone would have observed it."

"But that is exactly what happened," said Li Du. "The killer did stride across the pastures in plain sight, and the killer *was* seen. Seen, but not recognized."

"A disguise?" The question came from Lumo.

"A strategy to avoid being noticed," Li Du answered. "It was Yeshe who told me that in places where the distances are wide and the weather is cold, people become associated with their coats. If a coat is unfamiliar, its wearer is anonymous."

Paolo Campo shifted uncomfortably in his seat, furrowing his brow at Andruk's rushed translation. Andruk concluded, then looked at Li Du. "The person in the dark coat," he said. "That was the killer."

Li Du nodded. "Under normal circumstances, an unfamiliar coat would have attracted attention, but on that morning the valley was unusually full of strangers. You and Yeshe both saw the figure in black, but it did not arouse your curiosity." He addressed the group again. "This is an old, wealthy house with attics full of forgotten possessions. Perhaps the killer found a discarded coat among them. Perhaps it was already among the killer's own belongings."

Li Du turned to Sera. "A third person saw this figure," he said. "You recall the shadow you perceived in the forest near the hot springs?"

A small shudder passed through Sera's shoulders, but her self-possession wavered only for an instant. "I should not have crept away," she said. "I might have prevented a murder."

Doso's deep voice followed Sera's. "Who was it?"

Li Du took a moment to consider his words, then spoke. "Three people saw a person whom they could not identify. Consider that there is one person here among us who went to the hot springs that morning but was *not* seen, someone who would have been recognized even at a distance in his robes of yellow silk."

Eyes turned slowly to where Rinzen sat. He regarded Li Du with an expression of mild surprise. "Is it of any consequence that no one happened to see me? Yes, I went to the hot springs that day. I admitted it to you freely."

Li Du met Rinzen's eyes and held his gaze. "That is not entirely true," he said. "You did *not* admit it to me freely. You confessed that you visited the hot springs only after I confronted you about your tarnished ring. Had I not questioned you, your presence at the pools on that day would have remained your secret."

Rinzen frowned. When he spoke, it was in the authoritative tone of an official addressing an inferior. "I was under no obligation to speak to anyone here on the subject of my movements that day."

"Perhaps not, but if your actions were innocent, why did you make such an effort to conceal the yellow garments that identify you? Why did you wear the black coat?"

"I did nothing of the kind. I went after Dhamo that day with the intention of engaging him in a private conversation. The nature of my communication with him is confidential. I will not discuss it in this public setting, and I am astonished that you would make such a demand of me."

"You did not go after Dhamo," Li Du said, quietly. "You went before him. You wore the black coat so that, in case the apparent suicide was not believed, you would not appear to have any connection to the events in the forest."

Rinzen opened his mouth to speak, but Li Du continued in a firm, clear tone. "When your tarnished ring placed you at the hot springs, your plan to disassociate yourself from the area where the murder took place was thwarted. You thought quickly, and you invented, for my benefit, a collection of half-truths and lies. You claimed that you followed Dhamo to speak to him without being overheard. That was a lie. You could not tell me the truth — that you went *ahead* of Dhamo to the hot springs and waited for him in the forest — because it would have revealed that you knew he would be there. It would have revealed that it was you who emptied the cinnabar from the bowl in his studio in order to draw him away from the temple and the manor. It would have revealed you to be his murderer."

"This is nonsense." With tensed lips and lifted chin, Rinzen was a portrait of offended nobility. "I realize now that it was a mistake to confide in you. Clearly you have not only succumbed to a gross misunderstanding of the situation but also indulged in absurd fantasies that have no connection to truth."

"You deny that you killed Dhamo."

"I do, and I challenge you to offer any evidence that I did."

Li Du was silent. He lowered his gaze and rubbed the back of his neck. "I wish," he said, "that I had been able to do so before tonight." In the hush that followed, he turned and went to the stairs. He knelt, reached down, and picked up the the thangka and the book. Then he returned to the hearth and set them down on the floor, visible to everyone.

While the others craned their necks to look at the objects, Li Du turned his gaze to Rinzen, whose cheeks had become sunken beneath eyes that burned with fury.

"You waited for Dhamo at the hot springs," Li Du said. "You arrived there prepared to effect the plan you had devised days earlier. You already had in your possession the paint, stolen from the temple and folded in rawhide."

The muscles of Rinzen's throat were taut and visible along the column of his neck. "I had no reason to kill Dhamo," he said, but his affronted mien had deserted him. From the moment Li Du had retrieved the thangka and the book, the atmosphere in the room had changed. Rinzen was alone among strangers who were looking to Li Du for answers to their questions.

Doso spoke in a low, dazed voice. "How is this possible?"

"To explain, I must speak of empires," Li Du said. "I must speak of my own empire, and of its Emperor. In the forty years since the Kangxi began his rule, these mountains have never strayed far from his thoughts. Beyond them lies Lhasa, a city that taunts him, a beautiful city full of knowledge that he does not possess and strength that is not the same as his own. And so, in the course of those forty years, he has sent spies into the trade routes like beads on a tangled string. They appear as pilgrims and merchants and travelers. They watch and learn and make their reports."

Li Du paused, summoning to his mind a vision of the past. "A little more than thirteen years ago," he went on, "this place, this hidden valley, came to the attention of one of the Kangxi's most powerful spies in Lhasa: Rinzen Ngawang. He received a detailed description of it from one of the spies sent to search for a location from which messages could be taken secretly to China. When he heard of this valley — near to the main routes but removed from them, owned by an old family uninvolved in political intrigues — he concluded that it was ideal for his purposes."

Sera-tsering was sitting beside Lumo. She rested her elbows on her knees and turned her head to look at Rinzen. "How much you must know," she said in a low voice. She looked up at Li Du. "Then Dhamo was a spy?"

"No. Dhamo was, from Rinzen's perspective, another fortunate discovery. He was a brilliant thangka painter and a man preoccupied with demons. He was also highly suggestible. The code that was devised to conceal messages in thangkas might have been inspired by Dhamo's unique qualifications, but Dhamo knew nothing about it. He thought that he spoke to benevolent spirits. He painted what they told him to paint, and the completed thangkas were delivered to monasteries near Beijing where the Kangxi's agents waited to retrieve them."

Andruk had been watching Li Du intently, while dutifully and succinctly continuing his translations for a confused and exhausted Campo. Now he spoke. "But if what you say is true, then Rinzen is correct. He had no reason to kill Dhamo. It was Dhamo who ensured the continued success of his enterprise."

Li Du nodded. "That is also what I thought. I did not know that, only a few days before Rinzen arrived here, something happened to alter his situation. He and the

Chhöshe met someone on the road, some-one who had traveled from this manor."

"The pilgrim," whispered Pema.

"Yes." Li Du turned to Tashi. "You and Rinzen met a pilgrim who shared your fire. You told me that he and Rinzen conversed late into the night. When I discovered that this was the same pilgrim as the one who had commissioned a thangka days before, I came to the conclusion that he must have been a spy, and that he and Rinzen must have realized that they served the same cause. He would have told Rinzen about the thangka he had commissioned, and the message it contained. And it was in that conversation that Rinzen heard something he did not expect. He heard that the thangka being produced at that very moment in Dhamo's studio contained the news that the Kangxi's highest-ranking spy in Lhasa had shifted his allegiance to the Dzungars and could no longer be trusted."

"How did you discover this?" The question came from Sera.

"By finding the thangka where Rinzen had hid it, and by decoding its message with the codebook I located among his belongings."

Rinzen was staring at Li Du, his eyes bright with hatred.

"Where was the thangka?" The question

came from Andruk.

"Rinzen concealed it within the wrappings that shrouded Dhamo's body," Li Du replied. "I thought at first that someone had stolen the thangka, but that was not exactly true. Rinzen did not want to possess it — he wanted to destroy it. Every moment that the thangka remained in its frame was an opportunity for someone to take it or to read its message.

"But he was constrained by the activity at the temple following Dhamo's death. The body was being wrapped and the pyre was being built. He was surrounded by people. He could not throw the thangka into a fire — the hearth in Dhamo's studio was cold, and the flames of the butter lamps were not enough to destroy thick cloth and paint quickly. His search for a flame that would consume the thangka is what gave him the idea of where to hide it. He knew that Dhamo's body would be cremated. If the thangka was hidden on the body, it would be destroyed with it. The message it contained would be lost or, at least, delayed. An opportunity presented itself when the Chhöshe went to circumambulate the high shrine. While he was gone, Rinzen cut the thangka from its easel. He wrapped it around Dhamo's body and covered it in another layer of shroud."

A log broke in the fire. Li Du watched Rinzen through the sparks that burst from the blackened wood. "I think," Li Du said, "that if we were to go to the place where you and the Chhöshe camped that night, we would find the body of that lone spy not far from it. I suspect you killed him while the Chhöshe slept. From that moment, you began to plot Dhamo's death."

"And Sonam?" Kamala's voice came from the corner where she sat with the children.

"Sonam had witnessed the murder. He knew only that Rinzen had killed Dhamo, not why he had killed him, but what he knew was enough to threaten Rinzen. It was Sonam who suggested the cave as a meeting place. Pema had shown it to him, and he knew they would not be disturbed there. Rinzen came to the place Sonam described, but he did not know what it was. He knew only one painter in the valley, and he assumed that the cave was Dhamo's secret refuge, not Pema's. He thought the body would never be discovered."

"But what about the white mirror?" The question came from Sera. "What is the meaning of the white mirror?"

Li Du kept his eyes on Rinzen. "He told me what it was, but I did not understand.

The white mirror was a warning. It was a symbol in the code that had never been used before. It was to be used only in one situation — to command the spies to destroy the network, to scatter to the winds, to burn their codebooks and to disappear. Rinzen needed time to escape before the truth of his betrayal spread and reached Beijing. He knew that any pilgrim who came to the manor and asked to commission a painting from the recluse in the temple would hear the terrible report of Dhamo's death. They would receive the message of the white mirror long after Dhamo's body was gone. The paths of the spies would dissolve, and Rinzen would gain the time he needed to save himself."

Rinzen was sitting at the ornate desk in his room writing by the light of a candle. A fur rested on his shoulders. His brush moved silently across a page. When Li Du came in, Rinzen looked up and set his brush down. Its handle clinked softly on the porcelain rest. Rinzen stood up and gestured for Li Du to take a seat in a chair of carved and lacquered wood cushioned in crimson silk. Then he slid the paper he had been writing on to the edge of the desk, turned the chair, and resumed his seat, now facing Li Du.

"I was overcome by my emotions earlier this evening," he said. "I hope you will pardon me for becoming overwrought."

Li Du looked behind him. Following his look, Rinzen said, "I know that the door is watched. The Khampa muleteers reveal their usefulness. But I have no intention of running out into the night. Such dramatic behavior would be unsuitable."

"You asked to speak to me."

"I did. I understand we are to travel together."

"Kalden Dorjee has agreed to escort you to the next official outpost."

"Where I will be put into the custody of officials who serve the Kangxi, or those who serve Lhazang Khan?"

"Whichever we come to first. You have betrayed them both."

"And you will tell them the truth?"

"I will tell them what I know."

"Which, I think, is a great deal. I am surprised the Kangxi allowed you to go after he pardoned you. I would think he would find your services invaluable. A servant who speaks the truth is as valuable as —" Rinzen paused. Amusement glinted in his eyes like a golden fish deep beneath dark water. "As a mirror."

Li Du did not respond. Rinzen continued.

"The Kangxi Emperor is powerful. He had a worthy opponent in the Great Fifth. He has not found one in Lhazang Khan."

In spite of himself, Li Du was curious. "And you believe the Dzungars are a threat to him?"

"The Dzungars," said Rinzen, "are the enemy of his secret nightmares. It is from the north that the next great army will come, as it always does. The cycles of history can be predicted. The villages go on, unchanged. The capital cities shift with the whims of emperors. The foreigners come and, like the one who is here now, they scurry away, cold and hungry. So it continues until power grows in the north. Genghis Khan survived what should have killed him, and with ease took more land than all the emperors in their palaces can imagine. It will happen again. I side with the power that makes even the Emperor of China afraid."

Li Du had heard enough. "Your alliances are of no concern to me."

"No. You want justice for Dhamo, a mad painter whose mind was half in another world already. And for Sonam, a coarse and greedy man who probably cut more throats than I ever could."

"You could have traveled north to the Dzungar lands. You did not have to kill

Dhamo."

"I needed time. I could not risk the thangka arriving at its destination before I was far enough away to escape detection. The system I built was an efficient one. The paintings traveled quickly."

Li Du nodded. "As did Sonam. He threatened you through me, but I did not see it at the time. When he asked me to tell you that he could bring your correspondence to Lhasa faster than any caravan, he was communicating to you the speed with which he could bring about your destruction."

"Yes." Rinzen's tone was sour, but Li Du read satisfaction in his expression as he continued. "I told Sonam I would give him the silver he wanted. I told him to find a place where we could not be overheard. It seemed to be my good fortune that he brought me to a hidden cave, the abandoned fancy of a dead man. I had no idea the painter's apprentice cared so much for the art."

Several moments passed in silence, Li Du in his patchwork coat, Rinzen seated in his frayed silks, the room still except for the smoke that rose in thin spirals from the brazier and incense sticks.

When Rinzen spoke, the suddenness of his words startled Li Du from his thoughts.

"I asked for you because there is a matter I wish to discuss, one that relates to your own situation as much as it does to mine."

Li Du felt a change in the room. They were alone. Rinzen had not moved. But Li Du had the sense that he was being circled. The back of his head prickled with apprehension, but he kept his eyes on Rinzen, resisting the urge to look behind him.

"Why didn't you accept the Emperor's invitation to return to the Forbidden City?"

For the second time that day, the question caught Li Du off guard. "I wished to travel," he said.

Rinzen's gaze did not waver. "You wanted to go somewhere? Or was it that you did not want to go home?"

"What is your purpose in asking me this question?"

"I will tell you my purpose soon. But allow me to suggest that your reasons for not returning to your home have something to do with the death of your friend and mentor, head librarian and scholar at the imperial library, who was executed for conspiring to assassinate the Emperor six years ago."

Li Du stared.

Rinzen gave a small, bitter smile, and Li Du perceived the anger behind the other man's eyes, the rage and frustration of failure. "You have a talent for deduction," Rinzen said. "But you have overlooked several points that, to me, seem obvious. I admitted to you that I was in the service of the Kangxi. I spoke to you in the attic room of my high rank in Lhasa. And now you know that my loyalty is to the Dzungars. Do you really think that I, who hold the secrets of *three* rulers, do not know about you? I know about Shu. I know that he was your teacher. I know that he confessed his crimes. And I know that you were exiled because you were his friend."

Li Du's fingers, hidden in his sleeves, were curled so tightly that his nails bit into his palms. But he kept his voice calm. "You speak to me of what I also know. Why?"

"Because I have something that you want."

"What is that?"

"The truth."

Li Du's silence seemed to please Rinzen. He gathered the heavy fur more securely around his shoulders. "While you have studied the inhabitants of this manor in your search for a murderer, I have studied you. I see that you walk with despair as a companion. Your exile clings to you like that patched coat you will not mend or replace. I wonder, do you enjoy the pain that the cold brings?" Without waiting for an answer, Rinzen continued. "You are tormented by confusion. How did you fail to see a lie that was so close to you for so many years? If you had seen it, could you have turned him from his path? Could you have saved him?"

Li Du tried to clear his vision. Rinzen's white beard was bone yellow in the light. His eyes were black stones. Li Du blinked. "I should not have come," he said. "I am very tired, and we have no more to say to one another."

Rinzen smiled. "But we do. I will tell you something now — something known to very few who are alive. Your friend Shu was loyal to the Kangxi. He knew nothing of a plot to assassinate the Emperor." Wearing an expression that reminded Li Du of a merchant in a market, Rinzen said, "If you can arrange for me to be taken safely to my allies, I will give you what you need to understand what occurred six years ago. If you do not, then I will take the secret with me to my death."

Li Du looked for the lie in Rinzen's face, but he did not find it. "Even if I believe you —" Li Du heard his own voice as if it belonged to someone else. The repercussions of Rinzen's words expanded painfully through his thoughts. "How could I protect you? I do not know the path north beyond the plateau to Dzungar lands. I have no authority."

Rinzen waved a hand. "Authority in these mountains comes from the words you speak and the language in which you speak them. Surely you still carry a seal that can stamp a document with a look of importance. You are associated with power — you can do what I ask. Do it, and I will tell you what happened to your friend. Fail, and you will never know."

CHAPTER 28

Li Du did not sleep. When he felt the air becoming light he went outside to watch the dawn. With his belt pulled tight around his coat and his hat pulled down over his ears, he watched the sky pale and the stars disappear. There was already smoke coming from the Khampa caravan, smudging the blue air.

He caught movement to his right, and turned to see Kamala come from the stream, two of her children round and bundled beside her. They were carrying buckets of water. The smaller child — the younger boy — held just one bucket in front of him with both his hands, determined to succeed on his own. As he walked, his knees knocked its base and water sloshed over the sides.

When they reached Li Du, Kamala greeted him. The pink scarf around her head glowed, a prelude to the sunrise, and her eyes were bright. She touched the children's shoulders lightly. "Go bring water to Yeshe," she said.

She set her buckets down, watching them as she spoke to Li Du. "I did not understand the danger that surrounded Dhamo, but those pilgrims always frightened me. Now I understand why."

"This valley will never be used for such a purpose again," Li Du said. "The circumstances that cohered were too fragile. The painter, the hidden valley, the manor with two small sons . . ."

Kamala looked pleased. "In that case," she said, "you have my gratitude." She smiled and picked up the buckets of water. "Come in by the fire," she said. "We are making a good breakfast to prepare you for your journey."

Paolo Campo was fretting over the difficulty of organizing and packing his possessions. Li Du entered the room to find equipment, journals, clothes, and trinkets scattered across the floor like autumn leaves on the surface of a pond. Campo raised his eyes to Li Du with the look of someone exhausted by the cumulative effort of inconsequential decisions.

"What I do not know is how best to

distribute the weight," Campo said, "and how to protect the equipment that is most fragile. I cannot wrap it in my heaviest blankets. I will need them on cold nights when we must scrape away the snow to sleep." He sat down on the edge of the bed with a weary sigh. "I tried to organize it all yesterday," he said. "But the task over-whelms me."

Li Du picked up a book from the top of a pile and opened it. *Given three angles, the use of the sector in drawing the perspective representations of objects . . .*

Paolo Campo's voice drew him away. "How do you punish your criminals in this land?" he asked. He was looking in the direction of Rinzen's room.

Li Du closed the book and set it down. "His punishment will depend on who judges him for his crimes. If he is taken to Beijing, he will face a magistrate. If he is taken to Lhasa, I do not know what will happen."

"And if he faces a magistrate in your city? What then? I have heard that several Jesuits have suffered cruel imprisonment in the Forbidden City."

"He will be executed," Li Du said, quietly.

Campo shook his head and sighed. "Un-baptized, he will go in the realm of fire."

Li Du looked around the room at the

carefully polished objects arranged with no clear purpose or use. His gaze lingered on a slumped heap of dark fur half covered by a toppled pile of books.

"The muleteers with whom I travel have a certain genius for packing," Li Du said. "I have seen them secure packages of every shape to a mule's saddle using only a few scraps of rawhide. Since we are to travel some way together, why don't you ask them to carry these objects to the courtyard? The snow is gone, and it will be easier for you to arrange your saddlebags there."

Campo looked uncertain. "But can they be trusted?"

"I assure you that they can. And while they work, there is something I wish to show you at the mountain temple."

Campo surveyed the room wearily. "I do not want to be shown anything," he said. "I am too tired of everything in this country. I want to go back to Zogong and find Achille. And then I want to go home."

"What of your work?"

"My work?"

Li Du indicated the instruments arranged across the floor. "Your maps. Today is a rare day in the mountains. There are no clouds. If you come with me now, you will be able to see the relationships between the peaks with a clarity we may not experience again in our travels."

"But I have seen the mountains," said Campo.

Li Du smiled encouragingly. "A friend of mine once told me that an object exists in as many forms as there are perspectives from which to view it. This is our only chance to see them from this exact place on this exact day."

Reluctantly, Campo agreed. With another look at his half-consolidated cargo, he followed Li Du.

The morning was a still, violet blue as Li Du climbed the stairs for the last time. Behind him, he could hear Campo wheezing slightly. When they paused, Campo said through gasps, "How is it that I have walked in these high places for so long and still am not accustomed to the air? It does not sustain my breath."

Li Du ignored the other's complaints. They continued up. The sun rose higher, and the violet retreated from the sky, leaving it clear and blue. They came to the prayer flags, windows into worlds of different colors. Instead of leading Campo in the direction of the pyre and the temple, Li Du continued past them, following the route he had seen the Chhöshe traverse from the high shrine. Soon Li Du saw it ahead of them, waiting, a weathered sentinel on a crumbling summit.

A final, short ascent separated them from the shrine. Li Du could see that the angles of the mountain were about to change, to open into the expanse that was not visible from the manor or the temple. He lingered on the rocky path, allowing Campo to pass him.

Campo arrived at the shrine and stood for a moment facing the rough stone structure, which stood a little taller than he. The wind whipped his coat around his knees. As Li Du watched, Campo reached out a hand to touch the stone. Then he turned away and looked out at the sky. He uttered a soft cry, and sank to his knees.

Li Du hurried upward toward him, his feet sliding in loose scree. Campo remained where he was. He didn't seem to notice that Li Du had joined him. Breathing hard, Li Du turned to see what Campo saw.

A line of peaks extended from one end of the horizon to the other. Even across the vast distance, it seemed to Li Du that they filled the sky. He traced them with his eyes, trying to incorporate their enormity into his understanding of nature's dimensions. Then he stopped, his moving gaze arrested. The sky behind the peaks was not sky at all. It was a mountain.

Li Du felt his own knees weaken, and his mind trembled in its effort to comprehend that a body so immense could be encompassed by the world. He looked beside him to where Paolo Campo kneeled, his face shining with tears that spread across his cheeks and dripped from his chin like melting ice. Silent sobs racked his shoulders.

Li Du lifted his eyes again to the mountain. He knew that it had a Chinese name and a Tibetan name and perhaps a thousand others given to it by hidden villages filled with people who did not think often of empires.

But you do not mind what you are called, Li Du thought as he looked at the mountain. *Secret names, names given to you, new names and changed names and names forgotten. To you, these names are like chips of rock that fall away from your slopes unnoticed, and tumble down streams until they are smooth.*

Campo stood up. He wiped the rock dust from his coat and pressed his fingers to his eyes to stop his tears. "I did not think to find Him here," he said. Then, with a little sigh and shake of his shoulders, he turned and started purposefully away down the path.

The mules were packed and Andruk was in the courtyard overseeing the loading of surveying equipment onto Campo's mules. Measuring tapes, folding grids, sextants, and compasses were still scattered across the ground.

Paolo Campo strode to where Doso stood. He summoned Andruk to translate, and cleared this throat. "I have decided," he said, "that the weight of these objects is too much for the difficult journey ahead. By the time I reach Lhasa, these instruments will be rusted and bent, and of no use to anyone. If you will permit it, I will leave them in your care."

Doso listened while Andruk finished the translation. He looked surprised, and began immediately to protest. "A host cannot accept such valuable items," he said.

But Campo was adamant. "God's will is mysterious," he said. "I am confident that this is correct in His eyes. Allow me to do as my feelings dictate."

"In that case," said Doso, in a formal tone that concealed any bewilderment he may have felt, "I will preserve these items carefully for your future use."

Campo's expression changed. His green eyes seemed almost tranquil. "There is no need," he said. "I will not come this way again. I am returning home."

There were steps on the kitchen stairs and two people emerged from the barn, Tashi in his robes and Pema with a bag strapped to his back. Campo was forgotten as Doso turned to look at the two together. None of them spoke. Undiscerned machinations had altered the trajectories of two boys who had grown into men. The silence between the father and his sons was filled with echoes of events that never happened.

Doso's voice was hoarse. "After many years, you two are not so different from the brothers who were always up to some mischief." He turned to Tashi. "Will you return to Drepung?"

Tashi placed a hand on Pema's shoulder. "We will travel first to a monastery I know that houses painters and their apprentices. If Pema finds his place there, then I will turn my thoughts to my own future. If he does not, we will continue on together until our paths become more clear."

Doso's deep voice was steady, a father's voice. "We will make offerings for your safety," he said, to both of them, "and for the fulfillment of your wishes. We will burn juniper and sandalwood. We will offer flour and butter and tea to remove obstructions in your way." Doso embraced them both. "And when the wildflowers fill the fields," he said, "and the new calves are born, you will remember the home of your ancestors."

As the caravan started down the pasture fields, Li Du looked behind him and saw a cluster of figures coming to the manor from the direction of the village. He caught a glimpse of crimson and yellow. The village lama was on his way to counsel the family and preside over the funerals. Winter would come, followed by spring, and thoughts would turn from remembered death to new life.

"I have a question," said Hamza, squinting into the sunshine. He and Li Du walked together a short distance behind the others. "Why did Rinzen try to kill Paolo Campo?"

Li Du emerged from his own thoughts. "He didn't."

"In that case," said Hamza, "who pushed Campo from the precipice?"

Li Du hesitated. "Do you remember what Andruk told me about Campo's behavior on the day Dhamo died?"

Hamza considered. "Campo was upset because Yeshe and the children didn't want

462

to listen to him."

"Yes," said Li Du. "But his appearance was not that of a person who is merely embarrassed or annoyed. Andruk said that he was collapsed in the snow, unable to speak. It was not the interaction in Yeshe's cabin that felled him. It was something else — something he saw."

The furrows across Hamza's brow were partially obscured by his hair, which had grown long enough to emerge in dark curls from under his blue hat. "What did he see?"

Li Du drew in a breath. "Last night I said that three people observed Rinzen between the manor and forest. In fact, there were four. Paolo Campo saw him returning to the manor after having killed Dhamo."

"But if Campo saw the person in the black coat, why didn't he say anything about it? And why did it upset him?"

"Because he recognized it. He was the only one who did."

Hamza looked baffled. "He recognized Rinzen?"

"No," replied Li Du. "He did not. He recognized the coat. It was his own."

"His own coat?" Hamza came to an abrupt halt. "If you are going to communicate in this opaque manner," he said, "we must stop walking. I cannot simultaneously think and choose where to put my feet. You are saying that the black coat with the long fur at its shoulders belongs to Paolo Campo?"

"It does now," Li Du said. "But it did not always. It was the coat of Achille di Spiritu."

Hamza stared ahead of them on the path to where Campo sat astride a mule. "I do not understand. Why does he carry the coat of his friend?"

Before Li Du could answer, Hamza gave a long sigh. "Achille di Spiritu is dead."

Li Du did not have to affirm it. "There was a storm on a mountain," he said. "A storm far worse than the one that delayed us here."

"He said that his companion was in Zogong," said Hamza. "Why did he lie?"

"He didn't lie. Achille di Spiritu never reached Zogong, but Paolo Campo would not admit that his friend was gone. He carried the coat, as he carried all of the surveying equipment that was Achille's, but he hid from himself the significance of these items."

"How did Rinzen come to wear the coat?"

"His room was next to Campo's, and Campo's possessions, you recall, spilled out in a jumble into the hallway. Rinzen found the coat and decided to make use of it. He

464

assumed that only Campo would recognize the garment, and he thought he could avoid Campo's notice for the short time he had it on. Campo *did* observe him, but Rinzen was lucky. Instead of pursuing him with accusations of theft, Campo fell to the ground. Rinzen was able to continue on to the manor, remove the coat in the dark entryway, and proceed across the courtyard as himself. He returned the coat to its place amid the clutter. Campo remained where he was, near Yeshe's hut, where Andruk found him shortly after. Campo thought he had seen a ghost."

"The hot springs," said Hamza. "He went to the pools to look for Achille."

"Yes," said Li Du. "I thought you would understand."

"He went there because of the story," said Hamza. "The one he heard in the village, a story of dead souls waiting in enchanted pools."

Li Du nodded. "He believed he had seen an apparition. It did not occur to him to remember the coat he carried among his own things. His mind went instead to the story he had been told in the village. When he heard Doso tell me how to find the pools on the following day, he decided to go to them himself."

"And his struggle —" Hamza did not finish the sentence.

"Two nights ago," said Li Du, "you suggested that the problem facing us might not fit within the rules to which scholars adhere. Perhaps you were right. Campo's struggle was with himself — beyond that, I cannot explain."

They began to walk again. Li Du looked ahead at the procession of mules, bright with bells and colored yarn. The animals moved placidly, apparently content to be on a path. Li Du reached up a hand and patted his own mule's shoulder.

"But that is very sad," said Hamza. "Do you think he will keep searching ponds for ghosts?"

Li Du hesitated, thinking of the white mountain, and of the weight Campo had left behind at the manor. "I do not think so," he said. "I think that, with help from our caravan, Paolo Campo will travel over the mountains and see his home again."

CHAPTER 29

Two weeks later, the caravan stopped outside of Markham, a town governed by a local Tibetan lord in command of a small
army allied with Lhasa. They had traveled
well, past temples carved into mountains,
around blue and green lakes, and through
valleys surrounded by stone-like fortress
walls. It had not snowed again, and the
mules were content.

Pema had been in good sprits from the
moment the caravan left the valley, but early
on Li Du had noticed that Tashi was quiet.
He still wore his monk's robes. He accepted
his role as temporary caravan lama with
poise, and with an earnest desire to offer
comfort and counsel to the travelers who
were still shaken by what had happened.
But his eyes were worried, and at night
when Hamza told stories at the fire, he
retreated into his own thoughts.

On the evening after their third day of

travel, Li Du had observed Tashi in close conversation with Hamza, the two perched together on a high crag like eagles looking out at the mountains. Hamza had walked back down to the camp, leaving Tashi alone, a silhouette in the moonlight.

Li Du had asked Hamza what they had been speaking about. Hamza, after attempting to wave away the question, had shrugged. "I merely told him that it is possible to be chosen by miraculous signs, and to be a bad monk, just as it is possible to be overlooked by the astrologers, and yet to be a good monk. I told him that even though a liar told the boy that he was something he is not, he is not banned from a religious life. He simply has the freedom, now — and the challenge — of deciding for himself."

After that, Tashi's mood had lightened. He said his prayers and made his offerings, drank wine with the muleteers, joined in their songs, and exchanged memories with Pema of their adventures as children. On the fifth day, Pema and Tashi had parted from the caravan to follow a path southwest toward the monastery of painters.

Now in sight of the Markham walls, the camp was set as usual, the mules unburdened, the tents constructed, and the hearth built. The sky was becoming overcast, and they worked quickly to prepare food before nightfall. When the dark did come, everyone drew close to the fire.

Hamza spoke of how people used to be birds. Sera told a story of the ghost of a slain king who tried to warn his successor of danger by entering his dreams. Hamza criticized her for the cheerless subject matter and told a third story, of a princess who survived a shipwreck and swam to an island, where she outwitted a family of enchanted tigers, released a castle from its curse, and became queen.

When the travelers began to disperse, Li Du remained at the fire. He glanced in the direction of the tent that had been assigned to Rinzen. Every night since they had left the manor, the travelers had taken turns staying awake beside it, with the exception of Paolo Campo, who it was agreed was not equipped for the task.

Tonight, Li Du had no place in the assigned order of keeping watch. Aware of his exhaustion, he was about to retire to his tent when Andruk appeared out of the shadows and joined him beside the fire.

"Tomorrow we will be in Markham," said Andruk. He tilted his head back a fraction in the direction of Rinzen's tent. "Will he be taken to Lhasa to face the judgment of

Lhazang Khan?"

Li Du did not answer immediately. When he did, he spoke in Chinese, in a voice too low for anyone other than Andruk to hear. "You had hoped," he said, "that we would reach a Chinese magistrate first."

Without looking at Li Du, Andruk gave a small shrug. "Why should I care what happens to him?"

"Because," Li Du whispered, "you would see him punished by your Emperor for his betrayal."

Andruk had been reaching out to adjust a log in the fire. He pulled his hand back. "How long have you known?"

"Since I read the command associated with the white mirror. An agent who sees it must change his clothes and his name and burn the book he carries — the book of symbols and their meanings. Rinzen did not burn his copy of it, but a copy of it was burned. I found a scrap that had fluttered out of the brazier fire. You did as the white mirror instructed."

"How did you identify me?" asked Andruk.

"Campo told me that you intended to commission a thangka," said Li Du. "But when I mentioned it to you, you denied it."

"Ah," said Andruk. "I had forgotten. Yes

— I came to the manor with a message to send. It was not nearly so important as the one I carry now." His eyes moved again toward Rinzen's tent.

"Paolo Campo had been directionless for some time when he met you," said Li Du. "It was easy for you to take advantage of his confusion and bring him where you wanted to go."

Andruk turned disdainful eyes to the tent in which Campo was already asleep. "He is less uncertain now than he was before. He wants to go to Lhasa, and from Lhasa back to the West."

"Then you will go to Lhasa also?"

"I will go where I am required," said Andruk, with an unkind smile. "You will understand if I am not open with you. The Emperor may trust you, but I trust no one." He stood up. "Tomorrow we will see what the lord of Markham will do." Then he hunched his back and shoulders against the cold, and left the circle of firelight.

When Andruk was gone, Li Du turned back to the fire. *What the lord of Markham will do is his own business,* he thought. *But what will I do?*

He searched the fire for wisdom. Cracks through the coals glowed like written words, alternately validating and condemning his thoughts. He could speak to the lord in Markham. He could proclaim himself an advisor to the Kangxi and display the letter of transit that bore the Emperor's seal.

Wind muttered through the ashes. A pebble gleamed at the edge of the embers. He reached down and picked it up. It was obsidian black. On its round surface the reflected flame twisted like a creature caught inside the stone. He pocketed it and returned to his contemplations.

Rinzen had reiterated his proposition during each period Li Du was assigned to watch over him. With level, watchful eyes Rinzen waited for Li Du's response, and rebuffed any attempt to glean more information from him. Their whispered exchanges were brief, and ended in silence.

During the days, Li Du had several times caught Rinzen directing a speculating, assessing look at him. He knew that Rinzen was waiting for an answer. But he had no answer to offer. He could not allow a murderer to go free. Neither could he bring himself to dismiss what Rinzen had offered.

Li Du stood up, rubbed his neck, and searched the shadows for the pale shape of his tent. When he found it, he hurried across the frozen ground and ducked inside. Fatigue claimed him as soon as he had wrapped himself in his blankets, and he fell into a deep sleep.

It seemed only a moment before he blinked awake, but the dawn had come. It was a shout that had woken him. Disoriented and cold, he struggled out of his tent and stumbled, half asleep, toward the noise, almost tripping over the embers that had crumbled and collapsed on themselves during the night. The cry had come from Norbu, who was now gesturing to the others and pointing.

Li Du had not yet reached the tent when he comprehended the words being shouted around him and stopped. He did not need to join the cluster of people gathering to look inside. He did not need to see.

He turned around and scanned the camp. The place that had contained Andruk's tent and saddlebags was empty. Andruk was gone. Justice, a swifter justice than Rinzen would otherwise have faced, had been done. The secrets of a man who had deceived two kings were forever silenced.

CHAPTER 30

"Andruk could not allow Rinzen to be taken back to Lhasa," Li Du said. "The secrets he carried held too much power."

It was evening. Li Du and Hamza sat together in the courtyard of the Markham inn. The sounds of the town drifted over the low wall. An herb seller passed the gate, trailing fragrances of angelica and snow tea from the baskets on either side of her mule's saddle. They were drinking cups of a plum wine purchased that day.

Hamza took a sip of wine. "And the vanished Andruk? Where has he gone?"

"To make his report. Rinzen damaged the Emperor's web, but he did not destroy it. I am sure Andruk has means available to him." Li Du recalled Rinzen's words when they had stood together outside the manor door in the gusting wind, and wondered how many windows of communication existed between the Potala Palace and the

Forbidden City, hidden within palaces, mountains, and monasteries.

Hamza directed his attention to the sky, where stars were beginning to appear. "So Rinzen promised you information about the death of Shu in exchange for your assistance. Now I know why you have looked so preoccupied. You should have discussed it with me earlier — I would have told you what to do."

"What would you have said?"

"I would have advised you not to escort a murderer across a freezing plateau to a camp full of enemies of your Emperor." Hamza picked up the bottle of wine and refilled their cups. "And I would add that if this conclusion was not obvious to you, then you will not be making any decisions in future that relate to our safety."

Li Du started to speak, but Hamza was not finished. "Rinzen may have known nothing beyond what he needed to get your attention. And even if he did have information, his promise would not have stopped him from killing you at the earliest opportunity. Are you so unfamiliar with the minds of villains?"

Li Du raised his eyebrows. "Are you so well acquainted with them?"

Hamza gave a self-satisfied smile. "I have

said it before. I'm as old as the oldest in my stories, as young as the youngest, as benevolent as the kindest and as cruel as the most wicked."

Li Du's expression became serious. "I did not want Rinzen to escape punishment. But neither did I relish sending him to Beijing or to Lhasa, where there would have been more interest in torturing secrets from him than in meting out justice. I have no wish to assist the Emperor or the Khan in their plots against one another. That is one thing Rinzen and I had in common."

He sighed and picked up his cup. "I wonder if Rinzen's loyalty to the Dzungars was genuine. I believe the reason he gave us for going to Litang was true, but perhaps it was his own desire for power that drew him there. Finding the seventh incarnation of the Dalai Lama would allow him to manipulate all three contenders for Tibet. Of course, he might have found nothing. The incarnation might not be there. The Sixth may not have died on the road to China."

Hamza traced a constellation with a fingertip. "There will always be a story that he lived," he said. "And there will always be a story that he died. Both stories will be repeated, and there will be many others."

Li Du looked up at the stars spread across

the sky like pebbles in the Game of Many Eyes. Reminded of it, Li Du drew the pebble from his pocket and set it on the table.

"The tale you told," he said. "The tale of children and the dune."

"Ah," said Hamza, with a gratified expression. "You can read a book and listen to a story at the same time."

Aware that his mind was beginning to float on stars and plum wine, Li Du continued, slowly. "Each day, one child was endowed with the powers of a king, but it was a fleeting majesty, no sooner acquired than lost."

"That is true," replied Hamza. "But there was one child who went on to have other adventures. Her brother insulted a hearth spirit, and to protect him she was obliged to challenge the spirit to a contest of wits —"

"That was not my point," Li Du said. "I meant that —"

Hamza pointed a finger up at the sky, as he often did when asserting imagined authority. "One day we will journey together to the libraries in the far west, where the monks decorate their books with tangled snakes and acanthus leaves and wheels of flame, and bind them in silver instead of silk. We will travel to the ancient city ruled by statues of white marble and polished bronze. We will see the golden doors that are called the gates of paradise."

Li Du turned to Hamza. "These places you describe. There are times when I think you cannot have lived enough years to have seen them all before."

Hamza studied the clear surface of his wine. "I have not seen them all," he admitted. "But I have met travelers who know the way."

Li Du studied the man across from him. He saw again the contradictions written across his features, the suggestion that he had lived not one, but several lives. After a long moment, Li Du settled in his chair and pushed his hat back on his head. "I would like to see these illustrated tomes and statues and golden doors," he said. "But before we go west, I must return to the Forbidden City. It is time for me to resolve the questions I had thought to leave unanswered."

Hamza looked dubious. "The Forbidden City," he said. "There will be dangers for you there. I will accompany you."

Li Du smiled. "This is a task I will face alone. We have arrived in Markham, where the paths of the Tea Horse Road divide. You will go west with the caravan. Paolo Campo is without a guide, and I believe that with your help, he will find his way home. You will have good company."

Hamza gave an incredulous sniff. "Good company in Campo?"

Li Du shook his head and gestured to the door of the inn, from which Sera was approaching. She held her patched and embroidered bag in one hand and a silver bowl of wine in the other. "So you plan to go east," she said to Li Du, "to the Forbidden City, where the drum towers ring the hours through the night and every breeze that stirs a silk curtain whispers a secret."

"You see," Hamza said, "why I enjoy her company so much."

Sera smiled. She sat down, leaned forward over the table, and picked up the pebble. "Thank you," she said. "I won so many from the storyteller last night that I lost count of the pieces."

Hamza's expression soured. "I begin to agree with Paolo Campo. She charms the pieces to change color." He addressed Sera. "What have you found in Markham?"

Sera shifted her shoulders inside her voluminous coat. "I have discovered this plum wine," she said. "And I have spoken to several travelers with news to share from the east and west and north. But I have spent most of my afternoon helping your friend Kalden Dorjee."

"Helping Kalden?" Li Du and Hamza both waited for her to explain.

She leaned her elbows on the table. "I am too competent in my former duties to give Kalden those papers that the unfortunate thief brought to sell him. They are in the possession of the city's lord now, who promises to take action against the corrupt official Fang. But I am not unsympathetic to your caravan leader. I have negotiated a good deal for him on his taxes. He and the others are celebrating their fortune."

Hamza smiled. "They will still be drunk in the morning."

Li Du turned to Sera. "What is the news from the north?"

She raised her bowl, sipped, and set it down with a faint tap of metal on stone. "The Dzungars are regaining strength after Galdan's defeat. Some are saying that they have recognized a Seventh Dalai Lama and will no longer obey the false Sixth who sits in Lhasa."

"And in the east?"

"The Emperor of China has sent a delegate to the court of Lhazang Khan, but they say he has come in secret to make a map for armies."

"And the west?"

"The foreigners are leaving Lhasa. They have declared its conversion impossible, and will go home."

The three of them were silent. A path of stars had appeared across the sky.

"I meant to visit the Forbidden City once," said Hamza. "But I became distracted when I met a beggar who told me that he knew of a city with a princess who had vowed to marry the next man who could answer three riddles, and pose one to her that she could not answer."

Li Du woke to a clear morning. After receiving a final round of advice and instructions from the Khampa, he packed his saddlebags and settled them onto his mule. As he considered the road ahead, his mind took him back to a day thirteen years in the past.

It was summer in Beijing and time to sun the books. Li Du had just sat for a round of examinations, and was still silently reciting the *Spring and Autumn Annals of the Sixteen Kingdoms.* As he went in and out of the library carrying neat piles of books, he felt his mind begin to relax.

Outside, books and poem slips were clipped like clothes to a clothesline and the courtyard was filled with the rippling melody of fluttering pages and buzzing cicadas. The books that were too fragile to hang were spread on long wooden planks.

Shu was setting a jade paperweight on a curling corner of parchment. It was carved in the shape of a lion. He bent to look at it and clicked his tongue. "This warrior has defended many books in his time. See how he has lost an ear?"

Li Du leaned forward and saw the chip amid the jade waves of the lion's mane. "I remember when he lost that ear. It was when Duan was preparing for his final exams and had not slept in three days. The day before the exam, the Emperor requested that all of the books on mapmaking be pulled out and indexed for his immediate perusal. Poor Duan was responsible for that section. He fell asleep in the middle of his work and knocked the lion from the table."

"And," said Shu, joining Li Du in the memory with a faraway look, "Duan failed his exam because his hand was shaking so badly that the examiner could not read his writing. You students must take time to rest. Look at you. You have finished your exam and you still look as though you are standing in the dark instead of the sunlight. Go fetch one more set of volumes, and when you return we will drink tea. We did a good job last year. No bookworm tunnels through the pages."

Li Du returned to the cool stone interior of the library and made his way through its polished and painted corridors. He knew the paintings so well that each was like a window opening to a place that he had visited. When he emerged with the final stack of silk-boxed volumes, Shu was lying on a wooden chair covered in pillows. His hat was pulled down over his eyes, but he raised a hand and beckoned Li Du over to sit in the other chair. On the table between them, tea steeped in its pot.

"As I was saying," Shu said, as he lifted himself up slowly and filled their cups, "it is important not to spend too much time worrying when you are young. I am very content, you see. I have read all these books. Because I have read them, you might say that I have consumed them. And because I have consumed them, they are in my belly. And with a belly full of books, I too need to be sunned." He leaned back in his chair, closed his eyes again, and smiled at his own logic.

Li Du settled into his own chair and looked up through the canopy of pages illuminated by sunlight. He could distantly picture the book that Shu had borrowed the joke from, but decided not raise the matter.

Shu was beginning to lecture Li Du on the importance of allowing the books to cool before returning them to their places when suddenly they both heard a light patter of footsteps outside the courtyard wall. Shu's two grandchildren came running in, their cheeks bright red.

Shu put up a hand and raised an eyebrow in mock censure. The children stopped their headlong rush and stood like soldiers at attention. "Loyal scouts," he said, "what do you have to report?"

The little girl spoke with grave authority. "Grandfather, you told us to play on the highest hill there and to tell you if we saw any clouds. I have seen —" She opened her little hand one finger at a time and held it up to him. "— four gray clouds."

"In what direction?" Shu looked at the little boy, who pointed to the east.

"Ah," said Shu. "Then we face a grave emergency and I must make you and your sister librarian lieutenants. Show me your hands." He inspected their hands and pronounced them sufficiently clean and dry.

For the next hour, they worked hard, carrying the planks into the inner sunning room and climbing ladders to unclip books from the silk ropes. Just as they were carrying in the final set of pages, the rain began to fall, turning one patch of stone after another dark gray. Inside, Shu delighted the children by recounting to them the stories depicted by painted screens. After a servant took them home, Li Du stood with his friend looking out at the courtyard, which had become a single, square puddle of water.

"This is why," Shu said, "I have always recommended that we sun the books in the first month of autumn, when the weather is less changeable. We will have to begin again tomorrow." But his tone held no annoyance. It had been a good day. As Li Du looked out at the soothing gray and the drops pinging in the teacup that had been forgotten on the table, he felt his anxiety leave him.

Shu was scanning the courtyard for forgotten books. Satisfied that there were none, he put on his hat and prepared to go home. He turned to Li Du. "If you did as well on your exams as I know you did, you may be honored with a position of magistrate in an important city."

Li Du lowered his head, feeling slightly embarrassed. "I hope that I did well on the exams," he said, "but I have been thinking that I do not want to be a magistrate after all." He hesitated. "I have been thinking that

I would very much like to be a librarian."

In the courtyard of the Markham inn, Li Du shouldered his pack, glanced at the sky, and picked up his walking stick. Beside him, his mule dipped her head and shook her mane in the sun. The ground was covered in fine, sparkling frost. With a determined little nod, he straightened his faded hat and set out on the path to the east.

ABOUT THE AUTHOR

Elsa Hart was born in Rome, Italy, but her earliest memories are of Moscow, where her family lived until 1991. Since then she has lived in the Czech Republic, the U.S.A., and China. She earned a B.A. from Swarthmore College and a J.D. from Washington University in St. Louis School of Law. *The White Mirror* is her second novel.